THE MEN'S ROOM

Ann Oakley is a sociologist and writer. She is deputy director of a London University research unit, doing research into the health of women and children.

Her previous books include *The Sociology of Housework*, which helped to establish housework as a legitimate area of academic study; *From Here to Maternity*, which charts women's experience of first-time motherhood; *The Captured Womb*, a history of medical care for pregnant women, and *Taking It Like a Woman*, in which she combines autobiography with the fictional presentation of several themes which emerge in *The Men's Room* as fully the subject of a novel.

Ann Oakley lives in London with her two daughters and son.

ANN OAKLEY

THE
MEN'S ROOM

Flamingo
Published by Fontana Paperbacks

First published in 1988 by Virago Press Limited

This Flamingo edition first published
in 1989 by Fontana Paperbacks

Flamingo is an imprint of
Fontana Paperbacks, part of
the Collins Publishing Group,
8 Grafton Street, London W1X 3LA

Printed and bound in Great Britain by
William Collins Sons & Co. Ltd, Glasgow

FOR CATHERINE

'As a matter of fact, man, like woman, is flesh, therefore passive, the plaything of his hormones and of the species, the restless prey of his desires . . . In those combats where they think they confront one another, it is really against the self that each one struggles . . .' –

Simone de Beauvoir, *The Second Sex*, p. 413

CONTENTS

1 ✳ PROMISES

'It has been asserted time and again that woman is pleased to acquire in the infant an equivalent of the penis, but this is by no means an exact statement' – *The Second Sex*, pp. 222–4

She was looking at him in the half-light from the window, at the way his chest rose and fell beneath his carefully crossed hands, and at his face, and especially his nose, which stuck up into the morning air emitting a noise like a broken exhaust pipe. She ought to be used to it, she'd been married to him for twelve years and lying beside him most of that time. But she still couldn't understand how someone could make a noise like that and not wake themselves up. It seemed a most unnatural contradiction: to be at peace, yet to fight with the air, making thunder out of it; to withdraw from the world yet be so manifestly in it. Looking at him made her remember her friend Claire talking about her own husband's private habits, how he blew his nose so noisily in the mornings that everyone looked round for the donkey. Charity, like Claire, both found this funny and minded men's animal intrusions. But there was nothing, really, to be done about it. Men had to behave like that, and women must define their positions in relation to men: to mind or not to mind, to share a bed or not, even to creep into his head from time to time, have a quick look round and get out again before he's had time to notice the true nature of his possession.

The door crashed open as Rachel, aged six, Charity Walton's only daughter and fourth child, came into the room. Rachel dumped a plastic bag full of toys on the bed. 'I'm hungry,' she complained.

Charity put her arms round Rachel's thin body. James Walton stopped snoring with a final ghastly croak, threw back the bedclothes, put his feet on the floor and his head in his hands, and groaned. Rachel took no notice of this performance. She was used to it.

'This bed smells of Mummy and Daddy,' she said. 'Why does it smell?'

James groaned again.

'All beds smell,' said Charity, firmly.

'Mine doesn't,' insisted Rachel. And then, inconsequentially, 'You know Gavin?'

'Yes, I know Gavin.'

'Do you know what Gavin did?' incited Rachel, giggling.

'Tell me.'

'He took his sister's goldfish, and then he forgot about it, and he found it in his pocket three weeks later. It was all dead!'

'I bet it was,' said James. He was pulling on his track suit. 'Have you remembered we're going out tonight?' he asked Charity.

'Of course I've remembered. I'm superwoman, and one day I'm going to fly out of the window.'

'You shouldn't make bad jokes in the morning. It doesn't suit you.' And then he was gone, leaving the shadow of his unshaven face for them to remember him by.

'Come on you, we'd better get moving.' Charity pushed Rachel out of bed, took her to her room, and dressed her in a bright pink T-shirt and flowered skirt. She brushed Rachel's dark hair; the pink of the T-shirt picked out mahogany lights in it.

'Mummy.'

'Yes, darling.'

'Who do you love best?'

The question was neither original nor innocent. Charity had often wondered where the idea of children's innocence had come from, for children knew more than anyone did. 'I love you all differently,' she said. 'I love you differently from the boys, but of course I love them too.' Her speech was well rehearsed, and somewhat mendacious; the truth was that Charity would never forget the moment when the midwife had said 'It's a girl', using that special triumphal tone doctors and midwives resort to at such times. So Charity Walton had held her infant daughter and wept, inchoately, without knowing why or for whom she was weeping.

Rachel was born in 1974, when feminism was in full swing again. There was a newspaper, *Shrew*, the voice of the women's liberation workshop, and the magazine *Spare Rib* had entered the cookery section of newsagents' shops. Nineteen seventy-four was also the year Richard Nixon resigned over the Watergate affair, so that the relevance of feminism was highlighted by the obvious decomposition of male politics. They were strident times, full of metallic demands and easy notions of utopia. Visions floated like balloons – wherever you looked, several of them, silver or white and full of air, lingered buoyantly above the prickly treetops. Women's groups listed the political requisites for their liberation: free contraception and abortion on demand, free childcare, increased family allowances, equal pay and opportunities at work, proper paid maternity leave, no more discrimination in tax and social security systems: there was a lot to be done. Meetings and conferences abounded. But, partly because the voices that were raised were not in unison, few agreements could be reached about the political strategies needed to correct the problems. And while all this was going on, beyond the public gaze other groups of women were asserting their right to know things about their bodies only men had known before. The female cervix uteri turned out not to look like a nose after all.

The year Rachel Walton got to her feet and walked, some progress was made: the Sex Discrimination Act became law, and the first successful commercial feminist publishers, Virago, emerged to challenge the male media supremacy (and offend its sensibilities) by choosing such a name. But Rachel's mother, occupied with childrearing, did little more than note these happenings. She did so in the same spirit as events such as the establishment of chemical factories or nuclear reactors might be noted as having major theoretical implications for personal health.

Charity had had four children because she wanted to. Tom in 1968, the twins Dan and Harry in 1970, and then Rachel. The four of them, taken as a package, represented their mother's first understanding of her place in the world. Though they might suffer for this in various ways, they would also benefit, for the only state of affairs that's better than being what someone else wants is to be what you want yourself, and this is as rare as pearls in a sewage plant.

On this particular morning in May 1980, Charity found some weetabix for Rachel, and then took her daughter to school. The Waltons lived in North London, habitat of semi-radical intellectuals and people who prided themselves on the kind of superior aesthetic wisdom which meant that they all had the same arrangements of pine bookshelves, houseplants and white sanitaryware decorated with selected Victorian tiles. Rachel Walton's school, the other side of a busy main road, now had a crossing manned by policemen as a result of a vociferous parental uprising led by a father who was an actor in 'Z Cars' and a mother who was a writer of vegetarian cookery books. A sign on the school's main door was in advance of its times by saying 'no smoking on school premises, please'. The children's paintings and essays hanging on the walls inside made it clear that this was an establishment which tolerated poor spelling, rather than more contemporary mistakes such as racism.

After taking Rachel to school, Charity came back and stood for a moment in the hallway of the house, savouring its emptiness. Though silent, it seemed full of voices, of growing children and plants, songs and burnt breakfasts, lost socks and renditions of happy family life: this was where Charity lived and had her being. It rarely occurred to her to consider whether she liked this way of life or not. She had chosen it, after all.

Charity was thirty-two, and in possession of an olive-skinned body, dark hair and a classic facial profile that would have done well as the prow of a ship. This was the only prow-like thing about her, for otherwise she was a quite unexceptional woman.

The only surviving child of Florence and Frederick Dawson, two stolid citizens of Kent's commuter belt, she possessed in determination what she lacked in intelligence – not that she wasn't clever, for she was, but the cleverness was because of her culture and not in spite of it. Her mind and her spirituality fitted the culture's regular contours; there were no jagged edges of innovative thought or pathbreaking passions to contend with – or be proud of. People, looking at Charity, didn't always see this. They saw an ambitious woman. 'Unbearably organised', 'very successful', 'incredibly ambitious' was how they described her, the choice of such epithets revealing the very limitations of Charity's success in adhering to one model of womanhood. They really said nothing at all about the person behind the stereotype.

If Charity knew the truth about herself, then she didn't let anyone in on the secret. But she *was* humanly frail and vulnerable. She was capable of committing sins and errors – the frailty seeped out sideways in moments of agitation in the kitchen or suffering in the privacy of bath or bed. It was said that she had a temper – an affliction, like acne, that disturbed the peace from time to time, though what affected Charity more than anything else was the feeling she had in the midst of these tempers that there *was* no other reality.

She'd been working for some years in a university department of sociology. She did this as a necessary change from domesticity, the other half of the successful woman image, though perhaps selling flowers or climbing the Himalayas would have done as well. The essence of Charity's attachment to academia was that she saw it as a place with infinite promise. Possibilities of promotion lurked there, and the hope of improving one's mind and soul. The universities were uncontaminated by commercial greed and moral turpitude. God reigned there: God the scientist, God the knower. An incidental benefit was that, if you had a good relationship with God and were very lucky, you could get this thing called tenure. Tenure meant that you were paid to worry about other people's futures instead of your own, which was an expensive method of fund-raising, given the generally unproductive nature of worry.

Charity quite fancied herself as an academic, especially as she fled from Chalk Farm to King's Cross on her bicycle in the morning. This activity gave passing motorists promises of a succulent and unobtainable heaven in the shape of her sleek pink thighs; Charity felt there was was something nicely incongruous about the conjunction between the life of the mind and the life of the thighs. The bicycling kept her fit, but her body was relatively unmarked by the experiences of childbearing, except for a few dozen silver insignia on her stomach and thighs, and a slight flagging resistance in her right breast, which was the one all her children had preferred. She often remembered with horror and fascination reading about an African tribe where suckling gave the women such extended breasts that they threw them over their shoulders to get them out of the way. Despite this, Charity knew she fitted another cultural stereotype too – that of an attractive woman. This wasn't a great deal of help to her, except when her self-esteem was low, and then she might use it to comfort herself, along with Mars bars and *Woman's Own*.

She arrived at the department at ten o'clock. A corner building in a Georgian square, with newly painted blue and white wood-work, it housed the overflow from Regent's College, one of the colleges of London University. As the college had grown, its premises had not, and the sociology department had been moved round the corner to a separate residence. The reason why soci-ology had been singled out for this special treatment was not that the other departments thought especially highly of it, but rather that they tended to discount it and could do so more easily if it wasn't there any more. But the effect on the sociologists of having a separate existence was to give them a quite audacious sense of their own grandeur. They might have become like a gentleman's club, swanning time away in armchairs under tomes of Durkheim, had there not been one or two disturbing ladies in their midst.

Charity parked her bicycle round the side of the building, and detached her bag from the saddle. Steve Kirkwood, a junior lecturer, a wearer of eroded 1960s corduroy jackets, came up the front path.

'You're early, aren't you, Charity?'

'Usual time.' She smiled maternally at him. 'Some of us have to be well organised, you know.'

'Did you read the *Guardian* this morning?' Steve wasn't changing the subject, he just wanted to contradict Charity's position in a roundabout way.

'Listen, Steve, you know I don't have a chance even to *see* the paper in the morning!'

'Oh yes, I forgot.' He opened the front door for her with a theatrical gesture. 'Well, read it this evening. I take it les enfants do give you some peace in the evenings? Get the old man to do the washing up. Put your feet up and broaden your mind. What I was trying to say was there's an extremely odd piece by Barnes about the biological basis of modern marriage. He's either nuts or on to something, I don't know which. I'd be interested to know what you think.'

'I suppose you think everything has a biological basis?' She squinted at him in the dark brown light of the hallway.

'Certainly.'

'I'll argue with you later, Steve.'

He grinned at her. This attitude of his that she was a liberated woman who needed to be put in her place was a piece of play-acting between them.

Charity's desk was at right angles to the window overlooking the square. Her father, whom she'd believed for longer than anyone else, had once told her that you should always place your desk at right angles to the light; if you were right-handed the light should come from your left, and if you were left-handed, from your right. In the middle of the square, whose full dimensions could be seen from the window, was a garden where pink and purple hydrangeas bloomed. Around the square, constipated cars moved in vain pursuit of a spare parking meter. She watched them distractedly, wondering if the twins had got to school alright. She always wondered this. But they refused to go with her, and their dual resistance had been too much for her almost from the start. As babies, they'd done everything together – eaten, cried, peed, pulled out handfuls of marmalade hairs from next door's sluggish wandering cat. Sometimes she regarded them as being in collusion against her, and she nearly always felt they didn't belong to her as Tom, her firstborn, or Rachel did.

Charity had just started to draft a report to the Social Research Council on the first year of her research project, when Mavis, the departmental secretary, knocked on the door. You could usually hear Mavis approaching because of the jangle of her bracelets, and the aurally uncertain balance of her weight on outdated stiletto heels.

'You haven't forgotten, have you, dear?' asked Mavis.

'Forgotten what?' Charity recalled her comment to James this morning about ever-mindful superwoman flying out of the window.

'Professor Carleton. It's his first day today. We've bought some champagne. He should be here about lunchtime. Drinks in the common room.'

'Damn. I wanted to finish this. Alright, Mavis, thanks for reminding me.'

'Should be pleased, dear. Ought to be excited to meet him. I am. Could do with a new face round here. There are some interesting rumours about him. Should liven the place up.' Mavis's laugh tinkled scandalously away down the corridor.

Professor Mark Carleton, lately of Tuxedo University, Texas, had been one of the early stars of ethnomethodology, a school of sociology whose contribution to an understanding of the universe was obscure. Having identified himself as a flickering star in the ethnomethodological firmament in the mid-sixties, Carleton had vanished to the States, where he hoped to find a more appreciative soil for his ideas. But, although churlishly he had blamed the British lack of imagination, the Americans hadn't proved to have any more. They had liked his tweed jacket and his accent, and had some respect for his superlative lack of interest in the undergraduate teaching he was hired to do, but they had never really understood what he was on about.

His arrival that morning in his new academic home could be heard the other side of the square, since he first of all drove his car on to the pavement, hitting a motor cycle, then dropped a box of books in the gutter on his way out of it, and finally slammed the front door loudly behind him, dislodging a noticeboard from the wall. Seminar announcements and advertisements for yoga teachers rained down as he galloped up the stairs to the music of voices and the clink of glasses. As he reached the landing, the door to the common room opened, and he was given a view of a room peopled with blurred pointillist outlines and movement: the movement of hands gesturing, of mouths opening, of hair swinging, of action and inaction combined in a muddled concatenation.

'Here he is!' Dr Alan Pascoe, the department's most senior resident, held out a gesturing hand to the new professor. 'Welcome! You see, we've prepared a little ceremony for you. Do you know everyone?'

Carleton didn't. He had met Pascoe once before, and Mavis, the brassy secretary, and he had also encountered Steve Kirkwood on a previous visit.

'This is Dr Swinhoe,' said Pascoe, 'our crime and deviance person.' Carleton shook Swinhoe's hand and noted that it was sweaty. 'Howard Denby teaches class and stratification, doing some very interesting research on the class position of politicians' wives, perhaps you know him from the States?' Mark didn't, but recognised the type. He would be called Howie and make Woody Allen-type jokes. 'And this young man is our local mechanic.'

'Computer programmer,' interpolated the young man, who wasn't really so young. He fingered a red beard, and managed a wise smile. 'Mack McKinnon, pleased to meet you.'

Carleton took off his jacket: the room and the day were warm. The corks came out of two champagne bottles.

'Dr Margaret Lacey, our most recent acquisition, from Cambridge,' continued Pascoe relentlessly. He put a hand on the shoulder of what looked to Carleton like a fierce female with doctoral eyes and a tight chest. 'How do you do?' said Margaret. 'I hope you'll be very happy here.' She spoke like a clock.

Pascoe next brought him face to face with Charity Walton.

'Hallo.' He shook her hand politely. He was always anxious to be liked by women. Charity, not anxious to be liked by men, asked him if he'd had a good trip.

'What?' Carleton couldn't at first think what she meant. 'Oh yes, yes. We haven't settled in yet, of course, but it's good to be back. I've been away ten years, you know. Didn't think I'd be coming back at all, but in the end the British intellectual tradition got me where it hurts the most – in the head. American universities are high schools really – no challenge there at all.'

'Refill?' inquired Pascoe. More pale liquid was poured into Mark Carleton's glass. He stood there, holding it and looking at Charity Walton. He raised the glass to his lips and drank slowly. Some of the champagne dripped off the stem, making a little rivulet on to his blue shirt, which matched his eyes, but he didn't notice. He found himself next watching Charity's mouth, because it looked as though it were about to formulate a question. Suddenly his whole existence became focused on that mouth, about to frame an utterance as meaningful as the Bible or as trivial as the tabloid press; he was just terribly anxious to hear what that mouth was going to say.

'I hear you're about to publish a new book,' said Charity finally. It hadn't really taken her very long to get the words out; the waiting was in Carleton's head. He went on watching her mouth, but her warm beige lips had settled into a smooth line, and there was apparently nothing more immediately forthcoming from them.

'Well, not quite. I'm still writing it,' he said. Thinking he ought to say something else, he laughed anxiously and added, 'My reputation precedes me, I see.'

She ignored the laugh. 'I enjoyed your last one,' she said. 'Although I thought some of the parallels you draw with the psychology of revolutionary movements weren't quite on target. It's stretching the point a bit, I think. But I didn't agree with the BJS review, that was really very unfair. I always suspect the criticism that one isn't being sociological enough. I wonder whether Comte or Durkheim or Wright Mills would have passed the test?'

Carleton was surprised and impressed with this woman, whatever kind of woman she was. When she talked and even when she didn't, she managed to hold his attention in some quite intangibly erotic way – an eros of the mind and of the body.

'Yes,' he said, 'I do agree with you, about the reviews, I mean. But don't you think all reviews are unfair? I usually give them to my wife to read first. She says my ego isn't strong enough to take them!' He laughed again and sipped his champagne. He felt he didn't know what else to do.

'Is your wife in the academic world?' asked Charity.

'Jane? No. Jane doesn't believe in shared interests. She's a music teacher.'

Charity was unwilling to inquire further into the mystic interior of Mark Carleton's marriage. Other people's marriages were only marginally less boring than one's own.

Carleton pondered on the reason for Charity's reserve, for she let herself out in measured droplets, her essence trickling into the atmosphere, so the chances were it would evaporate in the air. Was it shyness? Arrogance? Equally striking was the lack of emotion in her voice and on her face. He looked at her sideways as she was talking to someone else. Those beige lips moved like liquid cream.

Charity had already fulfilled her own initial intention, which was to challenge Mark Carleton intellectually. The department which Carleton had joined had an international reputation for mediocrity; Charity didn't want this reputation to tarnish her own standing in Carleton's eyes. She was well aware of her ability to fit stereotypes as well as to resist them.

When she was very small, maybe five or six, Charity's father had taken her to the National Gallery one day, to look at great paintings: Titian, Rubens, Raphael, Holbein. Charity had stood with her face very close to the thickly oiled surfaces, and had marvelled at their undulations (she imagined the artist's paint-brushes getting stuck in the pot, as her own did when the water dried up). In her Startright sandals, she'd walked past the violent reds and blues of the Italian Renaissance painters: Uccello's *The Battle of San Romano*, Botticini's *The Assumption of a Virgin* (with a little wizened wife in black to one side); she'd commented, as a child would, at paintings of Mary with one white breast extruding from her dress and the infant Jesus with a nipple-sized penis on him. But in the middle of all that Renaissance grandeur – all those vistas of battles and creamy-faced Marys with blue cloaks – Charity's infant eyes had spotted a small unpretentious picture, almost hidden in a corner of the room. Most of the picture was white light entering a window and brilliantly coating the wall behind; in the foreground an outline of a fat man in a cap standing next to a piano gave it its necessary material subject. The painting was by Rembrandt, and was called *A Man in a Room*. Charity had led her father to the picture and told him she liked it better than all the others. When he'd asked her why, she'd said it was because you didn't know what to think when you looked at it, you could think a whole lot of different things, and they might all be true.

On her way home that day, Charity found herself thinking with interest about her meeting with Carleton. She thought of him watching her, of the way he hadn't noticed the champagne's passage down his blue shirt front. She recalled his hands, which had thick veins on them, and the way they had knotted themselves round the champagne glass. She remembered his attentiveness, his receptiveness to her utterances, his perplexed expression. What kind of man was this? A flicker of sexual excitement passed through her body, but, wrapped in the carcinogenic cling-film of the academic encounter, it was gone again as quickly as it came – its entrance and its exit both taking place entirely without warning.

In the Walton house in Chalk Farm everyone was home, except James. Beth, the mother's help, was in the kitchen frying bacon. 'You do want me to stay tonight, don't you?'

'Yes, yes, I'm sorry, I forgot to leave you a note. I'm going out to dinner.'

Rachel pulled at her arm. 'Come and look at something, Mummy. I want to show you something.'

They sat on the floor and looked at Rachel's arrangement of Sindy dolls, who lay on their backs covered in tissue paper. 'Do you know what they're doing, Mum?'

'No. What are they doing?'

'They're *sick*. They're in hospital. They're having babies, some of them. That one's broken her head' (the head was indeed lying on the carpet beside the doll) 'and this one's got to have an operation for something really nasty. Where are your kidneys, Mummy? Are they up here?' Rachel put a chocolatey finger up under the plastic point of a Sindy chin.

'I think she's been watching that ITV programme about hospitals,' observed Tom from the doorway. 'Have you seen my football shorts, Mum?'

'I wasn't,' said Rachel, crossly. 'I didn't, really!' She turned round and looked up at Charity with an expression of innocence arranged on her face.

'I'll tell you about the location of kidneys later. And no, Tom, I haven't seen your shorts.'

'I have.' Rachel leaned forward, so her hair fell in a curtain over her face.

'Where?'

'Not telling.'

Tom lunged at his sister, who shrieked with anticipatory delight. 'You tell me, Ragey, or I'll do something dreadful to your Sindys. They'll never be the same again.'

'Dan took them. He left his at school.'

Tom disappeared, yelling for his brother.

Charity went into the kitchen and finished making the children's supper. She looked at the four of them round the table. They were good children, healthy, bright, exhausting. She poured herself a large drink and told them she was going to have a bath. As she went upstairs, drink in hand, she knew that when she came down she would find that Rachel had left all her bacon, Tom would have eaten half his brothers' food, you wouldn't be able to get into the hall for all the childhood paraphernalia, and the telephone would be ringing. The expectation of such chaos filled her with satisfaction. She enjoyed the glow it gave her of being used, of using herself, in the interests of other people's welfare.

The friends they were to visit lived in Notting Hill Gate. Sally

Lawrence had been a student with Charity, but their paths since then had moved in different directions. Unimpressed by Charity's immersion in the world of the nursery, Sally had chosen not to have children. Instead of babies, she had her work as a publisher, and she had lovers, each the final solution, but, one after the other, disappearing in a dustcloud of disengagement from her emotional intensity. Now there was Eric. Eric had moved into Sally's house without any determination to succeed where others before him had failed.

Sally opened the door in a dress sprinkled with flowers the colour of those in the window boxes: red geraniums and blue cornflowers.

'I'm late,' said Charity. 'Is James here?'

'James is not here,' said Sally, 'and neither is Eric, and neither are John or Nick. Let's have a quick drink before they all arrive.' She drew Charity into the kitchen. 'You look tired. Or do you look how I feel?'

'I'm exhausted,' said Charity. 'I don't think I can cope with my sixteen roles any more.' She laughed mildly, amused at her own fraudulent disclosure. 'I'd like a simple life. I mean a *really* simple life. Just the children or just work, but not both.'

'Or just a man?' offered Sally hopefully. 'You know, Charity, you have a lot of unused potential. I've thought that for a long time. It's wasted on James. He doesn't really notice you. Not as a woman, I mean.'

'Maybe not.' Charity was surprised by the directness of Sally's remarks. 'How's work?'

Sally lit a cigarette and leaned back in her chair. 'Busy. We've started a new series on family life. I think I'm going to be put in charge of it. It'll be a challenge. But right now I feel what I need is a holiday. Eric and I are going to the South of France for a month in the summer. I can't wait.' She certainly seemed tense tonight. Her straight red hair was drawn tightly back in a band behind her ears, so her eyes and cheeks seemed to follow the angle of her hair, and her face had none of its usual radiance, but was set in a repressed and anxious mould.

It wasn't until nine o'clock that they were all assembled round the large pine table in Sally's lovingly tended garden. James and Charity, whose communication was assumed rather than manifest, John and Nick from Sally's publishing house, and Sally and Eric, who treated one another to a string of endearments and gestures of passion, though their eyes scarcely met. The assembled company ate asparagus and baked grey mullet and a strawberry tart. The evening changed its colour with the deepening of the sky to navy blue and its display of half a moon, sitting in a format of a cheeky Dutch cheese up there waiting to be eaten.

'Alright then, Sally,' said James, pushing his plate away from him, and putting his head back into the undergrowth behind him. 'Tell us how the publishing world is doing these days. Have you found a new recipe for fertilising our imaginations and expanding your profit margins? Or are we going to have more of the same?'

'The trouble with you, James,' said Sally, 'is your profession. Economists think the meaning of life exists in figures. A positive balance is the only proper objective. What about great literature? Isn't it important to find the really good authors, to nourish them and allow them to produce themselves through art?'

'You sound like a Marxist.' James intended this as a criticism, but Sally, who possessed the evanescent wisdom of the media world, knew a fashionable ideology when she heard one. 'In any case,' continued James sagely, 'there's no money in great literature. It's a pity, but there it is. We might as well all be pragmatists. Or Jackie Collins. All the great writers were poor. In order to be immortal you have to die first. Unfortunately.'

'As a matter of fact,' said Sally quietly, 'I've just found a new author, who's good. Very good. He writes well. He writes great literature, and he's going to make money for us.'

'Oh yes? What's he going to write about? Six months on a desert island alone with his fantasies and a few bananas?'

Charity listened and observed. Then suddenly, for one appallingly long moment, as the moon's cheesey light filled the small urban terrace, she saw her husband occupying the persona to which Sally had referred earlier that evening. She saw James, economic management consultant, father of four, husband of one, with his sculpted upper-class face, the whites of his eyes cleansed with early morning jogging, the creases of his suit falling into artificially untidy lines around his carefully managed body, and she saw that he was boring. Boring. There was nothing to this man, nothing at all. He was a caricature of the human condition. In his very solidity (the characteristic she had first admired in him under the heading of consistency) he was no statue of liberty, but rather a condition of imprisonment, the unimaginative stump of Cleopatra's needle staring eyeless over the black Thames at night. She couldn't think why she'd married him at all. Except that she'd been so young at the time, only twenty, and age (too little or too much of it) was sometimes a just defence. Had she loved him? She couldn't remember. Did she love him now? She didn't know. She was too much occupied with her own life to think about him. If she had feelings for him, she didn't know what they were. Perhaps he did. Perhaps she should ask him some time.

She watched him eat a piece of bread. She saw the way his cheeks bulged, and his mouth, emitting words, also emitted wet crumbs, and allowed everyone to see the grey fillings in his back molars. As he leaned back in his chair, to make a point, a blue budleia flower hung limply over his ear.

'Who do you know who still reads books, anyway? I bet you never read a book from start to finish. Look, this house is full of books,' he gestured wildly in the direction of the little house holding Sally's white shelves, the paperbacks mixed with pink china owls, glossy hardbacks jostling up against jasmine and ivy plants, 'and most of them you've never read. They're just a symbol. A cultural symbol. A product.'

'Who sounds like a Marxist now? Such materialism, from the lips of a liberal economist! Come on Charity, let's go and look at the roses.'

At the bottom of the small paved garden, Charity and Sally sat together on a wooden seat. Behind them were other gardens, carved jealously out of polluted stretches of urban living, and in front of them rose the backs of the houses in Sally's street: dark squares, with smaller yellow squares in them like children's pop-up books – here an arm, there a shape undressing, here an argument, there a lullaby.

'You're right, he can be awfully boring, my husband,' reflected Charity, referring to the moment she'd just experienced.

'I don't dislike James, you know. Not at all. I think I was just making a general observation about marriage. But maybe anything would make me irritable tonight.'

'Why, what's the matter?' Charity's attention reassembled itself on Sally's face, milk-like in the moonlit garden.

'I want to have a child,' said Sally.

'So?'

'I don't think I can.'

'It takes two to make a baby,' said Charity reflexively: it wasn't funny, but it did make a point. '"*I* want to have a baby," you said. But reproduction isn't something women do for themselves, surely?'

'I'm getting older,' went on Sally, ignoring her. 'Thirty-five. It hits us all. The biological clock.' She stopped and brushed some monochrome crumbs off the red flowers on the skirt of her dress. 'Actually, I don't know whether I want to *be* a mother. But I want to *have* a baby. I want to have a big belly, and feel a life inside me, and I want to go into Mothercare and buy little pastel clothes – white bonnets, lemon stretch suits, soft pink cardigans. And I want to go into hospital and be called "Mrs Lawrence". I want a label on my hand which says that I'm a mother, and who I'm a mother of. And I want to look down at my breast and see a baby lying there. Sucking and holding me with its tiny hands like a warm pink flower.'

'*You* want, *you* want,' repeated Charity. 'You want a hell of a lot of things.'

'Well, what's wrong with that?' Sally was angry. 'I didn't want it when you did. And now I do.'

'I got married,' pointed out Charity.

'That's got nothing to do with it. You're drunk.'

'Alright. It hasn't got a lot to do with it. But what I mean is, *how* are you going to do it? You can't do it all on your own, can you?'

'That's not the problem. Eric isn't keen on the idea, but he's just about prepared to go along with it. But that's not the problem, either. I had my coil out six months ago. Nothing's happened yet. That's the problem.'

'And what did you expect?' asked Charity, moved to anger. 'Instant conception? It's not like opening a bank account or getting a job, you know. You can't just decide. The intellect has nothing to do with it.'

'I know, I know.' Sally sighed. 'That's what's so unfair. If we can decide *not* to have children, why can't we decide *to* have them?' She paused, looked at the moon. 'Charity, tell me how to make a baby, I'm becoming obsessed.'

She put her arm round Sally's shoulders. 'Try not to worry about it,' she said lamely. 'Time. It takes time.'

The sharp feel of Sally's shoulders under the thin silk dress accompanied Charity on the drive home and inserted itself into her dreams. When they were in bed, James turned to her, pushed up her short white nightdress, and hurriedly penetrated her. She was not ready, but he did not wait. As he came, he clutched her left breast wildly, much as he had gestured towards Sally's white shelves.

She dreamed of bones bleached in the moonlight. She thought she saw a witch fly across the face of the moon, but she wasn't sure. And then suddenly she was at a terribly polite party talking to a very nice blond young man. She stroked his cheek. No-one thought this remarkable. The young man laughed. 'I've suddenly realised something I've known for eleven years,' he said. 'Fucking's clever.'

At first she didn't know what he meant. Then she did: 'Because it's clever not to think it silly,' she said.

'Exactly,' replied the young man.

The next morning at work the dream came back to her. She was standing drinking coffee with Mark Carleton, and was saying something to him about the organisation of teaching in the department, when the conversation with the blond young man returned to her. She felt herself flush, and thought she discerned in Carleton's eyes a crystallisation of his attitude towards her. But she turned away from it, in a sudden flush of adolescent embarrassment.

Carleton was enjoying the start of his new life. He was the kind of person who needed to make changes from time to time; these changes gave him his characteristically electric energy. Changing jobs, moving house, having children and, not least of all, having affairs, were his very life-blood. For example, his father's death last year of a stroke had, of course, been distressing, but it had given Carleton a vital message about the brevity of life and the need to get on with it while you still can. Accordingly, he had immediately started an affair with a young Californian student, and had launched himself into a book on the social construction of everyday life. The student, Lorraine, had a hard golden body and an air of nonchalance about everything which had impressed him greatly. But she had an unfortunate habit of chewing gum, even in bed. She would move the gum to the side of her mouth when Carleton kissed her, but still he would sometimes encounter it. His tongue would thrust itself into a ball of stickiness and, with a predictability that amazed him, his erection would subside, and he would have to think of some excuse for his poor performance.

Lorraine faded, and the book was not finished, though it was ultimately to generate an expensive and reasonably interesting research project. Carleton wasn't worried, either about the demise of the affair or about the uncompleted book. He possessed a comfortable arrogance towards women (the world was full of them), and he confidently believed that the longer books took to write, the greater they would be.

The theme of his unwritten book continued to occupy him, and he knew it was important: the idea was that the individual's social identity is created not only by other people (a traditional sociological argument) but also by oneself, through two strategies: management of self and presentation of self. Each of these two strategies is performed countless times in one's ordinary daily existence. But mostly they aren't articulated, defined or recognised to be ways in which identities are created. They need to be reconstructed, by being put into words, by being part of a conversation. For this reason Carleton had started to interview people about their daily lives. He had developed an extraordinary degree of interest in such details as the first actions people performed on waking (some people turned off the alarm clock, some removed their ear plugs, some farted: there was no end to the variety of initiatory movements), and in how people thought about, and structured, the needs of their bladders (there were those who emptied them as one would fill the stomach of a baby, every four hours, and there were those who did not appear to be aware of anything except a need to pee maybe twice a day).

It was Carleton's hope that this latest change of job would provide him with an opportunity to finish his book. In the States he'd had to do an enormous amount of teaching. At the Regent's College Department of Sociology he thought he could get away with delegating most of the teaching and administrative chores he disliked to others. Having met all his future colleagues he could now see why the place lacked dynamism. The men were either boring or weird. Pascoe, for instance, seemed to be a man of extraordinary mediocrity, and the gleam in Swinhoe's eyes was positively criminal. Carleton made a mental note to ask young Kirkwood about his thesis, something to do with the street life of unemployed school leavers in the East End of London, he believed. Did they have it, and was it a good thing? Denby's review article on 'Political Marriages: Conflict and Collusion' came back to him dimly from the unread recesses of the *Sociological Review*. He supposed he would have to take an intelligent interest in that as well.

The women were more interesting. (Women, he suspected, always were.) Like his own reputation, Margaret Lacey's preceded her. She was said to be a very clever woman, a leading advocate of feminism, unmarried, but interested in sexual liaisons. People said she liked men. While Carleton didn't give much thought to the meaning of this phrase, it worried him slightly, because of the possible synonymity between being liked and being used.

And Charity Walton interested him, too. Yet he was puzzled

as to why. In the first place, she wasn't his type. She was dark, and he liked women with fair hair that swung in the wind and carried the sun in it. She was too tall. She was married, and he knew from some remarks Steve Kirkwood had made that she had several children. His policy was to avoid becoming involved with women with children. He already shared his own wife's attention with their two daughters, and he didn't wish to share anyone else's.

They had a seminar that afternoon at the department, the first of the term. Mavis had appeared in Carleton's doorway earlier.

'Egg or cheese?'

'I beg your pardon?'

'Sandwiches for the seminar. I'm just popping out to buy them. Would you like egg or cheese?'

'Are those the only two options?' he had asked.

'Oh no, Professor, of course not.' Mavis got a kick out of being deferential. 'It's just that we all seem to be vegetarians here, and you never know where meat has been, do you?'

The seminar was on social class and ethnicity: methodological and ethical issues. The man who gave it, a lecturer from Cardiff called Brian Partingdon, made the fatal mistake of trying to eat his egg sandwich at the same time. The egg got in the way of the differentiation between ethnic and ethical. Carleton found himself concentrating with difficulty and nearly falling asleep, a habit he was trying to rid himself of, since it moved him over the border from eccentricity to rudeness. To keep himself awake, he watched the dusty afternoon light encircling Charity Walton's head. Today she wore a green cotton dress with splashes of red and black and white. Matching green earrings in the shape of parrots. She had nice ears, he noticed, lightly pointed and a delicate pale pink. He had just begun to reflect on the motivations women had to make holes in their ears, when Brian Partingdon consumed his last piece of egg and announced that he thought he would finish at that point, so as to allow plenty of time for discussion.

'Thank you, thank you,' mumbled Mark. 'I found that very enlightening. I'm sure we're all very pleased that you found it

· 21 ·

possible to give us this preview of your BSA paper. Has anyone anything they would like to say, particularly in relation to the main theme Brian raised?' Carleton had no idea what the main theme was, but he was sure there ought to have been one. If there was, then he would have said the right thing, and if there wasn't, then he would still have said the right thing, because he would have pointed out its absence.

The discussion proceeded. As it rambled on round him, Carleton decided to try to get Charity on her own as soon as he could. He wanted to get into her soul. He thought he might find himself there.

Every Thursday Charity worked late; James took over at home. This particular Thursday she planned to start a paper she had to write for an international sociological conference in Amsterdam later that year.

As she formulated her plan for the paper, she gradually became aware of noises in the building that ought not to be heard. The sound of a chair being moved, of a typewriter bell, and then an almighty explosion, as though a structural collapse had occurred. She ran up the stairs and opened the door of Mark Carleton's office, to find him up a ladder in a volcano of books.

'Oh, it's you,' she said, 'I thought the building was empty. What on earth happened?'

He turned and nearly fell off the ladder. 'I'm trying to organise my books,' he said, 'alphabetically. But there were too many Bs, so I shifted a shelf along and everything fell down. I'm sorry, did I give you a shock?'

He came down from the ladder, wiped his dusty hands on the sides of his trousers and trailed one hand through his thick hair, leaving a grey snail's track across his forehead. 'I think I've done enough. I'll finish it tomorrow. I'll only drop more books and disturb you again if I go on now. Books – how I hate them!' He looked despairingly around at the scattered volumes. 'Oh well,' he wiped his hands on his trousers again, 'as I said, enough is enough. I have to get out of this place. Why don't we go and have a drink?'

So Charity Walton and Mark Carleton crossed Beaumont Square as the sun set behind the houses, filling the sky with an apricot glow. They went into a wine bar and Carleton, being the man, ordered a bottle of house wine. They sat down and started to talk. Whatever *she* wanted, Carleton had decided to find out about *her*. Nonetheless, there was a hesitation: although new liaisons weren't new to Carleton, he knew they never lasted, because he quickly tired of them or complications developed, and he was drawn ineluctably back to the calm of his married life with Jane. Jane was Carleton's stability and peace. If there was one essential view Carleton had of his wife, it was of her reading a book in her favourite chair, a wingback upholstered in a quiet blue velvet, against which the line of her glossy almond hair cut a Renoir image. Jane was a contemplative woman. Carleton saw her as a nun in another life: a chief abbess with cool eyes running the sunny stone recesses of a convent in Italy. He could just see it standing on the side of a hill, topping verdant Biblical olive groves. These female friendships of his were all just a temporary trick, a diversion from the mainstream. They'd been happening for so long, he regarded them as part of marriage. He didn't expect any of them to create more than a ripple on the surface of the marital pond.

Thus, slowly, Charity let Carleton know items about herself, about her marriage to James, her children, her domestic arrangements, her solitary childhood in the hop fields of Kent, her friendships, her interests. She even found herself telling him intimate stories about herself: how formative it had been being sent away on holiday to some aunts for a month when she was only five, and how she had minded, and had soaked the lavender-scented pillow with tears.

'You *are* an unusual woman,' he concluded, after this short and selective acquaintance with her. Yet what was really remarkable about her, of course, was her significance to him at that moment. 'I don't think I've ever met anyone like you,' he went on, mindlessly.

'There isn't anyone like me,' she replied, flattered to be called unusual, which is naturally why he had chosen to say it.

'*Of course* there isn't anyone like you. Women,' said Carleton, as though beginning a lecture, 'I'm fascinated by them, you see. I *have* to be involved in them. They're much more interesting than men, more vital, more profound. It's women who hold the power, you know. Not the economic power, not the silly things about voting and being an MP and dressing up like policemen, but the real power over us, over the human condition. We need you!'

Charity immediately understood from this speech that Carleton was a philanderer. Surely his involvement in women, whatever its philosophical base, must take the form of affairs?

'No, I haven't had a lot of affairs,' he told her, when she asked him, 'but I have had some. Why do you ask?'

'It doesn't matter.' She was embarrassed, not wanting him to know about her incipient interest in his private affairs. 'What about your wife, does she know?' she went on.

'Jane only knew about one of them. I'm terribly discreet. I'm very good at lying. Some people actually don't *want* to know the truth, you know. Even if they feel it in the atmosphere, they disregard it, turn the other way.'

'Why do you do it?' she asked, peremptorily.

'Do what?'

'Have affairs. Deceive your wife.'

'Those are two different questions. I've told you why I have affairs – because I have to be involved. I don't tell my wife because I love her. I *do* love her. I don't want to hurt her. I don't want to leave the marriage. Apart from anything else, the children would be upset. But I can't make myself turn away from new opportunities, new relationships. I think the meaning of life is there, in these encounters we have. Don't you?'

'You hurt by deceiving.' Charity wasn't about to be deflected from her main point.

'I don't think so. Why are you going on about this, anyway? Are you trying to prove something? That I'm a dreadful person, perhaps?'

'Yes,' said Charity. Her face relaxed, she laughed. 'Naturally you're a dreadful person. You're a man, you're abusing your power over women, even if you say we're the ones with the power over you. Besides which, you're a sociologist, you know it all. But it doesn't mean I don't like you.'

She looked at him across the table, and saw that she might mean it. Their knees touched, and she felt an unusual warmth flooding her body. Along with the warmth came apprehension.

'*Do* you like me?' He leaned across towards her, knocking over the little pot of roses between them. It spilled its pink liquid deeply into the layered tissue of the paper tablecloth and then dripped like a leaky tap on to the cold grey stone floor. At the same time, Carleton gazed earnestly into Charity's eyes. His own blue ones sent out narrow white beams of light, designed to enter her mind and discover the truth.

'I don't know you,' she said. 'I've only just met you. I'm a very cautious person. It takes me time to get to know people.'

'Charity, Charity,' he sang suddenly. 'Why are you called Charity?'

'From the Latin *caritas* – love,' she said. 'Not sexual love, but the generic love human beings feel for one another. My mother is a Quaker. A very gentle, unassuming person. She finds the world a disappointing place. People are always arguing, fighting, killing one another. I was her redemption. That's why she called me Charity. I hated the name when I was young. At school they called me "lavatory". Now I like the name, I like its sound, and its meaning.'

'Have you got another name as well?'

'Alice.'

'Alice in Wonderland,' he said. 'Very appropriate.'

'Or Alice Through the Looking Glass,' she replied, 'you never know, I might see everything the other way round from other people, or even be a cause of other people doing so.'

Carleton couldn't deal with this remark, so he remained silent.

'And *your* name?' she said, 'I suppose it's quite unre*mark*able?'

'Very funny.'

'Mark. It could stand as a symbol for a man, for men as a category,' she reflected, 'but I don't suppose that's why your mother gave it to you?'

'My mother's motives always were impenetrable to me. I was her only child, she wanted a simple life. So she gave me a simple name to go along with it. It means "war-like". She didn't know that, of course. She didn't know, either, that one of the first Marks invented shorthand. It wasn't a popular name until the nineteenth century. People were put off by King Mark in *Tristram and Iseult.*' He saw she was puzzled. '*Tristan and Isolde* to you.'

'What was wrong with King Mark?'

'More or less everything. I'll tell you one day.'

She looked at him sideways. 'I'm hungry.'

'Is that relevant? Okay, let's go and eat.'

'Don't you have to go home to your wife?'

'Don't you have to go home to your husband?'

'Don't pretend everything's equal, it's not.'

'Then don't be nasty,' he said. 'Your remark was out of place. It's just the two of us now. We don't need to bother with other people.'

They left the wine bar, and as they turned down a narrow street in search of a restaurant he took her hand. His fingers were like hawthorne twigs, angular and knobbly. He moved his hand in hers, and she felt the hair on its back, strangely soft, like angora. They walked to Soho and went to an Italian restaurant. As they sat there, holding their large green plastic menus, he put his down abruptly and asked her if she knew what was happening.

'Do you?' She watched him with eyes that appeared profoundly dark.

'Yes. We're falling in love,' he said.

'But I can't fall in love with you,' she protested immediately.

'Why not?'

'Because I don't fall in love. That's the first reason. Secondly, because I don't *want* to fall in love. And, last, because I can't possibly be in love with *you*; you're my boss, it wouldn't be right.'

He was amused at her rationality, at her odd notion of morality. 'Your arguments don't persuade me.'

She wasn't surprised to hear this. Nor that he made no obvious attempt during the meal to bring her round to his point of view. For he was confident that reason – her reasons – wouldn't prevail, and she, aware of, and attracted by, his arrogance, felt there was probably no choice to be made, despite the political position she had stated.

'Good God!' Charity looked at her watch. 'It's ten o'clock, I've got to go.'

'I'll drive you home,' he said.

'No you won't, I've got my bike.'

They ran back to the square. She went round the side of the building to fetch her bicycle from where she had left it, pinioned to the wall, in an earlier life.

'Charity, Charity,' he sang again, after her, inserting his thin body between hers and the wall, 'come here, Charity, I want you.'

'You have no right. . . ' she began.

'It's not about rights,' he said, and kissed her. He ran his hands lightly over her body, and then placed them like rocks on her shoulders. 'I promise you one thing,' he said, redundantly, 'I'll never lie to you. You're different from other women. Whatever else happens, I won't deceive you. I'll tell you the truth.'

'Why are you saying that?' Her eyes in the dark stone passage might have been frightened.

'Don't worry, it'll all be clear to you one day. And if it's not, then what I said won't matter anyway.'

2 ✳ FATE

'Women's fate is bound up with that of perishable things
. . . The real reason why she does not believe in a
liberation is that she has never put the powers of liberty to a
test; the world seems to her to be ruled by an obscure
destiny against which it is presumptuous to rise in protest' –
The Second Sex, p. 302

The water that filled the bay gleamed with the wide and honest
rays of the midday sun. Although the water was tidal, its meeting
with the creamy sands of the beach took the form only of tiny
immature waves, affectionately lapping children's feet, seaweed
and the debris of a long summer. The slant of the masts of sailing
boats pointed to the direction of the wind; there were at least as
many sailing boats as people in the bay. Later, when the tide was
in and the wind made the boats' masts sing, people would take
them out beyond the sandbank to where the water was deepest,
raise colourful sails in front of them, and exercise their stomach
muscles in an effort not to fall in.

Charity sat looking wide-eyed at the bay with Rachel beside
her, cross-legged, eating a biscuit. The little girl munched and
sang simultaneously. Silver dappled the incoming tide in the
blue distance: across the bay rose the contours of a forest. Grass
tickled Charity's feet, and the sun changed the colour of her
skin. It had taken an endless negotiation, this time alone with
Rachel in Sally and Eric's rented house in France, waiting for
Mark to come on his way to a 'conference'. She did not know
how it would be, and sometimes couldn't make herself even

believe she had chosen it. Was it fate? She knew she was already under some sort of a compulsion to see Mark. This was both a burden and a privilege to her.

In the weeks immediately following their first encounter they had kept themselves away from the rest of the world and met secretly in the misty evenings under a railway bridge, in a smoky pub, by a designated seat in a wet empty park.

'Charity,' Mark had ventured one evening, as they sat watching a group of football fans cavorting around outside a Soho pub, 'We're going to sleep with one another, yes?'

'Yes.'

'It's only a matter of where and when.'

'And what it'll be like.'

'Are you worried?'

'No.'

'I just want to say something, to get it out of the way, really.'

'I haven't got VD,' she announced.

'I would never ask anyone that question.'

'Have *you* got any horrible diseases, then?'

'Don't be ridiculous.'

'So what was it you wanted to say?'

'Contraception. What are we going to do about contraception?'

'I'm glad you asked. Have you noticed how in films and in novels people never mention that? They just leap or fall into bed and babies don't get conceived, or they do, and then everyone's amazed that such a thing could have happened.'

'I can't say I have noticed that.'

'It's true, I assure you. People in novels and films never pee, either.'

'I love you,' he said, 'but please answer my question.'

'I've got a coil. I'm permanently protected. You don't need to worry. Or wear wellingtons, either.'

'Fine.' A look of relief passed across Mark's face. He leaned over and touched Charity's soft olive cheek and thought that everything that she said was absolutely new, and quite amazing.

And then Mark Carleton went away on holiday with his wife

Jane, aged thirty-seven, and his two daughters, Joanna and Susan, aged twelve and ten. A couple of days later the telegram had arrived from somewhere in Austria: it plopped innocently on to the mat, and Charity's children picked it up and stood over her while she read it, thinking that someone was ill, or had died, or their mother had won some fabulous prize she might share with them. But all the telegram said was 'I love you', and Charity had crumpled it up and put it in her pocket, and pushed the children away from her with some excuse about a meeting she was supposed to go to in Paris that had been cancelled. Then, with her hand round the crumpled telegram, she had gone into the kitchen and put the radio on, and the trumpet solo from Verdi's *Aida* had burst into the room and hovered in the air above the littered surfaces and over the crinkled yellow roses in the middle of the table, and she'd been filled with a prodigious happiness far greater, she supposed, than any she had felt before. Mark Carleton loved her! Hadn't he said so in a telegram? She took it out of her pocket, and uncreased it, and held it up to the light to make sure it was real.

Now he had done this, Charity would tell him how she felt. How did she feel? She sat down and put her hands round the roses, cupping their declining gold. Nature decays, and it decays the human world as well. But before that we are treated to moments of iridescence, which are out of time and beyond our knowing, and this is the very fate of which we speak when we say there is nothing else we can do, or could have done.

Mark had telephoned her the next day and asked her to find some time to see him later in the summer. He knew she was planning to go to France: she and James and the children always did. But this year their plans had remained vague: Charity was still scanning the papers for somewhere to stay. She told Mark she'd try to fix something, and she had. After her lecture on deception, what had she done? She had deceived James, of course. She hadn't gone to him and said, I want to spend some time with my new lover, will you look after the children? She'd said, don't you think it'd be a good idea if you and the boys went off together for a bit? As long as she made the arrangements, that was fine with him. And so she did. But she didn't feel she could unload Rachel on

James as well, nor did she really want to. So Rachel would be there when Charity and Mark met.

'Mummy,' said Rachel, who had now finished her biscuit, 'when are we going back to the house?'

'Soon, when the tide's come in, and we've had a swim.'

'Are you coming in, then?'

'Of course.'

'Can I swim on your back? Do you think those little girls are coming today?'

The houses fronting the bay, standing low under the trees with aprons of grass in front of them, seemed to shelter an inordinate number of little girls, who from time to time would all burst forth in shiny swimsuits and rainbow hairclips and spring like jewels into the water.

Taking off her light cotton dress, Charity lay on her front in her bikini, burying her head in her arms. Rachel got up and walked around, humming lightly and watching the little French girls. Charity fell into the kind of somnolence in which past, present and future intermingle as the different elements of the earth can: as the water and light did now across the bay, lacing waves and sunbeams in a speckled pattern of fused and fragile energy.

How lucky she was. She was a woman who had everything. A husband, four children, a lover, and a soon-to-be successful career. What more could one ask for? Her body, soaked in the sun, reflected back into the water of the bay the gloss of comfort absorbed over the last few weeks with James and the children in France. They had camped in the Perigord, eaten truffles and *confit de canard*, and tried hard to have a successful family holiday.

'Did you know,' James had said, reading his guide book one evening, 'that the Massif Central is twice the size of Switzerland? It's a sort of stepping stone between the Alps and the Pyrenees. In fact,' he went on, 'if you forget about all these political considerations to do with country borders, then you start conceptualising places in a totally different way. For instance, this bit of France we're in is part of the Iberian Peninsula. In

1896 a German chap called Willkomm estimated that there were 5,660 different species of plants on the peninsula, and that 1,465 of them were exclusive to the area. Imagine that.'

Charity did. She put all 5,660 plants in the same confined space, a greenhouse perhaps, where they all seemed to be fighting for air. And the atmosphere was humid and breathless. Kew Gardens on an August Sunday morning.

Out of the corner of her eye, she could see Dan and Harry doing something unspeakable to a cat. They had this wordless habit of inciting one another. Dan held the cat's head between his legs and stood facing the tawny, slow-moving river as though he had nothing to do with anything. Harry crouched in front of him forcefeeding the poor animal a crushed geranium. Charity looked the other way. In the face of such criminal solidarity, she had always felt hopeless. They'd never seemed to need her, as Tom and Rachel did. Watching Dan and Harry together as babies – even now – she felt jealous of their intimacy, which was bizarre. Jealous of her own children's closeness to one another! Unable to imitate that in her own life, perhaps.

But if Charity looked outwards and observed the countryside, she was able to push both the material and the symbolic oppressions of the setting away. She could see, for instance, the Dordogne in its changing states and conditions: here wide and brown like an English schoolgirl's hair, there parched and bisected by channels of mud in which the stick-like figures of children played. The river's banks and bridges and overhanging flora observed a grandeur unknown in the regions of Charity's childhood, spent playing pooh sticks in a tiny river down the road from the farmhouse her parents bought to give her the childhood they thought she deserved – protected, peaceful and proper, as regulated as the proverbial English country garden. She went to school, the same school, for thirteen years, and came home again: did her homework and passed her exams. She learnt the violin, though never to play it well enough to give herself pleasure. She took dancing lessons, and riding lessons, and was better on the ground than on a horse. She could never really come to terms with its animality; its smell remained offensive, its uncontrolled evacuations disturbing. She felt at odds with it, as in general with all nature, which was very contrary of her, since her parents had placed her in a natural setting with the aim of giving her a good experience.

It was in Kent that her first sexual liaison had presented her with some of the same problems of communicating with another species that she'd encountered with horses. David had disturbed her regulated life, just as Mark was doing now; though then it was her mother's eruptions that she had feared. She remembered David as all women remember in a ritual way the first man who took their fancy. She remembered his seriousness, his solicitude for her, and she remembered now, suddenly, for no apparent reason, a walk they had taken one day in the Chiltern hills. David had just learnt to drive, and had borrowed his father's blue Mercedes, and they'd motored first into London to deliver a package to someone for his father, and then out down the A40. They had walked round an estate and been chased by the proprietor's alsatian, and Charity had been frightened and had wanted David's protection. She had put a hand on his arm in panic, but had felt his arm, his whole body, stiffen, in exactly the same anguish that had gripped her. 'Let's get out of here,' he'd said, and run on ahead of her, away. It had come as a surprise to her that he was as frightened as she. She'd never really recovered from the disappointment of finding that, at least in some respects, the condition of the sexes was the same. She had supposed them to be different, and wished to continue in this supposition.

When Mark arrived later that day, he almost fell off the train in his haste, clutching an old brown suitcase and wearing a rucksack on his back. His face was surprisingly tanned as it came towards her across the tiny, geranium-bedecked station.

'It's good to see you.'

'Yes,' she acknowledged.

'I don't see why you have to bury yourself in a place that's so difficult to get to,' he complained. 'I had to change trains three times.'

'But it's worth it, isn't it!'

Back at the house, Eric was barbecuing some Toulouse *saucisse*, and Sally was sitting reading. She stood up and held out her hand.

'So you made it! Charity wasn't sure you'd master the French railway system.'

'Nothing to it,' he said, depositing his suitcase on the crisp green lawn. 'Well, not a lot, when you accept that nothing happens as you expect it to. Trains are only like life, aren't they?'

'I'll show you to your room.' Sally led him into the house, a cool stone-floored building with grey shutters and a kitchen painted canary yellow. She opened a door off the kitchen. 'I've aired the bed. I should warn you that the basin doesn't work very well, and the bidet's really only for show.'

'It's perfect,' said Mark, 'absolutely perfect.' His face beamed and the angle of his body expressed an unqualified happiness.

'I'll leave you to get organised,' said Sally. 'We'll be in the garden, come and have a drink when you're ready.'

He put his suitcase down once more and peered round the door looking for Charity. She wasn't there. He stood still and listened: her voice came to him from the garden. He shut the door and washed his face, drying it with a clean white towel. He looked towards the bed, which was a magnificent wooden affair covered in a pink and green patchwork quilt. He wanted Charity in it. He wanted Charity.

In the garden, Sally was giving Charity her first impressions. 'He's certainly good-looking. Quite a ladies' man. I wonder where that phrase came from?' Her mind wandered. 'I know what it means, but how did it get into the language?'

'I don't think I care about that at the moment.' Charity made a face.

'But maybe I'm going to give you some advice, C.D.,' said Sally suddenly. The use of the childhood name, C.D., for Charity Dawson, made Charity listen.

'What kind of advice?'

'Don't expect him to change because of you. That's the mistake everyone makes when they fall in love. They think they'll be able to mould that person in their own image. But it doesn't work.' Sally's head nodded sagely in the late afternoon sunlight. 'Sorry. I sound very preachy, don't I? But I've been thinking about things a lot in the last few weeks, away from London and all the normal hassles. Love's only a temporary distraction from the real problems, you see. Look at me. I was in love with Eric. But now the real problem is that I want to have a child. He can't help me with that.'

'But love in itself is a kind of change, isn't it?'

'Love doesn't make the world go round. The laws of gravity do that. All love can alter is the surface of things: underneath everything stays the same. When you're in love, you want the sun, the moon and the stars, don't you?'

Charity smiled. 'I think I've got the sun, the moon and the stars. Or I'm about to get them.'

'No, you haven't. You only *think* you have. But wait and see. Have you met Mark's wife?' she asked suddenly.

'No. Why?'

'Because you learn a lot about men by meeting their wives. If you meet a man's wife you immediately see all his dependencies, all his weaknesses.' Charity thought Sally might be right about this. 'To learn about a woman, on the other hand,' Sally continued, 'you have to meet her mother.'

Charity laughed ruefully. 'Where's Rachel?'

'Down the bottom of the garden, helping Eric with the barbecue.'

The bushes emitted a thick smoke, infant squeaks and a protesting male voice.

A few minutes later, Mark joined them and started eating the various bits and pieces arranged on the aperitif table. Shiny olives – he threw the stones into the sunflower beds. Great bunches of radishes recently uprooted and washed, their feathery green ends opposing naked pink and white tips. 'These need salt,' he announced, abruptly.

Charity leapt up to fetch it, and Mark admired the way her hips moved down the garden. She was wearing a green skirt of some deliciously light material. Her golden-brown shoulders arose splendidly out of a black silk top. As she passed it on her way to the kitchen, a rampant blue hibiscus bush touched her arm gently, its vanilla centre anointing her, as Mark himself felt he should like to.

After dinner, Charity put Rachel to bed. The child was sleeping on a camp bed in her room, tucked between the fireplace and the desk, on which Rachel had arranged her pink plastic Sindy house and a series of synthetic coloured horses with pull-out manes and tails that recalled for her mother the evacuating horses of her childhood. Rachel fell asleep easily, thumb in place, dolls and bears enclosing her.

Sally, Eric, Mark and Charity decided not to have coffee.

'It gives you cancer of the pancreas, anyway,' offered Mark, discouragingly.

'Well, drink gives you cirrhosis of the liver,' pointed out Eric, not to be outdone.

'Don't you think,' said Charity, suddenly clear on the matter, 'that it's all a question of what we *want* to die of? We can choose the cause of our own death. We choose to drink or to smoke. We decide to eat aspirins, or drown in a cave, or to ride a bicycle in a big city. None of it's accidental.' She was impressed with her own logic.

Mark had listened intently to this little speech. 'You shouldn't ride a bicycle in the London traffic.'

'Why not? I've been doing it for years. It's good for me. Nothing's ever happened to me.'

'But it will, it will.' Mark saw Charity wounded and lying in a gutter, bleeding. It hurt him to think of her like that. It hurt him more than he could say.

'You're a pessimist, then?' Sally leaned forward, as if to read Mark's character off his face.

'No, I'm not, not usually.' He didn't actually consider himself a person who thought gloomy thoughts. He looked on the bright side of everything, trotting out such aphorisms to himself as 'everything works out in the end', 'every cloud has a silver lining', and so on. So he'd been taken aback by his upsetting intimation of Charity's mortality. He couldn't understand why he should have thought Charity might die. Moreover, the thought agitated him precisely because of her demise and not, less altruistically, because it might have occurred before a consummation of their love.

They extinguished the smoking barbecue and removed the remains of the meal.

'Why don't you go to the ocean?' suggested Sally. 'It's a clear night, you'll be able to commune with nature. Take my car. Eric knows the way. I'll stay with Rachel. I'm tired, anyway.'

Although Mark had in mind more of a communion with Charity than with nature, the three of them piled into Sally's Peugeot and steamed off to the ocean.

To reach the shore, you had to climb a massive sand dune. Eric told them not to worry about it, because it wasn't the biggest dune in Europe – that was three kilometres away. They climbed. The white sand was still warm, and it shifted as they walked, so the muscles in the calves of their legs quickly ached. Stars lit the scene, as Sally had said they would, giving radiance to the thick salty grasses and the violet thistles that lined their path. A few minutes of breathlessness brought them down to the boundless plane of the ocean shore. The waves moved gently, but apart from that there were no sounds. Charity lay down on the sand to study the stars. Mark stood over her, conscious of Eric's presence, of his own visiting status; but, most of all, of Charity's body spread out before him, like a map waiting to be read, describing passageways, tunnels, roundabouts, public and private rights of way. He thought he saw beneath the folds of her green skirt the space between her legs, and he longed to put his hand there, and on her breasts, which trembled with the lungs of the ocean and the star-filled sky.

He yawned. 'I'm exhausted,' he said.

She looked up at him. 'After your long journey, and all those changes of trains.' He seemed so tall, standing there, a shadow against the sand. She let her eyes travel from his English sandals, across the distances of his light brown cotton trousers, up his white shirt to his brown neck and magnificent face, which wore a quite pure expression of moonlit kindness: no hint of arrogance, of malevolence, of betrayal could be read into those soft lines – nothing but endless good inhabited them.

It was midnight when they reached the house. Mark didn't know what to say, how to ensure that his vision of Charity in his bed would materialise. Charity felt she couldn't say anything. So they said goodnight, and went to their own rooms.

In hers, Charity paced up and down in the blackness while Rachel slept, incognisant of her mother's panic. 'Oh well,' said Charity to herself, 'I shouldn't go to bed with him, anyway. This affair is doomed, a disaster. It's not the kind of thing I ought to do. I'm a respectable married woman.' Such protestations were, however, singularly unpersuasive, because she wanted to.

In his room, Mark stood looking out of the window into the black night. All the time he'd spent away with Jane and the girls had been a preparation for this moment. Fantasies had riddled his most ordinary actions: in opening a door, he had seen Charity walk through it, with her dark gleaming hair moving through the space he'd created; the coffee he'd prepared for Jane in their self-catering mountain chalet was made for Charity's smooth lips; when he stood looking at the alps, their white caps, which Susan had compared to meringues, were to him the symbols of something quite different. The train journey to France, so complained about, had in reality been an exciting adventure, laced with ideas about the union which was to take place; the slow rhythm of the provincial French trains had been the rhythm of their bodies, languorous and luxurious, scented and discerning.

He recalled an interview he'd done just before leaving London with an old lady living in the Cambridgeshire fens. He'd gone to talk to her about the routines of her everyday life, and had accidentally recovered from her an account which was far from ordinary. As an unmarried teenager, she'd given birth to a daughter who she'd then given up for adoption. She herself had never married, but had led an apparently satisfactory and active life in the village as a teacher, and as an aunt to many nieces and nephews. Then, when she was forty, her adopted daughter had traced her and come to see her, and this balanced and extroverted woman had been plunged into a deep depression which years of various therapies had scarcely lifted. The daughter, twenty-three when she contacted her mother, was clever, attractive and successful. Moreover, the two women had instantly liked one another and had felt a bond between them. No one could understand the mother's depression, why the daughter's appearance had precipitated it. Except the old lady herself, now, years later, talking to Mark Carleton in her little house in the flat landscape of the fen country: 'It was because I realised what I'd missed,' she said. 'I saw her, my daughter, who'd been brought up by another woman, and it was only then that I knew what I'd done when I'd had her adopted. I didn't know it at the time. How could I have known it, without seeing her? I had to see her to understand what I'd lost by giving up all those years of motherhood.'

So Mark's meeting with Charity had encouraged a different light to fall upon his life. Nothing would ever be the same again. And yet, despite this new vision, it appeared he was to sleep alone in this French house. He could not go to Charity's room because of Rachel. He *would* not go to her room, because, perhaps, after all, she did not desire him. She had to desire him. He realised with a shock that this mattered to him. Normally it didn't. A woman's presence was all that was required, since her presence meant an automatic receptivity. He removed his clothes, and climbed into bed. He didn't feel like brushing his teeth: the action would seem out of place, being designed to preserve a rejected body.

The shutters on the window had been left open, so that the remembered light of the ocean streamed across the table in front of the window, through the vase of purple and yellow dried flowers, across the worn matting on the floor, over the white sheets and the brown hairs on his chest, now interspersed with grey. His hand travelled with the moonlight through these hairs, and he allowed himself to wonder how Charity's breasts might feel against them: how her nipples might poke and rise in their undergrowth, and touch his skin and penetrate his heart. He thought he could see her there, standing in the moonlight: her body was entirely white, like marble, and it gleamed with the translucence of a bar of Pears soap; in fact, he began to wonder if he hadn't borrowed the image from the decadent 'Miss Bubbles' posters, in which cherubic little girls were pictured alongside orbiting bubbles of soap in fields of emerald grass. Yet images of art couldn't distract him from practices of life, and he felt his penis stiffen with a will of its own. His hand enclosed it, and experienced its silkiness, so strange, he had always thought, on an otherwise rough male body. As he held it, it seemed to grow enormous and become also an image in his brain: a cypress tree trying to reach the sky, the stamen of a blue hibiscus open to the sun. He thought he felt the air around the cypress tree and the flowers redolent with sexual meaning: butterflies passed nonchalantly through it, and crickets chirped knowingly and mockingly at his disappointment, so concretely expressed in this piece of flesh without a home.

The door opened. 'Are you asleep?' whispered Charity's voice. Mark stirred, said yes, and then no, and thought perhaps she was a dream. She wore a nightdress of some extremely fine cotton material: even in the dim light he could see it had roses embroidered round the neck, and a ribbon falling to her waist. He threw back the quilt, and she got into bed with him.

'I shouldn't be here,' she said.

He propped himself on one elbow and looked down on to her lovely face: he thought he had never seen such untraversed loveliness before. She was the only absolutely undefiled woman he had ever met and had the good fortune to gaze upon in the pale moonlight of a French summer night. Her face below him was like a child's in the thin light, unlined despite her years of scholarship and domestic administration.

'You belong here,' he told her. 'I was dreaming of you. I want you,' he said. 'See how much I want you.' He took her hand and placed it round his penis, where his own had been. 'See how huge it is, it's waiting for you. Oh Charity.'

They were standing in line in the Credit Lyonnais, waiting to cash their travellers' cheques.

'Now we've met, and fallen in love, and gone to bed,' began Mark, 'what happens next?'

'Let's think.' She looked at him, through the plate glass window, at the tourists in the hot streets. 'What happens in books?'

'I'll tell you what doesn't happen.' He spoke authoritatively. 'What doesn't happen is nothing.'

'What do you mean?'

'Things progress. Something happens. People don't just go on being in love, fiddling around with one another.'

'Is fiddling around what we're doing?'

'Don't be silly. You know this is passion,' he said, imperiously.

She noticed the patches of sweat under his arms, and the way his shirt hung out of his trousers at the back.

'Monsieur?' said the short-sleeved short-haired bank official pertly, 'qu'est que vous voulez?'

'Ah yes,' said Mark. His French was almost non-existent. 'Je veux changer one of these.' He waved his red book of Thomas Cook travellers' cheques under the official's nose, like a rag.

'Et votre pièce d'identité, Monsieur?' the official inquired.

'What?'

'Your passport,' said Charity.

Mark handed it over.

'Did you answer my question?'

'What?'

'Is that all you can say today?' They laughed. Sally and Eric came in with Rachel, who was clutching six enormous baguettes. 'Hi Mum,' she said casually. Mark turned round and looked down at the child.

'Did you buy those by yourself?'

'Of course not,' said Rachel, scathingly, 'I'm only six, and I can't speak French.'

'Oh yes.' He felt foolish, which happened often, but had remarkably little effect on him, because his ego was like a mountain, having the ability to rise untouched from any landscape.

Some days later they were sitting at a café table overlooking the southernmost part of the bay. In front of them was a plate of assorted seafood, and a bottle of cold *entre deux mers*. The water this evening was an extraordinarily deep blue. Rachel was jumping repetitively off the wooden frame of the steps down to the beach, wearing only a pair of red knickers and some shiny blue plastic shoes. After a while she grew tired of this, and came to sit on her mother's knee.

'I want something to eat.'

'What would you like to eat?'

'I don't want those things.' She made a disgusted face at the seafood. 'I want chips.'

'Chips you shall have, then.' Mark stood up to attract the waiter's attention, and, in so doing, sent the bottle of *entre deux mers* crashing to the ground. 'Oh Jesus, I'm sorry. How careless of me.'

'You fool!' Charity's voice was absolutely without anger. Sally looked at her sharply. Charity typically would complain, rant on about men's clumsiness and lack of co-ordination, how acts such as this proved their general incompetence. But no! It didn't seem to matter to her how Mark behaved.

'You've got children yourself, haven't you, Mark?' she asked.

'Yup. Two girls. Susan's ten and Joanna, she's twelve.'

'Are they on holiday, too, now?'

'No. They're back in England. They've gone to stay with my wife's parents in Oxfordshire. They enjoy that, they get spoilt. And Jane gets a rest.'

'So she's having time to herself alone in the big city?'

Mark hadn't thought about Jane since he arrived in France. Now he'd been reminded of her existence he felt suddenly guilty. He decided he ought to telephone her.

Inside the café he inquired (in English) about a telephone, and was directed to a public call box in the street outside. After dialling twice, he reached Jane. She picked up the phone on its fourth ring.

'Jane? It's me.'

'Mark! Where are you? How's the conference?' She sounded genuinely pleased to hear his voice.

'I'm in a call box,' he said. 'It's one of those hotels without phones in the rooms.' He tried to swallow his words. 'The conference is okay, not very inspiring.'

'Is Kelvin there?'

John Kelvin was an old enemy of his. He thought quickly. 'No, thank God, he isn't. Couldn't make it at the last minute.'

'Have you given your paper?'

He couldn't remember whether he'd said he was going to give a paper or not. 'Tomorrow,' he said.

'I hope it goes well.'

'Everything alright with you?' He frantically pushed some more money into the machine.

'Yes, the girls are fine, Susan's got tonsillitis, but my mother's in her element looking after her.'

'I'm sure she is.' Mark thought of Jane's mother without affection as a waspish, prying woman with bony legs and glasses on a chain. 'And how are you enjoying yourself?'

'I'm fine. I like being alone, you know that. I'm playing the piano two hours a day. Tonight I'm going to a prom. Debussy *Images*, Ravel's *Aubade of the Buffoon*, and some Sibelius.'

'Oh.' He wondered idly who she was going with. Probably her friend Lesley. 'I've got to go now, Jane,' he said, 'the money's running out. I'll phone you again in a few days.'

'Look after yourself,' she said, 'I love you.'

He was just about to answer, though he wasn't sure how, when the little square on the coin box registered zero. He put the phone down and stood there, wondering what had moved Jane to such an utterance. Did she suspect something? Vaguely he recalled an incident in Tuxedo when his liaison with Lorraine had been in full swing and Jane had bought him a present of a locket with 'Jane' inscribed on it in italic gold lettering, which he was to hang round his neck in native Californian fashion. He'd hung it there, and Lorraine had protested. So he'd spent the whole time taking it on and off. One night in bed he'd found Jane peering intensely at his neck. 'It's got a knot in it.'

'What has?'

'The locket chain.'

'Oh.'

It was with difficulty he'd got himself out of that one.

When he rejoined the table, Rachel asked, 'What were you doing just now?'

'I was telephoning my wife,' he said, with astounding simplicity.

'If you've got a wife, why isn't she here?' Her simplicity was quite astounding, too.

'Because she's in England,' he replied, lamely.

'But wouldn't she like to be here? It's nice here, isn't it? She'd like the sunshine and the wine. Does your wife like wine? And what about those smelly oysters? I expect she'd rather be here than in rainy old England.' The child looked perversely at him from beneath her fringe.

'I expect so, yes.'

'But she wouldn't like to be here with you and my Mummy, would she?'

'Rachel, come on, that's enough of that,' said Charity quickly.

But Rachel was not to be deterred. 'I saw you kissing last night,' she giggled, 'I spied on you. You were in his room,' she pointed a salty finger at Mark, 'and you thought the door was closed, but it wasn't. You didn't close it properly. You shouldn't kiss my Mummy if you've got a wife,' she ended, severely.

Mark issued a nervous laugh, and crossed and recrossed his legs. Sally and Eric busied themselves with the seafood. Charity held Rachel firmly on her lap, and resolved to talk to her later. But what should she say? So I loved your father once, that's the story, and then I grew used to him, and he to me, and I got tired without knowing it, but he didn't. To him I was the same as I had always been; I breathed in the same way, moved in the same way, received him in the same way, so that he could have no understanding that I might be different now. What would have told us that I was? My own mind and body, a pain in my heart? Or an ache in my shoulders from the angle I was required to set them at? Life with James was alright. Love was never talked about. It was assumed. And now childbearing is over, the metal coil protects me, but from what?

As for Mark, will it be a marriage? Is it an affair? I can't tell you, Charity said to herself, because I don't know. There's nothing immoral about not knowing. Knowledge isn't morality. It's just an accident. You either have it, or you don't.

'It's not going to be easy, is it?' she said to him later, after dinner, when they were alone in his room.

'No.' A cloud shuttered his face, then passed. He lay down on the bed, where she was already sitting, and turned her to look at him. 'But would you want it to be easy?' He knew for himself the awful truth that most of the complications of his own life had been put there by him. Whenever they showed signs of abating, he piled more in there, so he could once more enjoy wallowing in a puddle of confusion and difficulty. 'My Charity.' He stroked her hair, ran his hands down her back and thighs. 'You have an absolutely beautiful body, you know.' He pushed the skirt of her dress up and ran his long fingers round the edges of her pants, playing with the few brackenish hairs that dangled there; and afterwards he flicked the inner surfaces of her thighs lightly with the legato touch of a pianist removing a Chopin nocturne from old ivory keys.

'Mark,' she said, 'whatever it's like, I want it to be just like this.' He raised his eyes from the hair crested on her pelvis like the forest fringing the bay, and smiled. 'There's nothing we can do about it anyway, my love. Nothing.'

They took off their clothes. He moved her legs apart and took her wet sexual lips in his own, enclosed the little button of her clitoris in the curl of his tongue. 'Gently,' she instructed. And so it was, until her desire for him hardened into the demand that something firmer than his pink curly tongue be placed in there. He arranged himself in a kneeling position above her, and in the moonlight the outline of his penis recalled the directional stamen of a hibiscus flower. She took it in her hands, drawing it down and circling its tip in moisture from her vagina, until he started to push slowly but steadfastly to fit her around him in an enclosure at once comforting and arousing. When he finally lay down on top of her, enabling her to feel all of him, all his skin touching hers, his chest and belly and kneecaps, the small of his back with the moonlight pooled in it, she sighed with the completeness of the feeling this gave her. They moved slowly together in the most standard possible formula of heterosexual love, which would have been boring had they not both wanted it so much, but which, as it was, was simply the best thing that could have happened to them. Looking from eye to eye, from moonlight to the shadowed crevices of life-lined faces, they could guess each other's moments; she gasped, he nodded and smiled at her. What they felt was no thunder and lightning explosion, but a peaceful flowering, as petals open when it's rained, or the single bloom is brought to fruition by the sun.

Much later, Charity left the house and went for a walk, awakened, not sedated, by the sex. The delight of the sexual encounter: what did it mean? She was drawn to it, but trapped by it. It gave her bonds beyond the bed and the moment. Mother, friend, lover, manager of human relations: maybe she'd rather be a tree in the forest, or a little squirrel, pleased out of its tiny mind to hold a nut in two endearing symmetrical paws.

On Charity's left, a cropped cornfield extended down the side of the hill. Pine trees sheltered the path from the field, and in the spiralling dusk the trees were black ironwork against the sky. An earlier brief rainstorm had cleared but left its damp odour behind. Through the trees on the other side of the field, horizontal strips of pink could be seen, layered with grey and white like a birthday cake. Charity walked half a mile or so along the track, alternating her journey between the sharp tufts of grass in the middle and the untidy stones each side which rubbed against her sandalled feet. Then she came to a place on the track where another joined it, and ahead was a field with sheep ordered against the skyline. She saw a gate and a group of trees out of which came laughter bright and noisy, competing with the soft repeating voice of the wood pigeon which had started to sing behind her. She lifted her eyes to the skyline, away from the noise, and was sure, immediately, that everything had been meant to happen to her in exactly the way that it had. What she had gained and what she might lose: the problems and the possibilities, the conversations and perplexities, the deceptions and the arguments – they all reigned together in a mysterious and symbolic world of meaning to which she, as a most serendipitous privilege, for a while would belong. It was not up to her to do anything about this; she shouldn't try to impose upon the pattern any impression of her own will. For her own substance, her existence, was merely fabricated as part of the material order of things. She was nothing more or less than a grain of sand in the desert, which stretches on and on over all the horizons of the human condition. There was absolutely no point in seeing herself as a free agent, because even if she were, her freedom and her pleasure were not the same thing at all.

3 ✳ ROUTINE

'It is easy to see why woman clings to routine; time has for
her no element of novelty, it is not a creative flow; because
she is doomed to repetition, she sees in the future only a
duplication of the past . . . A syllogism is of no help in
making a successful mayonnaise, nor in quieting a child in
tears; masculine reasoning is quite inadequate to the reality
with which she deals' – *The Second Sex*, p. 299

After the summer, when they'd got back to England, Rachel had
mentioned almost casually to her father that another person had
been staying in Sally and Eric's house, that Mummy had liked
him, but he had a wife and two children of his own, whom she
rang up from telephone boxes.

For Charity, life was no longer essentially magical; it had been
overcome by routine. The children's schools started again on 2
September. In the preceding week, she was busy organising their
clothes; washing, cleaning, purchasing and labelling. She took
Dan and Harry and Rachel to have their hair cut, and sent Tom
down the road with instructions about what to have done to his.
Then she took Rachel to the doctor for her booster immuni-
sations. She also began to autumn-clean the house, turning out
cupboards and excavating under beds, pulling down curtains and
discovering dead plants. No cupboard was safe from her house-
wifely skirmishes, and even the goldfish got a new lease of life as
she bought an electronic test meter to determine the hardness of
the water in which they swam and had their being, and then
introduced to them a form of duckweed which, by means of its

rapid growth, would remove some of the excess calcium from their water.

Autumn had always been her favourite time of year: to her there was nothing depressing about the changing colours of the leaves on the trees; the yellowing, the curling, the falling and the rotting were simply a seasonable occurrence; they signalled the underlying structure which in its very repetitiveness reassured. It happened last year, it's happening now, and next year will be the same. Every year of your life will be marked like this: the natural world persists independently of the cultural one, the two have nothing to do with one another.

It was as well to believe this, since by the end of 1980 Thatcherism had really begun to get a hold on the quality of life in Britain, causing the beginnings of a structural collapse in the welfare state. In July of that year, for example, the statutory requirement of Local Education Authorities to provide nursery education and school meals was abolished, putting food and sociability back into the hands of mothers, where the Government considered they properly belonged. Mothers of Charity Walton's class ranted about this, but were not the ones who were really affected. In any case, Charity would survive all such declines because of her love affair with Mark Carleton. She had a sense of advance as driving and as unthinking as a steam engine. Mark was in America now. He'd gone to New York to explore the possibility of raising money for an international study of everyday life. His book wasn't going very well (partly because of his affair with Charity) and so he'd turned it into a more grandiose scheme, a wonderful project that would involve sociologists in a number of different countries interviewing peasants, labourers, professionals, citizens of all ages and types in fields, factories, homes and institutions, about the ordinary living of life. The interviews, perhaps twenty thousand or so, would all be done at the same time, and Mark was driven by an imperialist vision of sociologists in Italy and Iceland, Australia and Africa, Spain, Scotland and South London all stepping out into the field in a simultaneous rhythm and shared intention. Funded by some multi-million-dollar foundation, they would invade and document reality, so as to create a unique record for all time of the private underworld of life.

Mark could talk and gesticulate with wild enthusiasm about this project for hours. 'The world's our oyster,' he said to Pascoe one day. 'A sociological oyster, floating in a salty mess, absolutely waiting to be scooped out.' Behind these words, an image of seafood consumed on the blue edges of a bay in south-west France did uncomfortably remind him of his own unavoidable clumsiness in emptying a bottle of wine on the ground. 'I only hope I succeed in getting it funded,' he added quickly.

'Carleton,' said Pascoe, who alternately thought of Carleton as a genius and an idiot, 'are you sure you shouldn't go for something a bit smaller? More limited? I mean easier to do?'

Mark gave Pascoe a scathing look. 'I wasn't appointed to do small things!'

'No, of course you weren't. I only meant that perhaps the idea of an *international* study isn't necessarily the right one. International research is very hard to do, isn't it?'

'How do you know?'

'Well, that's certainly what I've heard. Do you know Washbourne? Who did the study of old people in sixteen societies about fifteen years ago?'

'Dreadful study.'

'It took ten years to do. At least.'

'I'll tell you why, shall I? Washbourne is an inefficient ape. He was so incompetent at getting his samples organised that most of his subjects were dead by the time the interviewers got to them. As a matter of fact, one old boy in Southern Spain actually died during the interview. While the General Health Questionnaire was being administered. There had to be a special inquest.'

Mark was not to be put off. On his fund-raising mission to the States, he wrote his first letter to Charity. The letter, sent to the department, was marked 'Private', and was handed to Charity by Mavis with raised eyebrows. In it, Mark complained that he felt lonely and was forced to sleep diagonally in king-sized beds and eat more cheesecake than was good for him. But Charity didn't feel very sorry for him. One night she rang his home. The cadence of his wife's voice was low and controlled: 'Hallo' repeated several times, and then 'is anyone there?' after which the receiver was gently replaced. Charity didn't know why she'd rung. It served no purpose except to make her ruminate on the nature of Mark and Jane Carleton's connection with one another, and why would she want to do that?

Mark came home from New York. The next day, to celebrate the success of his mission to the Whiteman Foundation, he suggested they all go to the pub after work. So off they trooped: Charity pretending not to know Mark too well, Margaret Lacey, looking as though she wanted to, Pascoe striding confidently ahead (something he was good at), McKinnon coveting the latest Apple microcomputer, its shiny brochure secreted in his handbag. Mark had quickly realised what an odd character McKinnon was, stalking round the department with his handbag like a magisterial cat, yowling loudly and rubbing himself up against the furniture, taking no particular notice of anyone. Howard Denby was there, too, with his usual neat bow tie, notebook in hand in case something worth noting might happen. People teased Howie about this, but he was as impervious to their criticism as they were to his limp jokes. Behind him lumbered Steve Kirkwood's corduroy legs, and Steve himself, trying to capture Howie's attention for a bit of serious dialogue. Last but not least came Ivan Swinhoe, with rancid hands fingering used bus tickets in the pockets of an overlarge dark overcoat.

In the Dead Duck on Mariner Street, Charity found herself sitting next to Margaret Lacey, whom she still hardly knew. Margaret was wearing her usual layer of black eye make-up and constricting black 1930s dress, retrieved from a jumble sale and decorated with a large amount of coloured glass jewellery. 'Did you have a good summer?' she asked Charity, over her ice-and-lemoned tonic water.

'Very good, thanks. And you?'

'Fine,' said Margaret. 'I went to this women's retreat in Northumberland. Marvellous country, very rugged and bare. I walked a lot. Had a chance to think.'

'You were there on your own?'

'I didn't go with anyone, if that's what you mean. It *is* what you meant, isn't it?' Charity nodded. 'But there were six or seven other women there, we shared the cooking and the chores; it meant you could talk to someone if you wanted to, but you didn't have to. I've been meaning to go to this place in Northumberland for ages. It really was very therapeutic.' Margaret stopped thinking about Northumberland and focused on Charity with a sudden rather severe look. 'You're not a feminist, are you, Charity?'

'No. Well, I don't know. What's a feminist, Margaret? I think women get a bad deal sometimes. Of course, I haven't. I've always been able to do what I wanted. I've never been aware of any discrimination.'

'Discrimination is structural first and personal second.' Margaret's hand tapped the sentence out on the table, to drive the point home. 'You don't have to be aware of sexism yourself in order to know that it exists.'

'Don't you? Isn't it something that has to be felt?'

'Your consciousness, Charity,' said Margaret didactically, 'is false. Ever heard of false consciousness?'

'Of course.'

'You're conning yourself that you're alright. But you're not really. You're just participating in the liberal male view which says women have got equality, there's nothing left to protest about.'

'Maybe. But if I don't agree with you, I just prove your point, don't I? Like the patient and the psychoanalyst. You believe you're right. So there's nothing I can say. Why are you a feminist, Margaret?'

'Because I simply couldn't be anything else. I couldn't be a woman and not be a feminist. All women are feminists, Charity, because all women are victims of patriarchy.'

'That sounds terribly simple.'

'It *is* simple. What's difficult is doing something about it.' Margaret smiled. 'There are a lot of women like you around, Charity.'

'What do you mean? How do you know?'

'I mean privileged middle-class women who don't see the need to adopt a political position on gender. You will, one day, of course. Either when it's become the acceptably radical thing to do, or when you find out for yourself in some personally painful way that women are oppressed.'

'Thanks very much!' Privately, Charity thought that it would take a lot for her to identify with women in dungarees who said shit all the time and drank beer in pubs. She didn't want to have anything to do with such images. She feared it would be a repudiation of warmth and softness and motherliness: qualities she valued in herself, and which she saw as having been transmitted directly to her from her own mother. She wanted Rachel to be like her, like her mother, and not to have cropped hair and lack finesse and argue all the time. She wanted women to give womanhood to women, and saw feminism as an attack on this.

'I don't mean to sound patronising – matronising!' Margaret seemed anxious to retain Charity's trust. 'But I do really think you'll come to understand what I'm saying one day, only then it won't feel like a particularly radical ideology any more. One of the problems now, I suspect, is that you've been taken in by the media caricature of feminism. You know what the media do, don't you, Charity?'

Charity didn't know what to say. She hadn't expected a lecture. Margaret looked terribly intense.

'No, what do the media do?'

'They deradicalise everything that's happened, because in order to communicate they must simplify in the only way that's ever possible, and that's according to the past.' While Charity was thinking about this, Margaret's voice became more strident. 'The rise of the mass media has effectively ruled out the possibility of revolution,' she went on. 'There's no point in being a revolutionary, because you can't hope to compete with the saccharine tirades of the newspapers and magazines, the TV programmes and the popular films. Ideologies are reduced to bland hymns; new practices and forms of living are made to look like old habits. Headlines are the opiates of the people! You're a child of your times, Charity. We all are.'

There seemed no point in denying this. All the same, Charity felt Margaret's speech shouldn't be allowed to pass completely unchallenged.

'But I'm no different from you, surely? We're about the same age, aren't we? Why are you the one with the superior wisdom?'

'We have different histories. That's important. You've been immersed in marriage and children. Work comes next. For me work is all-important. I'm in the male world and, being in it, have seen it for what it is. You're still in the female world, so you have a different perspective, which is to some extent the male view.'

Charity was beginning to feel upset, as well as confused. 'Why do you say work isn't important to me? It is. But I can't do everything, can I? There aren't enough hours in the day.' She began to think of all the things she had to do that evening, to make lists in her head.

'Of course there aren't. But think about what work is. Labour. Labours of love and labours of other kinds.'

'That's another problem.'

'What is?'

'Men. What's your position on men, Margaret?'

'I like them.' She laughed. 'No, correction, I *need* them. I don't really like them at all. They're spineless creatures. Their whole existence is designed to protect their fragile egos against the knowledge that, biologically and socially, they're completely redundant. Men don't know how to relate to women. They know how to fuck them, that's all. Mind you, some of them can't even do that properly!'

Howard Denby, sitting across the table, looked up sharply as Margaret said this. Swinhoe, too, was alerted, but turned away to study the deep red sham velvet brocade on the walls. Conversations between women were no concern of his.

'Heavy stuff, ladies!' said Howie. 'Talking about sex,' he interrupted, although he hadn't been, 'do you remember that sixties joke?' Margaret looked bored. 'He asked her, "Do you smoke after intercourse?" And what did she say?'

'I couldn't possibly guess, Howie, what did she say?'

'She said, "I don't know, I haven't looked!" And talking about men . . .'

'Which *you* weren't,' pointed out Margaret.

'Have you heard . . .'

'Only one more joke Howie, please!'

'. . . the one about public lavatories?'

Charity and Margaret exchanged a look of irritation.

'Public lavatories are like men: they're either full of shit, or occupied.'

Charity laughed. 'That's the point, Margaret. That joke and what you just said. You make me feel rather sorry for men.'

'I know. I feel sorry for them too. But we can't devote our lives to feeling sorry for men, can we? The object of feminism is to rid ourselves of the emotion of pity in relation to men. We must pity our own condition instead. Not ourselves, but our condition. And turn that into anger, and then the anger into action.'

'You talk as though men aren't human beings,' objected Charity. 'Aren't you being just as sexist as men who say women belong in the kitchen, and so on?'

'It isn't sexism, it's the truth. But I really think we should continue this conversation another time.'

Soon Mark told Charity that he wanted them to go away together for the weekend.

'You're crazy,' she said straightaway. 'How could we do that?'

'Why can't we? We're clever people, aren't we? We can find a way of doing what we want. We need some time, just the two of us alone together. Please, Charity.'

'It's too dangerous,' she said.

'It's dangerous, but it's not too dangerous,' he said.

'What will you tell your wife?' For some reason, she preferred to make Jane nameless by calling her 'your wife'.

'That's my business, it's nothing to do with you.'

Charity tried to accept this. 'I can't get away,' she said. 'How can I get away?'

'I don't know,' he said, 'that's your business, isn't it? Haven't you got a girlfriend you stay with sometimes, or a mother maybe? Think about it,' he said.

They went to Strawbury Castle, which was one of the many places in England that Henry the Eighth was supposed to have stayed in with Anne Boleyn. They had a room with a gold enamelled four-poster bed and a crenellated ceiling. The window of the bathroom looked out on the croquet lawn, where businessmen and their mistresses landed in helicopters from time to time.

On Saturday afternoon Mark disappeared into the town. 'I'm going to do some shopping,' he said. An hour later he came back with an array of fruit: strawberries, bananas, cherries, peaches, one or two each of the larger ones, half a dozen each of the smaller.

'What are they for?'

'You'll see.'

He opened the windows. Beyond the croquet lawn lay an English vista of cultivated parkland: stone-carved balustrades, trees cut in fancy shapes, orchestrated willows and other rampant greenery. The lawns sloped as they should, and on the terraces immediately below the house two moody peacocks flashed their tails.

The air was warm and feathery as it passed over Mark and Charity in bed. 'You have a wonderful body,' he said. 'Wonderful. I want to eat it.' Carefully, he opened her legs and covered her with moisture until she made her own, and then he sneaked some strawberries in there. With his long knobbly fingers he moved them around, watching her response. She was appalled, and in heaven.

'Is this hygienic?' she gasped. 'Did you wash them first?'

'You'll catch strawberry disease,' he said, taking a bite from a peach and dropping peach juice on her. 'The symptoms are a never satisfied desire and an unfinishable PhD.'

She was incapable of answering him. He removed the strawberries and ate them, declaring them to be delicious. Then on fruit-stained sheets he fucked her for what seemed like hours. She came many times, but he didn't. 'I can't,' he kept saying. He moved out of her, and she took his penis in her hand, and moved it gently, and then rapidly, and after a while he pushed her hand away, abruptly replacing it with his own. He knelt on the bed and masturbated, and the whites of his eyes rolled around frantically in his head, and then the muscles in his thighs visibly tightened, and he made a little noise, and she, excited herself, looked at him and beyond him at the serene countryside and then back at him, fixing the image in her brain. 'Look at me,' he said, 'look at me,' and he glanced down to show her what he meant, and then he came, the semen spurting out of the shiny raw tip of his penis over her head on to the pillow, and then across her breasts in an opaque trail of glistening stickiness.

He lay beside her, exhausted. 'God, that was amazing. I've never done that with anybody. Did you mind? Are you alright?'

'I love you,' she said, intending this to be sufficient answer.

Later they went downstairs, sat in the library where a log fire burned, with all the appearances of being a totally synthetic arrangement, and had cocktails served them on a silver tray by thin unctuous waiters. Oil paintings of infamous men looked at them. Mark wore a suit and a black bow tie, Charity a purple-sequinned dress and high-heeled shoes. A necklace of violet glass irradiated her throat, and her hair piled on top of her head revealed to Mark the extraordinary beauty of her elegant olive neck. 'We make a good couple, don't we?'

'As a cultural stereotype,' she said. 'Look at you, you could be any man behaving like a peacock.' His white shirt cuffs peeked out erotically from the dark sleeves of his jacket. 'Oh darling, I do love you.'

'While you,' he said, brushing this remark manfully off his exaggerated shoulders, 'look like a mannequin. I've never noticed your ankles before, for example. Nor the way your waist dips below your breasts.'

She ate a salted cashew nut as delicately as she could. 'It's sex, isn't it,' she declared, unexpectedly.

He peered round the ostentatious room. 'What is?'

'Us.'

'No it isn't. It's love.'

'Which is a defence against depression.' She looked sullen.

'How do you know?'

'I read it somewhere.'

'You shouldn't read those kinds of books.'

'It was your book,' she said.

'Oh. How funny. Of course I never remember what I write in my books. Once I've written it, that's it. It belongs to someone else then.'

'Mark, I'm trying to be serious.'

'Well, don't be.'

'Why not?'

'I don't want you to be serious.'

She leaned over and took his hand. 'Has this got a future?'

'If we have.'

'But what'll happen to us?'

'Do you want to know? I don't.'

'You're being terribly evasive.'

'Because I don't want to think about these things,' he said, more or less simply. 'I also know what you're going to say next. You're going to ask me whether I want an eternal liaison with you. Can I promise to love you forever? Can I make a commitment to you? Is this, what we have now, compatible with, even the same thing as, true love? And you're going to ask me if I intend to go on lying to my wife about us. That's probably uppermost in your mind.'

'Something like that,' she replied.

'I feel for you, Charity. I feel more for you sitting here now than I would ever be able to do for you in an ordinary existence, if we were living together. You reach my depths, whatever those are, from where you are now.' He was amusing himself now. 'You reach my essence. I give you my essence.'

'Which is an obsession,' she said.

'Maybe. But what's important is that I don't want you to see the boring bits of me. I want to protect you from my negativity, my ambivalence. I want this pure stream of light to go on passing between us – nothing more or less.'

'You're either talking nonsense,' she said, 'or you're wiser than I am.'

'Call it common sense,' he offered.

'Your table is ready,' simpered the waiter.

'Right.'

'I'm not satisfied,' said Charity.

'It's not in your nature to be satisfied, so that doesn't worry me,' he said.

After their erotic weekend, Mark felt quite masterful at work. He rang up a friend, a man who was secretary of a strange outfit called the Workers' Mental Health Federation.

'I've got an idea, Bob,' he said.

Bob Seaman, a laconic beanpole of a man with élitist social origins and an acquired socialist conscience, was used to Mark's enthusiasms. 'And you want some money for it, I suppose?'

'Well . . .'

'I ought to warn you we haven't got much in our research fund just now.'

'All I want is about £7,000.'

'For what?'

'For a junior researcher for one year to do some interviewing.'

'Better bung in an application then, hadn't you?'

Mark told Pascoe he was planning to hire someone to do some pilot interviews for the everyday life project.

'We haven't got any money.'

'I know that,' said Mark crossly. Why did everyone keep telling him about the shortage of money? 'I think I can get hold of some.'

'We haven't got any office space.'

'We don't need any. She'll be out in the field all day.'

Mark assumed the junior researcher would be female, as, indeed, she was. The post, when advertised, drew fifty-six replies, not because the job was a good one, but because there weren't many jobs around. Delia Cook wore black dungarees and an extremely determined expression. Mark hired her because he noticed in her a capacity for hard work. Her father was a bricklayer. She had a first-class degree from Sussex. Would there be an opportunity to register for a higher degree, she asked?

'What?'

'A higher degree,' she repeated, patiently.

'I hadn't thought . . .' Mark interrupted himself, conscious just in time of his unacceptable assumptions. 'Yes, of course.'

'Where will the interviewing be done?'

'Where would you like to do it?'

She tore a strip off him for this. 'You mean the parameters of the project haven't yet been defined?'

He corrected himself again. 'We've decided to use a stratified sample in inner London and Kent. To get the rural-urban divide, you see.'

'That sounds like a good idea.'

Delia was given a desk in the computing room. McKinnon wasn't pleased, and he showed his displeasure by dumping his handbag on it all the time.

The week after the trip to Strawbury, on the Thursday when Charity went home after supposedly working late, though actually walking by the river with Mark, she was met at the door by a slightly flustered Tom. 'Dad didn't come back,' he said.

'What do you mean, he didn't come back?'

'He didn't come home at 5.30. And he didn't phone. I don't know where he is.'

'Why didn't you ring me?'

'You weren't there,' said Tom, reasonably. 'But don't worry. I told Beth to go to her class. We had baked beans on toast. The twins were a pain in the neck, but I think they've shut up now. I made Rachel some cocoa. She's asleep.'

Charity was quite touched by Tom's talent for taking care of people. She was also more disturbed than she cared to admit by James's non-appearance. She went upstairs to look at Rachel, who was asleep on her back with her nightdress up round her waist. She closed the window, drew the curtains, picked discarded clothes off the floor, and covered her up. In their room Dan was reading, Harry was asleep in a tight ball, face to the wall. 'Where's Dad?' asked Dan immediately.

'I don't know, darling. I'm going to ring Peter in a minute, he might know. Don't worry,' she added disbelievingly, 'it's probably all a misunderstanding. Probably he told me he had to go out, and I didn't hear. Or maybe he forgot it's Thursday.'

'He never forgets it's Thursday,' said Dan gloomily. 'Harry said he could have had an accident. Do you think he's had an accident? How could we find out?'

She tried to reassure him, and then kissed him, and Harry, in case he was only pretending to sleep. She never knew with him. He turned over and pulled the sheet tightly across his face.

Downstairs Charity poured herself a brandy and stood looking out of the french windows to the garden that neither she nor James had ever had time for. Purple hollyhocks pushed against the window, and an uncut hawthorn tree knocked lightly in the wind. A fuchsia had given up blooming, but its drained tendrils still opened themselves to the sky. She wanted to ring Mark, but knew she shouldn't. Besides which, Mark would be at home with Jane, and Jane would probably answer the phone, which wouldn't help.

She picked up the phone and dialled the number of James's partner, Peter Sherman.

'Hallo, Charity. How are you?'

'Fine, thank you. I was just ringing because James is late home. I wondered if you had any idea where he is?'

There was a short silence. 'I don't think so, Charity. He wasn't in the office this afternoon. He went to see someone about a job in Hammersmith. He said he'd go straight home afterwards. At least, I think that's what he said. What time is it now?'

'It's ten thirty. I've just come in. James takes over from the mother's help on Thursdays. It's the first time this has happened. I don't know where he is. I don't understand what's happened.'

'Let me have a think, Charity. I'll phone you back if I come up with anything. Ring me if he turns up, will you?'

She put the phone down and looked out again towards the garden. She didn't know what to think, or what she felt, or what she ought to feel. It seemed stupid to mind, because she was, after all, in love with someone else. How could she reasonably object to her own husband not coming home? He might be having an affair, too. Why shouldn't he? It would balance the scales, after all. Nonetheless, she felt disoriented. She *did* mind. She was angry that James had let her down. Her domestic life wasn't like this: it had an order, a pattern, a predictability. And she was even more angry at herself for reacting like this.

Tom came into the room in his pyjamas. 'Have you heard from Dad?'

'No darling, I haven't.' As she said this, her eyes misted over and she knew she was going to cry. 'Go to bed, Tom. I'll come and tell you if I hear anything.'

'Goodnight, Mum,' he said, kissing her. 'Why don't you have a drink or a cup of tea? Shall I make you one?'

At 2 a.m. she went to bed and dozed for a couple of hours. Then she sat up with a start and knew there had to be an answer. There always was. She put the light on. Given that James's behaviour wasn't typical, either events had made it impossible for him to communicate with her, or he'd changed his character. An accident would, sooner or later, reveal itself, but a character change would already have left clues.

She went downstairs silently and opened the Victorian walnut dropleaf desk that stood in the corner of the sitting room, and in which James kept his papers. They were all very methodically arranged. Envelopes, postcards, air letters, stamps in one compartment; house bills in another; credit card statements in a third. Curiously, she took out his latest American Express statement and read it. Most of the entries were uninteresting; he used the card mainly to buy petrol and pay for meals and hotel bills when he went away for the firm. This last month he had also bought himself some new clothes – nothing remarkable about that, either. She put it back. The next compartment held his old cheque books. She took out the two last ones. James always ordered the old-fashioned kind with stubs. She flicked through them: 'Restaurant San Georgio, 6 June, £40.53.' That was the night he'd taken his mother out. The next stub was more perplexing: 'Vidal Sassoon, £35.25.' James had his hair cut once every six weeks down the road, at the same place to which she took the boys. Why would he have gone to Vidal Sassoon in Knightsbridge? Moreover, paid £35.25? She went on looking through the stubs, but there was nothing else that seemed odd. She put the cheque book away, and closed the desk. Outside, it was still dark. She went into the kitchen and made a cup of tea. She felt exhausted, uneasy. It didn't make sense. Nothing made sense.

She decided to sort the washing into piles ready for Beth. She was standing with a pair of Rachel's faded blue knickers in one hand and Tom's grey holey sock in the other when the front door opened. James came into the kitchen. His face was red, his tie was undone and partly over his left shoulder. He stood in front of her with both hands in his pockets.

'Where the hell have you been?' Panic was instantly replaced by anger. Here he was, there was nothing wrong with him: why had he put her through this turmoil, made her conscious of his significance to her, even falsely?

'I got drunk,' he said.

'You were supposed to be home at 5.30. You didn't ring. Why didn't you ring? Tom had to cope. The children were terribly worried about you, they couldn't think what had happened.' (She noticed she didn't say that she had been worried.) 'Dan and Harry thought you'd had an accident. And then you just turn up. You say you got drunk. You expect me to accept that as an explanation? You bloody idiot.' She threw the sock at him, it winged its way on to the dresser shelves behind him.

'It's the truth,' he said, closing his eyes momentarily as the sock passed through the air. 'I went to the pub, and I got drunk. And I didn't want to come home. I didn't want to face you. I've got a headache, I'm going to bed.' He turned and left the kitchen, and stumped upstairs.

If the children hadn't been in the house sleeping and protecting him from her vengeance, she would have followed him to the bottom of the stairs, and stood there and screamed up after him, 'You bloody bastard, I hate you. If I can't rely on you to do what you're supposed to do, then you're not worth having.' Instead, she made another cup of tea and fed the goldfish. They opened their mouths winningly at her, and this made her feel better, despite the oily look in their eyes.

At 7.30 she woke the children and told them James had come home very late, that she'd forgotten he had a meeting, that it was all, in other words, her fault. He wasn't feeling well, and would probably not go to work today. They should be quiet, because he was sleeping, just as she had been because they were.

Mark wasn't at work the next morning. Mavis said he was giving a seminar in Oxford. She left a note on his desk asking him to phone her when he got back.

At her own desk, she found concentration difficult. This mattered, as she needed to make rapid progress with the writing up of her doctoral research if she was to submit it next January; it was now October. Though all the introductory chapters had been written some time ago, and needed only minor changes and embellishments, the main part of the thesis existed only in sketchy draft form. Her interviews with thirty couples forced to live with the disease of multiple sclerosis had been transcribed, and she knew more or less what she intended to do with the material. But knowing now had to be translated into writing. She wanted to show what living with an incurable and handicapping disease revealed about the nature of relationships between men and women; what was the basis of their solidarity, of their intimacy, if these existed? And were there different patterns according to whether it was the man or the woman who was afflicted? Today, Charity stared at one of the case studies that particularly puzzled her. The man, himself a doctor, said he had had MS for twenty-five years, but had never had it officially diagnosed. He had had the disease through three marriages and many other shorter relationships with women. He was a highly attractive fellow, but his charm was largely the product of egotism. Charity sensed a pathology far deeper, more profound, than the illness itself. She thought he had used the disease to secure affection, because what was more interesting than a man with the life sentence of an incurable disease hanging over him? Looking through his accounts of his symptoms, it was easy to see how the symptoms tended to occur at moments of crisis or transition; he was having an affair, thus his eyesight went temporarily, so that he required his wife's ministrations and the mistress could be pushed away; he wished to have a woman desire him, and so he told her, in confidence, that he had an incurable disease. She was to tell nobody, for nobody else knew. This made him a figure of interest, not unlike consumptives who retired up Swiss mountains in the nineteenth century.

The man's pathology undoubtedly played a role in his present marriage, but it had also structured the entire genus of his relationships with women. One problem, from the viewpoint of the thesis, was the lack of formal diagnosis. The doctor had never been to another doctor to have his own diagnosis confirmed. Why not? If the disease wasn't real, did this matter?

She was puzzled about how to deal with this. She didn't know what decision to take, either about the man in her doctoral thesis, or about the man who hadn't come home last night, or about the man to whom she sometimes wished she could come home every day. In her overtired state, these situations were collapsed into one: what was her own role in each? How powerful a factor was her own imagination? The fabric of her life seemed to be in jeopardy. Yet was she not herself responsible for some, at least, of the jeopardising? She wasn't a victim, but a perpetrator of her own errors.

Charity pushed the thesis away. She looked at her watch: twelve o'clock. She decided to go shopping, buy food for supper. Mechanical actions might make her brain function again. There was a small Sainsbury's round the corner from the square. In it she bought only what would fit in her bicycle basket: Ribena for Rachel, cereal for breakfast, chicken breasts, fresh beans, and an apple tart for supper. As she came out of Sainsbury's, she bumped straight into Ivan Swinhoe. He looked a bit surprised to see her with her carrier bags. 'I don't usually do this sort of thing in office hours,' she remarked, semi-casually.

'We all have our little perversions.' He seemed in an affable mood, and suggested she join him for lunch at a new vegetarian restaurant that had opened behind Oxford Street.

Swinhoe ordered beetroot juice and parsnip quiche. Feeling unusually ravenous, Charity chose pasta and a gigantic salad. He watched her attack the food.

'Look as though you haven't eaten for a month!' He scrunched his shoulders up as though he were about to laugh, but he didn't.

She laughed instead, her mouth full. 'Sorry. I did eat yesterday, but I didn't sleep much last night. It seems to make me hungry.'

'Not an insomniac, are you? I am. Never sleep much. Up and down all night. Have these blasted ideas in the middle of the night. Think they're good ones, but they turn out to be dreadful.'

'You write them down, do you?'

'Got a tape recorder by the bed. Put it on while I make the coffee. Boring stuff. Strange how daylight turns nocturnal visions into trivia.' He moved a lock of black greasy hair away from the front of his thick glasses. There was something odd about the parting in Swinhoe's hair; quite a lot of it started off in one direction, and then changed its mind and went the other way. Charity would have liked to give him some advice on how to improve the situation, and so would many of the people with whom he came into contact, but nobody managed to, because no one was sufficiently intimate with him. Ivan Swinhoe's only intimacy was with his mother, a formidable, shrunken, eighty-one-year-old who lived with him, or, rather, he lived with her in his childhood home in Sydenham, a house of depressing design in a street of overwhelming suburban drabness. Charity knew all this because Margaret Lacey, who made it her business to acquire background data on people in the department, had told her. Margaret herself had been invited to have a cup of tea with Swinhoe and his mother one Saturday. They'd eaten angel cake, because the Swinhoe cat had a taste for it. The cat, which was black, with watery daffodil slits for eyes, was called Bertrand, after Bertrand Russell, who was one of the old lady's heroes: she was surprisingly radical for someone who had eked out the whole of her existence in Sydenham.

Charity told Swinhoe that she wasn't an insomniac: the reason she hadn't slept was because her husband had neglected to come home last night, and this had worried her.

At first Swinhoe said nothing. A stringy piece of parsnip was lodged between his front teeth, and he was occupied with shifting it. Then he asked what she had thought was the reason for her husband's absence.

'An accident. I thought he was dead, or at least injured. Isn't that a normal response?'

'There aren't any normal responses,' reflected Swinhoe, authoritatively. 'Could be lots of reasons. This is a big city with a great night life, you know.' Now he did laugh, convulsively. When Swinhoe laughed, his shoulders moved epileptically up and down while his head appeared to remain stationary. The effect was odd. 'Could have been committing a crime,' he continued, still laughing, 'or frequenting a dubious establishment.' He stopped laughing. Charity reminded herself that Swinhoe taught crime and deviance.

'James isn't like that,' she reacted. 'He's a very straightforward and honest person. Reliable and predictable.'

'Or has been until now,' commented Swinhoe. 'What does this man do?'

'He's an economist.'

'Nothing very fishy about that. Must be his character. Women always think they know men,' he observed, continuing to poke about in his mouth with an incompetent stubby finger, 'but they don't.' He started to laugh again.

When she got home, James was sitting at one end of the kitchen table reading the newspaper. He smelt of shaving soap and he'd put on clean clothes. At the other end of the table sat Rachel, drawing.

'Where's Beth?' she asked.

'I sent her home,' said James. 'There didn't seem any point in her staying.'

'Didn't you go to the office?'

'No, I slept until three, I needed it.'

'Daddy's better now,' said Rachel. 'He had a bug. What exactly is a bug?'

'It's something that makes you ill,' said Charity, feeling quite ill herself.

'How big is it?'

'Very small.'

'As big as the point at the end of this pencil?'

'Smaller.' Charity was distracted, she wanted to talk to James. 'Don't you want to go and watch television?'

'No.' Rachel looked at her parents with large brown eyes, and especially at the space between them, in which, it seemed to her, something interesting might be about to happen.

'Rachel, please go and watch television.'

'Why?'

'Because I want to talk to your father.'

'Are you going to have an argument?'

'We'll tell you afterwards.' James folded up his newspaper and smiled, it seemed for the first time in a long while.

Charity unpacked the shopping. Her back was turned to him when he said, 'I didn't only get drunk.'

'No?' She waited, with hands suspended in the act of taking the plastic wrapping off the chicken breasts. She looked down at the raw, pale pink flesh with testicular skin adhering to it.

'I slept the night with someone.'

She said nothing. She felt icy cold suddenly, and then she remembered. 'Vidal Sassoon,' she said.

'What?'

'Vidal Sassoon, thirty-five pounds, twenty-five pence. I looked through your cheque books last night.'

'You shouldn't have done that.' He was angry.

'I was looking for clues. I thought something awful might have happened to you. And then I woke up in the middle of the night, and I knew that if you hadn't had an accident I'd be able to find the answer somewhere in this house. So I went through your desk, and found that cheque stub. Who is she?'

'Who?'

'The person who went to Vidal Sassoon.'

'My secretary.'

Charity laughed bitterly. 'How clichéed.'

'You want me to apologise for that?'

'I don't want you to apologise for anything,' she said. 'I imagine you knew what you were doing. We're all responsible for

ourselves. We all have to take responsibility for our own actions.'
She spoke calmly, in order to believe that she was.

'If that isn't a cliché, or two, I don't know what is.'

The phone rang. James leaned over and plucked it off the
wall. 'Hold on a moment, please.' He passed the receiver to
Charity. 'It's for you.'

'Who is it?'

'How should I know. Some man or other. You have your life, I
have mine. That's what you just said, isn't it? I'm going to get a
drink.'

'What's the matter?' It was Mark, of course. 'You asked me to
ring you. Is something the matter?'

'James didn't come home last night,' she said.

'So?' He didn't get the point.

'I was upset,' she explained, 'I didn't know what was happening.'

'But he's back now, obviously.'

'Yes.'

'But you can't talk?' He still didn't understand.

'Yes, I can talk, I can talk and talk and talk.' Her voice rose to
a shriek. 'He said he was drunk, and he's just told me he's having
an affair. With his secretary! Can you imagine!'

There was a brief silence. Then, 'Charity,' said Mark, reasonably, 'James is only doing the same as you are. Probably less. And
the secretary thing isn't important, is it? Why does that upset you?'

'I can't talk any more now.' She could hear the door of the
drinks cupboard close. 'I'll phone you later.'

Mark's voice became urgent now, almost as urgent as it had
been when he'd first persuaded her to have an affair with him.
'Listen, Charity, please don't tell him about us. It won't help. I
can promise you it won't help.'

'Why shouldn't I tell him about us? It's the truth, isn't it? He's
told me the truth, why shouldn't I tell him the truth? Why on
earth not? Why do you want to hide it?'

'Please!' insisted Mark. 'I don't want you to tell him. It's just
between the two of us. I want it to be our secret; I want to keep it
like that.'

'Why? Are you ashamed of me? For God's sake, Mark, what do you mean? What are you saying?'

'I don't think we should talk about that now. Phone me later.'

She put the receiver back on the wall. James was standing in the doorway. 'Okay, Mrs Walton, perhaps you're going to tell me who that was?'

'It was Mark Carleton, from work.'

'Why was he phoning you?'

'To give me some advice about a paper I'm writing for a conference in Amsterdam next month,' she lied.

'I don't think so.'

'What don't you think?'

'I don't think that's why he rang you. I think he rang you because you're having an affair with him.' He swallowed most of his gin and tonic in one furious gulp. 'You are, aren't you?'

She said nothing again.

'You bloody whore! Here I am plucking up the courage to tell you about one night, one single night when I was unfaithful to you, and you've been carrying on with someone else under my nose for how long? How long have you been having it off with him?'

'I'm not having it off with him. I'm not going to tell you anything.'

'You must tell me. You owe me the truth. You're my bloody wife, aren't you?' He seized her arm suddenly, yanked her to her feet, and hit her across the face with a sound that resonated through the house and in which was the whole force of his long-accumulated violence towards her. 'How could you? How could you do this to me?'

Charity's face hurt, and now wore the red mark of victimisation. This gave her a mask to hide behind. James had turned against her. Though she had turned away from him by choosing (choosing?) to have an affair with Mark Carleton, now James had chosen to be unfaithful to her. Gender roles had been reversed: her decision had become his. Men were proprietorial in all things. Still, it was easier to be a victim than make someone else one. James had made her his victim. He'd not only been to bed with someone else, he'd hit her. There was a strange comfort in that. She would tell Mark. Mark would protest on her behalf. But even as she played the reel in her head, she knew it wouldn't happen; Mark would retreat. He wouldn't want to get involved in her relationship with James.

And so she was caught between these two men, one of whom was maltreating her physically, the other psychologically. Which was worse?

She started to cry. 'I need a drink,' she said.

James got her one.

'I must get supper.'

He sat down at the table and watched her while she peeled and sliced potatoes, wrapped six chicken breasts in egg and breadcrumbs, cut the tough ends off the beans, and submerged everything in boiling water or oil, the symbolism of which wasn't lost on either of them. Then she put the apple pie in the oven and sat down at the table herself.

'I think there's a bottle of wine somewhere,' she said.

He ignored this, and looked past her, out of the window. 'It's raining.' And then, inconsequentially, 'Women are so lucky. Did you know that? They're lucky because they always have things to do. Look at you just now. You busied yourself with food, with preparing and cooking a meal. I've just been sitting here watching you. I have nothing to do. My life is empty. Yours has structure: you produce things. You look after people. Women have the meaning of their lives given to them. Whereas men have to find it for themselves.' He stared beyond her with a frightening emptiness on his face.

She was amazed. She'd never realised he thought like this. 'You call this structure?'

'I call it structure,' he replied, 'because it's the framework for everything else. Everything you do, and are, fits inside it. It's got a meaning you can always turn to when things go wrong. You know what you're doing when you make a meal, don't you? You're keeping other people alive. I can't do that. I can only hurt them, destroy things.' He looked down at his hands, now folded peaceably on the table. 'I'm sorry I hit you.'

'I don't like violence,' she said.
'No. Charity?'
'Yes.'
'I'm very confused.'
'So am I,' she said.

4 ✳ MAGIC PHENOMENA

'Woman does not entertain the positive belief that the truth is something *other* than men claim; she recognises, rather, that there *is not* any fixed truth. It is not only the changing nature of life that makes her suspicious of the principles of constant identity, nor is it the magic phenomena with which she is surrounded that destroy the notion of causality. It is at the heart of the masculine world itself, it is herself as belonging to this world that she comes upon the ambiguity of all principle, of all value, of everything that exists. She knows that masculine morality as it concerns her, is a vast hoax' – *The Second Sex*, p. 311

'Katherine Mansfield said that she believed absolutely in monogamy, but there was no man perfect enough for her,' said Sally.

'I like that.'

The two women were sitting in the garden in the centre of Beaumont Square. It was the spring of 1981. In the garden, amidst the hydrangea bushes, tiny blue, yellow and white flowers promised to blossom soon, and on the lowlands of England lambs were being delivered by their mothers on to the wet green grass. But not everything was innocent procreation: in London, one unusually warm weekend in early April, crowds of angry young people attacked the police on the streets with stones, bricks, iron bars and petrol bombs. The scenes of looting shown on television were reminiscent of those in films of nuclear holocausts, put together in order to show the terminal breakdown of law and order. Scaremongers talked about a racial holocaust instead, and the Home Secretary ineptly attempted to defuse the situation by remarking that unemployment and poor social conditions weren't excuses for the riots, but factors behind them.

Far from the madding streets of Brixton, Charity and Sally watched the nannies and wondered when the crocuses might be up.

'I met Mark a year ago,' Charity observed. 'A whole year. I wish I'd never got involved in this.'

'No, you don't,' Sally told her, 'you don't wish that at all. You're just saying it for effect. As a matter of fact, things are quite alright for you at the moment, you're doing your juggling act. It's all balancing out very nicely.'

'That's what you think.'

Since the night of what she thought of as James's betrayal, Charity had certainly tried to retain the two halves of her life, gliding between them with the felicity of a well-oiled hinge. James had said there would be no more nights of absence without explanation. He'd started to bring her flowers on Fridays, normally thorny ones. But the emotion of guilt behind these acts at least impressed her with its authenticity.

In January, Charity had submitted her PhD, and at the end of March an oral examination had been held. Her supervisor and the external examiners, two superlatively clever men, argued with one another for several hours about whether it was intimacy or separation that held marriages together, and what exactly was the root of men's and women's solidarity with one another. Charity sat contemplatively by, waiting to see who would win. Her supervisor, who did win, bought her a drink afterwards. In return for listening to this male dialogue she became a doctor of philosophy.

The night she got her PhD she had one of her odd dreams. In it she'd knitted her mother a handbag in a soft pastel blue. But the strap of the bag was knitted on to it in such a way that the bag couldn't be picked up without the contents falling out. Her mother was absurdly grateful for the gift, and Charity was absurdly apologetic about the fault in its design. Yet even as, in her dream, she apologised for this minor matter, she was overpowered and then subdued by a vast sadness: a storm of weeping swept through her which she couldn't stem; it seemed as though she were crying for the fact of her existence, which was, in some essential way, lamentable.

Charity knew, therefore, that she was unhappy. The dream told her that, and also the compulsive development of her affair with Mark Carleton.

One night in January the pavements had frozen and the sky was black with snow. In the past week, more than twenty inches had fallen in parts of Britain. Mark and she had had a meal together. And then they were walking hand in hand away from the restaurant when it began to snow again. They took a walk across Victoria and into St James's Park. The little iron bridge looked like something out of a fairy story; a floodlit turret of the Palace even more so. It was extremely cold.

'I'm going to lay you down on the snow over there.' Mark pointed to a dip in the earth under a snowclad oak tree. 'And I'm going to make love to you. I've always wanted to make love to an ice-maiden.'

'Do you think it's a good idea to indulge in these fantasies?' she had asked, as he'd pushed her, weakly protesting, to the ground.

'Fantasies exist to be made real. Reality is fantasy. No, don't take your clothes off, I'm going to devour you, I'm going to attack you; I'm a bear in the forest . . .'

He nuzzled her with the whole force of his physical affection for her and then inserted a hand up her sweater, pulling her bra away from her skin, and taking her whole breast in his hand, squeezing it and massaging it, and next concentrating on the nipple, rolling it between his fingers, so that, what with his pressure and the atmospheric cold, it grew as hard as an icicle. She wasn't conscious of the snow, or of the uneven ground on which she lay, only of her desire for him, a desire that was produced by the very intensity of his physical action towards her.

He kissed her face all over and as each part of it, wet with his saliva, started to feel cold, he kissed it again. He bit her mouth gently, and with the hand that wasn't on her breast he stroked the inside of her tight-covered thigh rhythmically. Through the layers of clothes she could feel his erection. 'I've never felt so much a man,' he whispered. 'You know what I'm going to do to you in a minute, don't you?' he said, 'I'm going to stick my enormous cock in you, and you're going to come straight away, and then I will, but first,' with impressive speed he unzipped his flies and extracted his penis, huge and white, even against the snow, 'hold it' (she did) 'make me wet' (she did), and while she was wondering if he might come in her hand, he removed his penis from her, and ripped her tights with the explosive sound of twigs breaking in the snow, and then, his hand poised on the flimsy cotton of her pants, said, 'Are you ready?' She nodded. 'Are you sure you're ready?'

The noise of the cotton tearing filled the park, and he pushed himself inside her and she screamed and came together. 'I love you, I hate you, I love you.'

'Yes you do, you do, you do,' he said, moving urgently, 'and so do I. I've never loved anyone like this! I'm going to show you how much in a minute.' He grasped her buttocks with both hands, and plunged deep inside her and then, as she felt him going to come, he withdrew and shot hot semen over her face, in her eyes, in her mouth, and he looked down at her and saw her covered in him, and his fluid, and thought how he possessed her, had joined her to him as completely as he would ever be able to do.

Charity was shocked, but more by her own reaction than by Mark's behaviour, which seemed to her simply in character with what she had sensed about him. When she got up, she realised her back was actually frozen.

'This affair is getting out of control,' she told him.

'Nonsense. Why do you say that?'

'Because of what happened just now.'

'And what was that, my darling?'

'You were violent towards me.'

'I'm a man,' he said.

'Does that justify it?'

'No, but it explains it. I'll tell you what justifies it – we both wanted it.'

'You didn't ask me if I wanted it.'

'I knew you did. You enjoyed it, because you love me. Because you love me you want me, and you want me to want you. That's all I did. I wanted you. I didn't hurt you, did I?'

'No.'

He touched her cheek with an amazing lightness. 'I think you're hurt by your own response. Is it what you want from men that damages you, or men themselves? There is a difference, you know.'

'I know.'

'Go home and read your Freud.'

'Don't be ridiculous.'

It wasn't Freud, but the time and circumstances in the spring of that year which conspired to bring about a general change in Charity's own version of herself, which was eventually to affect her relationship with Mark Carleton. At the advanced age of thirty-three Charity Walton became a feminist. She would have the rest of her life not only to find out why it had taken her so long, but why she had done it now, at the same moment as she found herself knocked off balance by a totally new kind of sexual dispute with a man.

Margaret Lacey had put a note about a meeting on feminism and the family on Charity's desk at work. Margaret hadn't said anything about it, just put it there. The day of the meeting, a Saturday, Charity had got up early, gone to Sainsbury's, gone home, had a row with James, who hadn't cleared up the kitchen, another row with Tom who'd left his shoes in the hall so she'd fallen over them, and a near-row with her mother, who rang up and wanted sympathy because the new double glazing didn't quite fit and had let some of the winter rain on to the new Wilton carpet. Then, finally, sorting through the children's clothes for the washing machine, she found in Harry's pocket a scrumpled 'Dear Parents' letter that invited her, some six weeks ago, to see the teacher about her son's scholastic progress.

She stormed off to find him. He was in the garage mending his bike.

'Do you think,' she began acidly, 'you could *occasionally* remember to deliver these letters?' She brandished the yellow ball of paper in front of him.

'What's that, Mum?' His dark eyes opened innocently at her.

'You know perfectly well what I mean.'

'Oh, that. Dan had one, too. I thought he gave his to you.'

'You always blame everything on each other, don't you?'

'It's true, though. Honest, Mum.' He sat crosslegged on the gritty floor of the garage. 'And it would have been boring, anyway. Old Jellybeans would only've complained about us. Talking in class.'

'Where is Dan?'

'Gone to get a new puncture kit.'

'You're hopeless, aren't you?'

'Hmm.' He wrinkled his nose at her as he'd done as a baby. 'What's for dinner, Mum?'

'There is no dinner today,' she told him, surprisingly firmly. 'I'm going to a meeting.'

At her meeting, Charity could not help but be impressed by the wisdom of what was said. A young woman called Anna Mason gave a paper on the theme of 'Men: The Problem With Too Many Names'. There were other papers too, containing many wise assertions. 'Feminism and the conventional nuclear family are incompatible ideological structures.'

Yes.

'The conventional family is founded on the domestic labour and servitude of women.'

Yes, certainly.

'Within the family, women's hope of independence and freedom is like a faint light hissing on the gas stove.'

Yes, perhaps, but who would really ignite it?

At the end of the morning session, the lights in the hall fused, and an unfortunately all-male electrician was called in to repair them. The poor man was booed off the platform, and replaced with a female version. The organisers, a collective, had committed an ideological error. Yet this was paradoxically the very error that permitted Charity's own conversion to feminism: she became a feminist when the women in the overcrowded hall all clapped in unison as the male electrician was ushered off the stage. She knew then the power of sisterhood, the archetypal plastic splendour of a political solidarity with other women. The man's role in it – that it was a man who had been removed from the platform – wasn't perhaps all that relevant; he might as well have been a performing seal or a Chinese acrobat, or a genderless clown, except that everyone knows that clowns are male.

The next event of that spring was a scandal in the department. Ivan Swinhoe was caught shoplifting. He liberated six bottles of washing-up liquid from the shelves of Tesco's in Sydenham High Street. The manager, a sharp, upwardly mobile young man, had apprehended Swinhoe with all the dramatic routines of a soap opera: the heavy hand on the shoulder, the deliberately polite 'Excuse me, sir.' The strange thing was that Swinhoe didn't look like a shoplifter. He looked odd perhaps, with those little eyes behind thick glasses, and those brown open-toed sandals stepping gingerly over littered pavements, but he didn't look poor enough, or unhappy enough, or female enough, to shoplift. He certainly didn't seem desperate enough to be stealing the children's supper, nor did he have that bemused air of menopausal ladies on valium, who normally take chocolate, sailing half-asleep out of supermarket doors with caches of Kit Kats.

Why had Swinhoe done it? By the time the news reached the department, he'd constructed a plausible story. Everyone knew he'd been doing research on shoplifting for years. He occasionally wrote a languid paper about it, but mostly it just dragged on. So now he said he'd needed to expand his methodological approach to the study by engaging in participant observation. Thus, like Jenner, who injected himself with cow pox, Swinhoe had caused himself to be afflicted with the crime of shoplifting. This account made him a great hero; Alan Pascoe actually cheered when he heard it. Howard Denby roared with laughter ('I didn't know he was strong enough to lift a shop!'). Margaret Lacey allowed herself half a smile, young Kirkwood looked slightly impressed, and someone pinned on the noticeboard in the hall the headline from the *Sydenham Star*: 'Local Man's

Research Into Shoplifting Lands Him in the Dock'. Even Mark thought it a good story, and told Charity that the reputation of the department would now soar, for any news was good news in such a place, and Swinhoe's behaviour could be hailed as pioneering sociology. Naturally, the ethical implications remained to be thought out: what needed to happen was that the names of social scientists studying society by such means should be cleared of all criminal associations; their behaviour was professional, not personal. However, it was hard to see how the British Sociological Association would easily defeat the police and the law courts on that.

While the plausibility of Swinhoe's account of his crime impressed others, Swinhoe himself found it depressing that you could fool people so easily. Why was everyone taken in by it? The only people who weren't taken in were his mother and Margaret Lacey. After a time, even Swinhoe forgot the truth. But the two women knew it. Mrs Swinhoe knew that Ivan had been taking things from shops for ages. He'd learnt from his research how to do it, and had become quite skilled at it. The two of them never spoke about it, but it had dawned on Mrs Swinhoe years ago that the housekeeping money she gave Ivan for the shopping couldn't possibly stretch that far. Things appeared on the table that she hadn't put on her list: packets of greaseproof bags, matches, new cardigans, sheets, occasionally out-of-season raspberries. Although she knew these items were morally contaminated, she welcomed them as injecting an excitement into her mundane life. Each Saturday she'd get up thinking, with childish anticipation, I wonder what Ivan will bring me today? And every Saturday there would be something. It was now an integral part of the domestic routine.

Margaret Lacey, unfamiliar with Ivan and Mrs Swinhoe's domestic history, knew from the start there was something odd about Swinhoe. At first she thought he was a closet homosexual. She still felt this was possible; that his life might be punctuated and structured by furtive encounters in men's rooms. (She preferred the term 'men's room' to the more pungently descriptive 'men's lavatory' because men's rooms did, after all, belong to men, and to that genus of social and architectural places into which women are not allowed, and in whose interiors acts occur and plots are devised which women cannot themselves witness. The exclusion is primarily political, not hygienic.) Though Margaret Lacey thought this about Swinhoe, she had no evidence for her supposition. Knowing herself well, she also realised that she hung on to the idea partly because it horrified and fascinated her. She couldn't visualise the kind of place men's rooms were, and didn't really understand what happened in them. On the other hand, she had known many men quite intimately, which made it harder to understand why they should inhabit these secret visceral places from which emanated, apart from anything else, dreadful odours.

'Ivan,' she said to him one day, 'why did you do it? I mean why, really?'

He was sitting in front of the computer terminal staring at his Scottish shoplifting data. Everyone else was out; it was lunchtime.

Without taking his eyes off the screen, he replied in a monotone, 'You know why, Margaret, participant observation.'

She sat down next to him, attempting to interpose herself between his fixed regard and the orange figures on the screen. 'I know that's the official story. But it's not the truth, is it?'

'These figures are the truth, Margaret.' He gestured with his hands towards the screen. 'These are the only things that can be trusted. Raw data: numbers, percentages, hard facts. All the rest is merely a question of interpretation.'

'Well, my interpretation is that you didn't intend to be caught shoplifting,' she risked. She was anxious to know the truth for its own sake. She also wanted to help him.

'You're a brave woman, Margaret,' said Swinhoe, still with his eyes on the screen. 'But I'm not going to talk to you about this. I don't want to, you see.' He turned to her then, and took his glasses off so she could see that he meant it.

The truth was that Swinhoe was too depressed and repressed to get much fun anywhere. His experience of himself was of someone whose flow of personality had early on been blocked by insuperable obstacles, so that he had never been able to develop freely or properly. His metaphor for this was that of an eager and outgoing stream meeting a blunt and precipitous dam of stones before it's had a chance to get anywhere – to the slower, wider, more pensive stretches of the river, to the open sea, down a mountainside, into a charging waterfall or a valley that needs water, whose irrigation might be a pleasure for the stream itself. But being trapped in his own silly repressions made him want to hurt people. The problem was that, because he was so incompetent, the sadism often translated itself into masochism; he couldn't even get his vengeance on society right. The shoplifting, for instance, had originated in his impulse to destroy other people's order – the tidy array of items on the supermarket shelves, the local branch manager's reputation, the market economy within which objects are labelled with a horribly exact and arbitrary value; and he wanted to get his own back on the people, mostly women, who fished in their purses and paid these precise prices for things. For there was too much superficial order in his own life, order which had been put there to distract him from understanding and relieving his own unhappiness. He couldn't stand it. He knew the order had to be destroyed before anything could get better. But the project backfired, and he became the victim of his own destructive impulses.

So the core of Swinhoe's unhappiness remained, but life went on, in the department and outside it.

Mark raised some money from the International Social Science Research Organisation for an interim meeting on the feasibility of his international study. Apparently the department had never hosted an international meeting before. The prospect made Pascoe nervous, and Mavis got very twittery indeed about the practical arrangements. She spent hours doing sums about food and drinks and air fares, and in the end Mark had to take the arrangements over from her. This made him very cross. What made him crosser was that he wasn't any better at it than her. Fifteen people from ten countries were invited, or had invited themselves, to the meeting. Three of them failed to turn up because their air tickets didn't arrive in time. Two of them

were unanticipated vegetarians. Communication was also difficult, because Mark and the Icelandic sociologist Birgit Leifdottir
couldn't manage more than a few words of French, which was
otherwise the only common language.

'I told you so,' said Pascoe.

'Teething difficulties,' said Mark.

To make matters slightly worse, one of the tabloid newspapers
managed a small paragraph headed 'Government Money Spent
on International Social Science Party'. It went on to soliloquise
about the appalling waste of public funds on useless research
designed to find out what time people get up in the morning.
'Public money should be spent on scientific research of real
value,' it argued, 'for example, low-cost body scanners and
artificial kidneys or the British invention of an electronic
windmill which won the small business of the year award
reported in these pages last week.'

Mark got a letter from the Vice-Chancellor after this, which
he assumed was a reprimand, so he filed it in his tray marked
'pending'. However Mavis, who periodically moved the 'pending' pile into the 'to do yesterday' section, pointed out to him a
few days later that it was actually a letter of congratulation.

In June, Charity and Mark, along with two hundred other
people, went to another international meeting, a medical
sociology conference in Amsterdam. The bed in their hotel was a
wooden one with carved ends. Mark took one look at it and said,
'You know what's going to happen in that bed, don't you?'

'I can imagine.'

She could, because he'd already told her, and she didn't know
how she felt about it.

'But first I think we should go out for a meal. Why don't you
have a quick bath?' (He knew her predilection for baths.) 'I'm
just popping downstairs to make a telephone call.'

When he came back, she was still in the bath. 'Come on
Charity, I'm hungry.'

'Why do we always have to do everything your way?'

His face wore an innocently mystified expression. 'I thought
we'd agreed, a meal first, and then . . . '

'So you send me to the bathroom. Why? Because you want to make a phone call? Or perhaps it's because I smell.'

He sighed. 'Don't be ridiculous. You're a difficult woman, Charity.'

'By difficult, you mean I don't always do what you want.'

'Don't you?' He knelt by the bathtub and used his forefinger to trace the contours of her slippery breasts.

'Don't do that.'

'Why not?'

'I'm trying to have an argument with you.'

'It won't work, Charity. I don't want to have an argument. You can't have an argument with me if I don't want to have one with you. I don't want to analyse things all the time. I just want to enjoy myself with you.'

'That's one problem,' she said. 'The other one is that you can't defer your gratifications.' His hand moved down. 'You must learn how to. Every child must.' She slapped his hand, and the water hit his face. She stood up grandly, towering over him, a foaming statue of liberty. They started to giggle.

Outside in the streets of Amsterdam, it was a beautiful day. Mark and Charity walked by the canal, and Mark slipped off down a side street 'to get some equipment'. Charity studied the contents of shop windows nervously, awaiting his return. He came back with a tightly closed plastic bag, and led her back to the hotel.

'Is this going to be like Strawbury Castle?' she asked.

'Not quite. This time'll be different. Every time is different, you know that. Are you willing to put yourself in my hands?' he went on.

'Yes.'

'Undress, and lie on your front.'

She did so.

'Close your eyes.'

He opened the plastic bag and took something out and fiddled with it, then took off his own clothes and lay on the bed beside her with his feet by her head. He placed a wet finger in her vagina and moved it around. She became aware of the impact of the beer they'd drunk for lunch on her bladder, but found the effect exciting, and felt herself becoming rapidly wet. He then removed his finger and replaced it with something plastic and hard – of course, a vibrator. He turned it on. She'd never met a vibrator before. She suddenly remembered Rachel at the age of three sitting on a mechanical rocking horse in a department store and saying pinkly, 'It tickles my pussy'. Her own face, she was sure, was by now quite pink. She put out a hand to touch Mark's penis, knowing only vaguely the direction in which it would be, and would be pointing, and grabbed it wildly with disturbing greed. It was extremely hard. 'I want it inside me,' she murmured, her instinctive and depressingly repetitive response.

'No,' he said, 'not yet.' Leaving the vibrator in place, he reached once more into the plastic bag, and came out of it with something else. She felt one ankle being pulled, and realised he was going to tie her arms and legs to the bed. He did so, laughing, every now and then giving the vibrator a casual twist.

'Are you alright, Charity? This is lovely,' he said, 'lovely', reaching over her body to massage the whole of her surprisingly gently, and then, with that suddenness that seemed to give him special pleasure, he took out the vibrator and put himself in there – his whole hard vibrating penis, and he moved and moved and wriggled his arms round under her body so his hands were full of the mounds of her breasts.

'Are you coming?' he asked. 'It's time to come now.'

She nearly did, being unable to stop herself obeying his command, when he withdrew.

'I'm going to teach you a lesson,' he said. 'Good girls don't come. Good girls are frigid.' And he smacked her buttocks lightly with a sound that sliced through the calm air of the canal. With his other hand he rubbed his penis wildly. 'Oh my God,' he said, 'my God, Charity, you can't move, I can do anything to you!' And he plunged inside her again, and she felt herself nearly coming again, and then he pulled out just in time, and she cried, 'Please put it in again, I want to come, I can't bear it!'

'You can bear anything with me,' he said, 'anything. Any

passion, any pleasure, any pain. Because I am with you. I love you.' Then he stayed inside her, and they came together, though even that wasn't the end, because she had to pee, but she couldn't, because he'd tied her to the bed, and he didn't want to let her go, and so made her pee all over his hands and the bed, which pleased and worried her, but what else could she do?

In the evening it rained very lightly, and the sky grew a thunderstorm which then passed away without a sound.

They sat in the Leidseplein until well after midnight. Mark was overwhelmed by his physical involvement in Charity: no woman had ever created such feelings in him before; he felt propelled by a desire to do to her everything any man might ever think of doing to a woman. This he considered to be love, because he had no other name for it. He said to himself, 'I love Charity. That's why I desire her in the way I do.' But even saying it made him mildly conscious of the difficulty he had in reconciling this, that he called love, with his actual conduct towards Charity, and his other feelings towards her and towards women in general. Jane, for instance: he still could not imagine life without Jane (as Charity could not imagine life without James. There was more equality between them than either of them realised). Yet, as well now, Mark couldn't envisage existing without Charity. Charity had become a drug, to which Jane was the antidote; only Jane could calm the withdrawal symptoms he had when away from Charity. As to his sexual conduct, this he scarcely comprehended either. Charity was to him both subject and object – the object of his own lust, the subject of her own life and destiny. His wish to invade and provoke her body was a measure of his feeling for her. For he no more desired to hurt her than to clip a butterfly's wings, or tame the light in the eyes of a cat.

Charity's face was magnified before him as they sat there in the Leidseplein, so that other faces and figures, their outlines and conversations, acted purely as a background for her splendour – her eyes, stupendous in their sexual depths and glowing colour, the colour of life itself, of farmyard earth, of human shit, of cows meandering through pastures making milk, of chocolates, and chestnuts warm on the coals of Christmas – her eyes rose before him, giving him a knowledge of himself through her which absorbed him utterly. He might have wanted to make her in thrall to him, but the act of trying had reversed the subjugation. He needed her. Not only now, but always.

'Charity,' he said, 'I've just had a fantastic idea. I think we should agree to meet here, in this place, in the year 2000, whatever happens.'

She was surprised by this, but not in the way he thought. 'But don't you think we'll be living together then?' she asked. 'I *want* to live with you.' She grasped his hand tightly between both of hers.

'Do you really want to live with me?'

'I do, yes,' she said. And decided then that the situation was irreversible. She could not alter her shifting identification from James to Mark. She would leave James. It was the only thing to do. She would do it without any more intellectual agonising, without any more speculations about what morality – any kind of morality – might dictate she ought to do; she would do what she wanted. That, surely, was part of the feminist credo – a woman must do what a woman must do. And yet, in making this decision, Charity also knew that she was throwing herself into the heart of the paradox. At that same point in her life when she had started to call herself a feminist, she had made herself peculiarly the object of male power. Mark's sexuality, which had the appearance of being a natural product of his love for her, yet had a political character. Those closest of personal encounters, experienced with great joy and abandon at the time, could be reduced in retrospect merely to the painful trappings of patriarchy. And there was James's violence in the kitchen, too: the one domestic, the other passionate – how could these manifestations of masculinity be accommodated by her new feminist quest for an authentic personal identity? To be free, one must be free of relations with men. Men pulled one back into the old struggles: one was forced to regress into the language of childhood, the language of greed, of possessiveness, of exclusion and domination. Only with women could true advances be made. So the only really correct path was lesbianism. Thus

Charity instructed herself. But listening to her own arguments merely sufficed to produce in her mind an important justification for her conduct now – that a great deal of illumination of women's condition can be derived from the study of male psychology. Women's relations with one another reflect men's psychological structures: there are mirror images, refractions, even sometimes rainbows. So the soul of a man is the purest and basest place in which a woman may look for an understanding of herself.

At the beginning of August, Charity, James and their children went to a log cabin in southern Sweden for two weeks. It was all tremendously healthy, which had been the intention; the cabin was part of a holiday village built on the edge of a lake full of glistening fish amidst pines that swathed them in a scent that could have come straight out of an aerosol freshener.

Charity did a lot of cooking and reading and thinking. If she left James, who would have the children? She would. Perhaps James should give her enough money to pay for resident domestic help, maybe a nice placid Swedish au pair girl? Would she be lonely? She didn't ask herself that question, because she didn't think of herself as being alone. Mark would be there, somewhere. She would have Mark.

But she also liked the idea of herself alone, managing everything. The independent woman.

It rained a lot in Sweden. The rain intensified the smell of the pine forest: it smelt like Christmas. But each time you looked up and thought the sky might be clearing, it wasn't. It was either raining or about to rain.

One morning, Charity woke early. It had been light for a long time. She sat up, wide awake, on her side of the bed, and looked at the bit of smoke-grey sky she could see through the window, with branches of a tree across its lower part; and nothing moved, and everything seemed as if it had been waiting for that moment. She looked across at James. He was lying there with his eyes open, staring at the ceiling. This surprised her.

'I often wake early,' he said, 'but you're usually asleep. You don't notice.'

'Early morning waking is a sign of depression.'

He made a face. 'You don't say.'

'James,' she lay back in the bed and felt every muscle in her body tighten, 'I've got something to tell you.'

'Yes.'

'I'm going to leave you.'

He turned his head to look up at her; the angle was extremely awkward. 'Why?'

She'd thought about this question. 'Because I don't love you any more.' She didn't love James, she loved Mark. She wanted Mark beside her, nights of passion with Mark, she wanted to wake and look out of the window, and watch all this evanescent stillness with him.

'I was going to say the same.' James's voice was very cool, it sounded as though he was at a business meeting. 'I think it's time we went our separate ways. This doesn't work any more, does it?' His face wasn't tragic, but resigned to something. Moreover, it didn't look from the expression on his face in any way like an appalling fate. 'Are you going to live with Mark Carleton?'

'I don't know.' His framing of the question aroused in her the panic she knew was lying around inside her. Panic at the thought of change, of dissolution of the old order. The 'what if . . .' panic (what if Mark left her too? What if she couldn't cope on her own? What if she turned out to love James really?). Her throat felt tight, her heart flapped away like an asthmatic bird contending with the air for breath. She'd once read a novel in which the heroine had said, 'Panic is one half of me – the other half is love.' That was exactly what she felt now.

But why should he decide to leave her? She didn't believe James capable of decisions about relationships. (If she'd thought about it, she would have seen that Mark Carleton wasn't capable of such decisions, either.) While she was thinking about this, James's voice intruded again.

'Shelley's pregnant.'

'What?'

'I didn't know how to tell you. Shelley's pregnant. She wants to have the baby. It's my baby, of course. I think I love her.'

Shelley was his secretary, the one he'd spent the night with and taken to Vidal Sassoon's.

'Couldn't you have been more careful?' This wasn't the most relevant reaction, but her feeling of outrage was the easiest feeling she could get hold of at that moment.

'She said she was on the pill.' James's voice sounded slightly tired.

'Said?'

'Was.'

'So what went wrong?'

'I don't know. I think she forgot one or two.'

'How stupid.' Anger, loss, pain, love welled up together – she couldn't tell the difference between them.

'Christ, Charity,' he said, 'she's only twenty. She wants to have a baby. So did you when you were her age.'

'I had one when I was her age,' replied Charity.

'Exactly.'

'But she didn't have to have a baby with you!' she protested.

'She had a relationship with me. Has,' he corrected. 'She loves me, so she wants my child. It's simple.'

'It's not simple at all. It's bloody complicated.'

He sat up, got up, walked round to her side of the bed and sat down. 'It's alright for you to leave me, isn't it?' he said, coldly, 'but it's not alright for me to leave you. Is that your version of sex equality?' he inquired.

'It's got nothing to do with it.' But it was true that her decision to become an independent woman had counted on James's passivity. She had never imagined he might decide to leave her. Have affairs, yes; leave her and dissolve the marriage, no. Surely he saw how ridiculous he was, launching into an affair and a pregnancy with his secretary, a woman half his age. Jealousy surfaced. 'What's Shelley got that I haven't, anyway?' she demanded. 'Apart from a pregnancy?'

James stood up again and walked to the window. The sky still wore the colour of illuminated slate. 'I'll tell you what she's got,' he said, enunciating his words carefully. 'She's got charity. Something which, despite your name, you don't have. Your

· 90 ·

standards are too high, your expectations – ' he had to search for the word ' – are unbearable. There's no room for truancy in your life, no space for getting things wrong, no forgiveness. You decide what you want and then expect other people to fit in with it. I was part of your life plan, wasn't I? You chose me to provide you with children and a home, because that was what you wanted, wasn't it? Then you decided you wanted to be a successful academic as well. You thought I'd go along with that, too. You've got it all, haven't you? But you got it on my back. You never asked me what I wanted. You used me. I want a woman who doesn't use me. I don't believe in the oppression of women. It's men who are oppressed. And now I'm getting out, and you're going to be on your own. Which, apparently, is what you wanted.'

There was a nail in the bed. It had cut into her face and made it bleed. He was hitting her when the black waiter walked into the room carrying a tray with their breakfast on it, and, as the waiter turned from the table after putting the tray down, James pulled back the whole of the sheet, revealing her entire white body with the light streaming over it. 'Look!' he cried, squeezing one of her mountainous breasts in his hand, 'look, she's got milk in there!' He squeezed and squeezed until the milk shot up to the ceiling. She lay motionless on the bed, staring at the waiter. The waiter moved his long brown hand across to the zip on his trousers, and she saw why, when he took out his equally long penis, moved his legs apart as if to urinate, and looked at her, holding it, the whole of him proud and erect.

Mark came in. 'Charity, my darling, what are these men doing to you?' He was wearing her mother's apron, and his wild hair was sleeked down with a 1920s silvikrin perm. 'You shouldn't let men do that. What would your father say?' Gently he cradled her head in his arms. She wept, 'Mummy.'

'I'm here,' he said, 'I'm here, I'll look after you.'

She looked up at him through grossly tear-stained eyes. 'I'm having a baby,' she said.

'Of course you are,' said Mark, 'and I'm going to help you.' He spread her legs apart. 'Breathe slowly. Remember the air in Sweden? Breathe as though you were standing in that air. In and out. That's right. You'll be delivered in a minute.'

With a flourish, he pulled out a pale blue baby and held it up to the same light that had streamed over her naked body. 'Here's the baby. A very nice baby.' He carefully wiped it on his apron. 'Just cleaning it up a bit. The only thing is, dear, it seems to be dead.'

5 ✳ THE INDEPENDENT
WOMAN

'We rarely encounter in the independent woman a taste for
adventure and for experience for its own sake, or a
disinterested curiosity . . . she remains dominated, surrounded, by the male universe . . . ' – *The Second Sex*,
p. 391

So, when they came back from Sweden, Charity and James
embarked on that long drawn-out and discomforting procedure
known as divorce. They agreed that Charity would continue to
live in the house in Chalk Farm, and that Tom, Dan, Harry and
Rachel would live with her. Nothing would have induced
Charity to give up her children, particularly since James was
re-entering the project of childrearing with someone else. (In
retaliation, she sometimes wished she'd persuaded him to have a
vasectomy after Rachel's birth. They'd talked about it, and
Charity had had her coil inserted in response to James's refusal of
male sterilisation as a barbaric procedure likely to rid him of his
masculinity, a quality which, rightly or wrongly, he wished to
continue to have.) So far as his existing children were concerned, James Walton was actually appalled by the thought of
being made domestically responsible for them. He wished to
know they were being cared for, but not to care for them himself.

Charity had tried to excavate the nature of James's feelings for
Shelley, but had not so far succeeded. She was young, with legs
like a racehorse and breasts that still couldn't offer a safe haven
to a pencil. She had a waywardness which probably gave James a
reasonably low-risk challenge – that of subduing someone, of

regulating them for an end that he could conveniently say was not in his interests but in theirs. Whether the pregnancy had truly been Shelley's project, Charity didn't know; she only cared about this because she found it easier to think her husband trapped by another woman than freely choosing his fate. Each time the fact of men's autonomy confronted her, she turned away from it, preferring to stumble blindly around in a snowstorm of softer explanations. Feminist she might have become, but the earth harbours many different kinds of these. To be a feminist and still on the cutting edge of loving men requires a certain number of perpetual snowstorms.

James moved out of the house in October of that year, 1981. He took his clothes, the contents of his desk, including his cheque stubs, the stereo system, the car, the lawnmower, his books, the barbecue, six prints from the sitting room wall, and their French coffee pot. Apparently, he anticipated a need for strong coffee in his life with Shelley. Charity's lawyer stipulated that he should continue to pay the mortgage and give her £200 a month for each child. He complained, but agreed. He left a phone number on the cork board in the kitchen between a list of school term dates and a recipe for vegetarian lasagne.

Of all the children, Tom was the most upset. He developed psoriasis, and the doctor to whom she took him remarked that fourteen wasn't the best age for a boy to lose his father. When Charity pointed out tartly that death and divorce were hardly the same thing, the dermatologist just shrugged his shoulders and handed her a prescription.

Rachel was philosophical. 'I'll still see Daddy, won't I?'

'Yes, of course you will.'

'He wasn't here a lot, anyway,' the child remarked. 'He'll take me to the zoo now, won't he?'

'Why should he take you to the zoo?'

'Because that's what divorced fathers do. And to the planetarium and the cinema.' She'd been reading a children's story, one of those written with a therapeutic objective, about a girl called Miranda, whose parents divorced, and who subsequently led a rather nice life making cakes with her mother and going to the zoo with her father.

Charity went to the children's schools to see their teachers and explain what was happening at home. The news was received quite nonchalantly. Miss Genevieve, Dan and Harry's teacher, just looked at her and said, 'But, Mrs Walton, half the children in the twins' class are from single-parent families. There's no such thing as a normal family any more.'

There was a lot to do, but at the same time Charity's life seemed easier. If she didn't pay the electricity bill or phone the plumber or buy the weetabix, then nobody would. As a matter of fact, it also became clear how little effort James had put into their daily life. This was brought home to her one day when Harry, then eleven, solicitously said, 'I'll put the rubbish out and mow the grass, shall I? Have we got enough money? I could always get a Saturday job.' Disposing of the rubbish and overlong grass and providing cash had been the three essential tenets of James's existence with them. But he'd taken the lawnmower. She bought another one.

By the times James left, it had almost been forgotten that she was the one who'd first decided to end the marriage. She'd telephoned Mark from Sweden later that rainy summer morning in a crescendo of tears. Sitting at his desk in the department, he'd scarcely been able to hear her voice from the silver call box in the pine forest.

'Hallo, who's that?'

'It's me. Charity.'

'Who?'

'Charity.'

'Charity! Where are you?'

'In a forest,' she said. 'Listen, Mark, can you ring me back, I want to talk to you.'

She told him what had happened, without thinking how it would sound to him.

'But why, Charity? Why do you want to leave James?'

'Because I can't bear it any more. I can't bear the struggle of living with one man and loving another. It's driving me crazy.'

'You don't mean it?'

'I bloody do. When I decide something I mean it. You ought

to know that by now. As a matter of fact, I decided that night in Amsterdam.'

Mark recalled the superior blackness of that night, the bowl of stars above them, the treacly luminosity of Charity's face and eyes. 'You didn't tell me.'

'No, because I needed time to be sure and to work out what to do about it. But that was when I decided there was no going back. I love you, Mark.'

'I love you, too, Charity.'

His words filled her head and stayed there as she walked back through the forest: not even the plodding Swedish rain could evacuate them. But she felt that she didn't quite know what they meant.

Mark was terribly shaken by the information delivered to him from the pine forest. He wanted Charity for himself, but felt he already had that. It was even a cause of celebration that she continued to live with her husband but continually thought about him. He was there in her life, and he knew it, and that was what he wanted. For a short wonderful time she made almost no demands on him: she was curious about his marriage but, knowing she had no right to be, realised her questions would fall on stony ground and so did not expect answers. And he had not made promises to her, and was not required to do so, except for that one promise, made at the beginning, that he would never lie.

Why couldn't it be simple? He needed a simple personal life because his professional one was getting too complicated. Each day he was besieged by uncompleted missions, lists, demands, complaints. He'd forgotten he'd actually signed a contract with a publisher for a book on everyday life. They'd given him an advance of £2,000, which was unusually large for an academic book, and now they were demanding it back. Sod them. What was £2,000 to a large publisher? Mark examined his bank statements and then his nails, which were curably dirty.

And then there was that letter from Birgit Leifdottir, demanding to know where the report of the international meeting was. To be truthful, it was still in his head. Howie had given him a long draft of an article on gender, class and politics to read; attached to it was one of Howie's awful notes, 'Stand closer; it's shorter than you think.' Kirkwood wanted to talk to him about temporal structures in street life for a chapter of his thesis. The students were complaining that Pascoe kept cancelling his lectures. They were even demanding some of his, Mark's, time. The sun sets, the sun rises, people have watches or they don't, thought Mark crossly. What is time, when one has all the time in the world, which some lucky people seem to do?

Charity's phone call from Sweden had made Mark feel suddenly rather sick. He got up, rushed out of the building and went and stood next to a blue hydrangea bush in the middle of Beaumont Square, feeling (and looking) absurd. After about fifteen minutes, the nausea left him, but he continued to feel odd. He decided to go for a walk.

It was a hot day, and London was full of American tourists, pushing and shoving and buying and sweating. Mark walked away from Oxford Street down Wimpole Street. It was comforting to feel the traffic accompanying, rather than contradicting, his ambulations, for Wimpole Street was one-way in the direction in which he was walking. He walked with his hands in his pockets, looking at his feet. After a while, he found himself in Regent's Park, the less inhabited end. He turned left and walked towards the rose garden, for no other reason than that he knew it was there. Children were flying kites; it was the school holidays. By the canal some of them stood with packets of stale bread; the ducks were bored and obese. As he walked, Mark saw that the flowers, including the roses, were magnificent. Yet nothing of their beauty reached him; he could see, and know, but he couldn't sense. The boating lake was next. There were several boats on it; in one of them, quite close to him, were a man and a woman in love. The man had blond hair and blue eyes and a matching blue shirt: Scandinavian probably. The woman was English, she had long brown hair, not unlike Charity's, and he could see the colour of her eyes, which were also brown. She wore a bright green T-shirt, and he could see her heavy breasts through it, as could her lover, who not only saw but touched.

Mark could see he couldn't keep his hands off her. It was all touching, laughing, happiness. Their laughter surged through the atmosphere and hit him like an electric shock; he trembled and panicked, and felt an oceanic sweat that was odourless, falling off him down his clothes and trickling into the lake where love abounded, where what he wanted existed in its purest form and in the most perfect structure that could be created for it: on its own, away from everything, in a void, in the abstract, out of context; a boat could hold it, or a car, or a hotel room; an evening would contain it, pearls and oysters would nourish it, candlelight and sunlight would shine on it. But time and contiguity and possession would do none of these things. The light of love would go out: the couple on the boating lake would vanish, be eaten up, become as worms.

He felt totally despairing. This was what was happening to him. His great union was about to be over. Charity was no longer safe in her household: released from it, she could only become like other women, and would no longer be his Charity. Tears ran into and out of his eyes. He would have to do something about this; what should he do? He found a café and bought himself a cup of black coffee. He put six lumps of sugar in it and stirred them for a long time, feeling at secondhand through the metal vibrations of the spoon the substance of the sugar dissolve and become part of the coffee. When he drank it, it was too sweet and too hot; it burnt his lips and he could feel it going down his throat and into his stomach, where it did no good either. Nothing he did to himself did him any good today, he reflected. He didn't know how to do the right thing for himself any more.

There was a commotion in front of him. He looked up and saw Ivan Swinhoe.

'Hallo, Carleton. You going to the Wellcome meeting?'

Abruptly roused from his misery, Mark couldn't work out for a while who Swinhoe was, or what he was talking about; then he remembered there was a meeting at the Wellcome Institute, a few yards away from where he now sat, on funding medical sociological research.

'Um, no, actually not. I went for a walk. Got stuck in the

paper I was writing, I needed time to think.' It sounded a bit lame.

'Long walk, old chap,' said Swinhoe. 'Mind if I join you for a minute?'

Mark recovered himself sufficiently to ask Swinhoe how he was getting on with his article for the *Sociological Journal* on 'Participant Observation: A Shoplifter's Story', and Swinhoe told him there were a few legal problems; he would need to get the piece read by a good lawyer. He didn't like Swinhoe. There was something innately ridiculous about him. Now, sitting across the table from him in the rose garden, he felt an acute physical revulsion. The sensation of nausea returned, bringing with it the familiar desire to sleep. He closed his eyes.

'Been to the zoo recently, Carleton?'

'What?' Swinhoe's inquiry cut rudely into Mark's advancing somnolence.

'The zoo. Over there.' Swinhoe waved his large white hand in the direction of Regent's Park Zoo.

'No. Why?'

'Pandas.'

'I beg your pardon?'

'Most remarkable creatures, pandas are. Discovered in 1879. Live in the Himalayas, about 10,000 feet up. Not many left in the world. Useless in captivity, get convulsions. Can't reproduce. Take Lien-Ho – name means union, symbol of friendship between China and England.' Swinhoe's shoulders went into action at this paradox. 'Flew to London in 1946. Got her to the zoo, but she slept all the time. When she did come out of her den, just sat there with her paws in front of her eyes. Not very funny at all. You know why we like pandas, Carleton?'

'No, why do we like pandas?'

'Don't have a sex.'

'They must do.'

'Well, they do. But you can't see it. Look the same from the outside. That's why people haven't been able to get them to mate in zoos. Kept putting boys together or girls together and expecting them to have babies. Didn't work out, you see! Only the panda knows what sex it is!' He sighed. 'Same as parrots, actually. Can only tell the sex of a parrot with a general anaesthetic and lights inside. Chickens difficult, too. Ever heard of a chicken sexer?' He sighed again.

Mark stirred his coffee and squinted at Swinhoe in the sunlight, wondering why he was being treated to these zoological reflections.

'One panda, forgotten its name, in a zoo somewhere, a male alright, and interested, but couldn't remember how to do it.' Swinhoe found this deeply hilarious. 'And when they do have a baby, it's so small, looks like a rat, gets squashed by its mother. Can't see it, you see, especially not with its paws over its eyes.'

Mark felt slightly sorry for baby pandas.

'Mind you, they're not a lot better in the wild,' went on Swinhoe, relentlessly. 'Have to eat twelve hours a day just to keep going. Got the shortest gut of any carnivore, only five and a half times its adult body length. Can't digest, you see. Eats bamboo shoots. Awful stuff. Only digests 40 per cent of it. Spends the rest of its time shitting it all out again. Desperate life, really.'

'Why are you telling me all this, Swinhoe?'

'Moral is, Carleton, pandas haven't evolved. Disproves law of natural selection. Who selected the panda? Not adapted at all. Should be extinct, really.'

'Well, I can see that, but so what?'

'Like men, pandas are. Men I mean, not women. Wander around masticating, no time for anything else. Inefficient biologically. Confused, as well. Walking disaster, pandas are.'

'And you think men are, as well?'

'Oh yes. Look at me. What am I here for? Write a few articles, teach a few students things that probably aren't worth knowing. Feed the cat. Talk to mother. Talk to the cat. Feed mother. Don't want you to think,' he added firmly, 'I mind it. Quite happy, really. So are you, probably. You happy, Carleton?'

'No. Yes. I don't know.'

'Precisely. Done a lot more than me, of course, you have. But achievement's not the point, is it?'

'Isn't it?'

'Talked to your girlfriend about this, have you?'

Mark was shocked to understand that Swinhoe knew about his and Charity's relationship. He didn't know what to say. 'About what?'

'Function. And dysfunction. Biological evolution. Or devolution. Is devolution the opposite of evolution?'

'I really don't know what you're talking about, Swinhoe.' Mark was getting irritated now. He'd come out to get away from everything, not to get a lecture.

'Never mind, Carleton. Interesting woman, your girlfriend. Nice eyes. Got problems, though, hasn't she?'

'Has she? Well, yes, we all have,' added Mark hastily. 'How did you know we were, er, friends?' He had difficulty making up his mind which word to use.

'Saw you one night, didn't I? Remember the snow we had in January?'

Mark did, well. For a dreadful moment he thought Swinhoe had seen them in the park, in the snow; they hadn't looked to see if anyone was watching, but now he imagined he could see Swinhoe under the trees in a long grey raincoat, the snow dripping disconsolately off him.

'Saw you in the park,' said Swinhoe. Mark felt sick again. He looked around for a hydrangea bush. 'Walking,' continued Swinhoe.

Mark took a quick look into Swinhoe's eyes. They seemed reasonably clear, though it was hard to tell through all that plate glass. They *had* walked, hadn't they? They walked over the bridge and down by the river and towards the tree and then back again.

'What are you going to do?' asked Swinhoe. 'None of my business, I know, but what are you going to do?'

'I'm going to the men's room,' said Mark. He found one round the back of the café and threw up in it. When he came back, Swinhoe was still sitting there.

'You feeling alright?' he asked.

'Oh yes, thank you. I must have eaten something.'

Swinhoe took very little notice of this. 'If you'll forgive me saying so, I think you should marry her.'

'I should what?' Mark was appalled at what he thought he'd heard.

'Marry her. Clever woman. Loves you, too.'

'Does she?'

'Husband misbehaving,' said Swinhoe, 'she told me.' This didn't seem to be very much connected with the rest of the conversation.

'Yes,' said Mark, 'he's leaving her for another woman. Well, actually,' he corrected himself, 'Charity' (the use of her name started to make him feel ill again), 'Charity decided to leave him first.'

'Good one, that,' said Swinhoe. His shoulders started to move up and down; apparently he found it funny.

'It's not funny.' Mark had now recognised a definable emotion in his internal jumble of feelings: resentment. Why should Swinhoe derive amusement from their predicament? Why should his shoulders behave in that way?

'No, of course not. So, as I said, what are you going to do?'

'I don't know,' said Mark. 'It's not your business, is it? Anyway, I'm already married. I don't want things to change. Not really.' He looked around him, gesturing into the air as if the movement of his hands would preserve the moment. 'But I'll have to do something. You're right about that.'

The two men got up and walked in opposite directions: Swinhoe to the Wellcome meeting, and Mark back to his wife.

Jane wasn't there. The house was clean and tidy and shining, as it always was, exuding a feeling of smug contentment. There was a bowl of red gladioli on the dark polished dining-room table. The clock ticked. Mark decided he was still feeling ill, and went upstairs to bed.

He fell asleep immediately, without taking his clothes off, on top of the Liberty print duvet. It was such a relief to go to sleep. He should have done it before. His dreams were entirely trivial – they were about applications for research money, the new computer the department was buying, children's voices, the soft brushed hair of his daughters on their way out of the house in the mornings. Except for one image which kept printing itself out on his sleeping mind: the white landscape with the two figures intertwined under a tree, and another figure watching. Each time the image reappeared the tree was blacker and more skeleton-like, the cries of the figures under the tree more nightmarish, and the figure of the man watching more and more motionless and judgemental in its immobility. The scene which, in its original version, had been highly sexual and erotic – indeed, one of the most erotic episodes of Mark's life – now seemed drained of all physical experience; it had stepped sideways into another, more sinister mode: that of morality. This is the fate of those who follow their desires: to be under surveillance, to be viewed as the repository of wickedness, to be made to feel dirty and shameful, and in this very carnality to be seen to be doing what most people would like to do, but cannot be allowed to. Why should some be more privileged than the rest? It is a privilege, after all, to sin and get away with it.

The figure in the raincoat started to cackle at him, or Mark thought it did, but he woke up to see Susan and Joanna standing by the bed, racked with schoolgirlish laughter.

'Daddy, what *are* you doing?'

'What are you doing here? Why aren't you at work?'

The questions came simultaneously. In his reduced state of consciousness, his daughters personified to Mark the interrogative condition of women. It seemed to him that some woman was always standing there asking him questions or telling him something he didn't want to know.

That night he and Jane went, unusually, to a concert together. She wore a blue dress with a silver belt, and sandals that picked up all the colours of her appearance – the blue of her dress, the silver, the red-brown of her hair. It was Beethoven's fifth piano concerto, the one with all the nice bits. The soloist was Maurizio Pollini. As Pollini sat down at the piano, Mark noticed he had started going bald. He found himself checking his own head: age catching up with him, that would be the next thing.

Perhaps age was the cause of everything – his mindless pursuit of Charity, his sexual confusions and manipulations. One of the first violins was a young woman with hair like a ripe conker. As she held her violin, she seemed to rest her head on it, so that the chestnut gloss of her hair and of the instrument merged. Perhaps he should have an affair with a violinist, thought Mark vaguely. He sat up in his seat, then, electrified by the music: the conductor, a relatively unknown, also balding German, seemed determined to extract real music tonight. It was alive, and earth-shaking. Mark began to feel at one with something – certainly not himself. The lyricism poured over him, altered only by the proximity of his seat to the brass section, particularly the four French horns, and particularly the second horn player, who was exuberantly revealing sub-themes in the music Mark had never heard before. The conductor was flapping his arms wildly, his face was quite red, he looked like the advertisement for Kentucky Fried Chicken. Why do people want to conduct? To stand up there and wave a little stick around? By the time they got to the slow movement, Mark had stopped asking questions and had lost himself in the music. That sweeping sound; the black and white and brown and gold kaleidoscope of orchestral figures, even the conductor who, given the much slower tempo, now resembled a liquid sausage bending itself this way and that way in line with the music. Though Mark had watched such orchestral events many times, tonight he noticed especially the intimacy the musicians had with the music: the closeness, the stroking, blowing and patting of the instruments. It seemed a good deal better than making love. And then, at the end of the third movement, there was this marvellous passage in which the soloist and the orchestra had a conversation with one another. He played a bit and then they did and then him again. It was extremely meaningful, much more meaningful than anything that happened in real life.

In the interval, as they were drinking coffee, Jane asked Mark whether anything was the matter. He told her no, indeed he felt quite extraordinarily good about the music, but he hadn't felt well during the day. She scanned his face with concern. 'Do you want to stay for the second half? I don't mind if you don't. It was Pollini I wanted to hear, anyway.'

That was Jane. Kind, sympathetic, altruistic. Jane was one of the nicest people he had ever met. How could he possibly hurt her?

They went for a walk by the Embankment. The yellow clock on the Shell building beamed across the river. They walked as far as Waterloo bridge, where they stood underneath the backside of the stone lion while Jane talked about the girls' school, about problems with one of their teachers. Mark found himself looking up at the lion's stone testicles. These majestic balls reminded him of his own, somewhat slighter, ones. He felt protective towards them, anxious about their destiny: in whose hands, hereafter, would they be safe? He tried to concentrate on what Jane was saying, something about choices for O Level. Should Joanna learn Latin? At that moment, he didn't care a toss about whether Joanna learnt Latin. He only cared about himself.

'I've got this problem with co-operation,' she said to him, 'or rather lack of it. I'm afraid the response rate is only 50 per cent.' The voice was Delia Cook's. It penetrated Mark's consciousness like a cockroach sidling up to a pile of rubbish. 'I'm afraid you're going to have to give me some help.'

She was, of course, talking about the everyday life project pilot interviews. People didn't want to take part in them.

'Why aren't they saying yes, do you think?' he asked her.

'Different reasons. One, they get these letters from their GPs. That's enough to put some people's backs up.'

'Yes, I can see that. But I don't think there's any way round that one.'

'And I'm too young,' she offered next. 'Too young for people to take me seriously.'

He stared at her and could see that she was. 'Why don't you try wearing a suit and a wedding ring?' he suggested, suddenly inspired.

'Oh no, Professor Carleton, that would be a deception, wouldn't it? I'm not sure that would be right, at all.' She bit her

· 105 ·

lip. He knew that he'd made a mistake in appointing her: she had no sense of humour.

'Come on, Delia . . .'

'Don't patronise me, please,' she said firmly.

'It was only a suggestion. Perhaps the dungarees . . . well, perhaps the dungarees put people off.' He couldn't tell what she was thinking.

'There is another problem, too, I think,' she went on, opaquely. He waited. 'I think they don't think it's interesting. The project, I mean. No, that's not quite right. People love talking about themselves, as you know,' she glanced at him in order to acknowledge his professional superiority, 'but they don't see the *point* of it. Why do we want these accounts of everyday routines? What are we going to use them for?'

'Have you been telling them the truth, then?' he asked.

'The truth about the project? Of course. Isn't that what you wanted me to do?'

'Not really,' he admitted, faintly.

'But isn't it unethical to do anything else?'

'Delia,' he said, getting up and strutting around the room, patronisingly, 'life is full of ethical problems. So is work. Sometimes, in order to achieve the ends we want to, we have to be unethical.'

After he'd said it, he wondered if he was talking to himself.

One week after James vacated his share of the Chalk Farm house, Charity invited Mark to dinner. He had never been to her house before, and it would also be the first meal she had cooked for him, a fact which apparently meant something to her, although it meant nothing to him. He didn't really care what he ate, or who cooked it, so long as it stopped him feeling hungry.

She had invited him for Wednesday.

'I can't do Wednesday,' he said.

'Why not?'

'It's Jane's evening out.'

'I didn't know she had one.'

'She goes out with her friend Lesley. You know, I told you about her.'

'Okay, Thursday.' Her voice was a bit curt.

'I think that's alright. I'll just have a look in my diary. Oh, um, I'm afraid there's a problem about Thursday as well.'

She waited.

'We're going out to dinner.'

'Your social calendar's obviously too full to bother about me.'

He decided to try to take no notice of this. 'What about Friday? I can do Friday.'

She told him to come at eight o'clock. At eight ten he rang the doorbell. He felt slightly nervous. Behind his back he clasped some pink tulips.

She opened the door, wearing an apron. He had never seen her in an apron. He kissed her, handed her the flowers. Rachel stood in the kitchen doorway in her nightie, looking confrontational.

'Hallo, Rachel,' he said cheerfully, 'how are you?'

She put her thumb in her mouth and grasped a handful of her mother's apron, as Charity walked past her into the kitchen to find a vase for the tulips.

'Are we all eating together?' he asked, hoping the answer would be no.

'Of course we are. Don't you all eat together in your house?'

'Oh yes,' he said, knowing it wouldn't be a good idea to tell her about the late dinners Jane and he had after the girls had gone to bed.

He was amazed at the number of children she had. Of course he'd known it was four, but somehow he hadn't visualised them, arranged around the table like this. Tom, the eldest, was a large square adolescent boy. The next two, the twins, were formidable only in their duality. He told Charity he couldn't tell them apart, realising as he said this how foolishly unoriginal he must have sounded. 'Harry's the innocent one,' she told him. 'Dan is his criminal accomplice.' The twins looked as though they'd heard this before, but didn't mind it, as a reasonably accurate description of their differentiation from one another. As she sat down at the table, Charity said, 'I'll tell you a story about the twins, if you like.'

'Oh Mum, not that one!' It was either Dan or Harry who said this.

'When they were born,' she went on regardless, 'they looked the same to me. I was given one baby to hold and then the other, but they could have been the same child. A few days later it occurred to me to ask if they were identical. James, who was there at the birth, said he didn't know. He asked the doctor, but the doctor didn't know either, and they couldn't find my notes. So I don't know whether they are or not.'

'How *would* one know?' asked Mark, curiously.

'You can tell from examining the placenta. Or placentas. But no one knows, because no one looked.'

This seemed to Mark a nice comment on the social irrelevance of biological phenomena. He stored it away in his head for future use. But it didn't help him relate to the products of the incident.

At dinner, the boys commanded the conversation, talking noisily about November the fifth and what they wanted to do on it; Charity intervened in a remarkably matriarchal way. He had never seen her like this. It really was quite worrying, though towards Rachel she was endearingly tender. Later in the evening, just before Rachel's bedtime, the little girl arrived on his knee and asked him to tell her a story. They went upstairs, and he found himself in the middle of a gruesome tale about a giant. At the point where the giant was going round threatening all the women in the village with some bloodthirsty fate, he stopped and said to Rachel, 'Are you sure you like this story? Isn't it a bit frightening?'

She took her thumb out of her mouth and looked at him with big bright eyes. 'No, I like it. It's interesting. I want to know the end. You'd better read it quickly, though,' she added, 'before Mummy comes up.' She replaced her thumb.

When he'd finished the story he went downstairs, quite pleased with himself. It was nine o'clock. Charity had cleared the table; the boys had disappeared to their own rooms.

They took the rest of the bottle of wine into the sitting room, where they sat looking out at a wintry garden, like a married couple. The hawthorne invigilated them through the window. The atmosphere inside was a bit glacial. Charity put some Schubert on the record player. Mark observed six bare rectangles on the wall. 'What happened there?'

'James took the pictures. We had some nice eighteenth-century prints. I'll have to repaint it sometime.'

She'd said rather little about the moving-out procedure. 'Come here,' said Mark. 'Charity, come and sit here.' He patted his knee.

She came, tense, like a piece of wire.

He stroked her hair. 'I'm sorry. I find this difficult, coming here. I'm nervous. I don't know how to behave. This is your house. Yours and James's. I feel I don't belong in it.'

'*You* find it difficult!' She leapt up again, blazing with flames of anger he had never seen in her before. 'What do you think *I* find it? I threw my husband out because of you, and now I have to deal with all this on my own.' She waved her hands to indicate the house, the children, the cupboards full of food, the new lawnmower, the unpaid bills on the top of the undusted piano. 'And what do *you* do? Nothing. Bloody nothing.' Her eyes, he noticed, were wet. 'You don't do a sodding thing. You sit there in your nuclear family – everything's alright for you, isn't it? You see me by appointment, you fit me into your life when there's time. And what am I supposed to do? Sit here twiddling my thumbs, while you live it up with your beloved wife?'

'We don't live it up,' said Mark weakly.

'You live with her, that's enough.'

'I never promised you anything else.'

'You promised to tell me the truth.'

'This is the truth.'

'Exactly.'

'Sit down, please, Charity,' he said, despairingly. 'Now listen. I can see how things might seem to you. But I've told you, my relationship with Jane is purely domestic, that's all. Don't you remember, right at the beginning, we talked about all this? We said that each of us had to solve our own problems. We couldn't put pressure on one another. You must do what is right for you, and I must do the same.'

'Things were different then.'

'We were the same people.'

'Our situations were different – I mean they were the same! Oh God, I don't make sense any more!'

'Let's go upstairs,' he said.

'That's your solution to everything.'

He looked at his watch. Eleven o'clock. He should be home by twelve thirty, or Jane would worry.

When he went upstairs, Charity was lying in the 'marital bed', he actually thought of it as that. He could see she was wearing nothing. The window which looked over the garden had its curtains drawn back, so some moonlight entered the room. He undressed and got into bed, felt her soft body, and began to recover a sense of well-being. 'It's alright, Charity,' he said, 'it'll be alright.' He was talking to himself, but she didn't believe him anyway. 'We'll sort it out somehow.' He closed his eyes to forget that this was her home, and the bed where her husband had lain and copulated with her. Jealousy was not an emotion he wished to get into.

Their intercourse was surprisingly mechanical. In fact, it was a little like making love to Jane. Charity made no noise at all; she'd been quite noisy in other settings, under the tree, in Amsterdam. He couldn't even tell whether she had come or not. And asking her was something which, like jealousy, he didn't want to get into. He himself went on and on, moving in and out of her vaguely, but it was like a train in a tunnel without any light at the end. His eyes, closed, couldn't see the light, and so his body couldn't feel it. He began to feel exhausted, was aware that he was sweating quite a lot. His heart got very loud. But he remained expectant, hoping for a resolution. Each time he thought he might be coming he realised he wasn't, and then the next time he fought really hard to keep hold of it, and it eluded him again. He wanted to get into her flesh, to hurt her, he wanted to spill out his fantasies, to slap her, to call her names; for then he knew he would come, and he'd be able to get out of her bed and go home. But he couldn't; the house and its atmosphere were constraining; he was aware of her children sleeping, and of his immigrant presence in the house. He gave up, rolled off her.

'I'm sorry,' he said.

'It's alright.'

It wasn't. He still had an erection. He fingered it sadly in the partial moonlight. 'I've got to go,' he said.

'Have you?' She turned on her side, and he could hear her crying as he left the room.

'Damn it!' he said in the car, 'damn it!' He hit the dashboard so hard that his hands hurt. He was exhausted, frustrated and fed up. He wanted to run away from everything. He drove fast and erratically, jumping lights and shouting to himself. He wanted to cry on someone's shoulder, even between someone's breasts, but whose? With each mile he drove his tension got worse. 'Christ!' he shouted, 'Christ!' At the next lights he did a U turn and drove back through the awful night to Charity's house. She opened the door in her green dressing gown. Her face still looked wet.

'Oh God,' she said now, in her turn, 'Mark, Mark, I love you.' He kissed her wet face and then, upstairs, her body all over, and his penis became as tumescent as it had ever been, and this time willing to make its gift to her and to him.

Passion, which desperation made from time to time recoverable, sustained Mark and Charity in their difficult life. For months, one way or another, they were able to believe that they could go on loving one another, and that it would be worth it for both of them.

In 1982 Mark read Nancy Chodorow's book *The Reproduction of Mothering: Psychoanalysis and the Sociology of Gender*. This enabled him to understand for the first time why men fall in love with women and why women want to have children. Since these were the two basic facts he kept confronting in his personal life, reading the book was quite a revelation. Though he had attributed both the drive to love and the drive to reproduce to biology, it appeared, on the contrary, that both could be understood in cultural terms: men fall in love because they lose their mothers, and women want to have children because they don't. Boys have a hard time; brought up by women in a system which assigns childrearing to women, they eventually learn they must identify with men and not with women. What a nasty cultural trick! How can a man succeed after this? Women, on the other hand, can, provided they have children. Women don't have to break the 'primary identification' with their mothers, because they are women and will remain so. It's the fantasy of the symbiotic mother-daughter relationship that sustains patriarchy – the fantasy more than the reality. Give up on one's mother, and liberation's just over the next hill.

He and Charity discussed the Chodorow book. It was she who had suggested he read it. He was becoming quite worried about Charity. She kept writing papers, and two of them had already been accepted for publication. They were about feminism and the nuclear family. Whatever line she was taking on gender, it was clearly a popular one. She was also writing a book based on her research. She'd bought a new car, a smart black Renault with tinted windows, so she didn't need to bother about sunglasses in the sparkling winter sunshine. She'd taken on the organisation of a London-based workshop on feminism and the sociology of the family, which meant that she was constantly on the phone and dashing out to meet people in pubs. There were lots of things she was doing, and most of them disturbed him. He trembled at the prospect of her success. Charity's own reactions were much more cerebral. She was enjoying herself. Even though she'd planned them, her new competencies were surprising her to some extent. Reproduction, her first aim in life – success in the female world – had been replaced by production – success in the male world. What also surprised her was that she felt no inclination to change the direction her life was taking because of Mark's reaction. His irritation with her was childish. He would have to grow out of it, just as children had to transcend their greed in wanting all the sweets for themselves.

As a matter of fact, her relationship with Mark was getting more and more strained. He showed no more sign of moving in with her than a dead flea. One night she threw a cast-iron frying pan at him. He was terrified. The handle of the frying pan came off, but he found a screwdriver and put it on again.

So Charity came round, eventually, to another mode of action. She told Mark that, since he was unable to make a commitment to her, she would regard herself as an independent woman. A woman free to have other affairs.

He looked shocked, as she had expected. 'But you've got me,' he said. 'Why would you want to have affairs with other men? Aren't I enough for you?'

'I haven't got you; I've got half of you.'

'The best half,' he replied. Having metamorphosed the declaration of independence into a joke, he passed on to his new preoccupation, which was with the physical interior of her house. She had done nothing about the six bare spaces on the sitting room wall, in fact he was looking at them now. He said he would paint the room for her. And perhaps she would like him to fix the door knobs on the rooms upstairs? In other words, Mark wanted to raise the standard of her interior physical environment only because he felt himself unable to do anything about her psychological one.

In August 1983, two years after Mark and Charity met, and one year after the telephone call from Sweden, Charity went to a meeting on the sociology of chronic disease in Evian, France, of mineral water fame. She'd been asked to give a paper on her research, all expenses paid.

'But what will you do about the children?' Mark had asked, when she'd told him about the invitation. He hoped to have discovered a real obstacle.

'Why? Are you offering to look after them?' She scarcely paused, knowing the answer. 'They have a father,' she pointed out, 'he's going to have them.'

'What, *all* of them?'

'Why not?' James's girlfriend, Shelley, had had her baby in June, a red-haired boy with a painful cry whom they'd named Joshua. James had become a much better father since he'd moved out of the house in Chalk Farm. He seemed to appreciate his children more, make more of an effort towards them.

When Charity got to the airport on her way to Evian, she took the wrong exit, into Switzerland. The letter said there would be a car waiting to take her to the hotel. Once she had found the right exit, she could see a man standing there holding a large card displaying several names on it, including her own, DR WALTON.

The hotel was set in acres of wild gardens, in which deer were said to roam. Charity's room was on the first floor: it had french windows on to a balcony, where an ornate little table and chairs were placed to provide a view. She immediately flung open the windows to admit the balmy air into the room, which contained two double beds, a can of Evian water spray and, naturally, several bottles of the precious liquid. There was also a bowl of polished fruit, and another of immaculate roses, which she suspected of plasticity until she touched them and held their soft vegetable substance between her fingers. Charity went into the bathroom, vast and white, and ran herself a bath full of orange-scented bathfoam. She got into it with a large vodka and tonic concocted from the drinks cabinet which masqueraded as a piece of bedroom furniture.

The bath was very hot. She lay back in it feeling as though she were on holiday. She'd never been away on her own before. Part of her wanted to think Mark was in the other room, in bed waiting for her, or sitting on the balcony strumming his fingers on the table, getting impatient because she wasn't there. She smiled now, to remember him. His greed for her, the strange way he cared for her – mending the kitchen table, painting the walls, bringing her half-dead tulips. Yet she was beginning to realise that something in Mark's character was profoundly disrespectful towards women and wished to denigrate them. She didn't know what it was, nor how, properly, to regard it. But she did know she wanted to transcend it, even considered that she had, by making her life an independent material product of its own.

Men, she decided, not for the first time, lack self-knowledge.

It is the knowledge women have of themselves that gives them the final edge.

She got out of the bath. The water made a phenomenal noise as it dragged the orange foam down the plughole. She put on a startling new green dress for the reception that was to open the conference, and looked at herself in the long gilt mirror on the wardrobe door. She looked alright; her skin was soft and her eyes glowed; her hair had had its surface bleached by the summer sun, and fell in crescents on to the shoulders of her green dress. No one could call her beautiful, but no one could deny that she was a highly attractive woman, the sort of woman that men would fall in love with, because she was the sort of woman they would like to have been had they themselves been women.

At the reception she was introduced to Professor George Harley, an arrogant man in a navy pinstriped suit who often appeared on television talking about the social causes of ill-health, and the limits and therapeutic role of medicine. Harley asked Charity what kind of work she did, and expressed surprise that a sociologist who didn't know anything about medicine (as no one who wasn't a doctor could) would be able to write a thesis about multiple sclerosis. Hadn't she found it difficult? 'So you regard yourself as an expert on the subject now, do you?' he inquired, somewhat nastily.

'I don't believe anyone is an expert,' said Charity, 'except on the subject of themselves.'

After dinner, Charity went to her room feeling pleasantly alcoholised.

The phone rang. 'Charity?'

'Yes.'

'It's me.'

'Mark!'

'I just wondered how you were. How's Evian?'

'I'm fine,' she said, 'it's fine. Marvellous hotel, wonderful food.'

'Good,' he said, and paused. 'And how about the people? Who's there? Anyone I know?'

She told him who she'd met, knowing she wasn't answering

the question he wanted answered. He asked her then about her paper, and advised her to read it slowly, because nervousness makes people speed up, and some of the audience wouldn't understand English well. 'Have you got any slides?'

'No, overheads.'

'Go and make sure you understand how the projector works before the session,' he said, 'there's nothing worse than fumbling around with machinery with all those eyes watching you.'

She realised as he was giving her this spurious advice that he never phoned her at this time of day, except on Wednesdays, when Jane was out.

'Where are you, Mark?'

'In a call box.'

'Why are you in a call box?'

'I wanted to speak to you, and I can't do it at home. I said I was going out for a walk.'

'But you never walk!' She giggled, visualising him in the call box, probably standing awkwardly on one foot.

'No, I know. Never mind. You're alright, are you?'

'Never better. Don't worry about me.'

'No.' He sounded distracted. 'Okay, then, I'd better go. Haven't got any more money. Sleep well. I do love you, you know,' he added, consequentially.

'I know.'

Her paper was a success. There were many appreciative comments, and some helpful points that she might even take account of in the second draft of the book. One vociferous contributor was a curly-haired French doctor in the back row. By the end of the session, he and Charity were passing rapid quips back and forth, amusing everyone. She felt terribly pleased with herself. At dinner she sat next to him. His name was Sebastien Marcel.

'So you work with Professor Carleton at Regent's College, do you?'

'I do. Do you know him?'

'We were once at the same conference in California.' Sebastien's English was excellent. 'He gave a very humorous paper. What is it like, Regent's College?'

'It's not the most intellectually exciting place on earth,' she explained. 'But it's quite convenient for me. I'm divorced, you see, and I've got four children, so I have to work quite hard to fit everything in.'

She could see he was interested in this information. 'An independent woman?' he asked.

'An independent woman,' she confirmed.

They went for a walk in the gardens after dinner. Coloured lights were strung out round the hotel, and the green earth sprouted little illuminated gnomes. Sebastien talked about himself, and about his work as a family practitioner in a small town in south-west France. He had come to this meeting partly because he wanted to start some research with other doctors looking at how traditional farming communities deal with long-standing disease. He had an anthropological bent to him, and described enthusiastically some of the local farming and culinary rituals he'd witnessed, including the making of *confit de canard* in huge pots of boiling grease with women cracking jokes in the impenetrable local dialect. Sebastien came from Paris originally, so all this was as foreign to him as it was to Charity.

He asked her if she would like to go to the casino. There were many things she'd never done, and one of them was going to a casino. They lost five hundred francs in thirty minutes. The croupier and the other gamblers, who were conducting themselves with great seriousness, took a dim view of their behaviour. When they ran out of money, Sebastien ordered a bottle of champagne 'to celebrate all we've lost'.

'But how are we going to pay for it?'

'We pay for everything we do in the end.' Sebastien was waxing quite philosophical. 'But it's all worth it. At least, we have to believe it's worth it. Your marriage, for instance, it's over, but it was worth it, wasn't it?'

'Oh yes, of course. Are you married?'

'Good God, no. I don't have the concept!'

'How can you not have the concept but be a doctor?'

He laughed. She saw that he hadn't understood.

'Doctors are usually married.'

'Marriage isn't a part of medical training.'

'I don't know about that. The point is, medicine is such a conservative occupation. If you're looking for radical arrangements, you don't look among doctors.'

'It's different in France.'

'Is it?'

'I'm teasing you. No, it isn't different, but I am. Do you know,' he took her hand, 'you're awfully nice to tease.'

She laughed at the 'awfully'. 'Why do you speak like that?'

'Like what?'

'Like an English public school boy.'

'Because I am one.'

'That's the last thing you are.'

'I spent two summers with one, once,' he said. 'My mother insisted. She sent me away to learn English. I was fourteen.'

'How awful for you.'

'The most awful thing was the food. I couldn't stand it. Spotted dick. Custard. Mince. I thought I'd die, it was so awful. There you are, that word again! Are you hungry?'

'No. Yes,' she said, 'why?'

'Let's go and eat.'

'We've already eaten.'

'We can eat again. Gambling makes me hungry. You spend it, then you have to take it in again.'

They took a taxi into town, to a nightclub. Sebastien ordered snails and *sorbet au cassis* and another bottle of wine.

'I'm going to smell after this,' Charity complained, 'the garlic butter, I mean.'

'So?'

'So nothing.'

'That's a very English habit, you know. To worry about one's breath smelling of garlic. In France we don't worry because we like garlic. It's good to smell of it.'

Smelling of garlic, they danced, and Charity felt the wiriness of Sebastien's body next to hers. She'd grown used to Mark's body: how long had it been since she'd felt another man's? Sebastien had pinned himself to her, she could feel his ribs, the contours of his pelvis through his thin summer clothes.

The lights were dimmed, but still they danced. As the music stopped, he cupped her face in his hands and planted a kiss on it; the gesture was one of sowing a seed on the earth, not in it, but on it, so that it would lie on the topsoil where the sun and the rain would make it germinate – or they would not. Charity felt she would like to fall in love with Sebastien. It would be an escape; he could be her dream-man as Mark had briefly been, the elegant, immaterial lover sustaining life's provincial dreariness. Leon or Rodolphe in *Madame Bovary*. Emma Bovary's fictions of love kept her with Charles, her husband, in a state of perpetual expectancy: 'And all the time, deep within her, she was waiting for something to happen. Like a shipwrecked sailor she scanned her solitude with desperate eyes for the sight of a white sail far off on the misty horizon.'

Charity supposed it was the Frenchness of Sebastien that made her remember her nostalgic adolescent reading of *Madame Bovary*. But Sebastien certainly succeeded in bringing her back to earth later.

'I should like to make love to you,' he said in the foyer of the hotel, when they asked the tired-looking night clerk for their keys.

Mark's face appeared momentarily in front of Charity, like a vision. The vision recovered not only her love, but her anger, not only her gratitude, but her hatred.

'I think that's a very good idea,' she said, 'but I don't think I can. Thank you for asking me, all the same.'

She dreamed of Sebastien. Her dreams always told her something important, she paid attention to them. They were in a field of cornflowers together. His eyes matched them. 'You should live with me,' he said, 'let's run away together.' And then he sent her a basket of mouldy apples in which lay a letter, under a sheath of lecture notes, saying he didn't love her, after all. Shades of Madame Bovary.

She woke up to the sound of the telephone by her bed, and groped for it with a poorly controlled arm.

'Where were you last night?' demanded Mark. 'I called you over and over again. I called at ten o'clock, your time. Then at eleven, and twelve and one. You weren't there. Where were you?'

'Here,' she said. 'I was here. I went to the casino.'

'On your own?'

'We went to the casino. A whole crowd of us.'

There was a short silence. She could hear him wondering whether to believe her. 'It's not fair,' he said finally, and not very originally.

'What isn't fair?'

'I'm missing all the fun.'

'Come on, Mark, you decided you didn't want to come to the meeting with me, so why are you so jealous?'

'I miss you,' he said. 'I need you.'

'Maybe.'

'Don't do anything I wouldn't do.' He laughed with a nervous tension that hissed out of the receiver.

'I've got a hangover.'

'I'm not surprised. When are you coming home?'

'Tomorrow. The plane's at midday.'

'I'll ring you when you're back.'

She replaced the receiver and felt truly nauseous. She decided to miss the morning session, take two aspirins and go back to sleep.

When she went into the conference room at two o'clock, the only person there was Sebastien. He came towards her with the light behind him, and kissed her on the cheek. 'I missed you this morning. Where were you?'

All these men asking her where she was. 'Asleep. I had a frightful headache.'

'You should have told me, I've got some good pills for that. Being a doctor does have some advantages.'

Sebastien and Charity sat together through the afternoon papers, their knees touching as lightly as the kiss he had given her. The next day she flew back to London, and he took a train to Toulouse. They never saw each other again.

The evening Charity returned to London Mark came round. The

children were still with James, so the house was empty.

'I'm losing you,' said Mark. 'I lost what I really wanted when James moved out. I lost our secret. But this is worse. You're going to stop loving me.'

'I told you,' she reminded him, 'that I had to feel free to have other affairs, in view of your inability to leave your wife.'

'Did you? I didn't listen. But I knew something was wrong. Who were you with?'

Charity thought of denying it, and then remembered Mark's promise to her which, oddly, now reconstructed itself as a promise she'd made to him. It would be worse to lie. If women lied to men, because men habitually lie to women, the rot would start in earnest.

'You're right in your suspicion,' she told him. 'I'm not going to make it worse by denying it. There was someone. A French doctor. We had a brief affair. It was fun. It doesn't mean anything. And I did warn you.'

As she said this, she realised both that Mark would assume that she and Sebastien had slept together, and that she wasn't about to dissuade him of this notion. This discourse she was having with Mark wasn't about sex at all, it was about possession and control. The thought rose in her like bile, but hastily she swallowed it, consigning it to her intestines, where it would fester and create bad-smelling gas.

Thinking of Sebastien, her dream-man, she gazed at Mark as though he were a ghost. Indeed, she couldn't for some reason see his face or its expression: there was nothing but a blurred white space where his face should be. Yet she could see his hands; they were knotted together in anguish. She allowed herself to focus on those hands, willed herself to receive some feeling for him again. Some tenderness at last insinuated itself into her soul, sympathy for the pain he might be in. But there wasn't any guilt any more, for she knew he had brought this pain upon himself. His inaction, which did not go with his masculinity, had cancelled out the aggressiveness with which he had begun their affair; had he left his wife, there would have been no need for her to have considered going to bed with Sebastien.

· 121 ·

The space where he sat was empty. He was on the floor beside her, and he laid his head on her lap. 'Hold me,' he said. 'I don't know what to do. I don't know what to say.' He raised his head, and the clarity of the look that passed between them seemed to inspire him to a resolution of a kind. 'Yes, I do know. I'm not going to lose you, Charity. I'm going to leave my wife. Get a divorce. Will you live with me, Charity?'

'And be my love,' she said, because nothing else came into her head.

6 * THE CONCEPT OF A MIRACLE

'The engineer, so precise when he is laying out his diagrams, behaves at home like a minor god: a word, and behold, his meal is served, his shirts ironed, his children quieted. . . he sees nothing astounding in these miracles. The concept of the miracle is different from the idea of magic: it presents, in the midst of a world of rational causation, the radical discontinuity of an event without cause, against which the weapons of thought are shattered'
– *The Second Sex*, p.310

Some apparently empty statements contain nothing but the truth. Mark didn't regret what he'd said; rather he felt resigned to it. The tide of history merely seemed to him to be flowing over him, dragging him along in its every unalterable ebb and flow.

Of course, the whole thing, by which he meant his reaction to Charity's behaviour, had been foreseen in the telephone call from the Swedish forest the summer before. The panic that gripped his stomach then, and which led him to stand nauseated in front of the hydrangea bushes, had migrated into the knowledge that now he had to *do* something. He had to be a man of action. The very thought made him feel ill again.

He woke at five the next morning, and lay in the dark worrying. He worried about everything he could think of to worry about. Charity. Women. His children. Work. He shouldn't ever have left Texas. It was easier in Texas: people didn't expect so much of him. The sun shone, and university offices were furnished with bright pine desks. There were coffee machines everywhere, and typists with long hair who smiled. Here it rained and people had expectations. Consequently, he was much more likely to fail. Consequently? Sometimes Mark wondered whether he wasn't one of life's failures anyway, his successes only a veneer. He'd get found out one day. He allowed his mind to linger morbidly on this for a few moments in order fully to enjoy the genuine emotion of pity for himself.

Besides his specific personal and professional worries, Mark felt that things weren't going right in the department. He didn't seem able to make the place cohere the way it ought to. It wasn't responding to his dynamism.

Beside him Jane slept neatly on her back. The rhythm of her breathing, which normally he found comforting, annoyed him. What right had she to inhale and exhale along with all good-natured living things while his mind ran circles round itself in anguish?

He got out of bed and stumbled around in the darkness looking for his slippers. Jane turned over and at the same time the water hissed in the central heating pipes. He went downstairs and sat at the kitchen table, first releasing the blind from its entrapment over the window. He saw an anaemic dawn break over the rooftops; dark trees lightened into pinky gold, the desiccated apple trees in the garden revealed themselves in all their melancholic glory. Next door's tabby, a castrated overfed male, prowled across the fallen crimplene leaves seeking the scent of a half-remembered furry encounter. Curtains in other houses started to be drawn back and he imagined a thousand bleary faces peering into mirrors, masochistically re-engaging with the image of the early morning self – grey, unwashed, unwilling. He ran his fingers over his own face, feeling its roughness. He got up, knocking over a chair in the process, to look at himself in the hand-painted Moroccan mirror positioned on the kitchen wall by Jane for this very purpose. He didn't look at all nice. He put the chair the right way up, switched the kettle on, and stuck his hands deep into his dressing gown pockets in a disaffected pose.

Joanna came into the room wearing a large white T-shirt with a picture of Mickey Mouse on the front. 'Morning, Dad.'

· 124 ·

He looked at her abstractedly. 'Hallo, dear.'

'What was that awful noise I just heard?'

'What? Oh, I knocked a chair over. Sorry.'

'Oh Dad.' She sidled up to him, and softly angled her head against his chest. 'Why *are* you so clumsy?'

He sighed, put his arm round her and held her unexpectedly tight. 'I have a problem with co-ordination,' he said, meaning several things.

'Are you going somewhere special this morning?'

'No, why?'

'It's early. You're not usually up this early.'

'No. That's right.' He sniffed, and continued to hold her, wondering if he was likely to cry.

'Do you want some beans?' she asked.

'For breakfast?'

'Yes. First-class protein. Easy, too. Come on, Dad, you need feeding up.'

'That I do not.' He looked down at his stomach, a blue-towelled mound, and pulled it in so it was no longer on his horizon.

Joanna gave him a plate of red kidney beans and rice. She was in a vegetarian phase, which also entailed a merging of the nature of different meals. Jane came down at 7.45, while they were eating their beans, looking pristine in a yellow cashmere jumper. As Mark looked at her, the beans stuck in his throat. What did she know? How could he tell her? What would he say? Susan pranced in with the mail. 'Two for Dad, three for Mum, postcard for you, Jo.'

'You can't go to school in that,' said Jane, referring unkindly to the black sweater Susan was wearing.

'Why, because it's got a hole in it?'

'That's one reason.'

'Listen, Mum, no one's going to blame you for what I'm wearing. Don't worry about it. We all know how wonderful you are. Why don't you nag Jo for a change?'

The stance of Jane's yellow cashmere sweater was one of accepting silence. This, Mark felt, had been her attitude throughout most of their marriage. He decided to go to a library today in order to think. He felt anonymous in libraries, and the lack of interruption aided cerebration.

At ten o'clock he was positioned in a seat on the fourth floor of the Social Science library in WC1. He took a piece of paper from his briefcase and placed it on top of the fire notice bonded to the top of the desk. Then he drew a line down the middle so there were two columns on the page. One of these he headed 'me' and the other one 'her'. He intended to write down some of the ways in which he might tell Jane he was going to leave her, and plot against this her probable responses, from which he would then choose, which in turn would make it clear how he should broach the subject to begin with. First he wrote down: 'I don't love you any more.'

He imagined her face calmly regarding him. 'You're overtired. Why don't you have a nap?' Or: 'Of course we don't love each other the way we did eighteen years ago. But so what?'

That one wouldn't get him very far. He chewed the end of his pen and then suddenly had the most incredible urge to fart. Of course, the beans. Urgently, he got up to find the men's room. He locked the door, farted and opened the window. Much better.

He went back to his seat and thought of another strategy. 'I want to live on my own for a while. I've never been on my own, and I really have this tremendous longing for solitude.' No sooner had he finished saying this in his head when Jane laughed at him. 'What's that a quote from?' Quite right, it certainly wasn't a quote from him.

He looked out of the window. A television aerial on the building opposite had a row of crosses on it, resembling accusing female chromosomes. Beneath it, through the plate glass window, he could see a meeting in progress: men in their shirtsleeves, jackets hanging off chairs, one man waving his fists at a pile of papers. He wanted to fart again. This time he let it out slowly, in a controlled manner, without leaving his seat, hoping no one would notice.

The trees that had seemed dark red this morning now looked

violently yellow, the colour of Jane's sweater. Leaves dangled off them, look-alikes for gold coins of chocolate money on Christmas trees. His mind leapt to Charity, to Charity in bed with this man in Evian. Naturally, he was quite capable of dismissing the whole incident, of closing his mind to it. This was his usual response to unpleasant events.

He remembered visiting his mother in hospital in Derby just before she died, the grey circularity of the ring road, the twin black towers of the hospital complex rising like burnt tree trunks into the gloomy sky, the smell of the cancer that was eating away her body. Though the smell had been overlaid by the sanitorising odours of hospital, it had been there, all the same; had infiltrated his consciousness and stayed there in a box all these years. In the box next to it he came upon Charity and her French lover. He saw her face beneath his, saw her rhapsodic eyes and her long fingers indenting another man's buttocks with their little white insignia. Oh, Charity! He realised the most awful thing, which was that he wouldn't be able to shut Charity and her French lover away in a box once he'd left Jane. She was his security against unpleasantness. Without Jane, he would be totally dependent on Charity's love.

Mark got out his handkerchief and blew his nose loudly. Then he picked up his case and left the room and found a phone in the lobby. He only had a 50p piece, so he put that in, but when he had dialled his home number, nothing happened. He put down the receiver and waited for the 50p to drop down, but it didn't. He picked up the receiver, dialled the operator and explained to her what had happened.

'What is your number?' the voice inquired.

He peered at the box. 'There isn't one.'

'Look again,' she said. 'It's above the telephone on the right.'

'Well, it isn't.' He felt foolish. He'd been going to ring Jane and ask her to meet him so they could talk about it.

'Oh shit!' He slammed the phone down and walked out of the library.

Instead of ringing Jane again, he rang Charity from another phone box in Gower Street. Traffic roared past, so he put a finger

· 127 ·

in the ear he wasn't using for the phone. Charity was in the bath – she said she was in the bath, though he couldn't hear the water lapping round her white breasts.

'I don't know how to tell her,' he said in a rush.

'Tell who what?'

'Jane, about us.'

'And you expect me to tell you what to say?'

'I thought you'd be able to give me some advice,' he admitted faintly. The line was suddenly disconnected, though he had this time inserted several coins. Christ! He dialled the operator.

'Operator, can I help you?' He was appalled to hear the same voice that he'd been connected to on the library phone.

'It's me again,' he said, 'I've got a different problem now.'

'I don't know who you are, but I am certainly not interested in your problems,' the voice said sternly.

'Hang on a minute,' he stammered, 'I mean I'm in another phone box, and it's eaten all my money.'

'Yes?' said the voice wearily.

He pulled himself together. 'Please would you reconnect me to the following number, 459 0570?'

'Hold the line, please.'

Charity was still in the bath.

'We were cut off,' he told her.

'We were not cut off,' she replied. 'I put the phone down.'

'You what? Why did you do that?'

'You ring me for help with telling your wife you're going to leave her? You must be mad,' she exploded.

'Sorry, Charity.' He shifted from one foot to the other, like a schoolboy. 'But I don't know what to do. Sorry. I really am sorry.'

At such times in his life, Mark welcomed distractions, and one useful distraction was that he was summoned back to the States to talk to the Whiteman Foundation about the funding of his project on the sociology of everyday life. They were interested, but not yet committed.

He was assembling the necessary papers together at his desk when Swinhoe knocked at his door.

'You busy, Carleton?'

'Well, yes, actually, I'm off to the States tomorrow.'

'I see.' Swinhoe looked at him mistily. 'I just wanted a quick word with you,' he said.

'Go ahead.' Mark continued to shuffle papers around. Swinhoe sat down and wound his long legs around one another.

'There are a couple of things actually. The first is I've got a problem with the computing side of my shoplifting survey.'

Mark looked up, mildly engaged.

'It's McKinnon. Can't get him to produce the goods.'

'What do you mean, exactly?'

'Not getting on with the analysis. Data are all in, but nothing happens. Just not doing it.'

'So what is he doing?'

'I don't know. No one knows. Not here much. Haven't you noticed?' Mark hadn't. 'Always walking out the front door when I come in,' continued Swinhoe, 'with that handbag.'

'Have you discussed the problem with him?'

'Told him I can't get on with the writing up until he's done the analysis,' mumbled Swinhoe. 'Doesn't get anywhere. In one ear and out the other. What's the man doing? I don't know.'

'Okay, okay,' said Mark. 'I'll have a word with him. What was the other thing?'

'Want to apply for a readership,' said Swinhoe abruptly.

'Do you?' Mark couldn't remember how long Swinhoe had been in the department. A hundred years? The request struck him as absurd, given the shoplifting misdemeanour and Swinhoe's general lack of qualification for such an elevated and expensive position. 'There's nothing to stop you from applying,' he said, 'but are you sure this is the right time?'

'I'm fifty,' said Swinhoe, as though this explained everything. 'Can't wait for ever.'

'No, indeed,' agreed Mark. 'Well, what I suggest you do is prepare your application, together with an up-to-date c.v., and let me have a look at it when I come back from the States.'

Swinhoe didn't stand a chance, but you couldn't say that sort of thing these days or you'd be accused of discrimination, or at least of subverting the official policy of what was called staff development. People were supposed to be stretched like pieces of knicker elastic until they got to the top of the ladder. The only problem was that the ladder metaphor wasn't appropriate any more. There wasn't any room at the top.

'Thanks.' Swinhoe stood up. 'Oh, by the way, my article on "Shoplifting: A Case Study in Participant Observation", is coming out in the *Journal of Sociology* next month.'

'Good, good. Let me have a reprint, will you?'

On his way out of the room Swinhoe turned. 'Sorted out your own problem, have you?'

'Which one is that?'

'Women,' said Swinhoe. His shoulders started to go up and down with the birth pangs of a sardonic laugh.

'Not quite,' said Mark.

Before he left for the States, Mark confronted McKinnon, who maintained a) that Swinhoe was a highly unreasonable and unpleasant person, and b) that he was having to spend a lot of his time negotiating with the university for more effective computing facilities. This necessitated frequent visits to the central computing service twenty minutes walk away. He reminded Mark that in the forthcoming University Grants Commission visit computing was an area that had been earmarked for special scrutiny. Mark had forgotten the UGC visit.

He summoned Pascoe and asked him to deal with the necessary arrangements. Pascoe said he couldn't, because his wife was in hospital having a hysterectomy, and he needed three weeks off to look after her, and arrange things like special steps in the kitchen so she could reach the top cupboards without stretching. As a consequence of these conversations, Mark was wearing a desolated look when Margaret Lacey found him in the common room, leafing through some old *New Societys*.

'You look dreadful,' she observed.

'This place is going to pot,' he said, 'and I'm going to America.'

'Is there anything I can do to help?' Her green eyes regarded him languorously. She wore her usual constricting dress, and an antique choker wrapped her narrow throat. Mark's eyes were drawn to her bra-less nipples which faced him as tiny evocative protuberances through the brown velvet surface of her dress.

'Perhaps you could help. Yes I think you could.' Suddenly inspired by the dialectical notion of delegating his directorial responsibility to this perceived manifestation of female sexuality, he decided to suggest she organise the UGC visit. She was probably very capable organisationally: most women were.

'Actually, I can't stop now,' Margaret interrupted him. 'I've got to go home to let the gas man in. My cooker's got a leak. When are you off?'

'Tomorrow.'

'Why don't you call in for a drink on your way home?'

'Fine,' said Mark, doubtfully. 'Good. Okay. When?'

'About six.'

'Good. Fine. See you then.'

'I'll look forward to it.' She left the room with a soft Victorian swish.

As he made his way out of the building en route to Margaret's, he met Delia, looking flushed, on the stairs. 'It worked,' she said, 'I thought you'd like to know it worked.'

'Good,' he said, absentmindedly. He went past her and then turned back and looked up at her; something about her was different today. She wore a pink crimplene suit and black high-heeled shoes with bows on the fronts. She looked quite absurd. 'Good God,' he said, 'don't you think you've carried it a bit far?'

'I got these in the Women's Liberation jumble sale in Hornsey,' she said, as though this explained everything.

Margaret lived in a white-walled ascetic flat off the Caledonian Road. The pavement was scattered with squashed fruit and vegetables from the street market, and the gas man had gone when he got there. She poured him a vodka and lime. They sat down on a white tweed sofa, in front of a white rug (there was probably a white cat somewhere) and he launched into a soliloquy on the UGC and its underlying and overlying agendas, outlining the points of possible conflict, where the department needed especially to impress. It was a matter, he told her, of getting together a batch of documents about the external relations and internal workings of the department – its essential democracy and accountability, its worthy research record, the great teaching it did, its amazing *esprit de corps*.

'The most important thing,' he said, 'is our postgraduate degree record. You'll have to get Mavis to work out our completion rates, but that shouldn't be a problem. Also make a point of this new option we're doing on the social economics of the household – no one else is doing that, and the students quite like it. Oh, and don't forget, we're not doing badly with the overseas students, either. They'll want to know we're raking in the money.'

Margaret was attentive. She took notes, sipped her vodka and lime, and said of course she would take care of it all, indeed she looked forward to making a good job of it.

In the light from the dull black metallic lamp, he could still see the profile of her nipples. At the same time as he reached out to touch them, she leaned over and kissed him on the cheek, a most chaste and unerotic kiss.

'I think I ought to go now, Margaret,' he said.

When he got to New York he wrote Jane a letter.

'My dear Jane. There's something I've wanted to talk to you about for some time, but it hasn't been easy to find a way of doing it. To write a letter is cowardly, but I don't know what else to do, so please forgive me.'

He read this through and crossed out 'so please forgive me'. She wouldn't: there was no point in asking.

'This will hurt you, and I'm sorry, because hurting you is the last thing I want to do.' He paused and crossed out this last bit as well, because he could hear her mind thinking, well, if he didn't want to hurt me, why is he doing this? Some women could be appallingly rational.

'I didn't intend to hurt you,' he rewrote. That, at least, was true. Intention had nothing to do with it. But, 'I have to leave you, Jane. I'm in love with someone else, and the present situation isn't fair to any of us.' He thought about this. It clearly wasn't fair to Jane, because she was being deceived, and he assumed she wouldn't want to be deceived. Would she? 'When I come back,' he wrote, 'I'll move out. Please don't tell the girls. I'd like to tell them about it myself. I'm sorry, Jane. In many ways I still love you and I don't understand what has happened. Mark.'

He put it in a hotel envelope and took it to the reception desk.

'We don't sell stamps, Mister,' said the assertive black clerk behind the desk. 'You'll have to take it to a post office.' Mark put the envelope in his inside jacket pocket, and took a cab to the Foundation.

After the meeting, Roger Strangeway, the Foundation's Research Director, suggested dinner at his house. Mark was pleased, since he didn't fancy an evening on his own. He went back to the hotel, showered and changed. He whistled to himself as he shaved, which must mean that he was happy. The thought pleased him. Probably he was happy because he was sorting things out at last.

Roger Strangeway's dinner party was fattening and boring. The roast beef ran with blood, which meant that the sweet potatoes were tinged with pink. The lemon meringue pie was like a cliff hitting the clouds. Strangeway had three American children and a sheepdog called Reagan. Mark sat next to an overdressed administrator called Gina, who confessed to having got through three marriages and actively looking for a fourth. She wore a lot of rings, at least two on every finger, and a light gold chain round one ankle. Her teeth were terribly white. She offered to take him home afterwards. Strangeway said the hotel was on her way.

Gina had a yellow sports car with an acrilan monkey hanging over the dashboard. She talked nonstop on the journey back, and kept giving him white-teethed sideways glances to make sure he was listening. When she stopped outside the hotel she turned off the lights, and the ignition, and clearly expected to be asked up for a drink. The bar was closed. Mark complained.

'It's a quarter after twelve, Mister, the opening hours are up there. Twelve is closing time.'

'Haven't you got some scotch in your room?' inquired Gina, twisting some of her rings and looking heavily at him.

In the lift she reached out to touch the lapels of his tweed jacket. 'You know who you remind me of?'

'I can't think.' He couldn't.

'Richard Burton.'

'Good God.' It dawned on him then that Gina expected him to make love to her. Did all women want you to make love to them? What were women? Crocodiles with open jaws, smiling lions with the smell of fresh blood on their manes. Addicts grabbing the next needle wherever they could. And why him?

He gave Gina a glass of scotch. 'I'm afraid I haven't got any ice.'

She put the glass down on the bedside table and took her shoes off, adjusting her ankle chain slightly. 'I don't need any ice, sweetie,' she said, 'I need you to come and keep me warm.' She lay down on the bed. Mark sat down beside her, glass in hand. He looked out of the window. It was still raining.

Gina undid the buttons on her blouse and unclipped a tight, lacey bra. She cupped one breast in her hand and reached for him with the other. 'Come on, lovey, I've got a good body. I don't have any diseases, and I'm a fantastic fuck. I come very easy. You can do anything you like with me. Tell me what you want to do and I'll do it.' She undid her skirt and lay there in a pair of scarlet underpants. She put her hand in her pants and he could see one finger manoeuvring the flesh. Against his will, something stirred in him. He stripped his clothes off suddenly and stood, impressed with the size of his erection silhouetted against the black raining night.

'Oh baby,' Gina murmured, 'what a lovely cock! Bring it here! Give it to me!'

He stood over her and she took it in her red mouth. After a few moments, he looked down and wondered if he ought to be doing this. He withdrew carefully. There were lipstick marks round the base of his penis. He lay down, overcome by a wave of sudden fatigue. He closed his eyes, and for a few delicious moments his brain lapsed into sleeplike waves.

· 134 ·

'No?' Gina's spiky nails assaulted his cheekbones, and her dark eyes flashed all over his face. 'You want to fuck me, then? Okay. Go ahead, fuck me. Stick it in. Stick your big cock in.' The pitch of her voice was rising all the time. She rolled over, pulled him down on top of her, grabbed his penis and guided it in. He was amazed to find it still erect. He would have done anything to disown it. She felt quite cavernous, a cavern filled with noxious liquids. 'Oh,' she said, 'oh lovely, come on, more, more, I want to come, oh ah . . . I'm coming . . .' And she did. She paused a moment, and then said in his ear, 'More, I want to come again. Make me come again.' He moved a couple of times and she started screaming, 'Oh, oh no, that's good.' He stopped. 'No, no, baby, go on please, more, more!' She screamed again. 'Don't stop now, I'm going to die, go on!' He did, but unfortunately (he almost thought) she didn't. She dug her fingernails into his bottom so that it really hurt. 'This one's going to be loud,' she warned, 'it's wonderful, you're wonderful, I'm coming, I'm coming . . . Ahhhhh . . .' Mark began to feel a bit tired. He felt like a garage mechanic. He withdrew, lay beside her and reached for his glass. She came out of her orgasmic coma.

'What's the matter, baby? Don't you want to go on?'

'Well, actually,' he said, 'I've got this problem with my back. It gets me sometimes.'

'Oh dear. Then let me give you a massage. I'm very good at that. Jack, my second husband, used to say that was the thing he'd miss most of all. Turn over, lovey.' Mark did, and buried his face with relief in the pillow. It could now wear any expression he liked.

Gina's ringed hands moved over the lower part of his back. It felt good. She certainly knew what to do. 'Just a moment, baby, I know what would help.' He heard her get up and open her handbag. Then he felt some cold liquid on his back. 'Massage lotion,' she told him, 'this'll feel even better now.'

It did, although a powerful smell of musk oil and cocoa butter filled the air. He lay there peacefully. No need to think about love, commitment, responsibility. He could have any woman he wanted. Life was a series of sexual adventures, and that was all it was. The life of the mind, of the thwarted and striving intellect, was a deception: only the body never lied. He began to draft the questions about sex they might ask in the everyday life project (would the same questions work in Alma-Ata as in Amsterdam?) when he became aware of a change in his masseuse's behaviour. She'd parted his legs, and was sticking her moisturised fingers up his bottom. He didn't like that. Nobody had ever done that to Mark Carleton before. It felt dirty. In any case, she hadn't asked him if he'd wanted it. Then it began to feel rather different.

'Just finding your G spot, sweetie,' she said. 'Did you know men have a G spot, too?' He didn't, but whatever she'd found certainly had nothing to do with his normal excretory functions.

He groaned.

'That's it, darling. That's where it is. Just behind your prostate. If I go on doing this, you know what will happen, don't you?' He didn't, but his penis now projected into the mattress like a battering ram. Gina's other hand played with his balls. The whole thing was quite extraordinarily ridiculous. He was totally trapped with this woman from South Carolina's ringed fingers tapping his buttocks and her manicurised fingernails up his arse. He thought about Margaret Lacey's nipples. He thought about Charity in the snow. He thought about all the vaginas he'd known, and all those he hadn't, and Gina's fingers continued to massage his prostate and almost without any warning at all he ejaculated straight into the mattress.

'Everyday life is non-philosophical in relation to philosophy and represents reality in relation to ideality,' read Mark. 'The study of everyday life . . . exposes the possibilities of conflict between the rational and the irrational in our society and our time . . .' He paused, with his finger on the page, in order to think about the point. He was sitting in the New York Public Library reading Lefebvre's *Everyday Life in the Modern World*. Strangeway had told him his project lacked a theoretical rationale.

'Now, that doesn't worry me,' Strangeway had said, 'I'm against jargon, anyway. But I think it'll worry some people on the research board. We're talking here about something that's going to cost at least three million dollars. I think you need to tighten up on your theory.'

So that's what Mark was doing in the library, tightening up on his theory. First of all he'd struggled through two volumes of Henri Lefebvre's *Critique de la vie quotidienne*, an early Marxist text. The librarian, a young man with one gold earring, then brought him a later work by Lefebvre, which Allen Lane had kindly published in English under the title *Everyday Life in the Modern World*. Near the beginning of this, Lefebvre invited the reader to select a day at random from a 1900 calendar, and then to visit a library to read the news for that day. The problem with this approach, observed Lefebvre, was that it told you nothing about what ordinary men and women were doing. Quite so! Exactly! As to the conflict between the rational and the irrational, it wasn't hard for Mark to understand this in terms of his own life. The rational in his life was his work, his professorship, the solid spiral from the bottom to the top. His existence with Jane, the world of the family. This was the structure, and structures were rational.

He thought back to the early days of his marriage and, before that, to his first encounter with Jane in a teashop in Oxford in 1966. After a couple of years mucking around, he'd decided to do his PhD, and his supervisor, a weatherbeaten homosexual wine taster at St John's College, had just given him a real grilling. Not about the intellectual content of his thesis, but the manner in which he'd expressed himself.

'Your style,' Professor Dillon had told him, 'is constipated in the extreme. In fact, the early chapters are dreadful. You begin to get somewhere about three-quarters of the way through. On the last page of Chapter 8 one has a faint glimpse of what you begin to feel you might think. But then the whole wretched cycle begins again. You *can* think, I know you can think. The research, well, it's not original, but it's alright. In any case, it's what you do with the material, not where you got it from that counts. Research is like dressmaking. You need to cut the material in the right place, and it's no good having a mouthful of pins. You're full of pins, Carleton. You can't get the words out.

By God, man, you can't get it out or you won't, I don't know which it is!'

Mark had retreated with his bruises to the infantile comfort of a cream tea in a High Street teashop. It was served to him by a waitress whose competent and dexterous manner suggested precisely that relationship with the external world that he himself would like to develop. He didn't enjoy dropping things, or bumping into them. He would like to be able to forge links, to produce himself in a manner that made immediate connections with, and sense to, others. Jane's hair shone like bleached silk. She moved like a cat. Her fingers were fluid marble, admirably and carefully arranging the teacups and the plates and the beginnings and ends of his buttered scones.

They were married a year later. A year after that Joanna was born. Mark was glad the hospital wouldn't let him see the birth. He had his own view of the space between women's legs, and he wanted to keep this view, not have it sullied by the clatter of instruments and the sight of blood. Joanna, glimpsed through the glass by him at the age of thirty minutes, appeared to be regarding him with one baleful eye, winking almost. When he pointed this out to the nurse on duty, she said it was just a sticky eye, lots of newborn babies had it, it didn't mean a thing. But it did mean something to Mark, because his first acquaintance with his daughter had been coloured by this one-sided mocking look.

Susan's birth two years later was also part of a rational plan: each child was conceived and born on time. Susan had both eyes open. He was forced to attend this birth because hospital policy had changed in the interstice between the two deliveries, and fathers were now supposed to be there, watching or something. Mark had held Jane's hand in the delivery room, and felt hot and nauseated. The midwife ordered a plastic cup of water for him, and then a cold cloth for his overheated head. 'Mr Carleton's not cut out for this, is he, dear?' she was heard saying to Jane, as though his incapacity made him invisible, and to the doctor, 'This is exactly why I think the father's place is in the father's room. They've done their bit. Now it's the mother's turn. The fathers are only a nuisance here.' Later on, she pulled the baby

· 138 ·

out with a flourish and held it up like a chicken: 'A little girl!' In his weak state Mark saw the baby as anything but little. It howled loudly, and was prominently pink, like a chemically coloured doll. Jane cried. He was amazed. Crying was not part of her character. The midwife wrapped the baby up and gave her to Mark to hold. He gazed at her screwed-up expression, and saw in it all women again, making faces at him.

So women represented the irrational blood and agony of birth, and their irrationality could only be dealt with by annexing it to some overarching plan. A plan such as the family. Sexuality, however, did not fit in. He remembered someone saying – a journalist, he thought, at a Christmas party – that 'the main problem in life is that fucking and childrearing have absolutely nothing to do with one another.' Sexual forces were irrational not, of course, when they bound you to a marriage, but when they pulled you away from it. He was an animal. But he should not be. With Gina he was an animal. With Jane he was a human being, a member of a family. With Charity he took a risk, because he didn't know what he was.

Mark returned to London ten days later, having spent a week in Washington before leaving the States. When he got home, Jane was watching the news on television. She got up, kissed him, and fetched him a drink, a dry Martini with three pieces of ice and a mint leaf in it – a Carleton invention. He could discern nothing that was in any way different about her behaviour, though she should have got his letter by now. By the end of the evening, when she'd made no reference to it, he decided that she'd made up her mind to ignore both it and its message. Jane's intelligence was cool and strategic. She'd probably worked out that if she ignored the letter, he would never have the courage to broach the subject again.

In bed that night, Jane turned to him and took him in her arms. In the darkness he could feel her looking at him: she cared for him. Her tenderness was real. He found it quite soporific, and instantly took refuge in a well-earned sleep.

In the morning he found the unposted letter in his jacket

pocket. He took it into the department, where he tore it into little pieces and put it in the wastepaper basket.

Margaret Lacey was waiting to see him, anxious to tell him how well the UGC visit had gone. She wore an enormous blue mohair sweater: the central heating had broken down. McKinnon had booked an appointment later in the day to complain about Swinhoe's malevolence towards him. Mavis interrupted this to tell him her mother had been admitted to hospital with a broken hip. Then, at the end of the day, there was Swinhoe, with a copy of his application for a readership, looking mournful and applicatory. Mark's head hurt. He took a couple of aspirin and made himself a cup of tea with three spoonfuls of sugar in it. The telephone rang.

'The Newells have asked us for a meal,' said Jane, 'and I've got a babysitter. Okay?' He coughed an answer into the phone and put it down. It rang again immediately. He picked it up without saying anything.

'Hallo?' It was Charity's voice. 'Hallo?'

'Hallo,' he echoed.

'What's the matter, Mark?'

'Nothing. I've had a bad day, that's all.' Where was Charity?

'I'm in Oxford,' she said, 'remember the one-day conference on the sexual politics of research?'

'Yes,' he said, falsely. 'But . . .'

'Mark,' she interrupted herself as she often did, not content with interrupting others, 'how about meeting me for a meal? I know this fantastic place in the country where they have champagne on draught . . .'

Charity sat in her car outside the Carleton house in Islington. It was eight o'clock, a cold February night. There was ice on the windscreen, and condensation from her own breath inside the car. The radio played the ordered chemistry of a Bach cantata.

She was waiting to find out whether Mark was in the house. Once she'd realised Mark's letter to Jane announcing the end of the marriage had never materialised, she'd given him an ultimatum: finish the relationship with her, or I'll spill the beans to

Jane. He couldn't say he wouldn't see Charity any more, so Charity had told Jane that she and Mark had been lovers for three years and she had left her own husband for him. In return, Jane told Charity that she and Mark had continued to sleep together during the two years when Mark had said they hadn't. Thus everybody ended up hating everybody else. Jane hated Charity for disrupting her life, Charity hated Jane for telling her the truth, and Mark hated both of them for talking to one another. He also hated himself for his pathetic inability to be master of his own fate.

After this, he'd told Charity he was staying with a friend. She didn't believe him. She thought he and Jane were in collusion against her. She imagined them sitting together in their neat house talking about her, discussing her habits, how she cried because Mark had hurt her, how she moved in her sleep, or smelt in the mornings.

She cleared the windscreen and the window on her side, so she had a better view of the house. She studied the places where light flowed out: the large front window, covered in a white blind, had the outline of tall plants behind it, and human figures as well, perhaps. She couldn't really tell. Above, curtains: a bedroom? She caught a kingfisher flash of a figure in the window above the front door, but was unable to see who it was.

Her hands clutched the steering wheel, matching the set of her mouth in their tension; she had really worked herself up into a state now.

'Why don't you admit to yourself it'll never work?' Sally had said. 'He'll never have the courage to leave Jane and live with you.'

'Does living with me take such courage?' she had replied. 'He loves me. I know he loves me. Men do find me desirable, you know,' she stated petulantly, remembering Sebastien, and what might have been instead of what was.

'It's not a question of love,' observed Sally flatly. 'Mark wants love without commitment, and you don't.'

The front door opened, and Mark came out, wearing a raincoat and holding a bottle. So he was back there after all! A burst of anger made her want to act, to do something which would register her rage. Charity knew that Mark was going to Howard Denby's party, a party to which she, too, was invited. She watched Mark walking down the road. He didn't look like a soul in torment. Did he really think she would wait around like this forever, loving him and getting nothing in return?

Watching him, the fluttering of his raincoat, the slope of his shoulders, the self-absorbed jolt of his steps on the pavement, she conceived a hatred for him that was new. She wanted to annihilate him, wipe him off the face of the earth. He was not her lover but her enemy. She would like to be holding a machine gun, so she could knock him down as he sauntered through the streets, bottle under his arm, hands in pockets, living his decrepit and deceitful little life. He had no right to walk there as though he owned the place, as if it were his territory, while she cowered in desperation, locked in love and fury and loneliness.

She started the engine and drew slowly and quietly away from the curb. He hadn't noticed her, she was sure. Ice on the pavement glinted like steel. Her hands were cold, she took them off the wheel and rubbed them together like matchsticks.

Sally and she had drunk a bottle of cheap brandy together while Charity raved and Sally alternately consoled and instructed. Charity had not been able to stop either crying or drinking, so that she was drained and saturated. Nothing was left inside her except her sodden anger. Her anger was the only thing she owned.

Ahead of her in the freezing night, Mark turned the corner. Perhaps he would slip and fall and mortality would catch up with him? The bottle of wine would crash and splinter, so even if he didn't bleed, the wine would, running into the gutters and joining with the ice to freeze the sewers of London solid.

She turned the corner, too. Ahead the road was straight and silent. It was a road of new houses with garages, so there were few cars parked on the street. A sombre mood hung over everything, an atmosphere of suspension, like those science fiction movies in which there is about to be an alien visitation and everything is waiting for the vital moment when the great white spaceship comes gliding out of the blackness with its load of uninterpretable calamities.

Mark still hadn't noticed her. And then he turned to look over his shoulder, becoming aware of the car creeping along behind him. He would recognise the car. He stood still in the middle of the pavement, shifting the bottle of wine from under one arm to the other. He looked at her and his eyes were astonished. To see her there? To see the look on her face. But he couldn't see it, not through the black cold night, and through the frozen-up windscreen.

A streetlight threw a crystallised white light over his body. The light made a circle round his feet. Charity saw it as a devotional picture, the kind of cheap card you would buy in Catholic shops. Christ the saviour on his way to a party. Mark as Christ, but not the saviour. Charity laughed, a humourless cackle. Her cold hands wrenched the steering wheel left and the car's wheels hit the curb and then mounted it. 'I hate you, you bastard!' she screamed. Mark jumped, his face white like the streetlight, his thick brown hair standing straight up in panic. His raincoat flew out like bats' wings, taking him up and over the nearest hedge, so that he disappeared into someone's front garden.

Charity accelerated, returning the car to the road and screeching off as violently as she could, nearly skidding on the glazed surface.

When the sound of the car had disappeared, Mark looked nervously out from behind the hedge. He was shaking. The wine had gone; it had landed in a neighbouring bramble. He ran his hands through his hair and felt in his pocket for his wallet. The noise of his heart could be heard all over the garden. He stood up, tried to straighten himself out. Behind him a door opened. A woman peered out. 'Alan!' she shrieked, 'Alan, there's a man in our front garden!' She withdrew, slamming the door behind her. Curtains were opened and the garden was washed with yellow. The door reopened and Alan came out in his slippers. He took one or two paces towards Mark and said, 'What do you think you're doing? This is private property.'

'I'm sorry,' stammered Mark, clutching his raincoat wildly about him. 'My girlfriend just tried to kill me. She drove up on the pavement in her car. I had to run away.'

'A likely story!'

'No, really, it's true.'

'You're a nutter,' said the man flatly. 'Get out of my front garden or I'll call the police. I've got a good mind to call the police anyway.' The shrieking woman watched with smugly folded arms from the doorway.

Mark ran. 'She tried to kill me,' he repeated to himself. 'Charity tried to kill me.' As he said it, he became increasingly impressed by what had happened. He had been made a victim. A crime had been perpetrated against him. Charity had committed a public offence, an inexcusable, even illegal act. What she had just done to him wasn't allowed. It was against the law. There you are, it was actually against the law for anyone to behave like that! He felt vindicated, triumphant. By running her car on the pavement and trying to kill him, she had made irrelevant all his own actions against her, for whatever he had done, however bad it was, it had at least not been contrary to any law. By becoming a victim, he was ultimately victorious. Her anger put him in the right.

Mark's shoes were not made for running, and especially not for running in a hazardous environment. He skidded on a patch of ice and ended up against a postbox. His bottom hurt, and his back, and all the air was forced out of his lungs by the impact, so that for several icy moments he couldn't breathe, and thought he would never breathe again.

He leaned against the postbox and gave himself up to fate in the form of women and icy pavements. Then, just as he had made the decision to give up, his lungs jumped into action, and their alveoli became pink with oxygen. Life flowed on. Mark started to cry. It was good that he was wearing his raincoat. He hadn't cried since his mother died. There was a moment in the starchy hospital when, alone with the old lady, he had realised it was no longer the moment before death but the moment after, and he had taken her hand and held it. It felt as lifeless in death as it had in life, not more so. He had found himself crying then, and he wasn't crying for her but for him. He had lost his mother, and knew that it would be even harder for him to grapple with the problem she represented. Her death made the problem abstract, and it was on that level that he would have to contend with it for the rest of his life.

Crying startled him, because it was so difficult to begin and so impossible to stop. To cry made his very existence fluid; its edges appeared to run into his habitat, and he couldn't tell where he started and the air or the concrete surfaces around him ended. He felt completely protoplasmic, just a bunch of random unlucky cells.

Whenever Mark cried he knew why he didn't bother the rest of the time. But he was also astonished at the superfluity and the fecundity of his own tears. Not like some other secretions one might mention. As the tears left his eyes Mark knew what he was crying for – he was crying for love, for the loss of love, for the disappearance of passion into the weary mess of everyday life. He cried for Charity as well, or rather for the woman he thought Charity was: warm, maternal, self-effacing in her sexual splendour, autonomous and cherishing. Where had that woman gone? Off into a freezing fog of arguments about who belonged to whom, and who had lied to whom about what: distracting disputes about who had loved and who had deceived, and who had been tricked and what should be done. Oh Charity. Where are those moments now, the moments when we breathed and heaved together, when the interlocking of our bodies was connection of a kind we had never known before, or since? The gardens and the peacocks of Strawbury Castle, the taste of torpedoed strawberries, peach juice on a silken body, substances driven without explanation across the sheets. Snow in St James's Park: the violation of twigs and other materials breaking. Her farmyard eyes in Amsterdam already misted with his nostalgia. Nights spent, nights wasted in multiple conversations and convolutions; discord, decorum, denouncements and denigrations. Charity, how could you do this to me? What have you done? What have we lost?

After a while Mark got up and went home to Jane. He didn't feel in the mood for a party. He told Jane what had happened.

'Charity's mad,' she offered, 'she must be mad to do something like that.'

'She's mad,' he confirmed.

The telephone rang.

'Mark Carleton?'

'Yes. Hallo.'

'This is James Walton, Charity's husband, ex-husband.'

'Yes.'

'I thought you should know Charity's in hospital.'

'In hospital? Why should she be in hospital? What happened?'

'She had an accident. In her car. Last night. She drove into a lamp post.'

'Is she alright?'

'Of course not.' James sounded irritated. 'She wouldn't be in hospital if she were, would she? She's got concussion and a broken arm. Possible fracture of the pelvis as well.'

'Thank you for letting me know,' said Mark politely.

'The Royal Free,' continued James relentlessly. 'They're not keen on visitors yet, but she might want to see you.' He rang off.

Mark visited, but Charity, surrounded by machinery, wasn't alert enough to recognise him. She was in hospital for a month. They decided she hadn't fractured her pelvis, but her arm would take some time to heal. Mark knew why she'd had the accident. She'd had the accident in order to get him to leave Jane. He'd *have* to move in with her now. He'd have to look after her. It was her right arm she'd broken.

He told Jane the move was temporary. She told him he was a joke.

In July Charity had the plaster removed from her arm. It was strangely shrunken. She needed physiotherapy. Mark decided he needed a holiday somewhere warm where he didn't have to think about his personal life. He took a plane to Morocco, and spent a miserable week on his own in a four star hotel trying to lie still by the acrid azure pool, reading Jack Douglas's *Understanding*

· 146 ·

Everyday Life: Toward the Reconstruction of Sociological Knowledge. The Whiteman Foundation had decided they would almost certainly fund his project. They wanted a detailed costing by mid-August, so that the enterprise could start in earnest the following January.

He read and squinted at the sun and occasionally swam. He ate three meals a day, and walked by the ocean which was a lot less blue than the sky. One day he kicked a stone at least three miles along the road which ran by the sea where all the new hotels were being built. Agadir had not been his first choice. He would have liked to have seen a camel or two.

The strangest thing of all was that his sexual desire seemed to have utterly abandoned him, or he it. He wasn't troubled at all by the shapes round the pool, by the multitude of uplifted and expanding breasts, by the hundreds of buttocks cramped in nylon bikini bottoms. He didn't have any dreams, any fantasies, any urges at all. It was lovely. He began to fancy himself as an aesthete, but he knew he would never quite make it, because he was eating hugely in the hotel restaurant, inaccurately described in the brochure as 'the fairy setting of a thousand and one nights'. He got through bowl after bowl of spiced pasta, almond and honey puddings, large pieces of pink fish, probably still alive, drowning them all in multiple gin fizzes and warm pink wine. One appetite had replaced both. It was a lot simpler, but it meant he did still have an appetite; he continued to want to incorporate aspects of the world into his own existence.

The day he kicked the stone three miles he returned to the hotel and sat by the pool in his swimsuit reading a chapter on 'The Everyday World as Phenomenon' by two characters called Don H. Zimmerman and Melvin Pollner. The chapter talked about 'the member' meaning a human being. Mark smiled and ordered a chocolate milkshake with extra cream on top. 'For the member operating under the attitude of everyday life,' he read, 'the world offers itself as an *a priori* resistive, recalcitrant, and massively organised structure into which he must gear himself.' I couldn't have put it better myself, he thought.

The rest of July and August were occupied with costing the every-day life project. How much did notebooks cost in Alma-Ata? Sixteen plane trips to Trieste. Should Italian fieldworkers be paid the same as Swedish ones? What about the unions? He rang up his friend Bob Seaman to consult him about levels of trade union activity in different countries.

'Can't help you much there, old chap,' said Bob, 'other than advising you to pay local rates. And watch the Swedes.'

'Yes, but supposing we pay the Italians less and they find out?'

'Cross that bridge when you come to it. I should.'

'You're not very militant these days, are you?' complained Mark.

'Pragmatic, really. Pragmatic militancy. That's what'll win the revolution, old chap.'

Mark doubted it. He moved on to the next problem. How many interpreters were required to cope with the minority dialects of South China, supposing it proved possible to include South China? And what about the Asians in Bradford? As always, he felt irritated by the intransigence of the world which often didn't do very well as a sociological oyster: the oyster stuck to its shell, it had to be coaxed, smoked or yanked out. Why the hell couldn't everyone speak the same language? They could keep their different customs as long as they used the same words to talk about them. Life as a sociologist was really hard when you thought hard about it.

In order to get through the work, and because he couldn't think of any other solution to the rejections perpetrated on him by the women in his life, Mark now lived and slept at the office. He bought a sofa bed and a small microwave oven, into which he installed crumpets every morning. He cleared a filing cabinet of papers, and filed clean underpants, razors, unpaid electricity bills and long-life semi-skimmed milk instead. Mavis thought he was very odd. But he no longer cared what anyone thought.

One evening his daughter Susan came to see him. She wore a tight black mini skirt and a great deal of mascara.

'Listen, Dad,' she said, like a mini-secretary. 'I'll come straight to the point. We'd like you to come back home.'

'We?'

'Joanna and I would. And so would Mum. She's said so. We've talked to her. But she's too proud to ask. You don't look well, Dad,' she went on, solicitously, 'your shirt's dirty, and so's your face. You haven't washed your hair for weeks. I think you're getting thin.'

'Actually I need to lose weight,' said Mark, remembering the epidemic meals in Agadir.

'Please, Dad.'

'What do you want me to come home for?' he asked suddenly.

'We love you, Dad. We're a family. Mum's miserable. She's getting little blue pills for depression from the doctor.'

And so Mark packed up the contents of the filing cabinet and went back to Jane. It was nice to be home. He felt the world was not restrictive and recalcitrant after all. Every night he sat and watched television with the girls. They ate as a family. It all fitted nicely into Mrs Thatcher's pro-family policy, of which much was being made by the media at the time. Jane was a bit withdrawn at first. He persuaded her to stop taking her pills. It was only after she'd stopped taking them that she started to talk to him.

'You are a dreadful person, you know,' she rebuked him one evening. 'I really didn't know about Charity until she told me. I suppose you've had other affairs as well?' She looked away from him, sideways at the open door.

He didn't know what it would be advisable to say, but fortunately she said quickly, 'I don't want to know. I'd much rather not know. Have affairs if you want, if that makes you happy. But don't try to break this up again. We must try to make it work,' she went on, 'for Susan and Joanna's sake. They're at an awkward age. They actually *care* about our being together. It's only a few more years. And anyway you do love me, I know you do. It's not passion, but it is affection. Doesn't that count?'

Eventually Charity wrote him a letter: 'Dear Mark, your behaviour is in character. I think we should call it a day.

Everything we do is destructive, we're no good for one another. Thank you for the good times.' She signed it 'Alice in Wonderland', and enclosed some photographs he had taken of them on one of their weekends. He'd borrowed Jane's expensive camera, which had a delayed action mechanism, and set it to register their congress. One of the photographs was especially wonderful; it showed Charity's creamy thighs with his own member extruding out of her. They were glistening together.

After this, he tried resuming his sexual life with Jane. She informed him that she'd stopped taking the pill during his absence, and she felt so much better for it that she had no intention of starting again. She asked him to use condoms, and showed him the drawer in the bedroom where she'd placed the product of a bulk order for these very items. He hadn't used a condom for years, not since he was a boy. He associated them with fumbling and embarrassment.

The first time wasn't good. He drank a lot, and they put the TV set at the end of the bed in the pretence of watching *Casablanca* yet again. Jane turned the light out. He caressed her, but it was only by thinking about Charity that he was able to get an erection. He thought about Charity strapped to her bed in Amsterdam, and this did the trick, and then Jane handed him a condom, which she had removed from its wrapper and hidden under the pillow in readiness for this moment. He took it, unrolled it, and jammed it on, remembering Charity's own resistance, and then penetrated Jane, but it was like walking into an underground hole with no walls and no sounds and no scents, just nothing. His penis drooped, and the condom fell off to the right of Jane's neatly pursed cervix. Behind him, in *Casablanca*, Ilsa's face shimmered gently and the pianist intoned the magic words: 'You must remember this, a kiss is just a kiss, a sigh is just a sigh, the fundamental things apply as time goes by.'

7 ✳ FALLEN GODS

'A fallen god is not a man: he is a fraud . . . there are women who devote themselves to dead or otherwise inaccessible heroes, so that they may never have to face them in person, for beings of flesh and blood would be fatally contrary to their dreams' – *The Second Sex*, p. 349

So the family was subversive, after all. In more than one sense. It gripped one, and it also devitalised. Nineteen eighty-three became nineteen eighty-four. The everyday life project started. Mark was very busy. He was away from the department a great deal. To pacify Swinhoe, who almost certainly would not get his readership, Mark put him in charge of the undergraduate teaching programme, and arranged for the university to pay him a special responsibilities allowance. McKinnon resigned, saying that he wanted a change of career. He was going to retrain as a horticulturalist instead. Swinhoe was pleased, imagining him fouling up someone else's geraniums instead of the inorganic soil of the department. The post was readvertised, and a competent woman found to replace him: she was called Rose Goodenough.

Rose's first task was to unravel the shoplifting project. Swinhoe had years of unanalysed data on the social background and self-professed motives of several thousand shoplifters in towns across the country, including Glasgow, so Scotland wouldn't get left out. Since McKinnon hadn't managed to run off even the simplest tabulations, Swinhoe told Rose to do these first. The data seemed to be reasonably clean, and Rose managed the job in a couple of weeks. Swinhoe bore the green and white striped paper away excitedly, like a little boy about to be given the chance of building a model aeroplane. But he was back in Rose's office very soon.

'These correlations,' he told her, 'don't make sense. What's this variable, for instance? I don't recognise this variable at all.'

Rose flipped a disc into the machine. The screen flashed a command crisply at her. Her fingers flicked the keys. 'Height,' she said.

'Height? Whose height? We didn't ask height! It's not in the statistics. Why would we be interested in height?'

'Well,' she said, 'I'm afraid it's there. The height of your shoplifters. Broken down by age and sex.' ('Aren't we all,' said Howie, sitting with overstretched ears at the next machine.) 'And ethnic group. The Scottish shoplifters are particularly small.'

'Look at this,' cried Swinhoe, 'it's absolute nonsense! Height under and over 1.25 metres. That's only about four feet!'

Rose took the paper from him. 'Seventy-five per cent of small shoplifters take large mechanical items,' she interpreted, 'such as domestic video-machines, or hoovers. No, I agree it doesn't seem to make sense.'

'They're too small to take the weetabix,' said Howie unhelp-fully.

'Pardon.'

'It's always on the top shelf. Could take soap, though.' Swinhoe looked at Howie with his mouth open. 'What's the difference between a nun and a woman in a bath?'

Rose leaned back, away from the fictitious screen.

'One's got hope in her soul, the other's got soap in her hole.'

Swinhoe wasn't distracted by this. 'Not only doesn't make sense, never asked for it in the first place. Know what's happened, don't you?'

'No. What?'

'That wretched McKinnon. Mucked up the data. Knew he was no good. What do we do now?'

They tried to find McKinnon, but the friend he lived with said he'd inherited a legacy from an uncle in Cheltenham, and had gone to look at mountain plants in Bhutan. Swinhoe ranted and raved and kicked Bertrand around the kitchen. Mrs Swinhoe gave him some of her valium. In the office, Rose did her best, but it wasn't good enough.

Oddly, it was Margaret Lacey who tried to throw some light on McKinnon's subversive behaviour. 'He wasn't happy,' she stated baldly, to Rose. 'He didn't feel he fitted in here. So he exercised the only form of power he had – the power to make a mess of the data.'

'That's extremely unprofessional conduct,' remarked Rose severely. 'And try telling Ivan that McKinnon wasn't happy. He won't wear that as an excuse.'

'It's what women do all the time,' reflected Margaret, obscurely.

'What do women do?'

'Use their power subversively. Because it's the only power they have.'

Rose, whose consciousness of these matters was quite undeveloped, merely said, 'But McKinnon isn't a woman.'

As a contribution to the de-escalation of these tensions, Charity had relocated her research at another college. At her instigation, Mark had written a letter giving all sorts of spurious reasons why the research had to find a new home. After she'd gone, he thought about her a lot. He knew it wasn't over.

In June 1984 he saw Charity at the Royal Opera House with a man in a blue velvet suit. The two of them were sitting very close together three rows in front. Mark was sure their knees were touching. Their laughter was silver, like Charity's earrings. Jane, sitting in the seat next to Mark, didn't recognise Charity; why should she? Mark got quite depressed. He watched the man and Charity from behind a pillar in the crush bar in the interval. The man was attractive, with ruddy cheeks and a beard. Charity looked happy. Her hair was much longer, and curly. Her waist was smaller than he remembered it. He wanted to capture her, take her away from the bearded man and disappear into a forest with her. Instead, he dozed off and missed the whole of the second half of *La Bohème*.

The Carleton family holiday in Scotland in August was not a success. Mark was so depressed he hardly slept. He rejected all Jane's advances, sexual, culinary and miscellaneous, and was irritable with the girls. In the end she sent him back to London.

The first thing he did when he got back to London was to send Charity a telegram. Like the first he'd sent, it said 'I love you'. He waited for a sign of life. Nothing. Then he rang her house. Tom answered and said his mother was away. She was in Italy, and wouldn't be back until September.

'Where is she in Italy?'

'I don't know,' said Tom. 'She's travelling around. Hang on a minute.' He went away and then came back to the phone. 'Poste restante, Milan, that's where she said we should contact her this week if we needed to.'

'Is she with anyone?' Mark asked.

'Listen, man,' replied Tom aggressively, 'that's none of your business.'

'Thanks.' Mark bought a ticket to Trieste. He knew he was crazy, but he'd become so obsessed with the idea of seeing Charity again that he didn't care what he had to do to achieve this. Milan wasn't far from Trieste – he'd go and check up on the everyday life researchers there. Keep them on the spot. Find her. He sent another telegram, this time to Poste restante, Milan. It said, 'Meet me Hotel Europa Trieste, August 30, 6 pm Mark.'

The Hotel Europa was an excrescence on a rock miles from the town. Mark checked in on 29 August, having arranged to see the local fieldworkers from the everyday life project on the morning of the thirtieth. Dr Silvestri's English was rather unco-ordinated and difficult to follow. They had lunch, a chewy lobster, some frascati and grapes. Mark took a shower and paced his room for a couple of hours until he noticed the sun lowering in the sky. He took the lift down to the beach and walked out on one of the wooden platforms into the sea. The sea was playing games with the golden light, juggling it around, arranging it in different ways. He looked up across the bay; across the sun's watery path was another wooden promontory. There was a figure on it. Charity?

On the sand she said, after touching him lightly, 'You had no right to send that telegram.'

'As I said at the beginning, this isn't about rights. It never was, and it never will be. But I love you.'

She wept. Tears like diamonds across her glorious golden face. He moved them away with his hands, whose dear protuberant veins she remembered from the first time.

'I've missed you,' she told him.

'Yes.'

'You're not happy, are you?' she asked, or rather said.

'No. No.'

'You made the wrong decision, didn't you?' she said.

'What decision did I make?' For the life of him, he couldn't remember any decision he'd ever made except to give his life to this woman.

'You went back to your wife.'

'You are my wife,' he said.

'I'm sorry I tried to kill you,' she went on.

'Are you?'

'Not really.' She took his hands, so that they were joined to each other as the red sun at last fell over the edge of the sea. 'I'm not really sorry for anything. I feel it's all been inevitable, and will go on being so. Till the end of time.'

When he returned from Italy and tried to go home, it didn't really surprise Mark to find that he couldn't. The lock on the front door had been changed. Jane had excluded him technologically and thus physically and emotionally. The only remaining problem was that Charity, with whom he now had an incandescently wonderful relationship, didn't want him to move in with her.

'You must live on your own,' she said firmly. 'It's no good going from one woman to another. You've been doing that for years. Find out what it's like to be by yourself. Learn to be independent.'

It sounded horrible, and it was. He found a flat quite near to Charity's house. There was nothing wrong with the flat. There was something wrong with him. He didn't like waking up on his own in the morning. Of course some mornings he woke up next to Charity, since they saw one another regularly, but he wanted her there every morning. He couldn't handle the way everything kept breaking down: the phone, the refrigerator, the electric can opener, the central heating. 'Do you know,' he told her one Friday evening, 'I arranged for the electricity board to come and repair the meter, and they said they couldn't say what time they'd come, so I waited in all day and they never turned up! Don't they understand that people have other things to do, apart from waiting around for things to be repaired?'

Charity smiled unenigmatically. 'That's how the other half lives,' she said cheerfully. 'With difficulty.' Mona Lisa was a housewife, who knew all about gender divisions and waiting in for the repair man.

Mark Carleton was uncomprehending. He was lonely. He didn't like eating meals on his own. He would tell Charity that even when the refrigerator was working there was nothing in it. She would tell him to go shopping. She didn't take him seriously.

He had the freedom to see Charity when he liked, without covering his tracks with endless fables. He had the freedom to live as he liked; he could even have other relationships, for who would know? Sometimes he thought not about the deviations before Charity, but those after: Margaret Lacey's kiss, Gina's red mouth and agile metallic fingers. From these memories, he derived an uneasy sense of being manipulated by women into giving them what they wanted. Men want sex, don't they? Sex in the abstract. As a matter of fact, he wasn't sure about this. Although he had found the encounter with Gina exciting, she had actually (in a way) revolted him, and his reaction had brought out in him a discomforting brutality. It was in his mind to punish her for wanting him.

Even thinking about it made him anxious. The lipstick marks on his penis. Her oceanic vagina. Her crude American way of talking about sex. Her apparent knowledge of the male body: what gave her the right to invade him like that? If he thought about it for very long, he could develop quite acute feelings of hysteria.

But in relation to sex at least the thing that puzzled him most was his own psyche. Or rather the wiring between his psyche and his soma. Though he didn't like admitting it, he had been having increasing difficulty completing the sexual act with women he cared for: Jane, Charity. Each, at the beginning, of course, had not been like that: everything flowed – happiness, love, and all their manifestations. It seemed that when the initial strangeness had worn off, so had the willingness of his body to lose itself in theirs. This suggested that it was only the foreignness of women that aroused him, a message that was both bizarre and ominous.

With Gina he'd had no problem. He didn't care whether it worked or not. He didn't think about it, because he didn't care about her. With Jane, recently, he had completely given up and had been able to blame it on the condoms. Jane, recalling his earlier potency, blamed him.

But Charity was the real reason for his perturbation, for it seemed that Charity was the woman with whom he would end up. Charity was also the woman with whom he had had the best sex ever: both psyche and soma were agreed about that. Yet sometimes, increasingly, even with her the wiring went wrong.

Was it because he had never yet been wholly committed to Charity? Jane had always been around. Perhaps the wiring would sort itself out if he became truly monogamous? This was possible. But monogamy made him feel trapped. Monogamy? No, not monogamy, women. There was nothing intrinsically wrong with monogamy. It was women. If only it wasn't women he had to be monogamous with there wouldn't be a problem.

He went out one night on his own with the intention of finding a woman. His motives weren't particularly clear to him, but he felt he needed to take the initiative somehow. He needed to do something to women, rather than having them do things to him all the time.

He went to one of those places that advertise themselves as 'sauna and massage'. He picked one in the Marylebone Road next to an umbrella shop. It was November the fifth, a night he'd always hated because of the interminable ideological arguments British people had about nationalism and fireworks, or about fireworks, the dangers of. He parked the car in a discreet mews and walked the rest of the way. The night sky was full of bangs and psychedelic colours. He didn't feel at all safe.

Behind the counter, a tall blonde in an off-the-shoulder leopardskin T-shirt, a Gina look-alike, asked him if he wanted a sauna only, or a sauna plus massage. When he said the latter, she asked him what kind of massage he wanted. He didn't know how to answer this, so he asked her what she would recommend, and she said she would advise a whole body massage which would cost a whole lot of money, forty pounds.

He went to the bar first. There were five or six men in there, all wearing the same robes as he'd been given, and draped in various postures on faded red cushions placed on the floor against two of the walls. One was sitting on a stool by the bar. They were all talking and joking rapidly in a foreign language, which sounded like Swedish, being full of a lot of unpleasant gutteral sounds, like a Bergman film. Mark ordered a double whisky on the rocks. He sat down on one of the cushions and tried desperately to keep his robe closed round his genitals at the same time as arranging his legs to look reasonably tidy.

He drank his whisky and then got up to find the sauna. There was a naked woman in it. He started to back away, but she patted the space beside her, saying something encouraging to him in Swedish. He began to sit down with his robe on, but the woman giggled, so he realised he had to take it off. When he'd sat down, she threw a bucket of cold water on the coals, which resulted in a lot of hissing and a temperature rise of about twenty degrees. Mark rapidly began to sweat. The woman's leg was firmly pressed against his.

'You English?' she asked. He nodded, hotly. 'You been here before, then?'

'No, no. This is the first time.'

'You live in London?'

'Yes. I'm a professor at the university.' As soon as he'd uttered this remark it struck him as completely incongruous, but he could hardly take it back.

'I'm Anna,' she said, 'I live in Stockholm. I'm here at a convention.'

'Oh. Are those your friends out there?'

'My colleagues, yes.' She gave him a friendly smile.

The heat in the sauna was quite terrific, and he began to feel faint. 'I think I've had enough for the moment,' he said suddenly, and stood up, hitting his head on the ceiling.

'See you later, maybe?' she said.

He staggered out and put himself under a cold shower. Then he dried himself carefully, went back to the bar and ordered another two whiskies. He drank them in a couple of gulps. The men were still there. He headed for the door marked 'Massage'. He knocked.

'Come in.'

He opened the door a little. A woman with long straight black hair wearing nothing but a pair of frilly black panties was standing by a couch. Behind her was a shelf with a row of bottles on it. She had very large breasts.

'Come in, please come in. You want a massage?'

'Er, yes.'

She indicated to him that he should lie down on the couch, so he did. When he was lying down, she came over and smiled at him. 'You haven't done this before, have you?'

'No. How did you know?'

'I can't give you a massage with that robe on.'

He laughed. Same mistake again! She laughed, but not at the same thing. She helped him take it off.

'Whole body?'

'Pardon?'

'Did you pay for a whole body massage?'

'Oh yes.'

'I'll tell you what I'm going to do,' she said. 'By the way, my name's Ella.' She paused.

'Nice to meet you, Ella.' That sounded pretty stupid, too.

'I'm going to do your front first, and then your back, and then your front again.'

'Okay.' What did 'front' mean?

Ella took a bottle off the shelf. When she turned her back to him, her long black hair nearly met the top of her black pants. The effect was curious.

He lay there and closed his eyes. She poured some lotion over his chest and his legs (this reminded him of Gina's unbidden ministrations in the Reddaway Park Hotel) and began to stroke him, pressing quite hard in certain places. However, she restricted her attention to his chest, upper abdomen, arms and legs. After a while he opened his eyes. She looked at him. Her eyes appeared to be black as well. Her breasts hung over him like balloons. Mesmerised, he watched them. He knew he would like to touch them. Ella now had both hands on his inner thighs, which she had cunningly prised apart. He looked down and saw that he had an erection. She saw it too, but did nothing about it.

'Turn over now,' she ordered. He did. The massage was now thoroughly underway with a lot of very firm pushing and pulling. At times she leant right over him and he could feel her breasts sweeping over his back. She was doing something particularly enthralling with the balls of his feet. Nobody had ever been so nice to his feet before. He gave himself up to the sensation, and began not to care about what happened next: whether he would have sex with Ella (he actually didn't know what happened in these places) or whether he would have sex with Anna (were those really her 'colleagues' at the bar?); whether he would move in with Charity, what would happen to him. The moment took all his attention. The delicious ineffable moment.

'I think that's enough,' announced Ella. 'Would you like to turn on your back again for me?' He would.

She started with the same movements again, looking him in the eyes all the time. He became acutely conscious of his erection. When was she going to do something about it? But Ella was an artiste, a specialist in suspense, in the elevation and extension of the ineffable.

'You have a problem,' she said, looking at it.

'Yes.'

'You want me to take care of it for you?'

'I wouldn't mind.'

She took his penis in one of her belotioned hands. He closed his eyes again. He felt already very close to coming. He heard her doing something with a bottle.

'This oil is very good,' she said, 'very good at relieving pain.' A curious smell of almonds cut into the stagnant air. His penis felt wonderful, and almost immediately discharged itself into the almond oil.

Afterwards, Ella fetched a roll of kitchen paper and cleaned him up. 'Alright?' she asked, matter-of-factly.

'Fine,' he said. She turned away.

He got up, fetched his robe and left the room.

In the bar he had another whisky. What with the sauna and the whisky and the massage, he felt very lightheaded. Three Swedes were still sitting there, or rather four, if you counted Anna, who came and sat next to him at the counter with her drink, something bright green and clearly fizzy. She looked at him. 'Would you like to go somewhere and have a drink with me?'

When they left Sue's Sauna and Massage Parlour, the streets still echoed with the sound of rockets and shooting stars, jumping jacks and catherine wheels.

'I fancy a sparkler,' said Mark suddenly. 'Yes, that's exactly what I want.' His face lit up in a literal expression of anticipation.

'What is that, a sparkler?' asked Anna.

'A firework. Come on.' He took her hand. They must be selling them somewhere. Outside Baker Street station there was a news-agent with lights on. Mark ran in, and then out again. 'Let's take them to the park,' he said, 'we'll light them in the park.'

'In the park?'

'Regent's Park. It's just over there.' He waved his hands into the darkness.

'You have some lights for the sparklers?' She was obviously a practical soul.

'God, no.' He rushed into the newsagent's again.

Regent's Park was littered with groups of people having their own little fireworks parties. Mark stood still and breathed the smoky air, and realised what he wanted to do next. He wanted to take Anna-Ella to the boating lake and light the sparklers there. The place where he had looked and seen the couple in love the year before, when he had been in a daze and had wandered around London and then found there in that placid water the conundrum that was occupying him: love out of context, perfectly free.

They walked, very fast. Mark was anxious to get to the boating lake while the urgency of the idea still impressed him.

'Why are we in such a hurry?' asked Anna.

'It's just a place I want to go to,' he said.

There was no one on the lake. It was black. Black liquid, in a black earthy hole. Over the other side of the lake a gang of boys were throwing something into the water. Mark took the matches and the sparklers and lit them all at once. He gave six of them to Anna-Ella and took six himself. They held three in each hand. Mark waved his around in a demoniacal circuit, watching not only the bright lines of sparks as they left the sticks, but the continuous lines his eyes made of them as he waved them wildly through the black night. The whole extraordinary night was full of bright white circles. This was his childhood too, the grey garden in Battersea, where Agnes would only let him hold sparklers if he wore special gloves and she stood by with a bucket of water. Once she had thrown the bucket of water over him as a whole packet of sparklers ignited together in a little orange ball of flame; she was frightened that he would get burnt and damaged and changed forever by the fire he held in his hand. He never forgave her for that drowning of his excitement.

This was his childhood, but it was also his adulthood, him making light for himself, not for anyone else. He danced around, happily, engaged with his own strange mischief. When his sparklers died, he realised he had quite forgotten Anna-Ella. Her sparklers must have died too, but where was she? She had gone. Perhaps she thought he was mad. He laughed out loud. Above him and around him the black sky was full of fireworks, bangs, scattered explosions, chemicals, iridescent blues and greens and

· 162 ·

pinks and yellows, but nothing was quite as good, quite as pure, as the clean white light of the sparklers which he had held and used to carve patterns in the air around his own dancing body.

8 ✳ EXALTED TO THE SKIES

'This is the moment when love becomes a necessity . . . the loving woman can open her eyes, can look upon the man who loves her and whose gaze glorifies her . . . she no longer sinks in a sea of shadows, but is borne up on wings, exalted to the skies . . .

Every woman in love recognises herself in Hans Andersen's little mermaid who exchanged her fishtail for feminine legs through love and then found herself walking on needles and live coals' – *The Second Sex*, pp. 343–8

It was Christmas 1985, Mark and Charity's first Christmas together. Mark had now moved into the Chalk Farm household on more than a temporary basis. James, Shelley and Joshua had gone to live in California, where James had started a freelance economic forecasting agency. Jane had divorced Mark and gained custody of Joanna and Susan.

By twelve o'clock, the table had been laid with ten places and a red poinsettia plant in the centre. The duck was giving off a good odour, and the orange and watercress salad was resting happily in its white bone china bowl.

At twelve fifteen Charity's parents arrived, fussing. Her mother was cold – the car heater had given up half way through the journey, and she was worried about the mince pies. Her father was just cold.

They hadn't met Mark before. 'Pleased to meet you,' said her father, although Charity felt reasonably sure that he wasn't.

'You must be Mark,' said her mother, less formally and with more credibility.

They had drinks and opened presents under the tree. Mrs Dawson had given Mark a box of navy-blue handkerchiefs with 'M.C.' on them. 'Just a token,' she explained. Her father gave him another one, a bottle of scotch. Politeness reigned, covering everyone with a light layer of tranquillising whiteness, continuous with the snow outside. Then Sally and Eric arrived, and it was immediately obvious that they were drunk. They staggered giggling up the path; Sally had a piece of holly behind her ear and Eric's flies were undone. Charity marched them sternly into the kitchen. 'You're totally pissed!' she complained, 'and you just can't be, now!'

'But it's Christmas Day!' wailed Eric.

'I don't care what day it is. My parents are here, and they haven't met Mark before. It's all got to be *managed*,' she hissed.

'Don't worry, ma'am,' said Eric, saluting, 'I'll manage it for you.'

'Your flies are undone,' she pointed out.

Sally did his flies up for him. Charity was making coffee.

'What are you doing that for?'

'To sober you up.' She made them drink it, like children.

'Nice to see you again, Mrs Dawson,' said Sally, walking into the sitting room. 'Hallo, Mark.' Mark was sitting behind the Christmas tree on what appeared to be a heap of old newspapers. He grinned lopsidedly at her.

Charity got them all sitting round the table as soon as possible, and invited them to pull their crackers. Fortunately Rachel was still young enough to make them all wear paper hats and read out the jokes to one another.

'What would happen if pigs could fly?'

'I haven't got the faintest idea.'

'Bacon would go up.'

Charity put the duck on the table. 'What is that?' asked Tom.

'It's a duck.'

'But we always have turkey.'

'We don't always have turkey. This year we have duck instead,' said Charity firmly.

'Well, I'm not going to eat it,' said Tom. 'It looks awful. I think I'm going to be a vegetarian.'

'It's not awful,' said Mark, who quite liked duck, 'and your mother's stuffed it . . .'

'She could have stuffed it with sawdust . . . or snails or chocolate ice cream for all I care,' said Tom. 'I'm not going to eat it.'

'Now, now, Tom,' said Mrs Dawson, who was sitting next to him, and who had, after all, known him since he was a baby. 'This is Christmas dinner, your mother's made a big effort cooking this nice meal for us. Let's all try to be happy, shall we? Let's be nice to each other. Couldn't you make just a little effort for once?'

He glowered at her. 'They don't have bloody Christmases like this in California,' he said. He'd just finished speaking to his father, whose lifestyle could easily be admired at such a distance.

Mark carved the duck, not quite as incompetently as Charity thought he might. The vegetables were handed round: potatoes, glazed carrots, peas, fennel with butter. They sat and looked at their colourful plates. Mark opened the wine and poured the adults some.

'I want some wine,' said Rachel.

'You're too young for that, dear,' said Mrs Dawson, comfortably.

'Alright, just a little bit,' said Mark, who knew Charity's theory about depriving the young of alcohol being what turned them into alcoholics later.

'I don't think she should, dear,' objected Mrs Dawson, looking at her daughter.

'Oh please, Mum, just a little bit!' Rachel wasn't having this.

'Alright.'

'*You* never did,' said Mrs Dawson. 'I don't think it's right.' She folded her hands into the red linen napkin on her lap and waited to see what would happen next.

While this was going on, Dan and Harry had eaten all their duck. 'Can we have some more, Mum?' Harry pushed his plate forward.

Mrs Dawson sprang into moral action again. 'Manners!' she warned. 'Remember your manners. Some of us haven't had any yet!'

Charity sat back and surveyed the scene. Snow was settling on the branches by the window, and on the bush beyond, reflecting a white light into the kitchen. She thought of the past, and a flush came to her face such as had afflicted her shortly after she met Mark, when she dreamt an obscene dream. Had he noticed? Then or now? She glanced across the table at him. He was immersed in his duck. 'I don't know why I bother, really,' she thought. 'Whoever they are, in the end they just sit there eating my stuffed duck.' But, it being Christmas, instead of becoming angry, she just saw the immense, endurable pathos of it all – the passion, the vigour in the sheets, the refrigeration in the frozen grass, the love that passed between men and women coming to settle here around a table, around any table, as people eat to fill their stomachs, and argue to claim their identities, and drink to make themselves insensible – or don't – in order to prevent this fate.

Later in the day, they were drinking coffee in the sitting room when the telephone rang. Tom answered it and, with his usual stony expression, handed the receiver to Mark.

'Yes?' Charity could tell the voice on the other end had caused a cat's reaction of uprising anxiety in him.

'Yes, that's right.'

'I don't think that's fair.'

'Well, I understand how you feel, but Joanna . . .'

'No.'

'Okay.'

'Look, I don't think this is the best time to talk about it.'

'She's busy.'

'Alright, I'll ask her.'

'Charity,' he covered the mouthpiece with his hand, 'it's Jane. She's in a state about the present you gave Joanna, and she wants to talk to you.'

Charity had given Joanna a pair of black silk shortie pyjamas. She took the phone outside the door, and closed it.

'Hallo, Jane. Happy Christmas.'

'Well, it may be for you, but it isn't for me. I rang because I'm absolutely furious. I've just found the present you gave Joanna. I want to know what on earth possessed you to give her that thing!'

'She likes it – those are the kind of clothes young people of her age are wearing these days, you know. Or didn't you?'

'It's positively pornographic!' screamed Jane down the phone, 'Black silk, at fourteen!'

'Look, Jane, I'm sorry you're upset. I really am. But I don't think that's the real issue.' Charity took a deep breath. 'The real issue is that Mark has left you and he's living here, isn't it?'

'There's no point in being clever about it. You bloody intellectuals, you all psychoanalyse everything. You make it complicated when it isn't.' Jane sounded extremely cross, perhaps uncharacteristically a little drunk. 'There you are, you seduce my husband, you get rid of your own, and you persuade mine to leave me when he doesn't really want to – there, you didn't know that, did you? You didn't know what agony he went through, leaving me. He loves me, really. He didn't want to go, but you made him. How many men have you got through in your life, I wonder? I feel sorry for Mark, I really do. And now you try to corrupt my daughter. Leave her alone, do you hear me? Leave her alone. I shan't allow her anywhere near you any more.' Jane's voice had achieved an unpleasant soprano shriek.

'I don't need allegations from you about my behaviour,' said Charity. 'My behaviour is none of your business. But if you wish me to consult you about any presents I give your daughters in the future, then I'm perfectly willing to do that.' She, too, was angry now. 'It's absurd. You're absurd. The whole thing is absurd.' She slammed the phone down.

Back in the sitting room, her mother was positioned very close to the television trying to watch the Queen's Christmas Message to Her People. Her father was reading a book in the corner. Rachel was asleep on the sofa. The boys were nowhere to be seen, and neither was Sally. Eric and Mark were having an argument about the civil rights of the fairy doll on the top of the Christmas tree.

On New Year's Day 1986 Charity lay in the bath, contemplating her condition. Her body, first. It was thirty-six. It had put on weight recently: somehow the fact that Mark had moved in had given her a licence to eat more. She was mildly troubled by this, and pinpointed various areas – her midriff, stomach and upper thighs especially – that would have to diminish in size in 1986. Today she was bleeding: a good way to start the New Year. Pieces of her endometrium discharged themselves into the bath, some small, some larger, with crooked edges like flowers. One extra-large piece issued forth and self-destructed itself on the side of the bath. She poked it with her toe. It was spongy and insubstantial. She imagined it would be a good place for a baby to be nourished – warm, comforting and a pleasing colour. There was a lot of debris around in the water. Charity realised her periods had become heavier recently. Perhaps it was time to have her coil out?

Anyway, that was her body.

Her mind was doing reasonably well. She'd finished the book based on her research, and it was due to be published in a couple of weeks. Her present research contract was coming to an end, so she was applying for other jobs, with every expectation of getting one.

Emotionally, things could be better. The post-Christmas period had sent her into a depression, sparked off by problems with Tom, who seemed to have decided she was his enemy, and who went on and on about joining his father in California. Mark hadn't been responsive to her depression. She feared it was because he wanted to have one of his own. Was she never going to be allowed to be depressed and get sympathy from him? Were all the depressions to be his? She had put the point to him – that he was a great egotist, that he wasn't really interested in *her*.

He'd become quite broody about it. 'We're too alike,' he'd complained, 'we're both ambitious, self-centred psychopaths. You want to get your own way all the time, and so do I, and if we don't get it, we're impossible! I don't think either of us really cares about other people at all.'

'I care about you,' she'd said.

'No, you don't. You love me, it's not the same. You wouldn't care about me if I said I was in love with someone else now, would you?'

'No, I'd want to kill you.'

'Exactly. I wanted to kill you when you had that affair.'

'Why didn't you say so?'

'I don't always say what I feel.'

'You don't always know what you feel.'

'That's true, too. But don't think I've forgiven you, because I haven't!'

She didn't say anything at first, and then she said, 'There really isn't anything to forgive. I lied to you. Or, rather, I didn't lie, I allowed you to believe in what would have happened had it been you who'd had the affair.'

He stared at her. 'I don't know what you mean, Charity.'

'I didn't sleep with Sebastien. I thought about it, yes. I wanted to. But I didn't. I didn't not do it because of you, but because of me.'

'I don't understand that.'

'No, you wouldn't, would you, Mark? I think you would have survived my infidelity, even been gratified by it. But I – I would have been damaged by having sex with Sebastien, because it wouldn't have been making love, and love is what I want to make. In any case, I've had much more to forgive *you* for.'

'Such as?'

'For going on living with Jane, for example.'

'Jane was my wife.'

'That makes it alright, does it?'

'To go on with an old relationship isn't as bad as starting a new one.'

She laughed. 'Your morality makes no sense at all. All it is is a rationalisation of what you want to do anyway.'

'That's what morality is,' he said. 'Morality is aiming for the good. The good is pleasure. Being happy. Aristotle's *Ethics*.'

'That's not right. What about justice?'

'I suppose you think justice is always on your side, on the side of women?'

'I think justice is always more important than happiness,' she asserted, ignoring the provocation curled up in his remark.

'You and your feminism!' he shouted. This had become a perpetual complaint of his, as of many men. 'You describe the position of women in terms of moral censure: look at us, poor creatures, how oppressed we are, how wronged we've been, but when you talk about putting things right, you're not willing to admit any moral boundaries at all. Your definition of morality is something which benefits women. Mine is something that benefits the human condition.'

'How wonderful for you!' she cried. 'Listen to me, you pompous idiot, listen to this,' and she brought out from under a pile of papers her worn copy of *Madame Bovary* that she'd been rereading since the Evian episode which had sparked off this very conversation. 'Emma is with her lover, Rodolphe:

' "But you see, there are two moralities," he replied. "One is the petty, conventional morality of men, clamorous, ever-changing, that flounders about on the ground, of the earth earthy, like that mob of nincompoops down there. The other, the eternal morality, is all about and above us, like the countryside that surrounds us and the blue heavens that give us light."

'*I* am interested in the eternal morality. *You* are not.'

Mark sat quite still, looking at her. The words she quoted had moved him, but he didn't understand what they meant. 'Happiness takes a lifetime to attain,' he said, suddenly.

'Yes.'

'And I don't think you can choose to be happy. It's purely the product of events. Aristotle again.'

'Maybe.'

'You do understand – I'm changing the subject, now –' she said, 'you do understand how badly you treat women, don't you?'

'I think you get a fair deal from me,' he said pompously. 'I'm good-looking, I earn money, I'm not bad in bed, I buy flowers sometimes. Women like me.'

'That's downright arrogance, and you know it. You treat women like objects. You "have" them.'

'That's feminism. You've been indoctrinated. If I treat women like objects, it's because they enjoy being treated like that. You, for instance. Why did your love for James dry up and disappear? Because he demanded nothing of you, other than obedience to a certain pattern. You looked after the children, you cooked the meals, you were available when he wanted to go out. And I suppose he fucked you, too. He did, didn't he?'

'Of course he did.'

'And that was alright. It was just alright. It wasn't great, was it? Just a five-minute job. In and out. And off. "Thanks, I needed that".'

Her face reddened. 'What happened between me and James is none of your business.'

'It is. Of course it is! I live with you. Your past is in my possession, just as your future is. If I treat women like objects, how do you treat men? You plunder them and their resources; you crash into their lives and get what you want and then get out – you don't love men, you hate them!'

'Probably,' she conceded. 'But it's not a competition, is it? I'm worse than you, you're worse than me. Which of us exploits the other sex the most? In any case,' she reflected, 'I'm inclined to think that if men want to win competitions with women, they should stick to chess – they won't win any others!'

In the middle of January Charity had her coil taken out, and she got a job in a medical research unit in a London hospital. The job, which was to start in May, was to serve as the unit's sociologist: to give their research a sociological perspective, and do research of her own; also to teach medical students. Charity was over the moon about it. She liked the other people in the unit, and particularly its Director, Edward Alderson. She felt she would enjoy working there; even the teaching was something she was anticipating with pleasure, because she fondly thought that teaching people is a way of changing the world.

From January to May proved to be a troubled time, however.

She had a lot of bleeding and pain after she'd had her coil out, and needed to go back several times to see her doctor. Finally she decided that Charity should go into hospital for a few days for investigations.

Her consultant, a round jovial man in his fifties, joined her as the anaesthetist was about to put her to sleep. 'Don't worry, young man,' he told the anaesthetist, 'Mrs Walton's my patient, I'm going to sing her to sleep.' He started to sing, 'Baa baa, black sheep,' and as the drug knocked her out, she recalled thinking that he wasn't *au fait* with the politics of race discrimination.

She woke up attached to a plastic bag which was dripping blood into her. 'What happened?' she asked.

The young nurse answered blithely, 'Oh you lost some blood, Mrs Walton, we're just giving you a little bit to replace it.'

'Doesn't look a little bit,' muttered Charity. 'What did you find? What's wrong with me?'

'Don't worry, Mrs Walton. The doctor'll be along in the morning.'

'But I want to know now!'

'Sh! I'll just give you something to help you relax.'

'I don't want something to help me relax, I want to know what's the matter with me. Please tell me.'

'I can't, I'm afraid. I can't divulge confidential medical information.'

'But I'm the patient! It's my body!'

The nurse gave her a withering look and a small blue pill.

The next time she woke up, Mark was sitting by her bed reading Freud's *The Psychopathology of Everyday Life*. 'I knew I'd heard the title before somewhere,' he said, meaning the title of his cherished project.

God, she thought, this is some nightmare. I come round from this operation, and no one will tell me what happened, and this man, who's supposed to love me, sits there reading Freud!

'How are you?' asked Mark.

'I don't know,' she said gloomily. 'I don't know what's the matter with me.'

'I thought you came in here to find out.'

'I did.'

'Well, why don't you know, then?'

'They won't tell me. Perhaps,' she ventured, 'you could ask?'

Mark didn't like hospitals. But he went off down the ward, and came back a few minutes later. 'I'm not your husband,' he said, 'so they won't tell me anything.'

'This is ridiculous. I haven't got a husband any more,' she complained, 'and anyway he's in California. Oh hell!' She pressed the button by the bed, and another bright-eyed young nurse appeared. 'Listen, nurse, I want to know what's wrong with me. No one will tell me. This gentleman here is my lover. He lives with me. I don't have a husband. I'm divorced. Please could you tell Sister that Professor Carleton,' she paused to gain effect, 'would like to see A Doctor.'

The nurse scurried away. A few minutes later Sister bustled down the end of the ward. 'Good evening, I'm Sister Matthews. Professor Carleton? I gather you'd like to see The Doctor? If you'd just come with me.'

Charity lay looking at the green ceiling of the ward. Around her people talked, offered squashed grapes to people who didn't want them, or sat painfully on portions of other people's legs under the sheets.

Mark came back, it seemed like hours later.

'You took your time.'

'I had to wait for The Doctor.'

'What did he say?'

'She.'

'She. Okay, okay, let's not get into that one now.'

'She said you have an overactive endometrium.'

'A what?'

'Sounds like an upset musical instrument. She said something about a hyperplasic – is it? – endometrium as well.'

'That doesn't help very much,' observed Charity. 'What else did she say?'

'They don't know the reason for it. They're doing tests. Also, you had a haemorrhage, and they don't know the reason for that.'

'Do you think they know what they're doing?'

He shrugged his shoulders. 'How do I know?' Then, seeing the alarm on her face, he added, 'Of course they know. This is a good place.' He looked round the ward for confirmation of this statement, but its appearance was rather contradictory. 'It's a teaching hospital, it's got an international reputation. I'm sure you've got nothing to worry about.'

'Hitler had an international reputation,' she said.

He kissed her. 'See you tomorrow.'

'Mark! The children, are they alright?'

'Absolutely fine. Nothing to worry about. We're all eating choc ices and chips.' There was, current at the time, a television advertisement which showed a boy and his father being made to admire an elaborately packed and labelled freezer by a woman who was clearly the wife of one and the mother of the other, and who was going into hospital to become a mother again. This woman explained to the two males all the wonderfully balanced and nutritious meals they would be able to eat as a result of her labours in packing the freezer, but they ended up on choc ices and chips, which pleased them, because it wasn't what the woman had intended. Mark grinned and waved as he left the ward.

Charity felt a sudden flood of affection for him. He wasn't so bad, after all. He was a multiple role man when she had believed him not to be; he could be not only a sexual adventurer but also a housewife. Her children were safe in his keeping. She had nothing to worry about. She fell asleep, to be woken up two hours later by another nurse who was saying, 'Mrs Walton, Mrs Walton, can you hear me? Would you like a sleeping pill?'

Charity was in hospital for six days. They told her that they didn't really know what was wrong with her, but that it was possible she'd been pregnant – hence the state of her womb, which they'd found to be rather overfull when they'd forcibly evacuated its contents. They thought the haemorrhage had been due to their accidental puncturing of a blood vessel. They thought.

They also thought she ought to be okay now. She didn't disbelieve them, but felt extraordinarily weak and weepy.

It was lovely to be home. She went straight to bed, and slept deeply, without dreaming, only barely conscious of Mark coming to lie beside her. But she felt his arms round her, and was comforted.

The next day she got up and decided to do some gentle domestic organising. She sat on the floor in Rachel's room with the intention of tidying up her toys, but found herself playing with them instead: putting the Sindy in the Sindy house, Barbie in her most outrageous outfit, Ken in his diving suit, combing the ponies' manes and tails – there was no end to the infantile diversions of which she was capable. Next, she decided to take all the dead leaves off the houseplants. This occupied her for an hour or so. Then she moved on to clothes, and started making up a package for the cleaners. She took Tom's coat, and Dan and Harry's duffles, and her own winter coat, and Rachel's blue one with the velvet collar: it had to be the end of the winter coat season soon. She added a couple of rugs, and went upstairs to see if any of Mark's clothes needed cleaning as well. Going mechanically through the pockets of his jackets – a ten-pence piece, an old handkerchief, a scrumpled-up W.H. Smith bill – she came across an unidentified material item: curiously, she unfolded it, and it transpired to be a pair of underpants, used, purple and female.

She stood in the cupboard holding on to the pants, unbelieving. Then she dropped them with a cry of horror, and shut the cupboard door to prevent them escaping.

She sat down on the bed. Her head was swimming, and her palms, on the side of the bed, were damp. What did this mean? What should she do? Of course she realised the evidence was such that she could only believe the truth: Mark was having an affair with someone else. He might just as well have told her! It was unspeakable. An unspeakable crime. He was unspeakable.

She went to the telephone, and dialled his number at work.

'Hallo.'

'Hallo, Charity. Everything alright?'

'I just wanted to tell you not to bother to come home tonight,' she said.

'But I promised the children a McDonalds,' he protested.

'You should have thought of that before you embarked on your latest affair,' she replied, both with and without reason.

'What do you mean? Charity, are you alright?'

'I'm perfectly alright,' she said. 'It's you that isn't. Your wife was right. She warned me. She said you were incapable of being faithful. But how could you!' Her righteous indignation had not yet evolved into tears. 'How could you destroy what we've got like this? And now, of all times. You bastard! I hope you burn in hell!'

He came straight home. Since it was only two o'clock in the afternoon, the children were all at school. He let himself in apprehensively. She was in bed with a bottle of brandy.

'Go away,' she said. 'I don't want to have anything more to do with you.'

'Charity, please tell me what this is all about.'

'Open the cupboard door,' she said, 'and look on the floor.'

He did, and picked up the purple pants. He fingered them, clearly not with the same revulsion to them as she had.

'Oh.' He continued to finger them, perhaps hoping that they would answer back for him. 'Yes, well, what can I say?'

'Who is she?'

'It's not important,' he said, 'she's not important. She doesn't mean anything to me. She seduced me. I was drunk, and she seduced me. It only happened once. It wasn't much at all. Really. I can't even remember what happened properly. It just happened and was over. I'd forgotten it until you – these – reminded me. Really.'

'I suppose you think that makes it better!' she shouted. 'You do, don't you? But if it wasn't important, why the hell did you do it? I'll tell you this, if you slept with someone else, that's important to me. Tell me who she is.' Charity raised the brandy bottle to her lips.

'Stop drinking that stuff, it's not good for you.'

'I am the judge of what's good for me. You, obviously, are not.'

'I'm sorry.'

'That's hardly good enough.'

'No, I know. But, Charity, please believe me, it doesn't mean a thing. I was lonely, that was all. She was there. She wanted to have an affair with me, I think. I gave in. I'm weak.'

'You bloody fool. You just follow your prick, don't you? Blindly, like a nose without a bone in it.' She cackled, and drank. 'Bloody men. Alright, who was it?'

'Margaret Lacey.'

'Margaret! Mark, how could you? She's in the department!'

'So were you.'

'That's not the point. You're living with me. I left my husband for you. You left your wife for me. We mean something to each other, don't we? Oh God, I'm going to be sick.'

She rushed to the bathroom, and he heard her vomit violently and then flush the lavatory and run the taps in the basin. She came back into the bedroom with a face like a sheet of typing paper.

'I can't talk about this any more,' she said. 'I feel ill. I hate you.'

He covered her up, and she fell asleep. He took the purple pants downstairs, and put them in the dustbin, underneath an empty lemonade bottle and a mess of coffee grounds and eggshells. Then he sat down at the kitchen table and put his head in his hands. Why did he do this sort of thing? Why was he always ruining one relationship for another? When he came unstuck with love, he thought he wanted sex without it, and when he had this, he knew he didn't. It re-evoked in him the urge to locate the perfect woman who would give him perfect love, perfect sex, everything he asked for, except that he wouldn't have to ask for it. The only relationship he hadn't ruined for a long time was his relationship with Jane. Jane had understood him, had understood how little these affairs meant. In the overall span of human time one woman was much like another. They all had breasts, and wombs that gave them trouble, and they all opened their legs and complained and had double standards. I want a peaceful life, he said out loud. I want a world without women. Yet even as he said it, he knew it wasn't true. What he wanted was women, precisely. That was the problem. One wasn't enough.

9 ✳ LINGERING IN THE WINGS

'. . . when with her husband, or with her lover, every
woman is more or less conscious of the thought: "I am not
being myself" . . . With other women, a woman is behind
the scenes; she is . . . lingering in dressing-gown and
slippers in the wings . . . .

Women's mutual understanding comes from the fact that
they identify themselves with each other; but for the same
reason each is against the others' – *The Second Sex*, pp.
250–1

Mark promised that what he was having was not an affair with
Margaret Lacey. Charity had lunch with Margaret to talk about
it.

Charity began by telling Margaret that she didn't see how she
could square her behaviour with feminism. With any kind of
feminism. Margaret held herself very straight, and opened her
mouth to speak, but the waiter came over to take their order.
They were in an Italian restaurant.

'I know it's difficult,' said Margaret, 'and I really have no
defence. Except that Mark seduced me. Practically raped me, in
fact. I'm sorry to have to say that, but it's true.' She looked
straight at Charity as she said this. Her green eyes, contoured in
mascara, were uncompromising.

'I don't believe that. It's not what Mark said. He said quite the
opposite – that you seduced him.'

Margaret ignored this. 'I'll tell you what happened, if you like,
because I think you ought to know. It was before Mark went to

the States. You remember the UGC visit?' Charity nodded. 'Well, he asked me to take charge of organising that. He asked me at the last minute, and I had to go home because the man from the gas board was coming, my cooker had a leak.'

'It doesn't sound very convincing,' interrupted Charity, cynically.

'Charity, believe me, I'm telling you exactly what happened. Real life is like that. Seduction scenes are punctuated by gas leaks. Do you want me to go on?'

'Yes. Please go on.'

'So I suggested Mark come in on his way home to fill me in on the details. We had a drink or two. He said he wanted to make love to me. I told him not to be so silly. He said things weren't going well with you. I told him that was none of my business. I don't deny I was attracted to him. But I said no. He didn't take no for an answer. I decided not to resist. I was frightened. You must understand' – as she uttered this phrase, Margaret shifted her position on the chair slightly, so as to reinforce her solidarity with the indisputable material world – 'that I'm not easily frightened. I don't easily accept the victim role. But I don't think that then I could have done anything else in that situation. It has to do with power, of course, in a number of ways. The power of being a man. The power of being in authority over a woman.'

'Did you enjoy it?'

'Come on, Charity, that's not the right question to ask!'

'No, perhaps not. Is that all, then? According to your account?'

'That's all.'

'And has it happened again?'

'What?'

'Sex.'

'Of course not.'

Their food arrived. Charity looked at it. 'I don't know what to say, Margaret,' she said, finally. 'If I believe you, then Mark's lying. If I believe Mark, then you're lying. One of you has to be.'

'We are born, we live, we die in an environment of lies,' said Margaret pensively.

'What?'

'It's a remark of Antonin Artaud. Do you know his work?' Charity shook her head. 'He was crazy, an incredible person. Wrote poems, plays, novels, acted, did everything. He was an opium addict, in and out of mental asylums all his life.'

'Oh really.'

'Sorry, Charity. What I meant was that we *are* all surrounded by lies. Your problem is you've got two versions of the truth to sort out, mine and Mark's. But they might both be lies. Gender may make a difference. But understanding the difference gender makes may still not give you the truth.'

'I don't feel very philosophical at the moment.'

'Okay, then, which one of us would you like to believe?' A curly piece of squid on Margaret's plate stared accusingly at Charity, waiting for her answer.

'Of course I would like to believe him.'

'Would you? Why?'

Charity realised she had probably offended Margaret. 'I mean,' she added quickly, 'now I'm sitting here with you, of course I'd like to believe you. It feels to me as though you're telling the truth.'

'Yes.'

'But on the other hand,' Charity was now fumbling for the right words, 'I can see you've got a reason for lying.'

'I have?'

'Yes. You might not want to admit that you'd persuaded Mark to, to, to . . .' She didn't know which words to use. 'To have sex with you.' Why was language so inadequate? Whatever Mark and Margaret had done or not done, they hadn't slept together, hadn't made love, hadn't passed a night lying intermingled in the intimate solace of snoring and sweating unconsciousness.

'I don't know why I wouldn't want to admit that, if it were true. Let me tell you something, Charity. You said just now I couldn't square my behaviour with feminism. Let's assume for a moment that Mark and I did have an embryonic affair. Just for the sake of argument, let's assume that. Now why would that be unfeminist? What do you think feminism is, Charity?'

'Feminism.' The word sounded odd, the way quite ordinary words sometimes did when you repeated them over and over again. 'Feminism, feminism.' It would do very well as a mantra, if one could forget its politics and render it transcendentally meditational. 'I suppose feminism is about two things,' ventured Charity. 'It's about understanding that women are an oppressed social group. Then it's about strategy. I think feminists put women first, or they should do.'

'I'd agree with that,' said Margaret.

'You would?'

'The point is,' continued Margaret, 'that according to that definition of feminism, I don't think there would have been anything unfair about my behaviour had I gone to bed with Mark. If I'd been attracted to him, why shouldn't I have slept with him? He wouldn't do it unless he wanted to. He's an adult. He has responsibility for himself. If he didn't want to sleep with me because of you, he would only need to say so. I would respect that. But if he didn't, why shouldn't I get some pleasure screwing him? For centuries, women have been told to believe they don't have a sexuality – that the only sexual drive that matters is the male's. We know that's not true. So why should we pretend?'

'What you're saying is reasonable. But I can't help feeling there's something wrong with it.'

'I'll tell you why you're confused, shall I? Think about yourself and Mark and Mark's wife. When you embarked on your affair with Mark, did you think about Jane?'

'No. Falling in love isn't a thinking state. You might as well say he didn't think about James. Our situation was equal at the beginning.'

'We're not talking about his point of view. We're talking about yours.'

'I'm not sure this whole thing is about feminism at all,' sighed Charity. 'Perhaps it's about how human beings ought to behave towards one another.' Her eyes moistened, and she started to cry. Large tears rolled into the remains of her spaghetti. She reached for her table napkin, but it had left her knee some time ago. She picked up the corner of the tablecloth and started peering around on the floor for it, hoping vaguely to glimpse something white and crumpled.

'I'm sorry you're upset,' said Margaret. 'Here, have mine.' She passed it over. Charity blew her nose on it. The waiter appeared, frowning.

'Any dessert, ladies?'

'No thanks,' said Margaret, 'just coffee. Two black coffees, please.' Then, 'Listen Charity. It's difficult for me. Mark may have lied to you. Or I may have done. But remember that if Mark's lied he's lied because he loves you. Therefore his lying – even what happened – they're not important. You should cling to that. Forget the whole episode. I really think that's the only thing you can do.'

The only thing you can do, repeated Charity to herself, walking home from the underground station. It was a crisp March day, with the kind of sky you hoped for in August but never got: wedgwood blue, with white ducks of clouds skimming lightly round the edges.

She found it difficult to come out of her mood of self-pitying anger, jealousy, or exclusion – yes, she supposed it *was* exclusion she felt. Mark was keeping her out of part of his life, a part occupied by another woman. Climbing up the hill, she reached the point where the angle changed, and you could see beyond the houses a slip of green, the edge of the heath, where in a few weeks there might be daffodils. Seeing the green made her realise something. This exclusion she felt had happened to her as a child. She'd always felt cut off by her father from his relationship with her mother. They'd had a private life, the two of them, a life determined and controlled by him, which daughters had no place in. When her parents shut their bedroom door at night, she'd felt fear, for she was alone and they were together. Somewhere inside her, she couldn't stand the thought of sexual union because it cut her out. Yet something also drove her towards it, as though by having it and doing it she would understand it and get it to admit her to its secrets, and it might then cease to be a problem to her.

When she got home, Tom was in the kitchen. 'What are you doing home in the middle of the day?'

'It's not the middle of the day. Anyway, I didn't know you were coming home, did I?'

'Do you do this often?'

He looked at her sullenly. She noticed he hadn't shaved recently, and he had a collection of little greasy spots on his skin. His hair stood on end, perhaps it was meant to. He wore his school blazer, and his tie was technically round his neck.

'You look a mess,' she said, flatly.

'You're always getting at me,' he said. 'It's either my appearance or my behaviour.' (What else is there, she thought?) 'Why can't you just leave me alone?'

He pounded upstairs and slammed the door. Loud music fell in waves down the stairs. It was too much. How was she supposed to cope with an unfaithful lover and the storms of adolescence, all at the same time?

She made a cup of tea and put three spoonfuls of sugar in it. It reminded her of the tea she'd had after Tom's birth. Friends had said the cup of tea afterwards was the best part. It was. But in her eagerness, she'd put in too much sugar, and the rough exaltation of the moment had dissolved in a sea of sickly sweetness.

Funny, that. You pushed them out of you, slimy and defenceless and hungry and bawling, and they got quite civilised after a while. Smiled, went to the toilet, said 'please' and 'thank you' and 'I love you, Mummy'. And then they seemed to revert. Started looking all messy again, and became very demanding. 'I hate that!' 'Why can't I have it?' Banging fists on the table, loud music down the stairs – all the same gestures as the baby with its angry square mouth waiting to be fed. That's another thing. You feel such love at the beginning – such admiration and devotion, such inseparableness. You can't imagine how you'll ever be able to let that person go. And then, of course, during the first few years, you do get angry sometimes and you shout, and you might occasionally hit them, but then you kiss and make up, and you justify it all by saying it's much better for the child to know how its mother feels than to see her as a stuffed parrot yapping away.

· 184 ·

But when they get older, there are times when you don't feel love at all. You actually hate them. Because they're so threatening with their size and invasiveness. You feel like a bird in a nest, wanting to tip one of the young out and over the edge. You don't care where it goes, so long as you don't have to think about it any more.

She went upstairs to knock on Tom's door. She had to knock hard to make herself heard against the noise.

'Tom, please let me in. I want to talk to you.'

There was no response, so after a while she turned the handle, but the door didn't yield. At first she couldn't understand why, then she realised it was because something on the inside was preventing it from doing so.

'Tom!' she shouted. 'Let me in!' Her body was subsumed with frenzy suddenly, at the thought that he had deliberately locked her out, excluded her from his life. He must have bought a bolt, put it on. 'Tom!' She hammered with both fists on the door. 'Let me in! I'll break the door down if you don't!'

Still no answer.

Quite overcome by now, she could think only of how she might get into that room. Wildly, she rushed into the kitchen and pushed items around in the cupboards, looking for some tool or weapon that might help. Nothing – where were all the tools? She flicked on the light in the cupboard under the stairs: old boots, cobwebs, discarded children's games, furry anoraks looking like dead cats. She found a hammer, rushed back upstairs with it, and started beating with it on Tom's door. 'Let me in!' she screamed again, 'let me in! I won't have you behaving like this! I want some respect – you live here and behave, or else you get out!'

There was a sudden lull in the music. Tom unbolted the door. He stood there. Her Tom, his hair on end still, his tie loosely knotted over his adolescent chest. In comparison with her frenzy, he was astoundingly and provokingly calm.

'What *are* you doing, Mum? Are you out of your mind? Give me that hammer.'

'No,' she said, whimpering like a child.

'Give it to me.'

'Why should I?'

'You're nuts,' he said, 'absolutely nuts. All I've done is I've skipped an afternoon off school. Why is that such a crime? Don't you ever miss work? Don't you ever do anything wrong?'

'I take responsibility for myself,' she said, clutching the hammer to her breast as though it were a baby. 'If I do something wrong, it's my fault, I sort it out.'

'So?' he said, 'what makes you think I won't do that?'

'You know what you're doing,' she said, raising her voice again, 'if you go on like this, you're going to fail your A Levels.'

'So?' he said again, 'what's so awful about that?'

'Do you *know*,' she demanded, 'what kind of job you can get with no qualifications at all? Have you any idea?'

'You're hung up on achievement,' he said.

'I'm older than you,' she said, as though that explained everything.

'It's for me to judge what I do,' he said. 'Leave me alone, Mum. Get on with your own life, and let me get on with mine.'

He shut the door, and she was left there, quivering, still clutching the hammer.

In May, Charity started her new job. She had her hair cut short, and bought a hundred and twenty pounds' worth of new clothes.

Home had become a battleground. She began to hate going home at night. As soon as she got in, one of them would get at her, or she at them. It would be the washing up, or money, or lost front-door keys, or Dire Straits cancelling out any feeble parental attempt at Mozart. In the living room, the goldfish stank, and she couldn't understand why, until she found Tom feeding them huge quantities of goldfish food.

'You *know* they only need a bit. A few crumbs every few days. That's quite enough.'

'That's what *you* say. I think they look undernourished.'

She thought he was projecting on to the goldfish his own fear of no longer being nourished by her, but had the wisdom not to say so.

'If you overfeed them, the water smells, and it's got to be changed every few days. I don't mind you overfeeding them providing you clean the tank out *and* pay for the extra food.'

He didn't. Instead, to annoy her (so she thought) he took Rachel as an ally and the two of them spent hours trying to catch the goldfish shitting. He had a mechanical sort of mind, this son of hers, and he pointed out that if overfeeding led to water pollution, there had to be an intervening mechanism of some kind. They called it 'pooh spotting'.

So going to work became for Charity a positive delight. Only then did she feel at all real. Home was the unreal place. Years ago, it'd been the other way round.

'You know, Charity,' said Edward Alderson, her new boss, one day, 'I think you should do some research on young people.' He'd been listening to her account of her latest trouble with Tom. It was funny when she described it, and of course she exaggerated what had happened, but not necessarily to show herself in a good light. 'Young people are a growth area,' said Edward. 'They have all the problems these days. They smoke, and drink, and take drugs. They never get any exercise. The girls have painful periods – there's been at least a 70 per cent rise in dysmenorrhea in the last thirty years.' He was really getting excited now. 'The boys have dreadful acne – it's quite repulsive, really.' He fingered his own chin, protectively. 'And then they all fail their exams and they can't get jobs. They become depressed. Their parents can't stand them, and they can't stand their parents. But they can't get away. Even on the dole – Mrs Thatcher's made sure of that.'

Charity went home and talked about the idea of setting up some research on young people.

Mark had his doubts. 'You're too involved. You won't be able to be objective. And anyway, they're a very difficult group to research.' He shook his head sagely, so that dandruff flew out of it.

'So we're a difficult group, are we?' Tom had been sitting, or rather lying, on the sofa, reading an old *Beano*. 'That's typical. Isn't there any bit of life that's safe from you academics? Fucking patronising, if you ask me.'

'I didn't,' said his mother.

'That's exactly the point, isn't it?' He put the *Beano* down. 'No one asks us what we think. Perhaps we don't want to be studied? Perhaps we don't want to be part of one of your nosy research projects?'

'It would be for your benefit in the end. We *ought* to find out what you think about things like health, and jobs, and how you see the future. It's because we don't know,' she pleaded, vainly.

'I think it's wonderful the way, if you don't know something, you have to do research on it. You could try talking to the people around you. Like me, for instance. Research is a complete waste of money – that's one thing I agree with Mrs Thatcher about. It either proves something that everyone knows already, or it comes up with some fucking ridiculous answer that no one in their right mind's going to believe anyway.'

Charity retreated to the kitchen. It was wonderful how her children made her hysterical these days. She didn't seem able to upset *them* any more. Was this what adolescence did to parents? In return for what parents did to children?

She rang up Steve Kirkwood because he was already doing research on young people. She thought it might calm and instruct her to have an adult conversation about it.

'Great idea, Charity,' he said. 'I think you'd do it very well. The problem with my research is that its focus is too narrow. It's not jobs that matter to some of these lads. I think it should be, but it isn't.'

'Lads? You mean you're only interviewing the boys?'

'Well, yes, actually.'

'Steve!'

'I know, I know. I'm only a simple chauvinist at heart, Charity. Don't expect too much of me.'

'You are not!' she corrected him. 'And I do expect everything. If women don't have higher expectations of men than men themselves have, then how is anything going to change?'

The next day she told Edward she was ready to write an application for money to study adolescent attitudes. His blue eyes gleamed. He was a charismatic figure. People wanted to do things for him because they liked to please him, and he knew this. He was full of ideas, too full really, in sympathy with his stomach, which was having difficulty staying inside his trousers. Charity liked him, but the stomach put her off, physically. He liked Charity, but never touched other women, because he was too frightened of what might happen, and of his wife's reaction. He even sometimes thought he nourished his stomach as a defence.

'While you're getting on with the application,' said Edward, 'there are one or two other little things we need your help with. This, for instance,' he pushed a pile of papers in her direction. 'We're writing up this study we did of parents' attitudes to the medical management of childhood cancer. I'm not very happy with some of the data. Could you have a look at it for me? And the other thing is this trial we're about to do of knitting as a therapy for longstay orthopaedic patients. I can't work out what the control group ought to do. Clearly it shouldn't knit. But should it do something? Perhaps we should have two control groups. Or even two intervention groups?' He mused, stroking his beard. 'You know, knitting, and perhaps something else. Maybe basket-making?'

Despite these diversions, the application for money went in on time. Just after that her first book was published: *Living with a Time Bomb: Marriage and Multiple Sclerosis*. The phrase 'living with a time bomb' is how one man had kindly referred to his wife, who was a sufferer from the disease. The BBC rang Charity up when the book came out, and wanted to do an interview with her. Two women's magazines wrote, requesting articles. She started to get letters from sufferers and their partners, sad wounding letters pouring out tales of grievance against doctors and men, or women.

Mark was envious of the new Charity. Whenever *he'd* tried being interviewed on television, he'd made such a mess of it, they'd thanked him politely, paid him for his time and never screened it. He knew exactly what the problem was (and he knew it especially clearly when he saw Charity on the screen): he couldn't simplify what he wanted to say enough to get anything across in the time and style appropriate to the medium. When he sat there, and was asked these glib, pre-packed questions, the very asking of the question revealed to him anew the enormous inexplicable complexity of everything.

He was finding things quite difficult with Charity just now. There was a lot of tension in the house, and he blamed it on her. After all, nothing had changed in him. He still wanted the same thing from the relationship – perfect love, total passion, unfettered intimacy. The problem with Tom also got him down. In fact, what really depressed him was the level of noise in the house. He'd taken to going out in the car on his own in the evenings to get away from it. He'd had a new cassette machine installed recently, with four stereo speakers. He'd drive the car to some quiet street in Tufnell Park, or Crouch End, it didn't really matter where, slide a cassette in, put the seat into a reclining position, shut the car windows, and his eyes. Wagner was particularly effective, he found. Sleep restored him, but only, unhappily, to the same battlefields.

At work there were a few problems too. The official report on the UGC visit, which had finally arrived, had revealed a substantial deficit in departmental funding. They appeared to be paying out much more than their grant would allow, but when Mark looked at the figures he couldn't see at all where the extra money was going. Pascoe, who'd remained administrative head of the department after Mark's arrival, admitted to puzzlement. Mark suggested they call in an accountant. Pascoe said he would do this.

Books were also disappearing from the library. A 5 per cent annual loss was normal – all universities sustained some loss of this kind. But the departmental loss was now running at about 20 per cent. Mavis, who was in charge of the library, was perpetually complaining to Mark about it. He'd been inclined to dismiss her complaints, but Rose Goodenough, who couldn't find a key computing text one day, was persuading him not to. 'There really is a very serious problem,' she insisted.

'Okay. What do you suggest we do about it?'

'Heavier fines.'

'We can't fine them if we don't know who they are.'

'Make it a nonborrowing library.'

'We can't do that. There's not enough room to sit and read.'

'Form a library committee.'

'Okay. You arrange it.' Privately he thought there was no way having a library committee would make a difference. The wonderful thing about committees was the way everyone regarded them as a solution.

Most of the time Mark tried to shut the door on these petty problems, which included Swinhoe's continuing tempers about what McKinnon Had Done to his Data, and Margaret Lacey's uncomfortably flashing eyes. The only thing that really kept him awake was his everyday life project. It was going well. The tide of data collection was advancing in all six centres so far co-opted into the study: Minnesota, Stockholm, Trieste, Salvador, London and Paris. He was having trouble with Alma-Ata. He'd thought it would be a nice idea to include the city where the World Health Organisation had declared the goal of Health For All By The Year Two Thousand, but that city was at the moment refusing to co-operate. He thought he might have to jettison the Russians, and was still playing with the idea of including Shanghai. But were there any sociologists in China? He thought not. They'd all been abolished in the cultural revolution.

Maybe he should take Charity with him to Alma-Ata. She needed a break, and he needed to have her to himself again. Inspired by this idea, and by a few minutes spent in a cul-de-sac in Highgate listening to Isolde's outpourings in Act 2, he drove home fast, capturing a bottle of red wine on the way and planning to extract Charity from the kitchen and take her to bed like the old days. But when he got back he found the kitchen full of Tom and his friends. They were smoking, and the table couldn't be seen for beer cans. He coughed prominently in the doorway.

'She's gone to bed,' said Tom, flicking ash on to the tablecloth.

Charity was asleep. Couldn't she do anything for him any more – not even stay awake? He switched on the bedside light. Its cream glow picked up the white of her sleeping face, its

· 191 ·

eyelids welded resolutely together. He put a hand on it and moved it about affectionately. She stirred, brushed his hand away as though it were a stray fly. She turned over then, away from the light. He undressed and stood naked in front of the big mirror, looking at himself. He looked odd with glasses on, so he took them off, but then he couldn't see very much at all, so he put them on again. What he saw wasn't a bad figure of a man – lean, despite his appetites. Greying body hair, a grey and receding hairline further up. He pushed his hair back with the hand that had just fondled Charity. Then he moved sideways to examine his profile. Beneath his still-flat stomach his penis drooped wistfully, resting its head sadly on his quite elongated balls. He touched it, moved it gently, to see if it had any life in it. No response. He drew back the curtains and looked at the moon. The moon looked back at him. It wasn't in a terribly good state, either. He pulled the curtains together and got into bed with the wine and a corkscrew. Lying down he couldn't shift the cork, so he had to get out of bed again. He held the bottle between his legs, and pulled the cork out that way – it came out with a loud pop, and the top of the corkscrew hit his penis. 'Shit!' He examined himself carefully. It didn't seem to be bleeding. But it hurt. He poured wine into a tooth mug and got back into bed. He drank it with one hand protecting his penis from further assault.

He could hear Tom and his friends laughing in the kitchen, having a good time. The doorbell rang. A few minutes later there were noises on the stairs, giggling and whispering. The door of Tom's room opened, then closed. One of the voices was higher than the other. Mark listened intently. For a while there were no more noises, and then a sudden yelp and another giggle. He got carefully out of bed, tiptoed to the door, opened it, and made it out on to the landing, where he had a better chance of hearing what was going on. No light could be seen round the edges of Tom's door, but muffled laughter seeped out from under it – such laughter, Mark imagined, as might be suppressed by a young man and a young woman using a pillow to stifle each other's sounds. And then, unmistakably, he recognised the methodical rhythm of bed springs, up and down, up and down. He felt suddenly unbearably excited. His voyeurism and the moon stiffened his penis, and he held and stroked it. It was hard and bursting with heat. The rhythm of the bed springs accelerated. In, out, in, out. There was a noise from someone's throat, and then a final forceful movement and a higher cry like that of an owl in the trees.

Mark fled. He got into bed with Charity, and lay there charged with desire and guilt at listening to Tom and whoever was there with him. Charity lay still with her back to him. He knew there was no way he could go to sleep now. He would either have to masturbate or he would have to wake her up. He didn't want to masturbate. What was the point of living with a woman if you couldn't have sex with her when you wanted to?

'Charity?' He touched her on the shoulder. She stirred, but didn't wake. 'Charity!' More urgently.

'What is it?'

'I want you, Charity!'

'I've taken a pill, Mark. Can't you wait until the morning?'

This should have put him off, but didn't. Anger at her stupidity, at her lying there like a passive lump of flesh fuelled his urge to get inside her and get rid of this thing that was worrying him. He pushed her on to her front. She moved her legs apart, but she was terribly tight. It was as though she had no hole at all. 'Let me in!' he cried. His penis was still hurting from its encounter with the corkscrew, so he helped it with his fingers. Then he was in. 'Magnificent!' He plunged in and out, up and down. It felt as though it'd been years since he'd had any sex. As he moved, he thought about Tom. That was how it had been for him in the old days. He would get a girl to bed, or on the sofa, or on the floor, even in a field or the back of a car, and he would come in a few minutes. Or before that. He'd once gone ballroom dancing with a girl (his mother foolishly thought this was a good idea) and he'd been so wound up he'd come in his trousers in the middle of 'The Blue Danube'. But then he'd calmed down a bit and developed some control. Jane had taught him control. She always waited until he came, and then she came herself straight after. She'd done that for fourteen years. It had been nice, not having to worry about her. Whereas with other women, like Charity, you had to make sure she was alright. That could make you quite anxious. You hung on to your own orgasm until they'd made it, and by then you'd lost sight of your own.

He sighed. He was still inside her and even more frustrated than he'd been on the landing. His erection was just as hard. But he couldn't let go.

He would have to wake her up. He withdrew and turned her over, roughly. 'Charity! Wake up! I can't go on like this. I need you to wake up!' She opened her eyes and looked at him.

'What's the matter, Mark?'

'I want you,' he said, 'make love to me.' He put her hand on his penis and moved it around. She held it but didn't move her hand in return. 'Charity, please!'

'I'm sleepy, Mark. I've got a hard day tomorrow.'

I've got something hard on now, he thought grimly to himself. 'Can't you do anything for me any more, Charity?' he repeated out loud.

'Okay, Mark,' she said, 'just fuck me. Do anything you like. Get it over with, and let me go back to sleep.' She opened her legs and her arms and lay like Jesus on the cross.

He put it in again and poked and plunged and prodded, and thought about Margaret's exciting chest, strapped down in her sensuous black dresses, with her nipples standing out behind the thin material. He nearly came, but then it went again. Charity's eyes were closed. She did genuinely seem to be asleep. Oh God! He withdrew, deciding to masturbate. He rubbed and rubbed until his penis was sore, particularly where the cork-screw had hit it. But it didn't work. Eventually, he fell asleep, exhausted.

He woke at six with this unbearable pain between his legs. This time he decided on a strategy. He would masturbate until he'd nearly got there and then enter her. It would only take a few minutes. It couldn't fail to work. The mere thought aroused him. She was lying on her back, almost in the same position as she'd been last night. He knelt above her and got it nice and ready this time (remembering the scene in Gloucestershire with the peacocks and the forest) and then, when he thought he was close enough, he put it in. She opened her eyes. She knew what was going on, alright. She wanted him. In and out, in and out. But the bed springs sounded like Tom last night. He was fed up really, with all this fucking. It got you nowhere. He couldn't come. He would never be able to come again.

All day at work he was conscious of his unresolved desire. Looking through some back numbers of medical journals for some material on concepts of health and illness in everyday life, he encountered an extraordinary article on foreign bodies in the rectum, which gave him another erection. He read about a woman who lost a vibrator up her arse and had to have an operation to remove it. The motor was still running five hours later, 'a tribute to modern electric batteries,' said the article. He rushed to the lavatory to masturbate. But the stains around the lavatory bowl, the lavatorial nature of the activity put him off.

It came back again in the pub at lunchtime. He was drinking with Swinhoe, and watching the barmaid – he supposed that was what they were still called. She had very large breasts. He was sure Swinhoe would be able to see his erection. He wanted to pee, but didn't dare go to the men's room in case Swinhoe followed him and saw it.

By five o'clock he had become totally obsessed. His head ached, his balls ached and his penis leapt up and down like a zombie. He went to the lavatory and washed it with cold water. But instead of calming it down, this had the opposite effect, of making it grow harder and more resolute than ever. He wondered about going to hospital, but what on earth would he say? What on earth would a doctor do?

Suddenly he started to laugh. How ridiculous he was, disappearing into lavatories and standing on landings in the moonlight all the time. This obsession with ejaculation had to be some kind of displacement activity. He really had some other problem and he was focusing it all on sex.

Once he started to laugh at his penis it went down. It

· 195 ·

became smaller than it had ever been. Quite tiny, in fact. Like a dead maggot.

He put it away in his trousers and went home. On the way, he dropped in at Lewis's Medical Bookshop and found the sexuality section. He noted that it was full of extremely expensive books. He pulled down a few and scoured the index for his problem. But like the problem that women couldn't name in the 1960s, his problem had no name either: he didn't know what to call it. After a little detective work, he was able, however, to deduce it from the text; since his ejaculations were hardly premature, they must be the opposite of this – retarded. So his problem was called 'retarded ejaculation'. The book assured him that, apart from a few rare cases of physical disorder, the cause of this syndrome was the new assertiveness of women. Women were simply robbing men of their masculinity, and thereby of its manifestation in essential body fluids. On learning this, Mark didn't know whether to laugh or cry, but it wasn't very difficult for him to decide he'd better not tell Charity what he'd found out.

10 * APRIL SHOWERS

'A man who has begun to detest wife or mistress tries to get away from her; but woman wants to have the man she hates close at hand so she can make him pay . . .

Certainly woman's aptitude for facile tears comes largely from the fact that her life is built upon a foundation of impotent revolt . . . Tears are woman's supreme alibi; sudden as a squall, loosened by fits and starts, typhoon, April shower, they make woman into a plaintive fountain . . . He considers this performance unfair; but she considers the struggle unfair from the start, because no other effective weapon has been put in her hands' – *The Second Sex*, p.307

Mark had started waking at four or five in the morning, along with the birds that populated the Chalk Farm trees. His body would jerk itself convulsively out of sleep, and his mind would flood with the black treacly tides he supposed were his depression, though it felt more like fatigue to him – fatigue with his situation, with himself, with the repetitive character of his domestic relations, all now daily compounded by this jerky waking to the brash urban dawn chorus. The birds cut into his reveries like the twittering voices of women. Once awake, his anger fired itself at the small stygian shapes in the trees, but his miserable plans to arm himself with a gun and get rid of the starlings and the sparrows and the blackbirds were synonymous with the mental assaults he performed on women, none of which had so far worked, for the complicated reason that he felt he needed them.

He drove to work early some days, just to get away from the morbid enclosure of the house. Once in the office he would attack his papers with gusto, achieving a great deal in the first twenty minutes, and nothing thereafter, as the black monster, having worked out the route he'd taken, followed him there.

This particular morning in April 1987, he was in the office at six. His room smelt musty, as though someone had been smoking there. He opened the windows and went next door to Mavis's little room, to open her window and get some air circulating across the landing.

At first he thought she was dead. It wouldn't have surprised him. The things that happened to people these days seemed quite enough to kill them. But then her arms, extended across her desk, moved sideways like sedated crabs, and her head poked up, and her glasses fell off her slippery nose, and her eyes, thick with sleep of a kind, perceived but didn't recognise him.

'Mavis! Are you alright?'

'What? Yes. Where am I? What time is it?'

'It's six. In the morning. Have you been here all night?' He noted then the nearly empty bottle of scotch and the ashtray full of half-smoked cigarettes. 'You've been drinking, haven't you?'

She was still semi-conscious, and the room was full of her firewater breath. She slid her glasses back on. 'I'm sorry, Professor.' He waited for her to produce an excuse. 'I stayed late to finish typing a paper for Dr Lacey. Then I thought it wasn't worth going home. Mother isn't there at the moment, you see. She's in hospital. I went to see her this afternoon. Visiting ends at seven.'

'You'd better go home now,' he said.

'Yes.'

'Have a bath and get something to eat. Tidy yourself up.'

'Yes.' Her face had a slight green sheen to it, he noticed. The pores of her skin shone like field mushrooms. He'd never been this close to Mavis before, nor did he want to be again. She was another thing to deal with, another object cluttering his path. Bloody women.

When Charity rang him later that morning, he told her what had happened.

'But you knew she was an alcoholic, didn't you?'

'No.'

'Everyone else did.'

'Why didn't I, then?'

She might have suggested he was too preoccupied with his own problems to notice other people's, but was sensible enough not to say so. Instead she gently reminded him that Tom was coming home that evening. After a two-year sojourn with his father in California, he was coming home to do his A Levels. At eighteen, it was a little late to start that, but James had assured her on the phone that his son's years of educational apathy were over. He would get on with it now.

Charity felt curiously apprehensive about seeing Tom again. Her nervousness was the reason for her phone call to Mark; she wanted Mark to behave. There had been tension between Mark and Tom in the past.

Tom had insisted he didn't want to be met at the airport, so at 6.05 that evening she opened the door on a young man who was, she could immediately see, still her Tom, but also someone who knew his way around the world. He even said, 'Hi, Mom', as American young people were supposed to. He smiled a smile she recognised from his milk-stained face in 1969.

She flung her arms round him and held him to her. He smelt of distant lands, and cigarettes. As the front door banged, Rachel flew downstairs, leggy and excited. She flung herself at Tom, always her most-admired brother. When he'd disentangled himself from Rachel, Tom asked, 'Where are the others?'

'Dan and Harry are at a friend's. They should be back any time.'

'And Mark?'

'He'll be home later.'

He grinned. 'You don't need to be secretive, Mom. I know Mark's still around. It's not a problem for me.'

'No? Good.'

Charity was cooking Tom's favourite meal – roast beef and Yorkshire pudding, followed by apple pie and custard. She didn't like cooking much these days, she wanted to be doing other things.

Dinner was good. For the first time in several years, Charity had all her children with her, and was alone with them. She felt temporarily as proud as a mother hen.

After dinner, Tom lit a cigarette. He did it quite ostentatiously, but with determination.

'You smoke now, do you?'

'Yeah. I know you don't like it. But I do! Sorry, Mom.'

'That's alright, Tom.' She faced him. 'I know the last thing you want is a speech from me. But I just want to say that I'm sorry about the conflicts you and I had. I realise you were very upset by the divorce and by Mark moving in. I didn't handle it well at all. I'm really sorry.'

'It's okay, Mom. It wasn't all that bad. You're not such a bad mother, really!' He got up from the table and hugged her where she stood, at the sink, loading the dishwasher.

It was into the calm of this reconciliation between mother and son that Mark walked, looking suspiciously drawn and exhausted.

'Hallo, Tom. You got back alright, then?' He held out a hand, and the falsely bright tone of his voice resounded through the kitchen. He poured himself a glass of wine, and sat down. 'Tell me about California, then. Is it where we all should be, enjoying the illiberal sunshine? How are James and Shelley? The romantic pair?'

It dawned on Charity that Mark was drunk.

'They're okay.' Tom was hesitant.

'And little what's-his-name, the product of their union?'

'He's a nice little fellow, actually.'

'So it worked out for them?' said Mark, aggressively. 'Unlike some of us we could mention.' He poured himself another glass of wine.

'Mom, I think I'll go and unpack and maybe call a few friends.'

'Good idea.'

When Tom had gone, Charity closed the door and sat down with Mark.

'I could say how angry I am that you're trying to spoil Tom's first evening at home by behaving like this. But I won't.' She pushed her hair behind her ear in a Charity-like gesture of fed-upness. 'You'd better tell me what's the matter.'

'Susan's pregnant, that's the matter,' he said, drinking steadily. Susan was seventeen, and still at the upmarket private school in Hampstead Jane had sent both girls to after the divorce.

'You've only just found this out?'

'Jane called me at work. She's absolutely beside herself. Doesn't know what to do. Susan won't talk to her.'

'How does she know she's pregnant, then?'

'She started throwing up in the evenings. That's what Jane did, all the time, when she was pregnant. Susan's pregnant alright.'

'Oh dear.'

'Is that all you can say? Oh dear!'

'I'm sorry, Mark,' she said. 'What else do you want me to say?' It seemed to be the evening for apologies.

'I'm fed up with all this,' he remarked, almost laconically. 'All these problems and messes. I want a nice ordinary life. The kind of life I had before I met you. Organised. Peaceful.'

'Oppressive and boring.'

He looked at her. 'Charity, my darling,' he said with feeling, 'what's exciting about this? It's not even a marriage. If it was a marriage, I could put up with it, perhaps. But it's not. I've decided, Charity. I want a wife.' He banged his glass down on the table, and lay back on the sofa, his arms spread expansively and authoritatively either side of his body. 'I want a decent structure to my life. I want to be conventional. I don't want this half-way situation in which we talk about respect and equality and friendship. I don't want to be free. I don't want to respect your freedom. I don't want to be able to get out of the relationship when I want to. I want to be constrained. I want to have limits set on what I do. I want to know where I stand.'

He fell back into the cushions, overcome with his usual misplaced desire for sleep.

His speech numbed her, coming as it did on top of her anger at his spoiling her reunion with Tom. It was like her right to be depressed, which seemed to have to take second place to his. He managed to ensure that her children always got eclipsed by his. So now the pleasure of seeing Tom again was cancelled out by Mark's announcement of Susan's pregnancy.

'I'm glad you know what you want,' she said eventually, and with as much sarcasm as she could manage in the circumstances. 'That sounds like an advance, at least.'

The look she gave him expressed a mixture of anger and desperation. Buried in it was a tiny remnant of romantic response left over from the days when any man who talked about marriage was a knight on a white horse, who could reasonably expect to exit with her soul, if not actually her body and all her worldly goods. For she did assume that when he spoke of marriage, it was her he wanted to marry.

Charity took Susan for her abortion. Jane couldn't handle it; she was too angry with Susan, because Susan had shown her up as a deficient mother.

'Who was it, Susan? Who was the boy?' asked Charity gently as they sat waiting for Susan's pre-abortion counselling.

'A boy. Just a boy.' Susan had her hands in her pockets, and her shoulders were all hunched up, indicating she wasn't about to give any of the secrets of the world away. Without make-up, she looked about fourteen. Her face was white and silky, like a baby's.

'Was he someone you were in love with?'

Susan glared at her. 'Love? What's love? It's only your lot that talk about love. You do everything for love, don't you? And you think it's immoral when we don't. Well, I don't do things for love. I just want to have fun.'

'Did you have fun, Susan?'

'What do you think?'

A week later, Susan went into a nursing home in Crouch End for the abortion. Charity drove her there and went home afterwards to collect herself and her things before going to work. When she came back from the Crouch End nursing home, Mark was listening to the radio in the bedroom, lying on the bed fully dressed. She wanted a few minutes by herself and was irritated to find him there.

'Are you ill? Why aren't you at work?' He stared at her, the same look, exactly, as Susan had just given her.

A voice on the radio intoned from the Bible, Ecclesiastes, chapter 3: 'To every thing there is a season . . .'

The sun sprang out from behind the April clouds. Charity sat down on the bed and took Mark's hands in hers. She saw that his eyes had tears in them. 'Are you crying because of Susan?'

'It's my fault,' he said. 'She's done this because of what I did to her mother.'

'Nonsense,' said Charity. 'You shouldn't blame yourself. We can't blame ourselves. It doesn't help them, don't you see?'

'Why are you so bloody unemotional?' he shouted. 'There's my daughter having a baby dragged out of her, and she's only a child herself, and you don't seem to have any reaction at all. You don't care. You just don't care.' His voice collapsed in a pool of glumness.

Charity got up and started pacing the room. 'Mark, listen. This isn't about Susan, it's about us. You're angry with me because I made you leave your family. You'll always be angry with me about that. That's what it's about really. And you've got this absurd idea that you can't survive without a family. So you want to marry me. I don't understand you. Or rather I do, but you don't understand yourself. You're making things worse for everyone. I can't stand this sort of pressure.'

'Is that a threat?' He swung his legs over the side of the bed. 'Don't threaten me. I can't take it.'

Behind him, the sun picked up the dust in the atmosphere and turned it, irrelevantly, into diamonds. The sun outlined for Charity Mark Carleton's thick curly hair, the furry surface of his tweed jacket, his stubbly hands, this man whom she'd known for seven years and lived with for two. Looking at him now made her recall the image from her childhood: the painting, *A Man in a Room*. The light brought it back to her, the light and the man's resigned attitude, exposed and paralysed by a single illumination.

Where did these rules about men and families come from?

Surely they existed only as conventions – as places where one might live out one's life or not, and, if one chose not to, then there was no sense in continuing to measure one's behaviour against them. The thing was to advance, make new rules.

Mark had no insight into this. A man, in the men's room, might very well wander round with his hands in his pockets, looking at his feet and mumbling to himself, quite insentient of other rooms, ways of walking and forms of mumbling. Maleness was an enclosure. As caged lions, men saw the diameters of their cages and mistook them for the cavernous spaces of the earth – unconstrained, untainted, inviting and likely to be bathed in sunshine, always.

Mark stood up. 'Alright, Charity, I'm not in a fit state to argue. I've told you what I want. You don't agree. Let's leave it at that for the time being.'

When he opened the door of his office, Margaret Lacey was sitting there reading the newspaper. 'Mark! I wanted a word with you about something rather urgently.'

'What is it?' He was plainly irritated. He wasn't in the mood to have any more words with any more women about anything.

'I can assure you it's something you ought to know about.'

'Okay, okay.'

'I went round to Steve Kirkwood's last night.'

He waited.

'Mavis asked me to drop him in a copy of the paper she's typing for him on class identity and temporal perceptions amongst unemployed young people.'

'Oh good. We need some more publications in the department.' Mark opened a drawer of his desk abstractedly, wondering what he was looking for. String? Able labels?

'You're not listening to me,' objected Margaret.

'I am. Indeed I am.' He looked up at her, hand poised in the drawer, connecting with an empty tube of Uhu.

'He wasn't expecting me, you see.'

'Who wasn't?'

'Steve Kirkwood. *Listen*, Mark! I went in, he invited me in for a cup of coffee, and while he was in the kitchen I started looking around his sitting room – you know, the way one does.'

Mark didn't. 'And?'

'I noticed some of the books that are missing from our library. Three whole rows of them, in fact. Including the book on computing Rose couldn't find.'

'Well, he probably forgot to bring them back. What's wrong with that?' He shut the desk drawer and sat down, extending his legs in a straight line under the desk. The position relaxed him, he began to feel sleepy.

'Mark, some of those books have been missing for three years or more! They're not even in the catalogue as having been borrowed. Steve didn't borrow them. He *took* them!'

Mark looked at her. 'Did you say anything to him?'

'I didn't know what to say.'

'No, I wouldn't have done, either.' That, at least, was clear to Mark, even if nothing else was.

'I think you ought to pursue it, Mark. In your capacity as head of department.'

'But how am I supposed to know what you've just told me?'

'Say I told you. It's the truth. The truth is always easier, isn't it?'

'Is it?'

He asked Mavis to locate young Kirkwood for him later that day. Mavis was being very obliging at the moment. 'He's out interviewing in Whitechapel. I've left a note on his desk.' Mavis's eyes gleamed. 'Is it anything urgent, Professor?'

He hated her habit of using his title. 'Yes. It is.'

She stood in the doorway for a while, but eventually turned round and went away.

A couple of hours later, with Kirkwood sitting opposite him, Mark found it difficult to get round to the subject of book stealing. Mark cleared his throat and scratched his head. 'Kirkwood, there's something rather unpleasant we have to talk about.' Kirkwood said nothing. 'Margaret came to see me earlier today.'

'Yes, I know. And I know what she came about.'

'You do?'

'Yes. It's not true, of course.'

'It isn't?'

'No, it's not true that I've been claiming too much in travel expenses. I've only exceeded the travel budget by a very small amount this year. Fifty pounds, eighty-nine pence. We can substitute by taking some money from the "other expenses" category.'

'We can?'

'Of course.'

'That's alright, then.'

'There is a real problem though, I gather, with the departmental budget in general.'

'How do you know that?'

'The accountant was here the other day going through the files with Pascoe. I hope you manage to get it sorted out soon. It must be quite a worry for you.'

'Oh yes, it is. It is.'

Charity and Sally were in the Natural History Museum looking at the dinosaurs and discussing the latest complication in Charity's life: Tom Walton and Joanna Carleton were having an affair.

'Mind you, they do look lovely together,' remarked Charity. 'A beautiful couple. Two young people on the edge of the ocean of life.'

'About to dive in. Well, that's alright then.' Sally walked round the end of the dinosaur's tail. 'How did these creatures actually get around?'

'On lorries,' said Charity, absently.

'What?'

'Don't you remember that old film? *One of my Dinosaurs is Missing*. Peter Ustinov and Derek Nimmo. Somebody hides some formula on a dinosaur, and this gang of spies, or whatever, capture it and put it on a lorry and drive it through London in the fog.'

'How confusing.'

'It was.' Charity stared at the dinosaur. 'Sally?'

'Yes.'

'Why do I find it so upsetting that Tom and Jo are having this affair?'

'Because it means that what you and Mark did isn't original any more. All you did was start a trend.'

'We never were original. That was the last thing we were.'

'Okay. I'll try another one. You don't like it because you suspect that they're not really enamoured with one another, they're just doing it because of you.'

'Could be.'

'It's pure arrogance, of course. They're old enough to know their own minds. And, anyway, if something impelled you and Mark to fall in love with one another, perhaps the same thing has hit these two?'

'Biology,' said Charity, glumly.

'No, not biology, you nit. Socialisation, social processes, all that stuff.'

'I don't think I believe in that anymore.'

'God, you must be depressed!'

'Well, what has all that stuff, as you put it, added to our understanding or our ability to change things?'

'A lot to our understanding, not much to our ability to change things.'

'Exactly. Remember those heady days twenty years ago? When we thought we'd seen the light? Everything that our elders had done they'd got wrong, and nothing would induce us to make the same mistakes? God, it was exciting.'

'You didn't believe it for long,' reminded Sally. 'You went into the kitchen to make the same mistakes with your nappy bucket.'

'Alright. But when I did believe it, it was wonderful. Before I got locked into reproduction and domesticity, feeding the babies and the goldfish and other people's egos.'

'How are the goldfish?' inquired Sally.

'Do you really want to know?'

'Yes. I'm a brave woman.'

'Two of them have been in the back of the deep freeze for a year.'

'Why?'

'It wasn't my doing, it was Rachel's. First of all, they became horribly ill with something called cottonwool disease. They started losing their colour, and then their little fins started falling apart, and then their heads started disappearing. It wasn't at all nice to watch. They're in the deep freeze because Rachel read up about humane disposal of fishes in the library. It said the most acceptable method was to place the fish in a dish of ice cubes and then put the dish in the deep freeze. Every time I defrost the fridge, I take the poor little sods out and look at them and put them back in again. Next to the fish fingers.'

'I think I'd rather be a dinosaur.'

'Mark's very upset about it, our respective children having this liaison, I mean.'

'Seems to me Mark's upset about most things, these days.'

'Do you know what, Sal, he wants to marry me.'

'How nice. Let's go for a walk.'

A warm wind blew in the streets of Kensington, and the September sunshine whipped up a colour in the fading leaves. The two women stood gazing up at Prince Albert.

'Victoria was a monstrous woman.'

'Perhaps Albert was a monstrous man. I've just read Caitlin Thomas's autobiography. She says Dylan treated her badly, but she was in love with him, and women fall in love with the worst kinds of men. She actually says the worse Dylan treated her, the more she loved him.'

'I don't understand the connection. It doesn't sound to me as though Mark's treating you badly if he wants to marry you.'

'There you are, you're the same as everyone else,' observed Charity. 'You equate marriage with good treatment. Do you know, when I was married to James, he used to give me lists of things to do? I remember one in particular, it started with remember to put the lid on the jam in the mornings, and ended with remember to buy my mother a birthday present. Every time I got a breathing space for myself, he gave me another list. He was a great list man, James was. I think he did it to prevent me remembering anything that was at all important to me.'

'But James was such a *nice* man.'

'Even nice men make lists.'

'But what difference would it make if you married Mark now? You live with him. You share the same bed and the same jam pot.'

'But in a free union,' interrupted Charity, 'I live with him because I love him. I don't want to marry him. Why would I want to be a wife again? He'd probably start making lists for me. I'm through with men's lists, Sal. I only want my own from now on.'

'You know what you are? You're a feminist romantic,' observed Sally. 'You want to have your cake and eat it too. You want this vision of an equal partnership with a man which allows both of you to flower at the same time. But there's no such thing. It's a different kind of cottonwool disease you've got.'

'How come you're still with Eric, then?'

'I've lowered my sights. It's age. I'm forty now. I don't want to end up on my own. I want someone to hobble down the street with in my old age. You know, holding on to each other, me with my plastic handbag, him with his plastic stick.' She smiled. 'Besides which, I'm still trying to have a baby.'

'I thought you'd given up.'

'Far from it. We've had all the investigations. Eric's wearing baggy underpants and eating evening primrose oil. I'm taking this homeopathic stuff, and my temperature the whole bloody time. When it goes up, we rush upstairs, but those underpants are hideously unsexy. I'm going to be in vitro fertilised next. Two thousand quid, that costs. Can you imagine?'

'Is it worth it?'

'You know it's worth it,' said Sally with feeling. 'You've got your children. I honestly don't think women who've got children can understand this biological panic those of us who haven't get into. I went to a lecture the other day on reproductive technology. This woman harangued her audience for an hour about the evils of the new technology. All very radical consciousness-raising stuff. Then someone in the audience asked her why she hadn't said anything about the problems of infertile women! She said she couldn't. That wasn't what she was talking about. I think that's outrageous. Morally outrageous.'

The sun set behind the Albert Memorial. Prince Albert looked benignly down at the two women and kept his own version of the reproductive battle to himself. His stone sagacity watched more leaves, lemon-edged, apple green, auburn, mahogany, fall from the trees in yet another season, leaves which would be ungraciously ground into the earth by thousands of feet stamping their way through untidy lives.

Something was the matter with Rachel. She lay in bed, groaning. Charity had prodded her all over, taken her temperature. Nothing. No fever, no particular pain. After two days she still wouldn't move. Charity decided to take a firm line.

'Come on, love, there's nothing really the matter with you. Get up. You'll feel better once you're on your feet.'

'But Mummy, I feel awful,' wailed Rachel. 'I think you should get the doctor.'

Reluctantly, Charity phoned the surgery.

'Does she have a fever, Mrs Walton?'

'No,' said Charity, honestly.

'A rash?'

'No.'

'Any other definite symptoms?'

'No.'

'In that case, doctor won't want to visit. You'll have to bring her in.'

'But she won't get up,' complained Charity. 'I can't bring her in if she won't get up, can I?'

'How old is she, Mrs Walton?'

'Twelve.'

'Well, I don't know what the problem is, Mrs Walton, but it doesn't sound like something for the doctor. I can give you an appointment . . .'

'Thank you.' Charity put the phone down.

Rachel's huge dark eyes regarded her. She certainly looked pale.

'Do you want to go to the doctor's?'

'I'm ill, Mummy. The doctor should come and see me.'

'Well, he won't,' said Charity, 'so that's that. Come on, darling,' she tried again, 'get up, let's go out and do something nice. I'll take the day off.'

'Will you?' Her eyes brightened.

'Let's go shopping. You need a new dress.'

'Can we have lunch out?'

'Yes, why not!'

'Somewhere smart?'

'Anywhere you like.'

They went to look at girls' dresses at D.H. Evans and Selfridges and John Lewis's. Then Rachel went to the loo while Charity tried to work out the best place to eat. She was looking through her Cosmo diary for suitable restaurants when Rachel burst out of the Ladies.

'Mum, I've started!'

'Started what?'

'My periods. I'm bleeding!'

'Good God.'

'That must be why I was feeling so awful. I knew there was something the matter, something I hadn't felt before. Why didn't you believe me?'

Charity was filled with remorse. How could she have got that wrong? She would make it up to Rachel. 'Come on, let's go to Wheeler's. We'll have champagne and oysters. Remember when you were a little girl, and we went to France, you watched us eating oysters and you said, "I'm going to eat those when I'm grown up!" '

'Yes, I remember.' Rachel remembered the blue of the bay, being allowed to jump off the harbour steps without her dress on.

'We'll have to buy you some STs first. Come on, grown-up daughter.'

In Wheeler's, Charity ate most of the oysters, but Rachel had three just to make the point. They had half a bottle of champagne. Rachel thought they ought to have a full bottle, so they had a little argument about that.

Afterwards, they went and bought Rachel a red dress to celebrate. She was twelve years and three months old. She was over the moon. Her mother had taught her that this was something to look forward to, that menstruation was not a curse, but a blessing. Charity herself felt a mixture of pride, excitement and depression. She was proud and excited because Rachel's physical development was on course. She was depressed, because there was enough of womanhood ahead of Rachel without her embarking on it with quite such precipitousness. Childhood was sacred. Children were inviolable. Women were not.

So in this particular era of women's inviolability, Charity Walton gained a menstruating daughter, her first and last; she aided the destruction of her lover's grandchild, his first, but not his last, and repaired the strands of affection adolescence had broken between herself and her firstborn son. Through all this, Charity may have gained in knowledge a little, but the goldfish didn't move from their resting place in the freezer.

One day, when she went to work, she found a poem from Edward Alderson in a rainbow-coloured envelope on her desk. It wasn't a very good poem. She'd suspected for some time that he was in love with her. His dense aquamarine gaze bathed her in a bright blue light wherever she went; she seemed to him a precious thing, a washed jewel glinting in the darkness, the high, sweet line of a Bach cantata, the hard, beautiful but inedibly fruited magnolia grandiflora. He liked gardening, and often thought of Charity when he did it, out there in the free air away from his unit and his family, amid the felicitous scents of autumn, the hailstones, frosts and snowdrifts of winter, until the glacial surface of the earth was broken by the impertinence of bluebells, snowdrops, daffodils and soft crimson tulips the colour of Charity's cheeks, as he imagined they might look were they to be subjected to the impact of any most intimate embrace.

The poem was the first of many. She was a little concerned about how she ought to react to them, for she instinctively felt that to tell a man his poetry was bad might well be the ultimate insult, far worse than telling him his breath smelt, or he hadn't made you come. She filed the poems in a box file in her bedroom labelled Articles About Feminism (because she knew that whatever Mark might be trying to find out about her, he would never look in such a place). Nonetheless, Edward's pedestal-like affection for her and Mark's possessive physicality seemed to form a congruent whole: Mark took hold of her, Edward let her go. Edward smiled romantically at her, Mark glowered intensely; the one smouldered like a great fire in a wet Scottish winter, the other flickered gently like a white candle in a hot Scandinavian sitting room. It would clearly be so much more practical to love someone like Edward, just as it had been more practical to live with James. Edward would do the garden, he would be able to diagnose and treat one's minor ailments, and he might get better at poetry, if he wrote more of it.

'It would be awful to have an affair with a doctor,' she told Edward one day, after he'd remarked that the Worcester sauce she'd just had in her tomato juice was carcinogenic. 'Quite awful. I know enough about bodies, I know all I need to know. I don't want my head filling up with macabre details about what causes what and why.'

'You'd rather die ignorant, would you?' he asked. 'Or die because of ignorance.'

'I won't do that,' she said, 'I'll live forever. Anyway,' she went on, 'I'm not ignorant. Not about bodies.'

'Nor about faces. You know, you have a very expressive face, Charity,' he said, 'and I'll tell you the really strange thing about human beings. It's not anything to do with their bodies at all. It's the fact that they have this whole range of facial expressions. We don't need them, you see, because we've got language. But not only are we the only animals with language, we've also got this highly developed system of facial movements. Why do we show fear to an enemy, or surprise to an intruder? There's no point. Why does a baby smile?'

'Because it's nice to smile. People smile back at you.'

'But the first smiles of a baby happen when it's asleep.'

'That's just wind.'

Edward shook his head. 'It's not just wind. When a newborn

baby smiles in its sleep, that smile is associated with a measurable state of excitement in the brain stem.'

'You mean they did experiments on newborn babies? That's disgusting.'

'One must advance knowledge,' said Edward pompously, sitting back in his chair, 'and without experimentation we can't do that. And what's the point of life, if it isn't to know more?'

She took his hand, and held it tightly. It was white, white as paper, and covered with veins the colour of his eyes.

'Can we go to bed together?' she asked. It was a long time since she'd slept with anyone but Mark. Even now, she didn't particularly want to, but the thought of Mark and his current crisis was enough to drive her away, it didn't matter where.

'Can fishes fly?' he replied. 'Have you ever heard of the flying fish? It lives in the Western Cameroons. You find it in the salt marshes, cohabiting with the flamingo . . .'

'In a monkey puzzle tree.'

'How did you know?'

'I'm very wise.'

'As a matter of fact, it just happens, I can't think why, but my wife is away. She's taken the children to her sister in Wales for a few days.'

'How terribly convenient.'

'It is.'

'Have you got a spare room?'

'Why?'

'I'm not a flamingo, and I don't cohabit in marital beds.' She flicked her hair behind her ear, revealing a pretty red and silver earring. 'I'm allergic to them, actually.'

The spare room was near the sky, boarded in pine and thickly carpeted in white. Edward was a gentle lover. He stroked and kissed her and whispered in her ear. He had a very hairy body, she thought she might be in bed with a fur coat. He glided into her like a carefully piloted plane. She held him tightly. 'This is nice, isn't it?' he said, as he sped through the clouds. The novelty of the journey lifted her up and kept her dancing in parallel with him, they moved and thought their separate

· 214 ·

thoughts together. Unhappily, though, not even the most deliberate clenching of her muscles was able to push Charity beyond the point at which it was simply nice being in bed with a man. Was it through fear that he would be another Mark? Or that there would not be time to find out? That at least hadn't happened, and Edward's bearded face above her shifted itself rhythmically across the horizon of her closed eyes as she asked herself to release whatever internal spring was holding things up. Edward's manoeuvring was less deliberate now. His plane was no longer on autopilot, and he came almost silently. A slight whoosh of air from his lungs discharged itself on to her face.

This made him happy. He started to stroke her again and to sing. She looked up at the night sky and said it was time to go home — not to her husband, but to her lover. Who was reading Jung's *Modern Man in Search of a Soul* in bed. He looked up inquiringly as she entered the bedroom. She cut his inquiry short by laughing at him and telling him he shouldn't read psychology at night, it would keep him awake, like cheese.

She got into bed without having had a bath. She was excited still, and wanted Mark. Going to bed with Edward had merely served to prove the sad truth: she was imprinted on Mark, like the large white duck who'd clattered round after her Aunt Margaret on her childhood holidays in Cornwall. The duck had leapt out of its shell, seen Aunt Margaret, and never recovered from the shock. Perhaps she'd never recover from the shock of meeting Mark Carleton.

She turned to face him. 'Put down that book,' she commanded. He continued to read. She picked up his penis, a little warm worm, already half asleep, and held it loosely and felt it grow. Her vagina ached. Mark went on reading. She bent and put his penis in her mouth, tasting centuries of secretions. At the same time, she opened her legs and played with herself: Mark flipped the page, but his body registered what she was doing. At last he flung down the book.

'You want to be fucked, do you?'

She took her hand away and lay back on the pillow, waiting for him. He took one nipple between his fingers, and drew it out, and then he sat across her, taking both nipples at the same time, and laying his penis, like a Christmas present, on her abdomen. She took it again in both her hands and cupped it lovingly and hungrily. He looked down. 'That's right. That's for you.' He grew harder; he threw his head back and looked at the ceiling and howled like a dog. She put her hands on his hips and pushed him down, and in return he pushed up and into her, lunged into her with a force that Edward Alderson would never be able to manage, and as he rammed her waiting cervix, she came instantly, resenting, as she had grown used to doing, her own reflexivity.

This completed her conjugation with Edward Alderson.

11 * THE BRIGHT IDEAL

'Thus what bourgeois optimism has to offer the engaged girl
is certainly not love; the bright ideal held up to her is that
of happiness, which means the ideal of quiet equilibrium in
a life of immanence and repetition' – *The Second Sex*, p.167

In January 1989 Mark Carleton went to Alma-Ata to discuss the
progress of that particular arm of his sociology of everyday life
project.

Eleven years on from the signing of the declaration of Health
For All By The Year Two Thousand, not a great deal had
happened. In ten countries the rate at which women died in
childbearing had come down, but that still left a great number in
which it hadn't. A drop in the number of deaths of children in
the first year of life was another area of progress, but, to
counterbalance this, the uncontrolled pace of industrialisation in
the Third World entered children in the workforce and made
them victims of industrial and urban accidents. Instead of dying
of malnutrition, they died of machinery. This was called
progress.

A further 5 per cent of the world gained safe drinking water,
but 60 per cent still did not have it. Food, the raw material of
health, continued to be unevenly distributed. People died of
influenza and depressed immune systems in Africa, and, though a
cure for AIDS was still hoped for, it would be unlikely to reach
with any great speed the millions of sufferers in the forests and
bogs and rickety backstreet hotels of the world. The Chinese
brought their population down and their rice yield up; they

swopped acupuncture for aeronautics, which was not a healthy thing to do, though it meant they no longer had to fly people round China in disused Russian planes with loosely fixed seatbacks that flapped every time the pilot put the no smoking button on.

In such ascents and descents, the fortunes of individuals were navigated differently. Charity had passed her fortieth birthday, and didn't mind. She'd got the material from the adolescent project together into a racy book: *Who's Made a Mess of the World, Then: The Health Beliefs of 13–18 Year Olds*. Even Tom declared a grudging respect for the book. He took a copy off his mother's bookshelf and gave it to his tutor. He'd climbed the A Level fence and disappeared to the University of Essex, where Joanna Carleton, newly graduated from New Hall, Cambridge, did not follow him. The destinies of Charity's twin sons showed signs of deviating at last. Dan had remained scholastic, reading weighty red books entitled *Lectures in Physics* in his spare time. Harry was distracted by nebulous desires. He'd bought a second-hand racing cycle and special cycling clothes which he took great trouble to preserve in pristine condition by frequent washing. He'd had one ear pierced. Rachel did it for him. She was fifteen now, and spent a lot of time trying to enjoy doing nothing.

And, as for Mark, he had his work and his lack of marriage. One got better, and the other got worse. 'I'm nearly fifty,' he said (he was forty-nine), 'and where have I got?'

'You've got me,' she said.

'I've got half of you,' he replied.

'The best half,' she quipped, as he had done back in the good old days of 1981.

'But I want a wife.'

'A refrain like a music hall song,' she said. 'Why don't you find one, then? Find one in Alma-Ata, and bring her back with you. Set up house in a tenement in Acton. See how you like it.'

He frowned at her, and later that week flew to Moscow with a contingent of co-workers – the three fieldwork co-ordinators on the study, Rose Goodenough, and Sue Bridges, a secretary. In Moscow they met Roger Strangeway from the Whiteman Foundation, which for unsubtle political reasons was particularly interested in the Russian connection. They went on from Moscow to Alma-Ata, flying by night because the Russians didn't want them to see the raised details of the ground beneath, which included the main Soviet space science complex at Baykonur, two hundred miles north-east of the Aral sea.

The little party assembled in the foreigners' building on the tarmac of Moscow airport, in the careful guardianship of Mr Novopolin from the Ministry of Health. When Novopolin gave the word, they moved out across the tarmac in the warm black night. Mark was walking separately from the others, thinking about something else, when he heard this roaring sound behind him and turned to see a jumbo jet bearing down on him like a great bird. He ran away from it as fast as he could, fearing for his life at the same time as knowing he looked very foolish (an impression confirmed by the ribald laughter behind him). The episode served to confirm his worst fears that, in doing what he felt he had to do in life, he would always and inevitably be a figure of fun.

The sun rose at 3 a.m. and the plane, which hadn't been flying very high, dropped through the clouds for a moment or two, to reveal a miniaturised landscape of plains and snowy mountains. Mark read the bundle of material Novopolin had given them at the airport. He learnt that Russia was twice the size of China and spanned eleven time zones; however, only 53 per cent of Russians were really Russians. The rest were ethnic minorities. These included the Kazakhs of Central Asia, who'd been having conflicts of one kind or another with their Russian hosts since the sixteenth century. Kazakhstan had its own customs and its own culture, and was far enough away from the capital to carry on regardless; it had been created an autonomous republic by the Central Executive Council of the USSR in 1924. Together with Siberia, it formed about 70 per cent of the total area of the Soviet Union, although it contained at the moment only 16 per cent of its people.

They landed in a warm wet dawn. A party of grey-suited Kazakhs awaited them holding bunches of white flowers, and took them to their hotel, where there were microphones under the beds. In addition, of course, they had interpreters with them, and Mr Novopolin from the Ministry in Moscow, who acted as a sort of spy. Sometimes he joked and smiled with genuine camaraderie, but at other times he hung around the hotel or the research institute where they were working, smoking cheap cigarettes and emitting an odour of unsuccessfully casual surveillance.

The Kazakhs were oddly untutored in social research methods. It took Mark several long and painful meetings to convey to them the concept of a random sample, and even then he wasn't sure they'd grasped it. Despite their enthusiasm about the project on paper, they also displayed a consistent and unhelpful incredulity towards the idea that everyday life was worth researching, partly because they didn't seem to know what it was. They'd done some pilot interviews, but when Mark got hold of the transcribed versions, he found that these were almost all with local officials, professionals and other bureaucrats who talked with a sodden pomposity about the important decisions they took concerning the running of the city and its environs, and the control of the local population by means of regulations about street cleaning and restaurant hours. 'I am not interested in the agenda of the local politburo,' insisted Mark, with a typically advanced degree of political naivety, 'or the process of collective decision-making on the local health boards. What I, we,' he corrected himself quickly, seeing the faces of the other members of his team across the table, 'what we are interested in is what daily life is like for ordinary people.'

A rapid exchange in Russian followed. The interpreter turned to him. 'But what is ordinary? Dr Katechsky does not understand what this word, ordinary, means.'

Mark got out his Lefebvre. The fluid and rapid intonations of his voice, which the interpreter had constantly to interrupt in order to translate, carried across the room, the institute, the plain on which Alma-Ata was built, and probably, for all any of them knew, right over the border into northern China. Sociology, viewed as insidious by the communist state, retaliated by being so. The Russians nodded politely.

The next day, after several more hours of survey planning and international cogitation, there was an official party in the hotel. A banquet was laid on. There was to be dancing. But before that, at the end of the meal, everyone was required to stand up and sing. To Mark's surprise, Rose Goodenough turned out to have an enchanting voice, with which she treated the assembled company to an unusual rendering of 'The Bluebells of Scotland', in Gaelic. The Kazakh doctor on her left then stood up and poured out an astonishingly powerful love song in a minor key. Rose bloomed under the influence of these unexpected melodies, not to mention the doctor's splendid gold teeth. Strangeway took the stand next, with a version of some obscene Texan ditty about a cowboy and a cowgirl. By the time it came to his turn, Mark could only think of God Save the Queen. He couldn't sing in tune, but the others helped him.

He danced with the local Minister of Social Affairs, a bleached blonde Armenian in a blue synthetic costume. She wore a cheap scent which got up Mark's nose, and he started to sneeze uncontrollably. Madame Itkina sat him down and fetched him some Russian kleenex and another glass of vodka. He told her he had a mysterious allergy which always came on at this time of the evening and made him sneeze; the only thing to be done was to go to bed. Alone.

Above the microphone in the floor of his room, he took out the other book he had brought with him, Roland Barthes' *A Lover's Discourse*. He'd been meaning to read it for some time. He liked the title, and some of the stories he'd heard about Barthes' anti-social behaviour at dinner parties in Paris. In his tired but emotionally charged state, he was peculiarly receptive to Barthes' words, his description of the lover's discourse as one of solitude, a craving to be engulfed, 'because there is no longer any place for me anywhere'. This encouraged Mark to feel even more lonely. He read on: 'Historically, the discourse of absence is carried on by the woman. Woman is sedentary. Man hunts, journeys; woman is faithful (she waits), man is fickle (he sails away, he cruises).' Mark was stirred by this, not to a perception of its redolent chauvinism but to a deep appreciation of the sentiment it expressed: the arrangement sounded to him a good one, yet it was not, he realised, with a pain that seared his heart, one that he himself had. Charity was the woman who would not wait. It wasn't that he didn't love her. He loved her more than he thought he could love: too much. But he did not get in return for this love what he wanted, and so he would rather love less and get something in return.

When Mark returned from his mission to Alma-Ata, he took back with him a decision. If Charity wouldn't marry him, then he would have to find someone who would.

He went to work one morning, and there she was, his future bride. His eyes fastened on her with the stickiness of a fly in heat. She was slim, five foot seven inches tall, and had a creamy skin, creamy hair and very dark eyes with curling lashes. Her hair was tied back with a yellow silk ribbon, and she wore tight black trousers, boots and a yellow sweatshirt. She was standing in front of their new word processor, holding a manuscript in her left hand, and Alan Pascoe was standing next to her.

'Good morning, Mark. May I introduce my daughter, Tessa? She's come in to help with some typing for a few days. Mavis is ill again, and there's a dreadful backlog of stuff that needs doing.'

Mark shook her hand. It was long and limp. 'I didn't know you had a daughter, Pascoe.' He would have said something to her, but he couldn't think of anything.

This didn't prevent him from planning his strategy. First he equipped himself with details of Tessa Pascoe. She was twenty-four, only twenty-four. That made a quarter of a century difference in their ages – in fact she was only a few years older than his own daughter. Jane would say it was indecent. He couldn't bear to think of what Charity would say. Tessa also had a background of non-achievement. After she'd left school, she'd done a series of temporary nonskilled, mostly domestic, jobs. Her longest job so far had been in a nursery. She was said to love children. But the nursery had closed down, and now she was taking a secretarial course. She also had some sort of boyfriend who worked at Gatwick Airport.

He thought he would have to get her out to lunch first. But how? On the day of the weekly departmental seminar, he arranged for Pascoe to take the chair and he absented himself, saying he had to write an urgent report. He went into the secretary's office, and there was Tessa, typing. The ribbon on her hair was blue today. 'Fancy a bit of lunch?' he asked, trying to appear casual. (Tessa told him afterwards that she'd known exactly what he was up to right from the beginning.)

They went to a fairly smart pub. Mark drank grapefruit juice, needing to stay sober, and Tessa had half a pint of lager. They ate two pork pies. He tried to amuse her with tales of his trip to Alma-Ata.

'Can I ask you something?'

'Of course, anything.' He made an expansive gesture with his shoulders.

'I just wondered if you were married.'

'No,' he said, proudly. 'I'm not married, I'm divorced.'

'So you live on your own?'

'Not exactly.'

'What do you mean, not exactly? You're either on your own, or you're not.'

'I live with a friend,' he said. 'Charity. She's called Charity.'

Tessa giggled. 'What a dreadful name! Is she really called Charity?'

'Yes. She really is.' Mark recalled how glorious the name of Charity had sounded to him at the beginning. 'It's not her fault she's called Charity,' he added, defensively.

'Well, I don't like my name either, Theresa Pascoe. Ugh. My parents have no taste. There are some people like that – no taste in anything, names, interior decoration, meals, music, whatever. The only music my father likes is the theme music from Limelight. Just no taste. It's a dreadful failing. Anyway,' she went on, 'the reason I wanted to know if you're married is because I don't have affairs with married men.'

Mark was taken aback by her forwardness, otherwise known as honesty. 'Do you tell everyone that?'

'Most people. It saves complications later on. You see,' she leaned forward confidingly, so that he could almost sense the possibly delectable odour of her breath, 'you see I've reached a certain stage in my life.'

'Haven't we all,' he mumbled.

'No, I'm serious. I'm trying to say something important.'

'I'm listening.'

'I want to settle down.'

'Settle down?'

'I want to get married and have a baby. I want to have a baby, particularly. Women should have babies when they're young. The trouble with your generation,' she leaned forward again, and he could smell her breath this time (it smelt of marigolds), 'is that you left it all too late. You had all these theories about the dreadfulness of the nuclear family, and how children stop women having careers, and you got it all wrong.'

'Did I?' He couldn't remember whether he'd had any theories about that sort of thing. It seemed to him that it was the women who had the theories and the men just went about their business as usual.

'Now your Charity,' continued Tessa, 'I bet she's a feminist, isn't she?'

'Well, yes,' he admitted.

'Of course she is. She believes in sexual freedom and equality, doesn't she? And sharing the housework?'

'Well, yes.'

'And she has a career.'

'Hmm. But she does have children.' It was odd, this sensation he had of needing to defend Charity. He supposed it was a change from defending himself.

'It doesn't work,' announced Tessa. 'It simply doesn't work — having a career *and* having children. It's a dissipation of energy. Everyone suffers. The children, the women, the men, the family. Somewhere along the line children, in particular, got left out. And motherhood. I'd rather be a mother than anything else.'

'Would you really?' Mark found it hard to believe that she was serious. He thought she might be feeding him a line she knew he wanted to hear, and, like an idiot, he would swallow it and then be hooked for ever. Again. He'd had enough of being hooked.

'I'm absolutely serious. Don't you believe me?'

He could reply only by asking another question. 'Do other people of your age think like you?'

'Who cares?' said Tessa. 'I don't. I think like me, that's all I care about.'

'Anti-feminist individualism,' stated Mark.

'There's no need to label it,' she said crossly. 'Would you like another drink? I would. And I want another pork pie, too.'

A few days later it was Tessa who invited Mark out for a meal. He phoned Charity and said he would be working late. He didn't even feel a heel about it. They went to a dingy Indian vegetarian restaurant in Shepherds Bush. You took your own wine and shared a table with everyone else. Tessa seemed to know a lot of people. Mark felt a bit middle-aged. Before he got back in his car to go home, he kissed her. She tasted, not of marigolds, but of egg curry.

'I'm taking Rachel to Paris for a long weekend,' said Charity. 'She's always wanted to go to Paris in the spring, and if I don't do it now, I never will.'

Mark gathered that he was not invited. 'What a nice idea,' he said ingenuously, 'I'm sure she'll enjoy that.'

He still hadn't been to bed with Tessa. She wasn't working at the department any more, but he saw her regularly for meals, to go to the cinema, even to a party once. Pascoe didn't know. Pascoe himself had become a problem. Mark didn't want to tell Tessa what kind of problem Pascoe had become; indeed, he hadn't especially wanted to tell Pascoe. It seemed that there were more and more unpleasant jobs he had to do, and he felt less and less capable of doing them.

The accountant called in by Pascoe to examine the departmental finances had come to Mark with a most curious account of what he thought he'd seen in them. 'As you know, Dr Pascoe called me in to establish the nature of the deficit,' Gottlieb began. 'Of course, I'm quite used to examining institutional accounts. I spend most of my time doing it, after all. But quite frankly, Professor Carleton, I've never seen anything quite like this.'

'Haven't you?' Mark felt out of his depth. He had absolutely no idea what was coming next.

'No. Have you ever checked the accounts yourself, Professor Carleton?'

'No, I can't say I have. That's Pascoe's job. It's called a division of labour,' he remarked, irrelevantly.

'That may be. But the man's had a field day.'

'I beg your pardon.'

Gottlieb cleared his throat. 'Sorry, I'm not making myself clear. What I meant was that when I examined the departmental accounts, it immediately became clear to me that Dr Pascoe was in fact himself responsible for the discrepancy. The deficit. I explained this to him. It wasn't easy, you understand, but eventually he agreed. Indeed, I felt almost as though he was relieved that his crime was out in the open.'

'Crime?'

'Perhaps that's not the right word. Error? No. It was intentional. Dr Pascoe has intentionally defrauded the department of a large amount of money. I think you need to recognise that, Professor Carleton.'

Pascoe? Pascoe as well? Mark grappled with the thought. Surely Pascoe wouldn't be capable of inventive fiddling: he lacked the imagination. Too straightlaced. 'Hang on a minute,' he said to Gottlieb, 'how much money are we talking about?'

'About £45,000 over three years.'

'How the hell did the man manage that?'

'Capital expenditure.'

'But we haven't got any capital to expend!'

'Precisely. But that's what he called it.'

'What did he say he spent it on?'

'Refurbishings. New office equipment. A couple of CPT word processors.'

'But we haven't got any of those!'

'I know you haven't.'

'That can't add up to £45,000.'

'Well, there were one or two other items. A car, for instance.'

'A car?'

'A Toyota space cruiser. Cost £12,000.'

'What was that supposed to be for?'

'Interviewing.'

'Jesus!'

'And a new men's room.'

'A what?'

'A new lavatory. Or, rather, three.'

'Where is it? Are they?'

'In Dr Pascoe's head, I'm afraid, Professor Carleton.'

'But what did he really spend the money on? Where did it all go?'

'He did tell me, and I didn't really understand it, but I believe he was telling me the truth.' Gottlieb put the file of papers he was holding down on the ground and rearranged himself in his chair. This was a most unusual job. He didn't like it at all. He wanted to get it over with as quickly as possible. 'I do feel I'm in a difficult position here,' he said. 'But Dr Pascoe did give me permission to tell you. I expect you know his wife has been ill?'

Mark recalled Pascoe's unwillingness to take charge of the UGC visit because his wife had just had her womb out.

'She's really been quite ill, over quite a long period. Sounds to me as though most of it's been mental. Psychological, you know. Not that it's up to me to pass an opinion, of course. Dr Pascoe's been very concerned about her. He told me that she's been in and out of hospital having electric shock treatment for depression.'

'What has all this got to do with £45,000?'

'He spent it on her. He wanted to make her happy. He bought her a new house. A bungalow in Redhill.'

'Bungalows in Redhill can't cost all that much. What did he do with the house he already had?'

'He sold it. And they do, or rather this one did. It's very large. It has a separate extension for her mother. Dr Pascoe's mother-in-law, that is. And another separate flat for a resident domestic help.'

'Why didn't I know any of this?' Tessa hadn't said anything. Perhaps she didn't know, or suspect.

'Well, it's not good, is it?'

'No, it certainly isn't. But how did he manage it? Why didn't I notice?'

'I imagine,' said Gottlieb, folding his hands carefully on the trousers of his grey suit, 'you weren't watching. Most people only notice what they want to, you know.'

'I know.' Mark felt an urge to terminate these proceedings before he learnt anything else he didn't want to know. 'So what do you think I should do about it?'

'That's clearly up to you, Professor Carleton. But if I were you, I should expect Dr Pascoe's resignation. And repayment of the money in full, with interest of course.'

Mark felt confused. How could he make Tessa's father unemployed when he'd never find another job at his age, at the same time as pursuing his daughter into bed? Tessa would never forgive him. In any case, he wasn't sure Pascoe's offence was such a crime, after all. He hadn't done it for himself, had he? He'd done it for a woman.

Mark told Pascoe he wanted the money back and the budget straightened out. If Pascoe could guarantee that, he wouldn't take it any further. To his immense surprise and embarrassment, Pascoe had then wept in front of him, his face going an unpleasant pinky-red colour and his eyes disappearing into the surrounding flushed and engorged flesh. Before Mark could think of a way of getting Pascoe out of the room, there had come from between the tear-washed fingers enclosing Pascoe's head like a draughty crash helmet the words, 'I did it all for love, you see, Carleton. That was the only reason I did it. For love.'

'She did it all for love.' The same phrase, with the genders reversed, floated unbidden into Mark's head. But surely it couldn't be the same for men? Where was Pascoe's reason? His self-discipline? His moral responsibility?

'I couldn't bear to see how miserable she was, Carleton. It was awful, awful.' Pascoe spoke without looking at Mark, he was still mumbling into his wet hands. 'There was nothing I could do about it, except what I did do. What can men do for women, except give them things? We can't understand what they go through. I didn't understand. She knew that.' He paused, and looked up. 'It's a lovely bungalow, you know. Perhaps you'd like to come and see it one day? I'm sure my wife'd make you very welcome. She does like showing it off to people. It makes her anxious, though. You know, in case it's not absolutely presentable. Everything has to be in the right place. Of course, she is on anti-depressants and other drugs at the moment, quite high doses. Esperon 50 mg – that's the anti-depressant. They're white. And then Serenax, 25 mg. That's for her nerves: they're yellow, little round yellow pills – she suffers from nerves as well. The drugs make her rather uncommunicative, perhaps you'd better wait a bit to come and see us. The doctor's hoping to reduce them soon. It's the mixture, you understand, of depression and anxiety. The hysterectomy didn't help, naturally. She's been having these panic attacks. I remember one a few years ago . . .' His voice trailed off as he became aware that Mark had stopped listening to him some time ago. But when he thought he'd regained Mark's attention, he started again. 'I *am* sorry, Carleton. Not for what I did. Because it was the right thing to do from a personal point of view, you understand. But not from a professional point of view, I realise that. I acted unprofessionally. I'll sort it out, though. I don't know how, but I will. Thank you for understanding.'

Mark didn't. He did feel sorry for Pascoe, for what he'd done, and the squalid mess he'd landed himself in, but most of all for the lengths the man had gone to in the name of love. It sounded to Mark more like an obsession – all this providing of material resources for an already demented woman. In view of his confession, Mark hardly felt he could raise with Pascoe the subject of his relationship with Tessa. It wasn't on, really.

But neither was sex with Tessa. She had this strange idea that one ought to wait. He'd wondered at first whether she was a virgin, but she told him she'd had a promiscuous period when she was in her late teens, and after that she decided to be more discerning. Sometimes he felt she was very young, younger than his own daughters, and sometimes incredibly old.

Should he tell Tessa that Charity was going away and the house would be free, at least in the daytime? Or should he be very casual about it, and just take her there? In the end, he booked a table at The White Tower in Percy Street the day Charity and Rachel took off for Paris.

When he kept refilling her glass, she said, accusingly, 'You're trying to get me drunk. And I know why.'

'Why?'

'Because you're planning to get me into bed this afternoon.'

'Well, you said it, not me.'

'I know,' she said suddenly, 'I bet Charity's gone away, so you can take me back to the house. I bet that's it.'

He was amazed at her intuition.

'It's bloody obvious. You're bloody transparent, you are! Just put two and two together. This restaurant. The wine. I know you want to go to bed with me. But I'll tell you something,' she lowered her voice conspiratorially, 'the answer is no – that is, if you were intending to ask me.' She sat back and laughed mockingly at him across the table.

He gnawed thoughtfully on a piece of lamb. Then he took his glasses off and put them down on the table. He stared at her hypnotically, or what he hoped was hypnotically.

'And I'll tell *you* something, Tessa, the answer is not no. You've played around with me for long enough. I want my just desserts.'

She summoned the waiter. 'Could we see the dessert menu, please?'

'Oh shit, Tessa!' He stood up. 'I'm going to the men's room.' As he put his napkin on the table, he failed to notice the precarious position of his glasses on the edge of the table, and they flew to the ground, where they came instantly into contact with one of his feet. He scrunched off across the carpet to the sound of his future wife's laughter.

12 ✳ SECRET AGENTS

> 'Woman plays the part of those secret agents who are left to the firing squad if they get caught, and are loaded with rewards if they succeed; it is for her to shoulder all man's immorality . . . [to] serve as sewer to the shining, whole-some edifice where respectable people have their abode' – *The Second Sex*, p.312

Mark seemed preoccupied when Charity came back from Paris. At first she thought it was because he was having to manage without his glasses; it wasn't always easy to tell the difference between myopia and thoughtfulness. But when his new glasses arrived (with metallic frames, which made him look quite a new man: whatever had inspired the change of image?) he continued to stumble around wrapped up in a fog which floated out of his own head.

The fog's main symptom was that he had stopped putting pressure on Charity. She tried to talk to him about it.

'Problems at work,' he muttered.

'What problems?'

He told her that he was getting transcripts from the everyday life project that puzzled him. The ones that were coming in from the Stockholm arm of the study had so much structure and coherence that they were literally unbelievable. The Swedish interviewees didn't deviate, contradict or repeat themselves the way normal people did. Mark thought perhaps the translators had edited the texts too much.

'You complain about the absence of structure in your life,'

observed Charity, 'and then, when someone hands you some on a plate, you object that it's not credible. You can't have it both ways.'

She wondered if Mark was depressed. He didn't show signs of depression. There were some things he was very eager to do, and he'd even developed new enthusiasms. He'd started listening to jazz, for example, and going for late-night walks. 'To clear my head,' he'd say, but he might as well have said, 'to take the dog for a walk,' for all the sense it made. He came back from these nocturnal wanderings quite elated sometimes, as though he'd been talking to the crystal moon and the stars. Then he would take a long bath, so that, by the time he got to bed, she was asleep.

One night Charity awoke suddenly, aware of a peculiar noise. She lay still, alert for the telephone, thunderstorms, burglars or sick children. Then the dreadful realisation hit her: the noise came from beside her in the bed, and it was Mark, who was masturbating.

'Don't stop because of me.' Her voice sizzled like acid in the warmth of the bed.

'I didn't know you were awake.'

'Clearly.'

'Does it upset you?'

'What do you think?'

'I didn't want to wake you.'

'No, that's right. Not out of consideration for me, but for yourself.'

'What do you mean?'

'You don't want me any more.'

'No? I don't know what I do want, then.' He took her hand and placed it on his flagging penis, 'Do it for me. Please, Charity.'

She held him in her hand. She knew what she should do. She knew what he wanted her to do. But she did not want to do it.

'No,' she said.

Swinhoe knew what was going on. His mother always said he didn't miss a thing. What she meant was that he made up in terms of observation for what he lacked in experience, which was a lot.

Swinhoe had watched Mark over the years, and then Mark and Charity, and he'd lost touch with Charity because she'd left the department, but since he was there every day, he couldn't help but notice all the beginnings, middles and ends of things. He thought it was an interesting development when Pascoe brought his daughter into the office. At first he fancied that Steve Kirkwood might take her over, but he noted that Steve was irritated by Tessa, she was too direct for him. Steve liked women to be obscure and convoluted: he only really got on with those who talked in paragraphs. Then it struck him that Pascoe's daughter was going to be given a different niche as Mark Carleton's youthful saviour. The man had been looking quite jaded recently. A bit like a dog that got put out at night. Every morning, when Swinhoe greeted Mark at the department, he felt he wanted to put a plate of Lassie down for him.

He was there when Tessa and Mark came back from their first lunch, there to observe that she came in first and he followed five minutes later. The next time, the roles were reversed, and he was the first entrant. On the day Mark took Tessa to The White Tower, Swinhoe had actually followed them. He left them in the restaurant for two hours, and then came back to see what happened next. They staggered out, went off down Oxford Street, and then disappeared into an optician's for ages. Very strange. Particularly since Swinhoe knew Charity was away with her daughter in Paris, because Mark had mentioned in a loud voice to Pascoe how much he envied them.

This affair was taking an unusual course. Most of all, it was taking an awfully long time to get anywhere. When Tessa stopped working at the department, Swinhoe found out where she was working instead, as secretary to a children's charity in Soho Square. If he had a free lunch, he'd go there on his bike and hang around to see what happened. Once or twice she went off with a young man about her age, but although they seemed happy enough together Swinhoe felt quite strongly there wasn't anything in it. He cycled back to the department reassured for Carleton's sake. He wanted to say something to him, but of course he didn't.

· 233 ·

Not once did Swinhoe think he was doing anything unethical in following Mark and Tessa around. He was doing it out of interest, and because he cared what happened to them.

In fact, he developed quite an anxiety state about it. He realised he had to get closer to the core of what was going on between Mark and Tessa in order to expedite things. But how? If they noticed him listening to their conversation the cat would be out of the bag. Completely.

He went to a theatrical disguise shop in Covent Garden and bought a grey wig and a grey beard and a pair of tinted glasses. He also bought himself a maroon velvet smoking jacket – he'd always wanted one, but had never been able to think of an excuse good enough to prevent his mother having one of her fits about it. He kept all these things in a carrier bag in the cupboard of his room at work. When he sensed that the time was ripe, he would put them on and penetrate the heart of the affair.

His chance came in late June. He heard Carleton on the phone ordering theatre tickets. And then, by dint of an awful lot of hanging around outside Mark's door, pretending to wait for the photocopier, he heard him ring Tessa and suggest they meet after work in a certain pub to have a drink and something to eat before going to the theatre.

Swinhoe got there first, fully disguised. He bought a Wilbur Smith novel on the way, something else to hide behind. He secreted himself in a corner of the pub with a pint of beer and a packet of chicken and tarragon crisps, and waited.

They came in at 6.30. Tessa was wearing a pink silk dress with a silk flower on the shoulder. They sat down at the next table with two glasses of white wine and two plates of pasta and salad. What unbelievable luck! Swinhoe went on reading Wilbur Smith. As the noise in the pub built up, he found he could only hear odd snatches of their conversation:

'I will tell her, really I will. I'm not putting it off. I just haven't found the right moment yet.'

'Right moments don't exist. They have to be created.'

And:

'I told you, I'm not going to bed with you until we get married. If we don't get married, I don't go to bed with you. Simple.'

'It's not simple. It's blackmail.'

'I'm not blackmailing you. I love you. I love your' (he couldn't catch this bit) 'and your experience. I want an experienced man to be the father of my children.'

Swinhoe almost choked on a crisp when he heard this. What an extraordinary thing to say! As he coughed, Mark looked in his direction, but was far too preoccupied with Tessa to take in much else.

After they'd gone off to the theatre, Swinhoe ordered himself some food and wondered what to do. He didn't feel very sympathetic with Charity's angle. She'd had her run with Carleton, now it was someone else's turn. Anyway, it was clear that Carleton wasn't happy with Charity any more. She wasn't looking after him properly. Swinhoe thought for a moment with abstract fondness of his own mother in Sydenham, and how she'd always looked after him: there was always food in the oven, always beer in the fridge, always cloistered piles of bleached cotton underwear in his cupboard. Swinhoe fetched himself another beer and started to think about Tessa Pascoe having a baby. Reproduction horrified him. He didn't really want her to have a baby. But he did want Mark to have her.

It was obvious, really. He, Swinhoe, had to be the person to tell Charity. That was the only thing that would bring matters to a successful conclusion. He imagined ringing Charity up, but, as quickly as he began to construct the conversation, he shied away from it. Too personal. A letter? Too cowardly, perhaps. An anonymous letter? That was the answer. There would be nothing wrong with an anonymous letter, because there would be nothing to connect it with him. His own role in the affair was an anonymous one. His identity was unimportant. That gave him a good reason for concealing it.

He got out his notebook and began to compose a draft of it. 'Dear Charity'. No, 'Dear Dr Walton'. That was better, more distant. 'It has come to my attention.' No, too impersonal. 'You might like to know'. Would she? Probably not. When the solution struck him, he put his notebook away with a flourish. He would compose a couple of sentences out of words to be cut out of newspapers, thereby restricting both his vocabulary and any possible suggestion of his true identity. Perfect. He'd have another beer to celebrate.

When the theatre finished, and Mark and Tessa came out, there was Swinhoe lurking in the doorway opposite in his maroon smoking jacket. But, wrapped up in themselves, they didn't notice. They strolled off hand in hand, down St Martin's Lane. Swinhoe followed in the crowds. They walked down the left-hand side of the street and then up the steps of St Martin-in-the-Fields. Swinhoe watched them open the door of the church and go in. Could he follow? He felt he simply had to follow, now he had got this far. He sprang up the steps and round the side of the church. He turned the handle of the door. It moved. Gently he pushed it open and slid inside.

The body of the church was almost in darkness. Two small lamps lit the nave. At the point of maximum light stood Carleton and Tessa, kissing. Tessa's hair, which had started out the evening piled on top of her head, had been loosened from its fastening and now fell into a pattern of light and dark against her white skin under the two small lamps. Carleton had his hands on her shoulders as he kissed her, and his mouth moved down her long neck, and Tessa's white hands gripped the back of Carleton's linen jacket. As Swinhoe watched, Carleton pushed the pink silk strap of her dress, the one with the flower on it, right off her shoulder. She took his head in her hands, and kissed him. He took the other strap in his left hand and ripped it with a sound like a cock crowing betrayal – lust, infidelity, yearning – and then the pink silk had been torn away, revealing the sacramental beauty of Tessa's breasts, two uplifted domes in the lamplight. Carleton knelt on the stone floor, and, with a hand around each breast, rested his head against the folds of the pink silk: and then Tessa carefully unfolded his hands and moved them down and her own body over him, so that Swinhoe had this extraordinary vision of breasts sitting like cooing pigeons on the top of Carleton's head.

He rushed out of the church. As the door banged, Carleton and Tessa looked up, startled.

'What was that?' she said.

'God keeping an eye on us,' said Mark.

Swinhoe had fled, full of all kinds of feelings, and also far too much beer, so that round the back of St Martin-in-the-Fields he emptied the entire contents of his bladder with a vengeful noise like thunder on to the stones.

'Who is this woman?' asked Charity, furiously, holding the carefully composed letter from Swinhoe in her hand.

'Tessa Pascoe, Alan Pascoe's daughter.'

'And how long have you been having this affair for?'

'Six months.'

'So that's why you've been behaving so oddly. I might have guessed.' She took a deep breath and turned to face him. 'Alright. You can get out. Now.'

'I was going to, anyway,' he said.

Tessa's strategy had worked. She'd prised Mark away from his dreadful Charity (whom she'd never met and never wanted to meet), and he was there, on the doorstep of her tiny flat in Shepherds Bush along with his suitcases of socks, his books, his collection of old photographs and the various impedimenta of his life with various women. 'I'm yours,' he said, and gave her a bottle of Bristol cream sherry with the price label still on it to celebrate.

'But I can't marry you,' said Mark to Tessa, 'I can't marry you now. We must wait. I need time to get used to things. You've got me. I've left Charity. You'll have to be content for a while.'

She was in the kitchen, a mere cupboard, cooking a boeuf bourguignonne. 'I don't understand. Why can't you marry me?'

He sat down. 'Because it's too sudden. It would upset Charity. I don't want to upset her.'

Tessa was angry. 'You shouldn't care about her any more. You should be thinking about me now!'

'I am thinking about you,' he said. 'I'm here, aren't I? But one doesn't shut off emotions just like that. I loved Charity for a long time, nine years. I've been living with her for four. She was my great passion. I can't just block her out.'

Tessa's black eyes poured fury out of the kitchen at him. So did the clack of the wooden spoon with which she stirred the boeuf bourguignonne. 'You think I want to hear about Charity's feelings?'

'I'm telling you the truth. Don't you want me to tell you the truth?'

'No,' she said. 'I don't want the truth. Do you think, as a matter of fact, that women want the truth? If you do, you couldn't be more wrong. That's the last thing women want. You can forget the truth. I'm not interested in it.'

He admired her self-knowledge. The consistency of her position. The trouble was, he was transposing the flavour of one relationship on to another. But Charity wasn't Tessa, any more than she'd been Jane. 'I'm going out for a walk,' he said.

'Okay,' said Tessa, seemingly matter-of-factly. 'Can you pick up a bottle of wine for supper on your way?'

He wandered out into the streets of Shepherds Bush feeling emotionally and geographically lost. There was a pub on the corner, The Black Raven. He went in and had a whisky. Or two. Then he went to a coin box in the corner, dropped in 20p and dialled Charity's number. Her voice reached him over the vast distance between Chalk Farm and Shepherds Bush, and wrenched his heart. He listened intently as she said 'hallo' several times with increasing impatience. Then he replaced the receiver without saying anything.

He went back to Tessa's flat. 'Where's the wine?' He'd forgotten the wine. He went out again and bought it.

'Alright, Mark, I give in. We shouldn't get married yet. There are all sorts of hurdles to get over first. We haven't even told my father yet. But soon, we'll get married soon, won't we?' She had a few misgivings about saying this, but only a few. It was a strange anticlimax really. Here they were, Mark Carleton and the woman who would be his second wife, together at last in this cramped second-floor flat, number 20 Cressida Road, London

W12, and after they'd eaten the boeuf bourguignonne, and drunk their wine, although he couldn't marry her yet, there was nothing either of them could do but get into bed together. The bed was terrible. It was on the floor, and under it the bare boards seemed to let light and conversations up and into the room from the flat below. Tessa lit incense sticks and looked at him very lovingly.

Mark felt the pressure had been taken off him by her speech. He didn't react well to pressure. Nor to cheap red wine. He got out, or rather up off the bed, to fetch the bottle of Perrier water he'd also bought, and came back swigging it.

Making love to Tessa was alright. It worked in a way. 'It always works the first time, you fool,' he said to himself, as he climbed off her. She looked happy. He could see this because there was a street light just outside the window, which poured a great deal of unnecessary illumination into the room. On his way out of Tessa, he fell on the Perrier water and upset it all over the bed; it was all his own fault. In the morning, when the street light had been turned off, he felt he hadn't slept at all.

'That was Mark on the phone,' Charity told Sally.

'What did he say?'

'Nothing.'

'So how do you know it was Mark?'

'Who else would ring and say nothing?'

'Could have been a wrong number.'

'It was Mark.' She fancied she could hear his breathing, his confusion, even his longing for her. She was beside herself. Since he'd left, she'd cried non-stop. She'd kept the tears back until he moved out, and then they'd taken over.

'Come on, Mum, it isn't the end of the world.' Rachel tried to cheer her mother up. It was horrible to see her crying, and eating all the time. She always ate when she was depressed. Biscuits, chocolate, raw spaghetti, even Mr Kipling's cakes, and especially his cherry bakewells. Charity would sigh deeply when she came in from work, peer in the fridge, take out these disgusting cakes and eat them. Rachel tried to stop her mother, but every time she tried, Charity flew at her, 'It's the only thing I've got left. In any case, it doesn't matter if I get fat. There's no one to see me, is there?' And then she'd start crying again.

When Sally came round it was the same, because Sally was also in an eating phase. Rachel heard her tell her mother that the IVF hadn't worked – twice. What was IVF?

'There was no problem getting the eggs,' said Sally, sniffing (she had a cold). 'They got five the first time. They've still got two in the freezer. They're going to try again, but they want to wait a bit first.'

The two women shut the kitchen door and alternately ate, drank and tore off strips of kitchen paper to wipe their eyes and their noses. 'I saw it coming,' said Charity. 'You can't say no to Mark without him taking it out on you somehow. But I never thought he'd give up just like that. Didn't he understand why I wouldn't marry him? It's as though he never listened to anything I said. All those conversations about freedom and equality. What were they for? They were all for nothing!' She answered her own question, and blew her nose again. 'I think I'm through with men, Sal. Honestly. Just when you think you've got somewhere, when you've got a good relationship and you seem to be communicating, that's when you discover the bastards haven't understood a thing you've been saying. They've been off doing something else all the time. I knew there was something wrong. I knew it. But I didn't want to face it. He stopped putting pressure on me to marry him. I should have known it was because he'd picked up a floosy.'

'A what?'

'A floosy. F-L-O-O-S-Y. A loose young woman. A diversion. An absurdity. James moved on. He moved on to Shelley. And now Mark's done the same. Oh Sally –' she got up and stood at the window, looking out at the garden, with her back to Sally, so only the garden could see the exact measure of her distress, only the trees and the birds and the lawnmower, and the old bench James had found in someone's front garden and brought home with a cry of provident triumph one November evening when Rachel lay like a kitten in her cradle. 'Oh Sally, how unbearable it all is! We have their children, then our bodies sag, and our hair starts to go grey, and they look at us and say, "Enough! Time for the next one!" What am I going to do?'

'Accept it, Charity. Accept what's happened. The man's a bastard anyway. He's no good for you. How can you possibly go on loving him? It's sheer masochism. You'd be much better off without him.'

Charity didn't listen. She wrote to Mark to say she missed him and wanted him back. She was waiting.

She posted the letter on 21 July, the summer solstice, and then went to a neighbourhood party where everyone was talking about private versus state education, and how it was too late for the new Labour government to do anything about the mess the country was in. A tall architect, who lived in the next road, was lecturing her next door neighbour, a soft yellow-haired mother of three, about the evils of the party political system, and how what Britain needed was proportional representation. 'A vote for the government and one against it, that's not good enough. Democracy should represent the interests of the people. It's outrageous that in this country a party can get a reasonable share of the votes, but no seats at all, or only very few. Take the Liberals. Six per cent of the votes in the 1959 election, and only 1 per cent of the seats. Why should a vote in Billericay be worth less than a quarter of a vote in the Western Isles. You tell me, I don't know.'

The soft woman nodded. 'You're quite right,' she said. 'I've never seen it like that before.'

Egged on by her deference to his spurious authority, the architect went on in the same vein. 'Do you realise that the two-party system is actually less common than a multi-party system? Most countries encourage smaller parties. If you vote for them you've got a chance of seeing that party represented in Parliament. Of course Churchill said it was because the House of Commons was rectangular.'

After a few minutes of this, Charity could contain herself no longer. The encounter between the architect and the soft woman was simply a parody of sexual relations. Him talking, her listening. Her pretending not to know anything, but really knowing a lot more than him. Okay, he'd read up about proportional representation, and perhaps he'd even designed a few houses or petrol stations in his time, but did he know how to comfort a child with a nightmare, or how to make a home where people feel they can let their hair down and their secrets out, while someone else orders the groceries and gets the windows cleaned?

'You think you know everything,' Charity told the architect with extreme clarity, not even adding the conventional 'don't you?' which would have given him a chance to respond. 'You think you can stand there and lecture us on the ways of the world. Your arrogance is amazing. You're so bloody arrogant that you can't see you don't know anything at all. I suppose you think voting should be compulsory? It is in Australia and Belgium, you know. I wouldn't mind having proportional representation – the Nazis only got 37 per cent of the vote and it enabled them to get power. What a wonderful system! I'm all in favour of that! I don't know, though,' she bit her lip, 'it won't help us to get rid of people like *you*!'

He stared at her. The soft woman stared at both of them. 'The only things you know are the unimportant ones,' went on Charity remorselessly. 'Anyone can find out the things *you* know. But the meaning of life, what do you know about that?'

'I'll tell you about you.' She paused to get her breath back. 'There you are. You're thirty-nine, or forty-one. Your wife is over there in the bushes.' Charity waved vaguely. 'She's one of the ones who's talking about private education. You have two sons. One of them's probably even called Jeffrey.' She spat the word out and it hit the architect right in the face, where it hurt most. 'Their names are down for the minor public school you went to. You have a white Peugeot. You take your holidays in the Dordogne. You've just bought a house there, very cheap, only 80,000 francs. You squeeze the toothpaste tube from the bottom. You never go through a red light. Your wife has a part-time job. You give her mother a cheque for Christmas. You change your socks every day, but you never wash them, do you? No, you never wash your socks!' Her iron-encrusted smile gleamed through the gathering dusk. 'Shall I go on?' He opened his mouth to protest, but it was too late. 'You've had one or two minor affairs. Nothing too serious. Just in and out of bed once or twice. You wash after sex. You probably even say thank you afterwards . . .'

The soft woman tapped her on the arm. 'That's enough, dear,' she said. 'I think he's got the message. And if he hasn't, there's no point in going on at him. Poor man. Save your breath, dear. You never know when you're going to need it.'

Mark wrote to Charity from Stockholm at the beginning of September. He'd dissipated the summer, partly by taking Tessa away for the kind of summer holiday she wanted – three weeks in a four-star hotel in Cyprus on the coastal road between Larnaca and Limassol. Pascoe had recommended it; they'd told him eventually, or, rather, Tessa had, and after the first shock of the news had worn off, he'd taken a surprisingly positive attitude. Mark's generosity to him over the matter of the £45,000 helped him to do this. Tessa didn't know about her father's embezzlement, nor would she ever, for neither man planned to tell her, for different reasons.

The hotel itself could have been anywhere. The cuisine was international, and so was the sun. Mark took a vast quantity of reading matter and a pile of overdue book reviews. Most of the time he sat in the hotel garden under a cypress tree with the hotel cat, reading or writing. Tessa bronzed her body assiduously. She dragged Mark to the hotel discos, and fetched him at mealtimes. They made love in the afternoons, with the balcony doors open and the Mediterranean sun distributing itself in little yellow pools across the garish carpet. In bed Tessa was anxious to do everything she hadn't yet done, which was a lot, and though, despite these titillations, after a time Mark's old problem returned, she either thought it unremarkable or was polite enough not to draw his attention to it overmuch. He enjoyed her body: the economy of its curves and its resilience. In a general sense, he enjoyed being with her; he was absolutely ready to admire her youth, her exuberance, her vitality, her determination to get what she wanted and her most gratifying desire to please him. He watched her sometimes, as she sat at breakfast or in the cocktail bar, or came back with parcels from a shopping spree, and thought himself lucky to have found her. He'd traversed oceans, mountains and all kinds of dreadful and wonderful terrains, and ended up in a quiet backwater with Tessa Pascoe. He couldn't believe his luck. But at other times, he found her outrageously young and silly, and this plunged him into a mood of remorseful longing for the past.

In Cyprus, as the sun set in the same way each day, Mark Carleton became aware of the truth of the saying that the only true paradise is paradise lost. His effort of will, his intellectual decision to find a wife, had pushed his paradise peopled by Charity into history. And his present ahistorical existence was itself a burden to him. It was no solace to him to know that he'd chosen it.

How was Charity? Did she miss him? Had she replaced him? Or forgiven him? He re-read her letter, which he'd brought with him in his grey plastic Eurocheque wallet, and took comfort in her statement that their relationship would never be over. Though he himself had tried to bring it to an end, this contradiction, her adamant rejection of his action, was exactly what he wanted to hear. He read the letter over and over; it warmed his heart, and lay there next to it, a veritable lifeline, maybe even a return ticket.

They missed the plane back to London, because Tessa got the time wrong. She thought the whole thing was a huge joke. Mark didn't. He thought that neither Charity nor Jane would have done that to him. When they got home, the problems hit him in earnest. He took one look at the stuffy little flat in Shepherds Bush and said he was going out to make a phone call.

'Who are you going to call?'

'Jane.'

'Why are you going to call Jane?'

'Because I said I'd call her when I came back. I want to see Joanna and Susan, and I don't know where they are exactly.'

He left Tessa in Shepherds Bush and went to see Joanna and her boyfriend, who were staying in a house in Sussex. Susan came down, and he went to Brighton and walked on the pier with his daughters, one each side of him, and bought them cockles, and allowed them to push him into the hall of mirrors so they could have fun actually viewing all his distortions. He took them to dinner in the Grand Hotel and began to feel better.

On 3 September he went to Stockholm to meet the everyday life project team there. Strangeway had booked the two of them into a small hotel that he knew in Gamla Stan, the old town. Mark confessed to Strangeway the problem with the Swedish transcripts. 'The ones from Gothenburg are the worst,' he said.

'Talk to Johannsen in the morning. There's probably some simple explanation.'

The meeting took place in the hotel's conference room, round a pristine white table with pristine white jugs of coffee skating over its calcium surface. Mark felt awkward. Johannsen, the Swedish co-ordinator, didn't turn up. Birgit Leifdottir from Iceland (Reykjavik was on the brink of joining the study), who was sitting on Mark's left, took it upon herself to go and find out what had happened, since the other Swedish team members didn't seem to know.

Birgit was away an hour or so, during which time Mark took the translator carefully through the transcribed texts, checking to see how much editing had been done. It seemed very little. Birgit came back and passed Mark a note. 'Johannsen unfortunately had an accident yesterday. His wife's bringing in a letter he left for you.' The letter, which arrived at lunchtime, contained a jumble of melodramatic outpourings reminiscent of a Strindberg tragedy. But the long and the short of it, the bit that concerned Mark, was that no real people in Sweden had ever been interviewed for the everyday life project. Johannsen had himself invented the interviews, writing them out in longhand in Swedish and passing them directly to the translator.

You see, Mark said to himself, there's no point in trying to get things right. Even if I don't make the mistakes, other people will make them for me.

That night after dinner he took out Charity's letter, nearly decomposed with overuse.

'Dearest Charity (he wrote in reply). We all make mistakes.

· 245 ·

Mine was to be born a man and to live in a world of women who are all much wiser than I am.

'Do you know what I miss most of all about you? I miss the way you gave me an understanding of myself. I find I don't know who I am without you.

'On some level I still love you, Mark.'

At Heathrow Airport a week later he suddenly felt so tired and overburdened by it all that he checked into the Holiday Inn and fell asleep. At least it solved the problem of who to go home to. At forty-nine years and ten months old, Mark Carleton, Professor of Sociology and Social Studies at Regent's College, the University of London, England, the United Kingdom, was actually homeless. A vagrant looking for a place to rest his ageing head, get his socks washed and his psyche looked after. Not a pretty state of affairs, and certainly not one to be proud of. He wasn't even happy enough to be proud of the fact that he wasn't lying to anyone any more.

13 ✴ ALL SHE HAS ON EARTH

'From the depths of her solitude, her isolation, woman gains her sense of the personal bearing of her life. The past, death, the passage of time – of these she has a more intimate experience than does man; she feels deep interest in the adventures of her heart, of her flesh, of her mind, because she knows that this is all she has on earth' – *The Second Sex*, p.323

The phone woke her up. 'Did you get my letter?'

'Mark! Yes, I got your letter.'

'Can I see you, Charity?'

'You know you can.' She heard him exhale the tension in his lungs.

'When? Now?'

Relaxed from sleep, she laughed. He'd always made her laugh. That was what she missed most about him. Without him she had no comic figure in her life. 'Can't you wait? Where's Tessa? What's happened to Tessa?'

'It doesn't work, Charity. She's too young for me. It was a mistake. You said it was a mistake, and it was.'

'But where is she?'

'In Shepherds Bush.'

'Where are you, then?'

He swallowed. 'At the airport.' He wasn't. He'd gone to see Tessa, who'd found out by telephoning Mavis at the department when he was due to return from Stockholm, and had become totally distraught when he didn't materialise, and now didn't believe his story about the Holiday Inn. She was convinced he'd spent the night with some woman – Charity, even, for this was by far the worst sin he could have committed. The more vehemently he denied it, the more sure she was that he was lying. It was strange. He had no trouble telling lies to women; he only had trouble when he told them the truth. He'd kept saying to Tessa, 'But it's true,' and she kept saying, 'You expect me to believe you spent the night in the Holiday Inn at Heathrow on your own? Don't be ridiculous. You have to credit me with more intelligence than that.' He'd admitted his story sounded odd, but he had no explanation for its oddity other than that he had, in fact, done it.

After their dispute, he'd got up and dressed and left without a word, taking his Stockholm suitcase and a taxi to the department. But he couldn't bear to recite all these gory details to Charity.

'I'm at the airport,' he repeated, 'I've just come back from a meeting in Sweden. Can I come and see you now?'

It was Saturday morning. Charity had slept late. He'd be there in an hour, she guessed. Time to have a bath and wash her hair and get over the shock of hearing his voice again. She flung open the bedroom windows on the remnants of a mist that hung over the tops of the trees, and through which a ghostly white sun could be seen.

When the doorbell rang, she was standing in her underwear drying her hair. It was less than half an hour since his call. Rachel answered the door and came up to tell her. She grabbed a pair of jeans and a sweater, and from the top of the stairs she saw him in the hall wearing a raincoat and still holding his suitcase, peering around him as though the hall itself was full of fog. He looked like a travelling salesman.

She took his suitcase from him. 'Were the planes landing alright this morning?'

'What?'

'With this fog. Wasn't the airport closed?'

'Oh, no. I came SAS. They're used to landing in all kinds of awful conditions.' He put his hands in his pockets.

'Well, anyway, you got here very quickly. I wasn't expecting you so soon. I've just washed my hair.' She flicked a strand of it to show him, and felt strangely girlish and nervous. He, too, seemed quite awkward.

She made him coffee and they took it into the sitting room, and sat in front of the window looking out on to the garden. Fog still hovered over the apple trees. Mark didn't look well. There were lines on his face she hadn't seen before: his hands, his dear hands, trembled round his coffee mug. She could see that he didn't know how to start talking to her.

'So it's over between you and Tessa, is it?'

'Yes, it's over. I was in love with her, Charity; there was something about her that fascinated me.'

'Her youth,' she offered.

'Not only her youth. She was fresh and straightforward, there were none of these complicated dialogues I've had with other women. I didn't have to struggle with her. She's different from you, Charity. She's not stupid, Tessa's certainly not stupid, but her life hasn't been a success. She doesn't want to achieve things. She's not a success,' he said again, thoughtfully. 'You see, I wanted a simple life.' He said it like a supplicant, confessing the incurable sin of self-interest.

'The human condition,' remarked Charity.

Mark was startled. 'What did you say?'

'It's a great human weakness,' she explained, 'but you could almost call it a strength. To want to simplify things. Because complexity is unbearable in everyday life, we have to reduce what's going on to lists of manageable points; we can't ramble on about how we love and hate someone, we have to decide which of the two it is. And so on.' Her smile in his direction was generous. She suddenly remembered how one evening he'd got up from that very chair in which he now sat, and knelt beside her and pleaded with her to live with him. Simplification. The same impulse.

'Why are you being so philosophical this morning?' He put his cup down noisily on the lid of the piano. A little coffee dived over the top on to the polished surface.

'I've had two months to think about it. Anyway,' she continued, 'the point is, you're here now. You want to move back in, I take it.'

'Yes.'

'Well, okay, you can. But I want to say something first, Mark. This is my speech.' She pushed her hair behind her ear in that familiar gesture of determination, a gesture that made him feel that all he was was an unproductive dialogue with himself.

'Go ahead,' he invited. 'I'm waiting.'

She stood up, and walked over to stand at the window. She put her hands behind her back, and clasped them tightly together. 'I won't forget the last few months. Ever. I hate you for what you did. First of all for lying and making a fool of me. The whole world knew about your affair with that woman before I did.' (It wasn't true, he wanted to say, for it wasn't, but they had never solved the problem of who had sent that amazing cat-out-of-the-bag letter.) 'The second thing that was unforgivable,' she went on, 'was that, instead of talking to me about how you felt, about what you saw as your need for a wife and a new marriage, and all that, instead of discussing it with me, you just ran away to find it with someone else. You ran away from us, and what we meant to each other. You ran away from yourself.'

He was humbled by her dissection of his behaviour.

'The third awfulness was the chimera of youth. How could you,' she swung round to face him now, wearing a venomous look, 'how could you think you'd find happiness with a woman a quarter of a century younger than you, a woman young enough to be your own daughter? That was another insanity. I'm ashamed of you.'

He opened his hands on his lap in a gesture of moral hopelessness.

'So. You see, I won't forget. And I can't forgive. Not yet. But I do understand. I'm willing to try to put all that in a box, and put the lid on it, because I know that I love you and, unlike you, I'm not able to defend myself against that knowledge.'

He wanted to put his arms around her and tell her that he loved her. She was so sincere, so good.

'But I have one condition for allowing you back.'

He trembled at the thought. What could it be? Would he be able to meet it? He decided there and then that whatever it was, he would say yes. He would lie for the rest of his life to this woman if necessary. He was through with the truth, it did him no good at all.

'Tell me.'

'If I ever catch you having anything to do with Tessa Pascoe again, that's it.' For the first time she used her full name. 'If I ever have any evidence that you're seeing her again, it's over between us. That's really the end.'

'But you said in your letter it would never be over,' he protested, clutching at straws in his own inadequate defence.

'We all have our limits,' she said sternly. 'There are points beyond which not even I can be pushed.'

He doubted that.

Swinhoe knocked loudly on his door. 'There's a policeman to see you, Carleton.'

Mark was rummaging through his in-tray to see if there was anything interesting in it.

'I'm sorry to disturb you, sir. Police Constable Threshfield, from the station in Marylebone Road.'

Mark stood up. At the same time, his in-tray fell over, tipping unreviewed books, unanswered letters and unread student essays into the wastepaper bin.

Silently, Police Constable Threshfield bent down and handed Mark a sheaf of papers. Together they reassembled the contents of the tray.

Mark blinked at him. 'What was it you wanted to see me about?'

'I'm afraid it's bad news, sir. It concerns a member of your staff, Dr Howard Denby.' The Police Constable waited a minute, presumably to allow Mark to interject, had Howard Denby not been a member of the department.

'Yes?'

'Dr Denby's had an accident. His Volvo was involved in a

head-on collision with a newspaper van in the early hours of this morning.'

Mark was struck by the elision he heard between 'Volvo' and 'involved'. But such niceties were lost on Threshfield, who continued, 'Dr Denby wasn't wearing his seat belt, unfortunately. I'm afraid he went straight through the windscreen.'

'So he's dead?'

'Yes, sir. I'm sorry, sir.'

'Ah.'

'Did you know Dr Denby well?'

'No, no. Only since I joined the department. In 1980, that was. But I didn't know him well, not well at all. I don't think any of us did.'

'The strange thing is,' went on Threshfield, 'he doesn't seem to have any close next of kin. Not according to the papers he carried with him.'

'He was American,' pointed out Mark, rather unnecessarily.

'I know that, sir. There is an aunt in Atlanta. We've contacted the police there.'

'How do you know that?'

'About the aunt in Atlanta? Dr Denby had his passport in his car.'

'That's odd.'

'Yes, sir. It is really.'

'So what do you want me to do?' asked Mark. Somehow he felt the policeman *was* going to ask him to do something. 'I suppose I could phone the aunt. I could phone the aunt, if you like.'

'We can handle that, sir. No, what I really wondered was whether you'd be prepared to come and identify the body. And collect the papers and other bits and pieces that were in Dr Denby's possession when he died.'

'Of course. That's the least I can do.'

In the police morgue, Howard Denby's face was quite horribly smashed in, but undeniably his. When Mark looked at him he could only remember, with awful irreverence, some of the jokes Howie used to tell. They were his memoriam. Mark particularly remembered one Howie had told recently about camels in a desert.

'This man went to hire a camel. He was asked, did he want the 250 mile camel or the 500 mile one? "Better make it the 500 mile one," he said. Along with the camel, he was handed two bricks. He didn't know what to do with the bricks, so he threw them in the nearest watering hole. After 250 miles the camel conked out. He put it on his back and returned it, complaining, to the man who'd rented it to him. "Did you use the bricks?" he was asked. "No," he said, "I didn't know what they were for." "After 250 miles you were supposed to bang the bricks together round the camel's balls, and it would do this (the man made a sucking noise) and take in all this water. That would keep it going for another 250 miles." "But wouldn't it hurt?" "No. You're supposed to take your thumbs away at the last minute".'

At the last minute, Howie's humour transcended the dreadfulness of his accredited mortality.

'Here you are, sir.' Mark was handed Howie's briefcase, and several plastic bags containing the contents of the car, his clothes, his watch, etc, and a denture with six slightly yellow teeth on it.

Later, when he opened the briefcase, he got a much worse shock than any camel looking for water in an Arabian watering hole. First of all, he found photocopies of confidential documents belonging to the political wives Howie was interviewing for his research. Eleanor Gatesby, wife of Labour's Education Minister, was represented by a love letter from the Conservative Home Office spokesman, mentioning certain things Roger Scrafton would like to do to her tits. Deirdre Fell, who was married to the head of the Labour Party's Research Department, had her name on a bank statement with a lot of D's against it. A speech purportedly given by Ben Airdwell, a promising leftwing MP in the Midlands, had been annotated in red biro so that all the figures relating to a proposed nuclear plant in the area had been changed.

There was a whole file of such documents, including photographs and miscellaneous notes in Howie's careful italic handwriting, and lists of names and addresses, some of which were in Tel Aviv and Johannesburg. This was carrying research too far. But there was, of course, no reason why Howard Denby should have gathered such information in the interests of his research, none at all. It must therefore exist for another reason. Was Howie a spy? A spy for who or what? Could it be the CIA? Howie was, after all, an American citizen.

There was also a large notebook in a purple plastic cover. The entries, also in Howie's writing, began in 1977, which Mark knew was the year Howie had come to the department. In 1977 and 1978 there were comments about how Howie felt like an anthropologist studying a strange culture – the culture of Pascoe's paternalism and Kirkwood's unengaging youth, of McKinnon's intransigence and Mavis's high heels, of British filing cabinets and brown carpets and arguments about the location of noticeboards and political sociology on students' reading lists. But after this, observations about the strangeness of the environment tailed off. What followed were pages and pages of systematic observations, collected over a period of twelve years, on all the members of the department.

Mark's discomfort increased as he turned the closely written pages. 'Carleton behaving oddly today. Looked flushed and tense. Trouble at home? Keeps disappearing to the men's room. Went home early . . .'

'Margaret Lacey premenstrual. Don't women in the same institution menstruate together, like nuns? She's more provocative at this time of the month. Suggested we went to the cinema together. *Les Enfants du Paradis*. I declined. I don't want to get involved. Or enchanted. The main purpose of life is to preserve your disenchantment without letting it turn into cynicism.'

Or, 'Kirkwood took Whyte's *Street Corner Society* out of the library today. That's the sixth one this week. Why isn't anyone getting suspicious? He'll never bring it back.'

A week later, 'Mavis's mother ill again. 1 litre bottle of Beaujolais nouveau in Mavis's filing cabinet . . .'

And a few days after this, 'McKinnon working late. Waiting for Swinhoe to go, took files from his office. Heard him laughing. When does McKinnon ever laugh? Never at my jokes.'

More recently, 'Swinhoe's disguise isn't very good. I'm surprised Carleton and Tessa Pascoe haven't noticed . . .'

'Pascoe exchanged contracts on the bungalow today. Invoice for the space cruiser came, marked private and confidential. Pascoe here at seven to open the mail.'

'Swinhoe pasted bits of a newspaper together in the photocopy room. Who's he writing to?'

Then, 'Carleton's out on his ears again. If it wasn't serious, it'd be funny. I wonder if he knows what Lacey's up to?'

And then, in June 1984, came a long soliloquy. 'I never intended to keep this notebook, and there are times when I have more guilt about it than anything else. Why did I start? At the beginning it was an act of survival. A way of talking to myself. But then it became a necessity. I *had* to do it. And once it became that it was inexcusable: obsessions are at best understandable, they're never excusable.

'Even if they're all small-time criminals, these people aren't really doing anything wrong: whatever they're doing, they have a right to do in peace. It is their right. Just as it's mine.

'None of them knows what the others are doing; they're all nursing their risky secrets in private. But even if they don't know what I'm doing, I know. It weighs on me like a vast moral turpitude. I'm taking their secrets away from them, I'm invading their privacy. Without any possible justification except my own inner need for transgression. So I'm the worst criminal of all.

'All I can do is observe, make notes, decide whether to pass information on. Those are the limits of my autonomy, of my moral action. It's not an existence to be proud of. And it isn't even research, for the research itself has a double justification . . .'

There were several pages more which went on in the same vein about the ethics of social research and the bad habit of unintentional observations. Then there was an astoundingly erudite passage about people who treat themselves as fiction.

'Reality is the written word, these words. The French word *jouissance* means reading as well as orgasm: the entanglement of mental with erotic pleasure. I've been reading Roland Barthes again.'

Mark sat up, remembering the role *A Lover's Discourse*, read in Alma-Ata, had played in his own life.

'Barthes always said he would write a novel, but he never did. He was waiting for his mother to die. Are we all in a state of suspension waiting for our mothers to die? But whether he wrote a novel was irrelevant, because he wrote about himself in the third person. He wrote an autobiography, *Roland Barthes by Roland Barthes*, and then he wrote a review of that.

'Incredible. So this journal isn't only by me but about me. The other characters in it aren't real. I've invented them purely in order to complain about myself. I'm not acting as their consciences, they're acting as mine. I can only notice what they're doing, because I'm doing it myself. You great fool, Howie.'

Mark, sitting at his desk in his office in Beaumont Square, was terribly moved by this. He raised his eyes from Howie's contorted speculations and saw the sycamore in the square bending in the wind, with the wind, so that the whole of its shape expressed what the environment was doing to it. He got up from his desk, and opened the window wide so he could hear, as well as see, the wind in its branches. It was late, the traffic had abated, or the sounds of nature never would have reached him.

'You great fool, Howie.' 'Other people are only an excuse for complaining about oneself.' That's why we study them of course, thought Mark. That's what sociology is. The worst form of self-abuse.

Mark felt suddenly cold and white, like marble. He shivered. He experienced an identification with that body in the morgue. Howie had died. Poor Howie. Poor Mark. Howie had been observing Mark, observing them all. Howie had known exactly what they were all doing. He'd known about Mark's problems, about his liaisons, his intentions, about his bungled missions. His shady manoeuvres, his glorious ideals. The man he was and the man he wanted to be – yes, even his fantasies, capering about like quicksilver lambs in a still French garden.

Howie had known about the others, too. About Kirkwood's bibliographical mania, Pascoe's sentimental and financial derangements, McKinnon's demoniacal data distortions, and

Swinhoe. And Swinhoe? So Swinhoe had been watching them. Swinhoe, with his speeches about pandas and his deviations in the household cleansing sections of supermarkets.

What did it all mean? Why had it all gone wrong? Was it him, or was it these creatures who were there before him? Fate, or fatal weaknesses: what was the nature and name of these incapacities, that had driven each of them to engage in surreptitious and seditious attempts at sabotaging themselves and each other? It crossed Mark's mind to consider the fact that the agents of these activities had all been men. But instantly he classed this thought as planted in his head by some equally malicious influence, a product, as it were, of the same destructive forces that had wrought such havoc in his department.

On his way home Mark realised there'd been no jokes in Howie's briefcase. In real life Howie had been the ace joke-merchant, but this endearing and annoying characteristic, which they would all remember him for, was merely in itself a front, a most gigantic deception.

Charity went to a conference in Bradford for a few days. When she got home, Rachel said, 'Sally rang yesterday. Says she's absolutely desperate to speak to you. You'd better ring her. And one of the goldfish has died. I've put it in the freezer.'

'Oh Rachel, how could you? We haven't got rid of the other two yet. If we go on like this, by the year 2000 the freezer'll be completely full of dead goldfish.'

Charity rang Sally. 'What is it, Sal?'

'I'm pregnant.'

'That's wonderful! *How* pregnant?'

'Eight and a half weeks. I've just had an ultrasound. I've seen the baby's heart beating!'

Charity's stomach took a quick dip. She felt cautious, on Sally's behalf. Supposing something went wrong? Sally was forty-three now, this was her first pregnancy. She might need a lot of luck.

Over the next few weeks, Charity was given regular bulletins. Another ultrasound: the head had grown three centimetres.

Sally had stopped feeling sick in the mornings, and could look fried eggs in the face again. Another check-up with the doctor, who said she was fine, doing as well as a woman half her age. She wanted to know if she should take extra vitamins. 'If you like, if you like. Won't do you any harm,' he said. 'Probably.' He didn't seem awfully interested in the subject of what the mother could do to give her baby a good start in life. Sally saw a consultant privately, he wore a carnation in his buttonhole, had a double-barrelled name, a house in Burford, five sons and a horse. He wasn't the doctor who'd done the in vitro fertilisation; they had a division of labour these days. One took care of the conception, and another the gestation. Between them, they might get it right, and, if they didn't, they had each other to blame. The one who'd finally got the baby going had been terribly chuffed, said Sally, leapt up and danced round the room when he told her the thing had taken. 'Got the little bugger growing at last!' Sally would have preferred a more sentimental notice of her child's materialisation, but the doctor's crude announcement suited the agrarian attitude of the artificial reproduction industry.

The conception had cost Sally and Eric £6,400. Eric had sold his Porsche and bought a small gold Fiat. Sally had borrowed money from her parents. The bank manager had been helpful, too, once he'd known what the money was for. His own wife had been infertile for a while, so he knew at first hand how dreadful reproductive difficulties could be.

Sally gave up her job and stayed at home reading books about childbirth. When they met, she had lists of questions for Charity: 'When do you first feel the baby move? What does it feel like? When do you start getting really fat? Should I massage my nipples for breastfeeding? How long should I breastfeed for? Is it better to give birth standing up or lying down? Will the baby have hair when it's born? Is it true that you feel more sick if you're having a girl?'

It went on and on. The appetite for learning about motherhood, for deciphering the facts behind the fantasies, the orthodoxies behind the fairy stories. There was nothing that Sally didn't want to know except, apparently, her own, or her baby's, fate. She never voiced a single worry about whether the baby would get itself born safely and well. It was as if she repressed even in herself that secret that women are themselves born with, that lodges in their infantile ovaries along with all the eggs that exist in the hope of being enabled to grow, the secret knowledge that everything in life is ultimately or at some stage likely to go wrong. The pregnancy had released in Sally twenty years of pent-up longing for a biological experience and a social role. The longing spilt out of her now in tidal waves, and nothing anyone could say would stop it. She didn't even notice the caution that inserted itself from time to time in Charity's voice.

In the middle of February Mark was going to be fifty. A few days later it was Tom's twenty-first birthday. Charity decided to hold an enormous party. She would invite everyone she knew.

St Valentine's Day 1990. There was a frost that night. Charity woke early and watched Mark sleeping beside her. Unlike James, he rarely snored, but his sleep couldn't be described as the sleep of a baby. He was always restless in it, tossing and turning, uttering expletives, twitching, punching and grabbing the duvet. Sometimes he simply broke out into a sweat: his flesh would be cold, but running with dew. She woke him up. He looked at her with misty eyes. 'Happy birthday, darling.'

'What?'

'Half a century,' she said, 'of sleeping and waking, eating and digesting, loving and hating . . .'

'Okay, Charity, it's too early for that sort of thing.'

But he was pleased, she could see that. 'I've got something to tell you,' she said. 'It's a kind of birthday present.'

He sat up in bed and plumped the pillows so he could see out of the window. It was a greyish sort of day.

'I've decided to marry you,' she announced, brightly.

'Good God.' Mark's stomach lurched down the bed towards his feet. He wriggled his toes, tensely. Why were women always giving him shocks? They were like electricity, always going on and off, and arranging great voltage leaps and short circuits just to make sure people like him didn't get too much sleep. 'That's very nice of you,' he said, 'but tell me, what made you change your mind?'

'Marriage is a metaphor,' she replied, staring at the frost outside. 'I don't know what it's a metaphor for. But, okay, have it. Marry me.'

He didn't know whether she was serious or not.

'I'm completely serious, you know,' she said, offhandedly, and got up to dress.

Mark went to work. By the time Tom got up, the table in the sitting room, pushed back against the windows, was groaning with bottles of wine and fruit juice, and flowers which she'd ordered to be delivered to the house: gladioli and zinnia, irises and chrysanthemums and pots of cyclamen. He stood in the doorway munching a piece of bread. 'You're crazy, Mum, you know. What do you want to do all this for?'

'For you,' she said, 'and for Mark. For the two oldest and most brilliantly wonderful men in my life. Women sometimes want to praise men, you know. Not often. But sometimes. Let us now praise famous men and their fathers who begat us! Don't complain. It doesn't happen often. Just enjoy it.'

Around five, when Charity had sat down exhausted with a cup of tea, the doorbell rang. More flowers, addressed to Mark. She put them on the hall table and walked round them curiously. The little envelope attached to them had a staple in it. She went away and finished her tea. Mark came home a little later and he walked straight past the flowers in the hall. Upstairs, Charity gave him her present, a hardback edition of Dostoevsky's *Crime and Punishment* and a pair of opera glasses. He was pleased, both at the book, which he'd been muttering he wanted to read nearly all his life, and by the glasses, which gave him a new opportunity to see things.

'Did you see the flowers in the hall?' she inquired casually.

'No, who are they for?'

'For you. It's your birthday, remember?'

'Oh.' He went downstairs and she heard him rustling the paper and undoing them. He went into the kitchen and then came back upstairs.

'Who were the flowers from, then?'

He coughed, and headed towards the bathroom. 'From Tessa, actually.'

She went downstairs to look for the card, but of course he'd taken it. Fifty white roses lay on the table, their prickly stems in contact with her glazed gammon, her apricot-stuffed chicken and the fringes of her raspberry tart. She picked them up angrily, telling herself not to be a fool and make a fuss about it, and then swore loudly as the rosy thorns lanced her fingers. She opened the window and threw them into the garden. Then she went upstairs again and started getting ready for the party.

'Where are my flowers?' asked Mark, at five to eight, when they were having a preliminary drink. 'What have you done with them?'

'I threw them in the garden.'

He looked at her wordlessly, put his raincoat on and went into the garden. He came back into the house with his arms full of wet white roses just as Charity was letting in the first guests. Margaret Lacey and her current man, a golden-haired anthropologist from Paris.

Margaret looked at Mark. 'How lovely, flowers for the party!' Her friend shook Charity's hand crisply. Margaret took a little red parcel from her coat pocket and handed it to Mark. 'Happy half a century!' she said. 'I hope you like it.'

Charity could see that Mark was feeling completely unco-ordinated, what with Margaret's parcel and Tessa's wet roses and the belt of his raincoat flapping, and then the doorbell rang again and more people poured into the hall. She summoned Rachel, who was opening crisp packets in the kitchen.

'Darling, could you take these roses from Mark and put them in a vase?' Charity took off Mark's raincoat. He looked relieved. The party had begun.

By eleven o'clock the table had been desecrated and there were people everywhere. Charity was sitting on the stairs next to Ivan Swinhoe, who was chewing a chicken leg with one hand and pulling up one of his socks with the other. 'How are you, Ivan? I haven't seen you for a long time.'

'No, indeed.' Swinhoe gnawed at the chicken leg and looked intently at Charity. Had she guessed it was he who'd sent the letter? 'Well, life goes on, doesn't it? Much the same. Day after day. Haven't got my readership yet. Probably never will. Mother's had a bad bout of flu. Bertrand's been fighting again.'

'Bertrand?'

Swinhoe held the leg, flaglike, up in the air. 'My cat. Splendid animals, cats. Have a cat, do you?'

'No, we only have goldfish.' Charity always felt uncomfortable with Swinhoe. 'Can I relieve you of that bone?'

'What? Oh, yes, thanks.' He handed it to her, looking at her stickily. 'It wasn't me, you know,' he said suddenly, 'I wouldn't like you to think I wanted you to be unhappy.'

'Why would I think you wanted me to be unhappy?'

'Might do.'

'Ivan, what *are* you talking about?'

'Doesn't matter, dear girl. Got some more chicken, have you?'

As she made her way to the kitchen, Charity felt disposed to wonder why men were so obscure. Even invisible. Where was Mark? Nobody seemed to know. Edward Alderson was sitting under the kitchen table with Rose Goodenough. She could hear the conversation from under the tablecloth.

Charity lifted up the edge. 'There *are* chairs, you know.'

Rose smiled at her. 'Sorry, Charity.' Without her glasses she looked quite pretty.

Charity realised she had a headache. It was all that getting up early, stuffing the chicken and getting the ham glazed on time. She pushed her way through the people on the stairs and made it to her bedroom to get some aspirin. The door of the room was closed. She opened it very carefully, in case people were copulating in there. But it was Sally who lay on the bed, her hands folded across her stomach. Her eyes were open; she'd been crying. Charity sat down on the bed gently.

'I'm bleeding, Charity. I just went to the loo, and I'm bleeding. I'm scared. What does it mean?'

'Oh God, Sal, I'm sorry. I don't know what it might mean. You're about three months, aren't you? Sometimes you get a bit of bleeding at this stage. Don't get up. Stay there. I'll go and get Eric.'

'No, I don't want Eric,' she said quickly. 'Don't tell him. Just let me lie here for a bit. Perhaps it'll go away.' Her frightened eyes searched Charity's face for reassurance. 'Things still might be alright, mightn't they?'

'Of course, of course.'

Moving across the room to look for aspirin, Charity glanced up and saw Mark through the window walking up the garden path, wearing his raincoat. She knew instantly where he'd been. He'd been out to phone Tessa. To thank her for the roses. Bile rose in her throat, aspirin and anger mixed. This is it, she said to herself. From now on I watch him, and if there's any other sign of contact I throw him out. He can't fool me. As she left the bedroom, she glanced back at the bed with Sally on it groaning, trying to save a baby, and thought, we're all trying to save something, and we can't. Maybe we can't even save ourselves!

An hour or so later, Tom and his friends left noisily on motorbikes, destination a nightclub. Sally had been put to bed in the spare room, with 20 milligrams of valium inside her. Eric and Margaret Lacey were holding up the sitting room fireplace. Rose and Edward Alderson had started to dance; Swinhoe sat by the music centre, turning the volume up every now and then and changing the discs when they ran out. His shoes tapped whatever rhythm it was, and occasionally his shoulders went up and down as he saw or thought something that amused him. He'd put his gloves on – fingerless gloves – and was picking disinterestedly away at the skin of an orange. Mark was completely drunk. He followed Charity around with a bottle in one hand and a glass in the other. She, feeling horribly sober, carried a sack of rubbish outside to the bin, and he followed her there, trapping her in the narrow space between the houses.

'Fifty years,' he said. 'I've had fifty years. That really is something to celebrate, isn't it? I need a fuck to celebrate. I want a fuck,' he said. 'Charity, come and fuck me!' He giggled to himself. She could scarcely bear to look at him. He put the bottle and the glass down and started trying to kiss her. 'Come on, Charity Alice, a birthday fuck for an old man.' He slipped his hand inside her black silk blouse, and took out her breast and stared at it as though he'd never seen it before. 'Nipples,' he said. 'Wonderful! A nipple!' And he bent his head and licked it. She just let him get on with it, thinking what an old fool he was, until he reached that point, and then, despite herself, she wanted to continue this sexual connection with him. Why not? She'd use him for her own ends and then throw him out. Along with his dead roses.

He started to undo the buttons on her skirt. 'No, don't,' she said, 'let's go inside.' Holding her blouse across her with one hand, she took his hand with the other and stalked past the kitchen window and up the fire escape at the side of the house to a window she remembered opening earlier to get rid of cigarette smoke. She pushed him through it first, all arms and legs; she stood behind, helping bits of him over the window ledge, and fingering them through his clothes as she did so. Then she climbed in. By now there was someone in their bedroom, and Sally was in the spare room with her fetus. They went into Tom's room and locked the door. He pushed her on to the bed and lay on top of her moving in an exaggerated parody of intercourse, giggling happily to himself. 'It's an animal act,' he said, 'that's all it is. We're no better than the animals. But, my God, it's nice!' He opened her blouse and bared her breasts. The walls of the room, like her blouse, were black, and the bed was narrow and unmade and smelt of men. He smoothed her hair away from her face. 'I love you,' he said. He kissed her face all over, like a cat. He took his trousers off then, and his underpants, but forgot his socks, so that she saw him standing in her son's black room, in a white shirt and a white tie and black socks. A man in a room. She closed her eyes. He lay on top of her again, and this time she could feel his flesh. But if his mind was willing and his spirits were high, his flesh wasn't; it did nothing but droop. He didn't seem to be terribly aware of this. But after a bit he moved slightly, and put his fingers inside her and moved them cleverly, as if in a dream, and he put a hand over her mouth (which tasted of herself) and said shhhh, our guests will hear you, this isn't

· 264 ·

the time to shout and cry, it's a time to be silent, a time for sweet silence, to everything its season; and then someone dropped a glass below, and she heard it splinter and at the same time he entered her, very firm and manly he was, and he lay there, quite still and resplendent, and she thought how magnificent this lying together is, this embrace between man and woman, how timeless, how essential, how much I love him, how much I can forgive him now and for ever, and then after a while he started to snore in her ear, and she realised he'd been asleep for quite a long time.

14 ✳ TIME TO KILL

'He always has "other things to do" with his time; whereas she has time to kill; and he considers much of the time she gives him not as a gift but as a burden' – *The Second Sex*, p. 409

Since it was in the nature of Mark Carleton's relationships with women that their conduct continually surprised him, the letter from Margaret Lacey he found on his desk one day was merely part of a familiar pattern. As soon as he started to read it, he recognised it for what it was: another electric shock.

'Dear Mark,' he read, 'Enclosed with this letter is my official resignation from the department. I feel, however, that both as a friend and as my Head of Department, I owe you an explanation of my decision.

'It will no doubt seem sudden to you. But I've been thinking for some time that I am something of a misfit in the academic world. I have skills I can't use in it, or when I try to use them, I meet resistance. I think you'll know what I mean.' (Mark didn't have the faintest idea.)

'We only have one life, Mark. Mine is half over, so I'm going to make changes before it's too late. Mack' (here Mark didn't at first know who she was talking about) 'has asked me to join him in Bhutan.'

Jesus. McKinnon and Lacey. That was a combination he'd never thought of. Not that he was particularly good at thinking of combinations.

'As you probably know, he's inherited some money. It'll be

enough for us to live off for a time. I'm going to try my hand at writing. I'm surprised to find myself finally in love, but I don't need to talk to you about that, do I?'

Didn't she? The concept of Margaret in love felt to Mark like a contradiction in terms.

'I realise I should give three months' notice. But under the circumstances perhaps this could be waived. I'm planning to leave for Bhutan on Friday. Before that I can be reached at home.

'Yours, as ever, Margaret.'

Margaret's letter didn't encourage in Mark an enhanced respect for women's sanity. But he envied Margaret her decision. Not to live in Bhutan with a computer programmer-turned-horticultura-list, of course (what would the fate of the handbag be in Bhutan, he wondered), but the wonderful quality that enabled Margaret to decide what to do and then do it.

'Margaret's resigned,' he told Charity at breakfast the next day.

She looked up from her mail, a moaning letter from her mother, with an expression of interest on her face that he realised was rare these days.

'But why would she want to do that?'

'She's going to Bhutan.'

'With McKinnon? My God. I had no idea they were having a thing, did you?'

'No. But then you told me I never notice anything. So you see, we aren't the only ones, Charity.'

'To have a secret affair in the department?' A net curtain of nostalgia dropped momentarily across her eyes. 'No. Nothing we did was original, I suppose. But what's Margaret going to do in Bhutan? Collect orchids or whatever with McKinnon? I don't believe it. It's incredible, really.'

'She says she's going to write.'

'Well, I hope she succeeds. At least she's getting away from all this.'

'Charity,' said Mark, 'do you think you ought to see a psychiatrist?'

She stopped chewing her toast abruptly. 'Why do you say that?'

'I don't think you're very happy,' he ventured.

'That's true.' She put the rest of her toast down. 'Of course I'm not happy.' She started to cry. 'My God, how could I be? With you behaving like this!'

'Like what?'

'You know what I mean.'

'I think you should go and see someone. Do you want me to find someone for you? I think Margaret knows someone at the Tavistock . . .'

'Fuck Margaret.'

'Pardon?'

'You did, didn't you! And who are you fucking now? Why can't you stop it, Mark? Why can't you stop behaving like a bloody man and start behaving like a human being!'

He stared at her.

'And then you have the phenomenal cheek to suggest I go and see a psychiatrist! You know what kind of suggestion that is, don't you?'

He shook his head.

'Yes, you do. Of course you do. When men have problems, they offload them on to women, so they can send them to have their heads shrunk and they don't need to think about their own. There's nothing wrong with me, Mark. But there is something wrong with you.'

It crossed Mark's mind to remember Pascoe's wife's psychological disorder, not to mention the ineffable wisdom of Howie's secret diary. He got up from the table and put his coat on. He placed a hand on her shoulder. 'Don't cry, Charity. Think about what I said. I only said it because I thought it might help you. I don't want you to be unhappy. I've got to go. I'm sorry, but I've got to go to a meeting.'

She would have thrown something at him, but she remembered throwing a sock at James in that very room, and she didn't want to repeat history any more than she could help.

When he'd gone, she went out into the garden. It was mid-March: the grass crackled under her feet. As she breathed, the air made patterns with her breath. It was very cold.

Rachel stuck her head round the kitchen window. 'Mum? Where are my black tights? What are you doing out there? It's *freezing*!' The window slammed shut. Charity went inside. 'Are you alright, Mum?'

Charity looked at Rachel and saw herself many decades ago. 'Yes, darling.'

'You're not.'

This was a statement. Rachel put her arms round her mother. Charity buried her face in Rachel's soft black hair. 'Oh Mum, what's the matter?'

Charity sniffed and tried to laugh weakly. 'I'm tired. Didn't sleep very well. Or maybe it's my age.'

Rachel pushed her away and searched her moist face. 'It's not your age. You're still young and beautiful, Mum.'

'Forty-two.'

'So what? It's not your age, it's men, isn't it?'

'I suppose so.'

'I'll make you a cup of tea.' As she busied herself with the kettle and mugs, Rachel went on talking. 'You know what? I've decided to give up men. I just don't think it's worth it. It's too much hassle, isn't it?'

How could one decide to give up men at sixteen? At that age Charity hadn't yet decided to take them up.

'Why do you stay with him, Mum?'

'I love him.'

'So what?'

'Is that what you say to everything?'

'Not everything.'

'I need him.'

'A woman needs a man like a fish needs a bicycle. Slogan of the 1970s women's movement.'

'Yes, I remember. Well, I don't know what women need men for,' she said.

'Here's your tea, Mum. Drink it. It'll make you feel better. It's more reliable than men, tea is.'

Charity sipped her tea. Rachel sat down. 'Seriously, though, don't you think you ought to get rid of him? Properly? Find yourself a new man. Marry a millionaire. With a swimming pool. If you're going to have a man, you might as well do it properly.'

'Why are you so much more sensible than me?'

'Because I haven't been corrupted yet. You should listen to us, we've got it right. It's your generation that's got it wrong.' The tone of her voice changed slightly. 'Nuclear war, unemployment and poverty, AIDS. You haven't exactly made a great success of it, have you? It's a wonder any of us have survived at all. We all ought to be raving looneys.' She paused and noticed the worried expression on Charity's face. 'Sorry, Mum. Didn't mean to depress you. Why don't you take the day off? Go for a walk in the country or something?'

'I said all that in my book, you know,' she chided Rachel.

'Did you? I don't know. I didn't read it. Never read your mother's books, that's what I say. I mean that in the nicest possible way, Mum.'

'I know you do.'

She was watching television about two weeks later when Mark rang to say he would be late home. 'I've got to go and see Jane,' he explained. 'She wants to talk to me about Susan. Another crisis.'

After she'd put the phone down, she began to wonder. Following the abortion, Susan had had a couple of difficult years, but recently seemed to have calmed down. Moreover, Jane was now ensconced with a new man, and was said to be blooming. The idea that she'd call Mark at the first sign of trouble didn't really make sense.

She picked up the phone and dialled Jane's number. 'I'm sorry to trouble you, Jane,' she enunciated carefully, 'it's Charity Walton here.'

'Hallo, Charity.'

'I wondered if you could give Mark a message for me. He told me he was coming to see you this evening, and I need to speak to him about something rather urgently.' She was pleased with the even tenor of her voice. No hint of panic there.

'Did he? Did he really? Well, he's telling you lies, Charity.

He's not here. He's not coming here. I haven't spoken to him for weeks. You'd better face the facts this time, Charity.' The line went dead.

Charity tidied the sitting room and the kitchen, turned off the lights and went upstairs. Rachel was out, at a friend's. She undressed and got into bed and lay there in the darkness. She got up again, the bedroom was cold. She turned the thermostats on the radiators up and plugged in an electric fire. She switched on both bars and positioned it so it looked at her. The phone rang. She got out of bed again and unplugged it. Then she lay in the accumulating fug of the bedroom, pulling the covers round her, trying to comfort herself. The room was like a greenhouse now. In its fetid warmth, she began to feel a little more secure. I am tired, she thought, I've been working too hard. I've been struggling for too long. With the children, with Mark and, before that, with James. I've been struggling all my life. And for what? What have I got? I've got tired. I've worn myself out. I've published books, I've reared children, I've made beds and lain in them, washed a thousand dirty dishes and dirty bottoms, created decades of happy Christmases and Easters and smiles on other people's faces, but I'm not happy. I'm not happy, because I haven't cared for myself. I'm a deprived person. Emotionally deprived: perhaps I *should* see a psychiatrist.

It was raining. She could hear the rain dripping on to the rooftops and on and off the trees that were still clothed in the insignia of winter. It would be Easter soon, and spring. Buds would appear on trees, and pink blossom lighten the sky. Blossom, what an odd word. She repeated it to herself. Blossom, blossom. She remembered as a child walking in the country with her father one spring and seeing some and picking it and taking it home and putting it in a vase in her bedroom, only to watch it disintegrate under her very eyes. 'Why didn't you tell the child not to bring that stuff into the house?' demanded her mother.

'She thought they were flowers, I didn't want to disillusion her,' said her father.

'That's what life's about,' decreed her mother crossly, sweeping up the fallen blossom. 'She must learn to be disillusioned.'

Charity turned over, wanting to blot the scene from her mind. There was hardly anything she wanted to think about.

When Mark came home, a few minutes before midnight, he thought Charity was asleep. She lay silently, hardly breathing. He had been with Tessa, in her flat. He was tired. He got into bed and closed his eyes, thankfully. Charity listened to him going to sleep, and she heard the front door open and close again as Rachel came home. She herself felt wide awake. She had no idea what was to happen next. 'What happens next?' she remembered Mark asking in the bank in Bordeaux. 'Now we've met, and fallen in love, and been to bed, what happens next?'

What was that quote from Thornton Wilder? 'There are more people wanting to break out of houses than wanting to break into them.'

It had stopped raining. Mark was sleeping. Anger rose inside her like hot oil. She got up, put on her dressing gown, snapped on the light and stood over the sleeping Mark.

'Get out,' she said, 'now. I never want to see you again.'

Mark blinked. 'What? What did you say?'

'I'm getting rid of you. Finally,' she said.

'Hm.' He really was very sleepy and he wanted to go back to sleep. He was used to these nocturnal performances of hers. She was generally alright in the morning.

'Mark.'

He opened his eyes fully to the light.

'I mean it. Get out.'

'But I thought everything was alright?' The words stumbled out of him, half-formed.

'I told you, if I ever had the slightest suspicion you were seeing her again you'd be out.'

Vaguely he remembered this. 'But I'm not. It's only you now, Charity.' He extended a limp hand to her from under the bedclothes.

'Balls.' She didn't usually use words like that. 'You were with her tonight.'

'I wasn't.'

'You were.' He looked so useless and sickly lying there. She hit

· 272 ·

him on the face. He sprang up like a jack-in-the-box, alarmed by this change in the usual procedure.

'You hit me!'

She threw back her head and laughed. 'You don't believe it, you just don't believe it! Listen to me, Mark Carleton. You're not God's gift to women, after all. You're not the eighth wonder of the world. You're actually a walking disaster, a total mess. Get out of my life.'

He couldn't bear her laughing at him, so he hit her back. They were rolling on the floor like puppies when Rachel burst in.

'What the hell are you two doing?'

Shamefaced, Charity stood up. Mark, who was naked, grabbed the duvet, and held it in front of him.

'Can't you grow up? Can't you stop making a mess of your lives and everybody else's?'

Charity took a step towards her daughter and tried to touch her.

'Don't, Mum. I don't like you very much at the moment.'

'I'm sorry, Rachel.'

'Don't apologise, Mum. You're such a joke. You can't expect me to take you seriously.'

Mark got back into bed with the duvet. 'Get out of there,' shouted Charity.

'Oh come on, Charity, please. Let's talk about it in the morning.'

'We will not! I want you out now.'

Rachel tried to restrain her mother's flailing arms, but she might as well have tried to halt a windmill in a gale.

'Leave me alone! Stop patronising me! I know what ought to happen next, he has to go! I can't bear it any more!' She was wailing now, not shouting.

'You're pathetic,' said Rachel quietly.

'Oh, it's all my fault, is it?' Charity was shouting again. 'He has nothing to do with it, I suppose!'

'I didn't say that. But you've had something to do with him, haven't you? Too much, for far too long. You've made a fool of yourself, mother, it's time to stop now.'

'Don't talk to me like that! I'm your mother!'

'And a bloody awful one, at that!'

Charity grabbed Rachel's face in her hands. 'What did you say? Do you know what you said? You don't want me to survive this, do you?'

'Let go of me!' They were like two cats, clawing at one another.

Mark started to get out of bed, thinking that he ought to try to stop this thing between the two women. Rachel kicked her mother in the groin, and Charity folded up with pain and lay on the floor groaning; Rachel fled. He stood for a while looking at Charity, and then went downstairs and heated up some milk for both of them, and brought it upstairs with a packet of biscuits. He picked her off the floor and gave her the milk.

'You're right, of course,' he admitted. 'It is over. We both have to accept that. I'll go in the morning.'

It was a peaceful departure. He showered, dressed and packed a suitcase. 'I'll fetch the rest of my things later when you're not here,' he said, and telephoned for a taxi. When he'd given the taxi driver Tessa's address, he straightened up and looked back at the house. Charity was standing in the door in her green dressing gown. A faint sun shone sideways on her hair, her tautly folded arms, the houses with their coloured front doors, and the squalor and magnificence of the universe and the horrible passions of men and women.

Much later in the day, he clocked up the date in his head: April the first.

'She's in labour ward three,' said the duty midwife, her blue uniform matching the night sky. 'She's quite distressed. We've given her a sedative, just a mild one. We can't give her much, you see, because of the baby.'

'Yes, of course. Is her husband with her?'

'He was. He's gone now. Said he had to go home for something. Between you and me,' the midwife lowered her voice and watched the doorway carefully, 'Mr Lawrence wasn't much help. Some of them aren't, you know. It's like animals. The mare kicks the stallion away when she's in labour. Mostly the males keep away. Women get on much better without them.'

She showed Charity into labour ward three, having first given her a white gown to wear. Sally lay on her side watching the electronic monitor which was drawing patterns on graph paper. She clutched the pillow tightly. The needles on the graph paper leapt up and did a dance the shape of a hill. Sally's face clenched with pain, and her hands dug into the pillow.

'Sally, it's me.'

Sally opened her eyes. 'Aha . . .' she said, 'it hurts. They won't give me anything for it. I wish they would.' She shut her eyes tightly.

Charity fetched a stool and sat beside the bed. She picked one of Sally's anguished hands off the pillow and tried to comfort it. 'They don't want to give you anything much for the pain for the baby's sake, Sal,' she said. 'The baby needs every kind of help it can get.'

Another contraction seized the monitor and Sally. When it had passed, she said, 'I don't see how this baby's going to make it anyway. All this pain. It's like mountains. It's clamping down over the baby. I can feel it. My womb. It's my womb that's hurting the baby.'

Another contraction. The midwife came in. Charity moved away from the bed. The midwife held Sally's hand and checked her pulse against the upside-down silver watch pinned to her chest. 'Could you just move on to your back for me please, Mrs Lawrence? Just for a minute? I want to listen to baby's heart.'

Painfully, Sally changed position and the midwife pushed up the white gown and bared Sally's small globe of a tummy, the thin pigmented brown line of pregnancy streaking its middle. The midwife pressed the metal stethoscope to one side of the brown line, and leaned her ear against it. 'Ow!' shouted Sally. 'I'm having a contraction!'

'Alright, dear, just a minute.' The midwife went on pressing. She moved the stethoscope slightly, tried again.

'Oh stop it! Please stop it!' She took the instrument away,

covered Sally's tummy and moved her, not without gentleness, on to her left side. Then she flicked the graph paper up and away from the machine so she could look at it. After studying it for a few moments, she left the room.

Sally was sobbing. 'Charity, where are you?' Charity moved her stool back to the bed. It was herself she saw labouring there, herself, her own mother, her daughter, all women, going through this climactic pain in order to give life. She stroked Sally's hair. It was wet at the temples. 'Shhh.' She got up and found a washcloth in Sally's toilet bag, moistened it at the sink and carefully drew it across Sally's hot head. 'Sh . . . sh . . . It won't last forever, Sal, it'll be over soon, you'll see.'

'It's only twenty-six weeks,' said Sally, in a small voice. 'Only twenty-six weeks. Six and a half months. That's not long enough. My baby hasn't had long enough, Charity. It's not going to make it. It can't.'

'It might!' She went on stroking Sally's head and she looked at the clock – eleven thirty – and out of the window. She thought she could almost see a star.

The door clanged behind her. The midwife came back in, this time with a doctor in tow. 'Doctor's just going to examine you, Mrs Lawrence. Would you mind leaving the room?' She looked at Charity pointedly. Charity got up to go.

'Don't go, Charity, please don't leave me.' Sally's eyes were terribly afraid.

'Let her stay,' ordered the doctor. He was young. He looked quite nice. He went to work, washed his hands, put on gloves. The midwife moved Sally down the bed, shifted her buttocks to the edge of the hinged bit of the bed, that could be let down when people wanted to put their hands inside women to find out what was going on in there.

Throughout the examination Sally screamed. Charity held her hand and talked to her, but Sally didn't seem to hear. She was lost in the pain, away in a place of her own.

'Fully dilated,' said the doctor, 'call the paediatrician.'

The midwife flew to the phone on the wall. 'Bleep Dr Greenwood, please. It's urgent.' She replaced the phone.

'We'll have to use forceps,' said the doctor. 'Quick, there isn't much time.' The midwife scrubbed her hands and then, just as she was turning the taps off with her elbows, the doctor said abruptly, 'The head's on the perineum.'

Charity saw with fascination, and with horror at herself for this, the doctor's hands between Sally's legs, and then Sally almost insentient and beyond consciousness convulsing her body in an enormous push, and this tiny blue baby shooting out into the doctor's hands, scarcely bigger than one of them. As the baby was born the doors opened, and four or five people burst into the room. One of them took the baby and put it on some sort of machine. Charity couldn't see properly what was happening to it. There was a lot of noise and bustle. The doctor who had caught the baby was covered in blood, and the midwife was sticking a needle in Sally's bottom. 'She's having a bit of a bleed,' said the doctor. The midwife handed the needle to the doctor and leaned over Sally's still expanded tummy, felt for something and began to massage it. The doctor watched the stream of blood trickling down the bed. 'That's better,' he said.

Sally was white and crying. 'I'm going to be sick,' she said. Charity, the only unoccupied person in the room, found a metal kidney-shaped dish and gave it to her, and she retched into it, bringing up nothing but a few drops of fluid. She sank back. 'Where's my baby?' she asked. 'Is it dead?'

'I don't know,' said Charity. 'I'll find out.' She walked over to the group of white-coated doctors in the corner.

'Please keep out of the way,' said the midwife sternly.

'She wants to know what's happening to the baby,' said Charity.

'We're doing all we can,' replied the midwife.

'I don't know, Sal,' said Charity. 'I think they're trying to make the baby breathe.'

The clock on the wall moved noisily each minute, and many seemed to have passed before a tiny squawk came from the corner of the room. The squawk grew and expanded into a definite cry. The cry of a baby. Then everything was bustle again. The tiny body was wrapped tightly in white blankets, and the paediatrician flashed it in front of Sally's face. 'A little girl, Mrs Lawrence. She had some trouble getting going, we're going to put her in the skerboo. I'm afraid you'll have to wait to hold her.' And then they were all gone.

'What's the skerboo?' said Sally to Charity.

'I don't know,' said Charity. 'What's the skerboo?' she said to the midwife.

'Special care baby unit,' said the midwife, as though they were stupid not to know.

'I want to hold her,' said Sally. 'Did you see her, Charity? What did she look like?'

'Like a little old man,' said Charity.

Sally laughed. 'Oh, Charity! I've had a baby! I've had a daughter! I'm a mother at last!'

Sally said she was called Annie. She weighed exactly 650 grams or one pound seven ounces. You could have held her in your hand if you'd been allowed to, but she lay there resembling a monkey in a glass cage attached to all sorts of pipes and tubes and machines that sustained her premature life.

Sally spent hours by the incubator, willing her to live and stroking her tiny form with a finger whenever the nurses allowed her to. Charity spent a lot of time there as well, feeling that her presence might be some comfort to Sally, but also to herself, for Annie had turned into a focus for her own bereavement. Would the child live or die?

'About fifty fifty,' said Dr Greenwood, the paediatrician. 'She's been born in the right place. We're doing all we can,' he repeated.

'But is it enough?' whispered Sally.

When Eric visited the nursery he seemed to be in the way. His distress was for Sally, not for the baby, whom he hardly dared claim as his own. He bought a little pink teddy bear in one day. Charity couldn't help matching its colour to the blossom of her childhood, which had never managed to sustain its own picking.

Annie developed severe respiratory distress syndrome. Her lungs weren't mature enough to work properly. After two weeks, this seemed to be a little better, but by then she was severely jaundiced. The yellow tint of her skin was obvious even to the untutored eye. By now her weight had fallen to only fifteen ounces.

Day after day Sally laboured away on the breast pump collecting milk for Annie, which was sent to her stomach in a tube. After a few weeks, it became harder to get milk out. Sally was very anxious and tense. She wasn't sleeping. The hospital sent her home, thinking this might relax her. But back in the smart Chelsea house, standing in the carefully prepared nursery, Sally couldn't cope at all. Her milk dried up completely. 'Is there nothing I can do for my baby?' she asked Charity pathetically one night. 'Is there nothing I can do to give her a proper chance of life? I couldn't keep her inside me for long enough. I shot her out into the world before she was ready. And now I can't even give her the nourishment she deserves.'

'Don't worry, Mrs Lawrence,' said the sister in charge of the SCBU, 'we've got a breast milk bank here. Your baby can go on having breast milk because that's what she needs.'

'But I don't want her to have anybody else's milk but mine,' wailed Sally.

In the fourth week of her life when, if born then, she would still have been classed as very premature, Annie developed necrotising enterocolitis, which meant she had to have an operation to remove some of her intestines. It was beyond Charity's comprehension as to how such a tiny little being could survive such desecration, but she did. Thinner and paler than before, but still technically alive. The two women stayed in the hospital throughout the operation, and saw the baby afterwards. 'She's a fighter,' said the man who had plunged a knife into her doll-sized abdomen.

'She can't survive all this, can she, Charity?'

'I don't know. We must just wait and see.'

They were onlookers in a medical drama. Though one of them was the baby's mother, even she only had a walk-on part. Eric decided to talk to the consultant about Annie's future quality of life, should she make it through these grotesque crises.

'About a quarter of these babies have some sort of handicap, and some of those are mild. The rest are perfectly normal. I shouldn't worry, Mr Lawrence.' The consultant was a busy man.

'But what about Annie?'

'What about her?'

'Which of those groups will she be in?'

'Too soon to tell. All we can deal in at this stage is statistics, Mr Lawrence. Don't worry, we're doing our best.'

But was their best what Sally and Eric really wanted them to do? Was life always better than death? Whose baby was she anyway?

'I want her to live,' said Sally one day, gazing at the baby lying on its side, arms and legs sticklike, half-extended. 'I do want her to live. But I want her to have life. If she can't have life, what's the point? There wouldn't be any point in any of this.'

She surveyed the room full of sickly infants, dedicated health professionals and costly technology. Charity could do nothing except hold her hand and squeeze it with a gesture that said, I know what you're saying, and it doesn't only apply to babies. It's a general statement about the futility of certain goals, which become quite futile precisely at the point at which one knows they are the only thing one is pursuing.

On 24 May, Sally rang Charity and asked her to meet her at the hospital. She said Dr Greenwood had telephoned her and told her he was concerned about Annie's condition and would like to discuss it with her and Eric. Eric wouldn't be available till later: he was in transit from a meeting in Liverpool.

In the lift to the sixth floor, Charity had a sense of impending doom. Through the ward door she could see Dr Greenwood standing by Annie's incubator with his hand protectively on it. Sally's back was hunched hopelessly between the door and the guarded look on Dr Greenwood's face.

Looking at Annie in her little box, Charity saw that she looked different today, but didn't at first realise how.

'You've taken all the tubes away,' she said, half-excitedly, 'does that mean she's getting better?'

'I'm afraid not,' said Dr Greenwood. He had kind eyes, which resembled those of a spaniel in a television dogfood advertisement. 'As I explained to Mrs Lawrence earlier, we did a series of EEGs last night, and I'm afraid there's no sign of brain activity any more. We've agreed that the best thing to do is to take her off the ventilator. Haven't we, Mrs Lawrence?'

Sally didn't take her eyes off Annie. Dr Greenwood looked directly at Charity. 'Unfortunately, I gather Mr Lawrence isn't in London at the moment. But Mrs Lawrence wanted to take the decision now. Didn't you, Mrs Lawrence?'

He seemed worried. Charity put her hand on Sally's shoulder. Without moving or changing the focus of her regard, which was inexorably fixed on the little limp baby, Sally said, 'He means her brain is dead. Even if she lived she'd be a vegetable.'

The doctor nodded.

'But she's still breathing!' protested Charity, watching the rise and fall of Annie's chest.

He nodded again. 'That's right.'

'She won't go on breathing for very long, probably,' said Sally in a monotone.

'Mrs Lawrence.' The doctor now put his hand on Sally's shoulder. 'I wonder if you might like to hold her for a little while. Some mothers like to do that. And perhaps we could make a phone call for you, see when your husband is likely to arrive?'

Charity watched while the incubator was opened and Annie, still breathing, was given to Sally. A nurse went to phone Eric's office. They were shown to a little room, away from the main bustle of the unit. Sally held the baby very carefully. She stroked her cheek with her finger. The baby's eyes were closed. At the moment when Eric appeared in the doorway the other side of the unit, separated from his wife and child by a sea of incubators, Charity looked up and saw him standing there, and Annie died.

15 ✳ RESEARCHING LOST TIME

'In this perspective she reviews the past; the moment has come to draw a line across the page, to make up her accounts; she balances her books . . .

In particular, the woman who "has lived" knows men as no man does, for she has seen in man not the image on public view but the contingent individual, the creature of circumstance . . .' – *The Second Sex*, pp. 279, 296

The house was at the end of a track three kilometres from the nearest village. Near it was one other house, a new cement-rendered affair, built by a farmer with one adolescent son. They did shooting practice together, and the father was teaching the son to drive on the flaxen-haired field at the back of the house. These were the only sounds that disturbed the house's peace, save for the calls of birds and the winging of other wild life about the place, cows and sheep in neighbouring fields, and the expeditions of the mouse that lived in the kitchen. Apples fell when it rained or when the wind blew; the countryside was rich and fertile; its farmers were not poor, stuffing ducks for *foie gras*, manufacturing nut oil and selling their local *prune* – a racy plum liqueur – under the counter.

The main living area of the house had three views, south, east and west; two showed you hills blue in the distance, the other the track away from the house through fields in which, when it rained, people came out to look for mushrooms. Sally and Charity rented the house for three weeks in August. Charity wrote out a list of things to take based on what the agent had said about it:

coffee machine
music centre
small television, a video and films
2 duvets
3 lamps
box of candles
mousetraps
insect spray

They also took a box of books each. Sally brought: Patricia Highsmith, Dorothy Sayers, science fiction, including three books by the radical feminist science fiction writer Olanda Hughes, and some Jane Austen. Charity's selection was mostly poetry: Shakespearean sonnets, John Donne, W. H. Auden, Plath, Emily Dickinson. She also had with her the whole of Proust's *A la recherche du temps perdu*.

When they arrived, they stocked up on food and other necessities: cheese, eggs, vegetables, fruit, long-lasting *charcuterie*, long-life milk, two dozen bottles of the regional wine, a damson-tinted liquid, a supply of batteries for the music centre (since the electricity supply to the house was erratic), and a yellow chicken complete with head, to eat that evening. They didn't intend to leave the house very often. This was their siege on the external world, their chance to lock themselves up and untangle the meaning of what had happened to them. They had sustained two separate and different events, both involving loss. Charity's loss was that of the most important relationship she had ever had with a man; Sally's event was death, not only of a baby but of her hopes of motherhood.

When they arrived, Charity put a large photograph of Mark on the stone sill under the window with a view over the hills.

'What did you do that for?'

'It's a shrine – I'm going to light a candle to it every night!'

'You're not serious?'

'I might be. Anyway, I want it there now. I'll get rid of it after a bit.'

Sally opened her handbag and took out of it the black and white print the hospital had given her of her dead baby. She put it alongside the photograph of Mark. From their stone resting place the grinning man with the wild hair, and the little white baby with its crab-like hands folded across its tiny chest, regarded the two women as they moved around the house.

For the first few nights, they both took sleeping pills, because they didn't want to dream. But as the days passed, they began to relax and didn't need the pills any more. Life became simpler: there were few decisions to make; which books to read, which music to listen to, which film to watch in the evening, whether to eat a round or plum-shaped tomato.

They began to sleep, and, eventually, to dream. In ten hours or so each night, it seemed to them that they lived through hundreds of dreams.

After breakfast Charity took Proust into the garden. She was in the middle of 'Swann in Love', and had reached that part where Swann is captured by jealousy. Odette turns him away one evening, she has a headache and doesn't want 'cattleaya' – their pet word for love-making. After this rejection, Swann goes home, a disappointed man. But then it strikes him that Odette might have been expecting another lover, so he returns to the house and sees a light behind her shutters. Knowing the truth, his 'torment' becomes less acute, simply because it's less vague. He recognises that understanding her deception carries an intellectual pleasure with it – it's *interesting* to be in love, to be immersed in the details of another person's life and the emotions one feels for them. Swann knows that knocking on Odette's shutters to notify her of his presence will make her detest him forever, yet his desire for the truth is stronger than his wish to preserve the relationship. So he does knock, and they turn out to be not her shutters after all. Swann has got the wrong house.

The man was absurd, he'd made a mistake; any other writer would have left it there. But Proust dredges everything he can out of Swann's mistake. Jealousy is the shadow of love; from then on, every time Odette smiles at him, the scene of deception, which was actually a scene of not-deception, will come back to him. The actuality is used by Swann's imagination perpetually to support a passion he already had – the passion to be jealous of Odette.

Charity sees herself in Swann. Her love for Mark was jealous; somewhere along the line jealousy became its dominant mode. This meant that her gratification, external to their relationship, became the only truth in which she was interested.

Now she wonders whether what she did was right. The jealousy was hers; the fault, in this particular case, not his. At the same time as she wonders this, she thinks what kind of world it is that gives women back the bad feelings they have, and says to them, these are yours, they're nothing to do with us. No, she was jealous because Mark *made* her jealous. He had other women, she lined them up in her head. Mark's women. She did not count herself among them. But rendering them as objects enabled her to take a simplifying perspective; in the light of which her jealousy amazingly dissolved itself like the sugar in a pan of boiling redcurrants.

She stared at the ashblond field ahead of her, stared and stared. A lapwing called from a pine tree, and then another. They brought to mind another scene, the forest in Sweden where she had awoken early and told her husband their marriage was over, and he had then told her the same thing, in his own voice.

On the night of the day Charity imagined Mark and Tessa had got married (she didn't really know when it was to be) she came upstairs immersed in a tiredness of such proportions that she fell on to the bed and slept straightaway in her clothes, surrounded by books, a torch, an empty yoghurt carton, dried flowers. Her first dream then was of her father's study in the house in Kent, a small upstairs room, a highly privileged place. A men's room, of a kind.

Her second dream was not of a room but of a field, a seemingly open space. But in the field Mark was standing, wearing his oldest clothes, looking quite dishevelled and disreputable. The sky was full of clouds. Next to him there was a group of women wearing white wedding dresses and giggling amongst themselves. There was space between them and Mark, and the field sloped at that point, so that the women were at a lower level than the man. Mark was watching them. The sun came out from behind the clouds, but strangely low on the horizon, as though it were about to set. In response to this, Mark took off all his clothes. The women turned and looked at him, still giggling. Then they stopped giggling, and there was complete silence: all the commotions of the universe ceased. It was exactly that silence that happens during an eclipse of the sun. All the sounds of natural life are stilled as the darkness tells the birds not to sing any more and animals not to howl with hunger or happiness. The women threw back their veils and looked at Mark, but, horribly, their eyes, this time, were all his: each woman's face was decorated with a pair of Mark's eyes. So his eyes looked into his eyes, and at the same time his white thread of a penis moved and grew until it was quite gigantic and pointed directly at the sun. He placed one hand on it, but his hand wasn't big enough to go round it, and it became very heavy, so he had to move his legs apart in order to sustain its weight. Something odd happened then to the women: they shrank in size to become white flowers in the field mingled with the grass in which Mark's feet were planted, and in which this monstrous malformation of a man now stood.

Charity awoke from this dream highly aroused. Since Mark had left, she'd been leading a sexless existence. Her emotions had become detached from that part of her body. But now she awoke with this unbearable sexual hunger for the man who had gone. The hunger was only for him. Her hands between her legs explored an area she had no longer wanted to know, but despite this she gave away instantly to a powerful orgasm, and then another; and then she took a decision to rid herself of Mark with the next one: its contractions would totally expunge her sexual memory of him. She took herself to the plateau before the exploding moment, and held herself there, as he, in her dream, had held himself, unable to proceed because the enormity of the task defeated his expertise. The difference was that she knew she could make it.

With the last orgasm, the light of the dawn came with a blinding flash, and then was over.

'Was that you crying in the night?' asked Sally the next morning.

'It could have been.' Rachmaninov number one poured out of the music centre – the new laser technology had improved the sound one could get out of these very small machines.

'In my dream,' sighed Sally, 'I had a baby again. Two of them, this time. The hospital said I had to choose. They said one was dead and one was alive, one was a boy and one a girl, but they didn't know which was which. Remember that game when you have something in one hand and you hold up two clenched fists and people have to guess which hand it's in? It felt like that. Oh God, I'm fed up with all these dreams!'

Charity was staring at Sally. 'I've just realised there's no mirror in this house. We're going to be here for three weeks, and then we're going to emerge and we won't have seen ourselves for three weeks. Now you, Sal,' the music roared into the atmosphere, so she had to raise her voice, 'you're beginning to look quite awful. You've been wearing the same clothes for a week, and your hair needs washing!'

'How can I tell that if I can't see myself?'

'You can't. You have to do it by smell. My hair smells, or something about me smells. It's time to get washed, I think.'

'I think we're going mad, actually.'

'Could be. Now,' Charity moved to point out of the window, 'that tree out there is obscuring our view. I can't bear a place without a view, can you? I'm going to get a saw so we can get rid of it.'

She got in the car and drove to the nearest town. She went to a likely-looking shop. 'Avez-vous une scie?' she asked.

'Pour quoi, exactement?'

'Pour couper des branches.'

He raised his eyebrows. 'J'ai celle-ci, une peu petite, ou celle-là.'

'Non. La petite, s'il vous plaît.'

She drove straight back again, and stood on a chair under the apple tree. The saw was effective. Sally held on to the back of the chair. The tree cracked suddenly. 'Look out!' Charity sprang back as the branch fell on top of the chair. They collapsed against the side of the house.

She went upstairs to examine the effects of their labours. 'That's better,' she declared, 'but I need to get that one now' –

pointing at a huge lichen-covered branch arching out over the fields. She went to work again, but after a quarter of an hour's vigorous sawing the branch had refused to budge. 'We need a rope, Sally. Go and see if you can find some rope – or string, or anything.'

Sally went to the barn, which was full of dusty wine bottles, and found some lengths of thin rope. They tied some together and put a stone on one end. Charity threw the end with the stone on it over the branch she'd sawed through, and the stone got stuck. She hit it with a piece of dead wood, jumping up to reach it. 'This is ridiculous,' said Sally, 'the whole thing is absurd. This apple tree doesn't even belong to us. It belongs to whoever owns the house, and they're going to be furious.'

'I don't care. It's in the way. We're doing the tree a service, anyway,' she stopped jumping for a moment, 'cutting off all this dead wood. This tree doesn't want this wood,' she proclaimed, 'it can't make use of it, and it can't grow any more while it still has this.'

They finally got the stone to hang down, and, taking both ends of the rope, pulled the offending branch until it severed itself from the trunk and crashed to the ground.

Inside the house, they celebrated with a bottle of wine. 'You realise all this stuff about trees and dead wood and views and things is all deeply symbolic, don't you?' commented Sally.

'Yes, doubtless. But it's making us feel better, isn't it? You know what I'm going to do next?'

'I can't imagine. Tell me.'

'I'm going to burn Mark's photo.' As she got up to fetch it, she saw the look of pain on Sally's face. 'But you mustn't burn the one of Annie. You should keep that. Here,' she took it from its cold resting place on the stone sill, 'take it. Look at it, look at her.'

Sally did.

'That was your daughter. That is your daughter. You conceived her and gave birth to her. You're a mother. No one can take that away from you. Losing a child is worse than losing a man. Men can be made to disappear, but children are for ever.'

Tears fell down Sally's face, and on to her crumpled dress.

'Put it away now,' commanded Charity. 'You've looked at it long enough.'

Sally put the photograph in her pocket, and wiped her tears with the back of her hand. She smiled wetly at Charity. 'You know, C.D., you have the right idea, sometimes.'

'I know. Now it's my turn.' She put a match to the photograph of Mark, and within a minute he lay in ashes. With her finger, she moved the ashes round the window sill. The gesture reminded her of Sally's finger stroking Annie's cheek as she died.

'You won't get rid of him just like that,' remarked Sally quietly.

'Do you think I don't know that? I'll never get rid of him. I'll learn to live without him, but that's different. There were three things I learnt from Mark, Sal. One, I learnt what I'm capable of in a sexual relationship with a man. I didn't know that before Mark. Second, I learnt that whatever happens, I'll survive. I'm not afraid of taking risks, now. Because I've learnt about the rottenness of my own dependence, the gangrene of what I thought of as my needs. We don't have needs, you see, not in the abstract. Our needs are created by our circumstances.'

'And the third thing?'

'That real love between men and women isn't possible.'

'I don't understand that.'

'It's all a chimera, an illusion. It's the most powerful illusion we have. You see it everywhere. In all the ads portraying love as an eternal hygienic answer to everything, in the rules of insurance companies, in the games little children play, everywhere. We're taught that a man and a woman together make the basic formula, and we must all strive for that.'

'Of course.'

'Mark and I were Héloïse and Abelard, and Lancelot and Guinevere, and Romeo and Juliet, and Antony and Cleopatra, and Tristan and Isolde – all of them. We were part of the myth. The point isn't love, its secret personal interior, but what the heterosexual couple stands for: we keep the myth alive. We carry the whole sad mess forward into the future for the next generation.'

'I'm not sure,' responded Sally, slowly, 'whether that isn't all a wonderful rationalisation of the fact that you haven't a clue what it was all about, and you're still in love with him. Anyway, romantic love is an exploitation. You've left out the political dimension.'

'It's an exploitation of women by men. Yes, I know.'

'That's not what I meant. When you discovered feminism, Charity, you learnt to treat men as a class, to see them all as the same as one another, the way they've always treated women. I don't think that's an advance. The only true advance is for all of us to see each other as individuals. Gender is an individual trait, that's all. You've lied and deceived and manipulated just as much as any of the men you've known.'

'Why are you attacking me? I thought you were my friend.'

'Friends are there to tell each other the truth. That's all I'm doing. You don't want to face it, though, do you?'

'It's not the truth. There's no such thing as truth. There's only the way you see things and the way I see things, and they might be the same and they might not. But you can't say that one of us is right and the other is wrong.'

'Shit, C.D., I don't believe that. I know what you're saying. But I think you have a problem about men. Or several problems. One of them is feminism. Feminist politics are incompatible with what you've just said. Feminists say men as a class oppress women – that they hold the power, that they lie, that they're incapable of crying, or whatever. You make these categorical statements. You know the truth. And how can that be squared with allowing men a point of view? Wouldn't Mark say that you had treated him badly? That you had lied? That you had had your own motives that weren't his, and that you didn't tell him about?'

'I don't know. I suppose so. But what he said was that I didn't put him first, I couldn't have the right kind of commitment to him because I was too selfish and because of my children.'

'I don't want to give you a lecture, C.D.' Sally could see that Charity was anxious.

'No, it's alright. Go on.'

'This is the most important point,' she said. 'I never understood your obsession with Mark. None of your friends did. None of us could understand why you loved Mark for so long and so desperately. It seemed crazy to us. A neurotic affair. On both sides, perhaps, but I never got to know Mark well enough to check that out.'

'Perhaps you understand it better now. As I said, Mark and I represented something. An obsession. All heterosexual love is obsessional: that's its nature. Ours was just a more complete version of the normal.'

'No. It wasn't normal. Mark and you were never kind to one another. You didn't really care about each other. You wanted to *have* him. He wanted to *have* you.'

'Men and children,' said Charity. 'Why can't we just be women on our own? Like this, Sal. This has been nice and peaceful, hasn't it?'

'It wouldn't work for long,' Sally replied, 'because it's in our nature to make connections.'

'Like electricity, or thunderstorms.'

'Yes. I've had my share of torrid affairs. I don't want to be in love any more. But I think you do.' Sally became silent. Charity looked at her. She was half-smiling.

'No, not now. But I may. The excitement, the danger, the closeness, that burning feeling you get in your toes.'

'Come on, C.D., we ought to go to bed. All that tree-cutting was exhausting. We've got rid of enough dead wood for today.'

An owl hooted in the blackness filled by woodsmoke. With the windows open, Charity could hear rain landing on the mossy ground. Looking from the lamp on her desk to the window, she could not at first see the division between the sky and the trees on the hills; she needed to focus the muscles in her eyes on the task of seeing the difference, though the outline of the stone church in the village across the hills recalled to her the knowledge of established order – that there *were* divisions between places, people, times and things, the order of stones and names, of earth and water, of gender and generation. Each morning the church bell rang at seven, a single black clattering notion of a sound, pealing the Angelus into the corners of the village, across the fields and into the vegetation, from the blue buttons of the cornflowers, to the heavy dejected yellowness of the sunflowers, from the homes of bats to the spreading arms of oak trees.

The Angelus, to call everyone to prayer, to rejoice in the beginning of a new day. Structure.

Now, at the end of the day, at the end of the affair, she needed to write Mark a letter. She wanted to tell him:

'We called it love. And yet, in using that word, the two of us did not mean the same thing. You did not want me, not really. You wanted love. Why did you want love? Because you did not have love in you. I was a way of filling an empty space. For you it was the space that mattered. Anyone could fill it. For me it was the other way around. You created the space that only you could fill, though I never understood how or why that happened.

'Remember that night in the snow? It is an external impression of that I remember now, the scene as it looked to an outsider, not as it happened to me. I am a witness, an observer of the snow against my body, of your driving warmth inside me. Was I ever really there?

'I'll tell you something. You may have married and started a new life, but there's not a moment of any day when you don't miss me. Defend yourself against knowing that, if you will (and you will) but it's only a matter of time. Time will make you reach out for me. Time. Time and again.

'I had a conversation with a friend the other day. She said she hadn't ever been tempted to any kind of religious belief. I said no, but what about mysticism? Surely mysticism is different. She said, what's mysticism? I said mysticism is what's beyond the sociology of everyday life. It's why people think of the sociology of everyday life last, and why the moment in the rose garden, when humankind, so T. S. Eliot says, knows that it cannot bear any more reality, comes first. Down there on the terrace, at the fringe of this French summer, are the last roses of summer. I should like to see them against the night sky, scarlet and sapphire in conjunction, and that would be a mystical experience, and I should like to see them with you. I couldn't have that experience of seeing a crimson rose against a sapphire sky without at the same time thinking of you.

'To look at a rose is mystical; so is being in love. We never stopped being in love with each other; that was the tragedy. We could never turn it into something ordinary. You said you didn't want it to be. There wasn't any point in saying that. I said you were wrong. I was wrong to say it. Is that why you had those other affairs? Why you lied about Jane, and Margaret Lacey, and Tessa, and God knows how many others? Sexual jealousy, which you knew you could fuel by denying its premises, was a way of retaining the purity of the emotion. You made me jealous so we would know we were still in love. But you also made me jealous because you couldn't behave in any other way. You probably didn't realise this, but whatever I did when I was with you was because of you, not because of me. You were the centre of my life, I was only a symbol in yours. You made me play your game and everyone got caught up in it: we made the world sick and unhappy with our manoeuvrings, and its relief is manifest, it's painted, even, across these golden hills.

'You know what we should have done? We should have only had an affair. For ever and for ever. Then we would have been able to keep hold of the mysticism. Mysticism is a recipe for eternal life. Everybody wants eternal life. That's why we fall in love, have children, climb the Great Wall of China, think we can write poetry, evade the washing up. That's the reason for everything. It's not our mortality that we have in common. It's our failure to take death on board, to believe death will ever happen to us. Life is a confidence trick, and love is the greatest confidence trick of all.

'Don't you want an eternal life, Mark? I do. You won't find it wherever you are now.

'I wonder sometimes what has become of your sexual problem. That's the first time in all the years we had together that I have called it your sexual problem. I never called it that when I knew you. I never even named it to myself. It was only after our affair was over I could recognise it *was* a problem – to me, to us, but most of all to you. You know why I couldn't see that at the time, don't you? Because I felt I might damage your psyche by seeing it. Men's sexuality is the most fragile thing, but women conspire to keep its fragility a secret. We love you, you see. Like children. That's the sad truth.

'I used to think about why you couldn't come. I used to think it was my fault – I wasn't attractive or titillating enough. When I thought that I couldn't bear it, because I imagined all these fantasies you might be having to help yourself, none of which did – or perhaps they did, one at a time, and once only, and then the next one had to be even more flagrant, yet more monstrous.

'Ours was a phallic relationship. Built around the phallus itself in the flesh, yours – I remember it, hold it in my hand every day of my life – and the phallus made of stone as an emblem of patriarchy, that time will not ravage except to darken its vessels and cover them with accumulated slime. A stone erection can't be dissembled by dread or panic: that phallus points always at the sun of life. It stands for vitality – the life force itself.

'Sex in the men's room. It happens. We all have sex in the men's room, whatever sex we are. Have you ever thought about that? Sex is something we are and we have, and that is how we think of it, that unless we feed the activity into the essence, the essence itself falls into decay. And, actually, sex in the men's room is the essence of sexual endeavour under patriarchy – distant, disabling, mechanical, hurtful, alienating, convenient.

'To put it bluntly, what I have understood is that you had a sexual problem because you couldn't entrust yourself to a woman. When you got to know one, and understood that you could care, you couldn't let yourself go within her, because you were frightened of losing yourself in her and you feared what she might do with what you had given her. A real man, who is phallic and patriarchal, must live in the men's room. A sexuality that is different from this teaches him that his masculinity is at risk. So he must either abrogate it, or fight on.

'You fought on. And still do, I imagine. You pursue the moment of orgasm because it's elusive, and because it is what you are supposed to strive for, but you fear its annihilation. You know in your heart (or wherever it is that men know things, if it isn't in the phallus) that to ejaculate is to vote – to connive with a political system that exploits, denigrates and punishes, and whose central and essential mode of communication is combative. You act, I respond; I attack, you defend; you fuck, I am fucked. I come and you do not. You cannot, you see, insist that I make you. I understand it, but the game doesn't work. I don't live here any more.

'Remember what you used to say? "You're too intellectual, Charity. You analyse everything."

'Or: "I need a woman who isn't as clever as you. You're too intelligent for me."

'I never knew what you meant. I could never say that to anyone.

'As a matter of fact, you were not too clever for me. I loved your mind. There was nothing wrong with your mind.

'As a matter of fact, Mark Carleton, you knew it all, but you defended yourself so admirably against this knowing. Adam in the Garden of Eden. Adam knew bloody well what Eve was doing. It wasn't her fault that he wouldn't talk about it. What a shame we have to be silent enemies. But there is nothing else for it.'

When she got back to London in September, Charity called in at the department one day and had a drink with Ivan Swinhoe. It was a warm golden evening. They sat at a white table on the pavement of a wine bar.

'They got married, you know,' said Swinhoe, à propos of nothing.

'I thought so. When?'

'August the fourteenth. Silly business.'

'Why?'

'Won't last. How can it?' He poured the wine. 'Running away from something, Carleton is. Don't know what. But something.'

'He's running away from himself,' she said.

'Aren't we all?' Swinhoe's shoulders started moving. 'Shouldn't be jealous, if I were you.'

'No?'

'Nothing to be jealous of.'

Only another woman /in his bed, and sharing his life, she thought, remarkably calmly.

'Forgive me if I say something?'

'Of course, Ivan.'

'Problem was, he never liked you and you never liked him.'

'No?'

'Didn't like him because he wasn't likeable. Not in an ordinary way. Devilish, yes. Attractive as a hornet's nest. Didn't like you for a different reason, though. Doesn't like women, Carleton doesn't. Makes it impossible, you see.'

'I see.' She blinked at him in the amber urban light.

'We're all animals, aren't we?' observed Swinhoe.

'Are we?'

'Not you, dear girl. Us men. Read *Madame Bovary*, have you?'

'Yes, I have as a matter of fact. But how did you know?'

'Didn't. Just guessed. In character. Remember, "all men are criminals". That's what she says. The only thing she got right. Better to get one thing right than nothing, though.' He looked back at Charity sharply. 'She's pregnant, you know.'

'Madame Bovary?'

'Madame Pascoe.'

'Is she? I didn't know.' That was something Charity hadn't thought about. 'Already?'

'Just. Pascoe's over the moon. Not about Carleton, you understand, he didn't think much of that, but there was nothing he could do about it. He wants a grandchild. That's what I meant.'

'Where are they living?'

'In Germany. West Berlin. Carleton's got a job there at the Institute for Social Research.'

'But he can't speak German.'

'Doesn't matter. They're all American there, anyway. Said he wanted a clean break. Awful place, West Berlin.'

'It is, yes,' she agreed. 'I've only been there once. But it was quite horrible. Well,' she paused, 'I hope they're very happy.'

'No you don't,' remarked Swinhoe. 'Still love him, don't you?'

'No, of course I don't.'

'Dear girl, you do. But don't say so if you don't want to.'

His unexpected kindness surprised her. He put his hand over hers. 'Cry if you like. But remember, he's not worth it. Men aren't worth the tears of women. Never were, never will be.'

A butterfly landed on his wine glass. Its wings had white stripes across them, and two eyes at the rear giving a quizzical look. Beneath the black-brown surface of its wings, a blue shimmer caught the evening sun. '*Apatura iris*,' he said.

'Pardon?'

'*Apatura iris*. Purple Emperor. A very sedentary butterfly. Likes sitting in puddles and on manure. Decaying flesh will do as well.'

'Do you know a lot about butterflies, then?'

'Some. Got a reasonable collection at home. On pins.'

'On what?'

'They aren't alive. Dead. On pins.'

'Yes, I see.'

Swinhoe hadn't changed after all. Charity hadn't really expected him to. Some things in life had to remain the same.

'Extraordinary things, butterflies. Start out in one form and end up in another,' went on Swinhoe, borne along by his interior dialogue, much of which, these days, took the form of acerbic observations about nature's logic and irrevocable decay. 'How would you feel,' he invited her, 'suddenly changing from a nasty creepy crawly thing into something lovely with wings?' Swinhoe nodded at the Purple Emperor vibrating its shimmering wings showily on the edge of the glass. Charity thought perhaps this was what she had done. 'Some of them never eat,' he continued. 'Moths, that is. Come out of their pupae, live a few hours, mate, but never eat, then die. Imagine that.'

Charity watched the butterfly flutter off to enjoy the rest of its brief existence somewhere else.

'Expect you think I'm weird, don't you?'

'No, Ivan, I don't actually. I think you say a lot of extremely truthful things. I'm not sure you realise how truthful they are sometimes, though.'

'Do.' The word sped out of his mouth like a highspeed butterfly, newly ejected from its chrysalis. But as soon as it was out, it was as though it had never existed at all. Swinhoe turned his head a little in the direction of the setting sun. 'Remind me of a Camberwell Beauty,' he said.

'What does?'

'You do.'

'Do I?'

'Most beautiful butterfly I've ever seen. Wonderful silky brown wings with lacy borders and rows of little blue spots. Quite wonderful.'

'If you say so.' She watched him quietly, protective of his difficulty in admitting to this subtle admiration of her. Her response, to feel protective, seemed out of place. Was this what the maternal instinct really was? A misplaced instinct of women's towards men?

Swinhoe leaned over the table towards her with a fierce expression on his face. 'What's it all for?' he demanded.

'All what, Ivan?'

'All this!'

'I don't know the meaning of life, if that's what you're asking.'

'*You* don't need to, do you?'

'No.' She realised she didn't, any more. Nonetheless, she wanted confirmation of this from him. 'Why don't I?'

'Look what you've done.' Swinhoe's eyes swivelled for once round to focus on hers. 'All those children, bright-eyed young things. You brought them up, sent them out into the world. Probably did a good job there. Don't know them, mind you, but I should think you did a good job. That's not all, though. Work, jobs, books, ideas, husbands, lovers.' He looked slightly gloomy. 'You're the one who's come out of this best, you know. Better than any of us. Can't think why Carleton didn't marry you. Out of his tiny mind, Carleton is.'

16 ✳ IN THE YEAR 2000

> 'The social structure has not been much modified by the changes in woman's condition; this world, always belonging to men, still retains the form they have given it' – *The Second Sex*, pp. 372–3

She moved her hand over the polished surface of the clock on the mantelpiece, feeling how its walnut curves were able to cherish the passing of time. Time revolving inside it, the sustained interpolations of time past, present and future in the universe outside it. From the time when she was a little girl, when the clock stood in her father's study and her mother dusted it for him, to now, the year of the millennium, when she took care of it herself. All the time she had lived, in different places and moods, with real people, ghosts, strangers, enemies, kittens, babies, clowns and criminals. Every minute was hers.

Either side of the clock were mementoes and reminders: an old birthday card of bright painted balloons, an invitation to a summer solstice party, a grey photograph of a little girl, a silver pierrot balanced on an unlikely glass base. She fingered each of these objects with distraction, at the same time turning to look out of the window: the London rooftops were glazed with morning sun, and displayed a surprising medley of colours. The sky was an urban blue, and generously calm. One of the new bright green refuse lorries swaggered its way down the street; the refuse lorries, with their brash colouring and enhanced metallic clatter, were one of the legacies of Margaret Thatcher's

England, which had lapped its insidious tidal wave well over the shore of the 1990s, leaving all sorts of scum behind it on the beach.

At ten o'clock it's time to go. Charity Walton is about to take a flight to Amsterdam, where she is going to meet someone she hasn't seen for ten years. A man whose existence once supported hers in a passion that passed understanding.

She checks the windows of the flat carefully. Everything is closed. She feeds Daisy, the arrogant black cat, and the three streamlined goldfish, Hook, Line and Sinker. Funny how habits one complains about, like the keeping of goldfish, stay with one, even when the necessity for them has passed into history. As she drops fishy crumbs on to the surface of the water, the three goldfish rush up and open their fetal mouths – for it is babies they remind Charity of, babies unborn, fighting for food in the dark, enclosed and not necessarily safe world of the amnion.

In the train to the airport Charity takes out of her bag the two books she's brought along: a volume of short stories and a new book by a feminist writer called *Being and Doing: Feminist Existentialism and the State in the Twenty First Century*. Charity's mood is not, however, up to the onslaughts of feminist theory. She puts it away, and instead dips into the less challenging but skilled Roald Dahl, an ominous story called 'Royal Jelly' in which a well-meaning beekeeper with a failing-to-thrive baby feeds it royal jelly and watches it turn into a bee. No one can accuse the beekeeper of deliberate malice; he's such a nice, kind, stupid man. All he wants is for his daughter to be a queen.

At the airport terminal Charity feels quite panicky. Standing at the check-in counter she wildly imagines she might go somewhere a long way away, like Hong Kong, or somewhere quick and safe, like Birmingham, though Birmingham is now much less so, with its present wave of student and Black riots. However, the airport computers they'd had so much trouble with back in the 1980s are working splendidly today, and she is apparently to be checked inexorably through to Amsterdam.

'Any seat preference for you today, Professor Walton?'

'I'd like an aisle seat, please.' They've stopped asking about smoking on aeroplanes now, because no one smokes any more. In 1996 it became a notifiable disease.

The young man behind the desk smiles, showing off his toothpaste and his synthetic olive shirt, part of a new look recently introduced by the British Airports Authority (now jointly managed by Trusthouse Forte and a government aviation organisation in a format resembling a traditional marriage where both partners lead secret and financially disjointed lives). The shoulders of his shirt are at right angles to his arms. A padded masculinity is in fashion again. 'The flight will be boarding at 11.45, gate 45. Have a nice day.'

He smiles his toothpaste smile again. Charity loathes that phrase, and the whole cultural merging that has made it part of the public language of the British. She buys herself a double whisky at the bar. Men stand round her, a black-suited afforestation rooted with briefcases to the sleek, carpeted lounge. They talk and move from one leg to the other like ninepins in a bowling alley. In the midst of this wood Charity glimpses one tree, the upstanding, blue-eyed, far from honourable Mark Carleton. A few dozen cameos of Mark-and-Charity speed rapidly through her mind as the whisky goes down her throat, and the real Mark Carleton prepares to embark on a similar journey to hers from some other airport in the world.

At the age of fifty-two Charity has become a sensible woman. She knows her own strengths and limitations, she values herself at least as much as anyone else does, and she has at last come to regard the world as a rational place that isn't out to get her. She holds a senior university position in social science research, a personal chair: not the one she had had her eyes on in the beginning, but another one, which will do just as well. She has published six or seven books, she heads the editorial board of a left-wing academic journal and has acquired a solid reputation as a theorist in the health and illness field. People listen to her carefully and students come and sit at her feet. No one doubts her reasons for doing most of the things she does – having a mortgage, going to work, visiting the British Museum, buying the latest Avocado word processor to help her research monographs on their way, sending presents to her grandchildren. Tom has by now fathered three daughters, Dan a son; Rachel has repeated her mother's history and given birth to twin boys. Now AIDS can be cured, Harry lives happily with his friend Martin in a small stone house in a field in Yorkshire.

But Charity's credentials for going on a mission such as the present one are another story.

The flight is called and the black forest moves towards gate 45. Now they have done away with all that walking at airports, and one simply stands on a travalator from the bar to the plane. Air travel is vastly cheaper, but its comfort hasn't increased in reverse proportion: there are no more free newspapers or free drinks or free socks, or eyeshades, and this is called rationalisation. On the other hand, to balance that, no one is afraid of flying any more. One might as well be afraid of going to the supermarket or visiting a leisure centre.

Charity's aisle seat places her next to a woman heavily laden with an expensive cologne. As soon as she decently can – that is, as soon as the seat belts are automatically unfastened – Charity escapes to the lavatory. In its blue confines (well charted by Peter Sellers in the 1970s movie where he had his leg in plaster but still had to pee) she examines herself and her readiness for the meeting ahead. She can see only the top half of her body in the mirror, which is just as well, because it is the best half. As one gets older, she often thinks, the extra flesh seems to sink downwards and cling to those parts that flesh has already reached in liberal amounts. As they used to say before feminism, and now can safely say again, a woman like Charity isn't bad for her age. Her hair has only recently gone grey, and it's still thick and soft to the touch, though it has now been cut short to prevent anyone thinking she is trying to look like a younger woman. Her eyes have the same depths – the depths of her childhood and coming of age; Mark had once cynically remarked they reminded him of cherry blossom shoe polish, the familiar cleverly designed tin as much as the luscious creamy polish within.

As the plane lands, her memory re-enters an old cosmic phase. She is on a beach with him somewhere, with the shifting silver

sand under their feet, the sand merging with a fertile ocean and
the ocean with an untroubled sky. It is warm; even the wind
coming from the ocean breathes warmly on them, and on a
donkey next to them, taking ice down to the fishing boats. 'I
wouldn't mind,' he had said, 'running away here, and living here
with you. No one would ever find us. We wouldn't need much
money. We could write. I would go fishing, I would bring you
bright fish and you would cook them on a wood fire, and we
would make love, and we would be happy . . .'

In a different city on the same day as Charity flies to Amsterdam,
Mark Carleton had a row with his wife. It concerned their
eight-year-old son Nicholas. Mark thinks that Nicholas has an
over-protective mother.

'What's wrong with letting him come home on his own?' says
Mark.

'What's wrong is that he's only eight!' says Tessa. 'You're
crazy. It's obvious, *he* may be okay, but what about other people?
He's an attractive little boy. This isn't exactly a crime-free city.
Anything could happen. You don't care, do you?' she went on,
changing the formulation, 'It's all up to me, just as it was with
Jane. You don't want any real responsibility. You're *incapable* of
really caring about anyone.'

Tessa's eyes were wet. As Jane's had been. 'Don't be ridiculous,' he said, 'I love Nick every bit as much as you do. I just
think you should allow him some independence. It isn't right for
him to grow up too close to you. He's your only child. I'm away a
lot. He could get too close. It would be bad for him. I want him
to feel in control of his own life.'

'*You* want! *You* want!' Tessa couldn't bear this. 'What about
what *I* want? Don't I count? You pushed me into this,' she said,
finally. 'You wanted to turn me into another Jane. You wanted
another woman to exploit. You've got to have a woman
somewhere in your life, haven't you, that you can point to and
say, she's mine, she'll do anything I want!'

'But you wanted a baby,' reasoned Mark. 'I didn't. It was a
kind of bargain – a baby for a home. You got what you wanted.

Anyway, you were the one who went on about marriage.' He paused, attempting to slide his arm round her shoulders, but was repulsed. 'You've had a good time. I've looked after you. It hasn't been too bad, has it?'

'You bastard,' is all she said before leaving the room and closing the door so the walls of the house shook.

Mark was glad she'd brought the duel to a temporary end. He sat at his desk and closed his eyes. To remember Charity as he had last seen her. Where was that? At her house in London, one morning, as the April sun made angles of pale lemon light across the street and between the houses, and Charity stood there in her green dressing gown, her morning flesh picking up the light, her long hair in limp spirals down her shoulders, her expression both caged and transparent.

The plan for this reunion had been born that weekend in Holland in the early 1980s. Margaret Thatcher was systematically eroding the quality of life in Britain, schools were shut much of the time, hospitals were closing, the universities had become bastions of relative poverty. Feminism – real feminism – was nearly underground. One evening, drinking a bottle of good wine in a pavement bar, Mark had been telling Charity episodes from his earlier life and had, in the midst of the flow of edited recollections, been inspired by a way of bringing the three sorts of time together: living now, sitting here, telling stories about time past, and at the same time wanting to know about the future, their future, if only to know that they had one.

He remembered what she had said. 'But don't you think we'll be living together in the year 2000? I want to live with you,' and she had reached out and taken his veined hand in hers, hungrily.

But he had asked her to promise him. 'Please, Charity. The first of June at six o'clock in the evening in the year 2000 in Amsterdam. I'll wait for you on that corner over there.' He had pointed. 'By the Kodak building, next to the hotel. We'll drink champagne and discuss the future of the world, and the impermanence of love, the only thing that really matters. Governments will have fallen, populations will have exploded and died, women will still be taking valium, men will still be boys – I don't know what the world will look like, but we'll still be here!'

Mark opened his eyes. He went downstairs to find Tessa in the kitchen. 'I'm off,' he said.

'Good.' The word emanated from her back, he couldn't see her face.

'I'll be back on Sunday. Maybe Saturday if the meeting's boring. I'll call you tonight. Give my love to Nick.'

Unwilling to leave it there, he moved towards her, towards the expression in her hunched shoulders. 'Come on, Tess, don't let's fight. It's not worth it.'

'Isn't it?' She turned to face him. 'Why are we having so many rows, Mark? What's happening to us?'

He didn't want to answer these metaphysical inquiries. 'I've got to go, I'll miss the plane. Oh, by the way, have you seen my blue silk shirt?'

'Why do you want your blue silk shirt?'

'Conference dinner,' he muttered.

'It's in the cupboard, but it's got a stain on the front. From when you went to Manila. I think it's wine, or perhaps blood. You'll have to stick a flower over it.' She turned back to the sink.

At the airport Mark felt that all had been lost. He looked up at the clock and saw with alarm that it read five minutes to one. His plane went at twelve. And then with relief it dawned on him: he wasn't looking at the clock after all, but at a mirror image of it at the opposite end of the departures hall. It was only just past eleven. He sat down, breathed deeply and tried to take control of himself.

The woman next to him on the plane had several enormous bags which were somehow attached to her body. She spent about ten minutes trying to cram a maroon-coloured one under the seat in front, which brought her into direct confrontation with Mark's foot.

'Can I help?' he asked. 'Perhaps you could put it in the overhead locker?'

'Oh no, I don't think so, it's very heavy.'

'Let me try.' The offer was made for selfish, not for altruistic, reasons. As he heaved the bag up, he felt his shirt disengage itself

· 305 ·

from his trousers, and he knew that the woman was looking at several inches of slightly sagging hairy tummy.

'Thank you,' she said, 'that's much better.'

When the plane was over the North Sea he took another look at her. She was flustered and flushed by the effort of travelling. Youngish, mid-thirties perhaps. A careful linen suit, quite inappropriate for travelling. A bright orange blouse, which resonated with the light in her brown hair as the plane changed direction and allowed light to enter its body. He couldn't see her eyes, they were enclosed in tinted glasses, but he enjoyed a moment of imagining them: green centres, he thought, in a Persil whiteness, and long hazel lashes.

It's ten minutes to six, the last minutes of Mark and Charity's decade. Charity brushes her teeth and puts a string of red beads round her neck. She feels sick, almost like vomiting, although she's eaten nothing since her free-range egg for breakfast.

On the way out of the hotel she sees in the lift glass that her hands are shaking; her face is tense like a cuckoo clock about to chime. Outside the hotel, music fills the square, a savage beating with rhapsodic undertones, entirely electronic as it all is these days. Celia Johnson and – who was it? – in Brief Encounter had had Rachmaninov; the music in Casablanca hadn't been bad either, and that old film about the Danish writer Karen Blixen she and Mark had seen together the night before they parted had had a similar emotional musical strength. 'Don't move,' she recalls Robert Redford saying as he lay on top of Meryl Streep, 'don't move.'

'But I want to move!' Streep had protested. And the music had burst like a cloud over their heads, and then the scene had changed to another pasture. 'Why don't you say goodbye?' he had asked (another he this time).

'I'm better at hallos than goodbyes,' she answered.

When Charity reaches the square, Mark isn't there. The pavement by the corner of the Kodak building is empty. Where he should have been is nothing: only the air remains expectant. And Charity wants only to be a spectator. She stands on the opposite corner watching the space where they should meet.

Mark is late because he has fallen asleep in his hotel room. He awakes knowing he has something to do, but not knowing at first what it is. The yellow counterpane reminds him of a field of buttercups, and, because he has more than once been in a field of buttercups with Charity, he is able to remember what he has to do. When he goes to the square he can't see Charity. He watches the space carefully for a few minutes to make sure she really isn't there. Perhaps she will materialise, be reconstructed out of the music and the happy crowds pulsating in the square.

He scratches his head, uncertain what to do. A few strands of grey hair come out in his fingernails. He spends a few moments cleaning his fingernails. Then, 'Charity,' he says, silently, as he has not said that name for years, 'Charity, where are you, Charity? I want you, Charity.'

Still nothing. He allows his eyes to leave the spot and survey the square, and then he sees her. It's real! She's here! It's happened! His knees weaken beneath him: he holds tightly on to the key ring in his trouser pocket, but the keys in his clenched hand are coated with sweat. This is Charity. Here she is. Shorter than he remembers, and looking more vulnerable. But smart, and intelligent, even at this distance. Oh how the intelligence of that woman had overpowered him! He had been swallowed up by it, been made to come up choking for air, looking for fissures of insensibility in the dense intellectualism she had created around her.

She wears a black dress, guarding a figure that had always seemed right to him, despite the fact that it had increased and decreased by several per cent in many directions during the time in which they had been lovers. At a certain point in the decrease he remembers her hip bone achieved a sharpness that hurt him as he lay on top of her, and then he used to say 'It's time to eat a little more.' Or, in other years, her right breast would have too much contact with the flesh beneath, and he would warn her of the dangers of obesity, actively withholding food from her and instead eating it himself. Together they had shared all the available excess weight and distributed it between them according to gender, appetite, inclination and power. In that respect, if in no other, it had been a most equal relationship.

Her shoes, her bag and her beads are red, a colour she had seldom worn ten years ago. Her hair, on the other hand, is grey. That's a bit of a shock, but it looks good on her. She isn't looking in his direction, though. Why is she standing there and not in the place they had arranged?

He moves across the square towards her. At the same time, she leaves her vantage point and crosses the street.

As her foot touches the pavement, she sees Mark coming out of the crowd. He wears a look of anguish and a creased suit. His hands, stuck in his pockets, push his shoulders up in a familiar attitude of suppressed resignation. Soon he will stand in front of her, so she will become aware of the smell of him, now and long ago. Without touching it, she can feel the material of his jacket, can predict the temperature and condition of the skin beneath.

He looks at her. She is the same Charity. He can see himself placing a hand on her shoulders in a gesture intended to claim her. She goes on looking at him.

On the first night there they are both tired. They eat a sandwich together, go to bed and make love. He goes to sleep almost straightaway. Charity tries to relax, but can't. The summer wind round the edges of the ill-fitting window, the hard bed, the street sounds, all disturb her by virtue of their unfamiliarity. And then she is disturbed by something else: lamentations and echoes from the past. She finds herself shaking and crying with a frenzy of longing for what she no longer has and, indeed, no longer wants. His face comes out of the blackness towards her, and his eyes penetrate hers, and hold her in an inflexible regard, and she feels herself wilting with pain and anguish. The agony and the ecstasy: 'And in the room the women come and go, talking of Michelangelo.' She knows she doesn't want him, and has done nothing to summon up this image. But no matter. He is there. Always will be. In her consciousness, out there in the universe, so long as he is alive he will be alive in her.

He moves beside her in his sleep, touches her thigh with his hand. 'What's the matter, love? Do you want to talk about it?' She clings to him, and he holds her and knows the nature of what she is feeling, that it is something to do with men, and her attachment to them – to him now, and in the past, and in the future – that she will never cease to speculate on her own place in this high-walled shadowy enclosure of the men's room. All her life it will occupy her, as a creature without a territory to call its own runs and scurries around prying into corners of other people's lives looking for a small warm place to lie down and rest in peace.

Sharman Macdonald

Night Night

Frances, tired of winter and dark days, dreams about the tattooed man who won't make her plead for love. Her husband, Joey, a gaunt and haggard boy of forty, chops down the Tree of Heaven she has lovingly planted, and dreams of a fat wife in an apron cooking bacon, eggs and fried bread for his breakfast. Aaron, their son, dreams of the Libyan bombings, of planes and explosives. Fat Mia, the baby, is sublimely indifferent. Only Nat-Nat, womanly and wise beyond her years, doesn't dream.

When Joey gives up his struggle to be a painter for the more financially rewarding work of a commerical artist, his world seems secure. Yet superficial prosperity doesn't hide a lurking malaise that climaxes with a random bomb threat to their home. As the neighbourhood empties to the village hall, and a panoply of superbly imagined, heartbreakingly real characters unfolds, Joey stands to guard his house and meet his fate.

Night Night is an exhilarating fantasy that interweaves domestic shambles with a menacing parable for the bewildered eighties . . . a funny suburban nightmare about loss of faith and direction.

'A surreal purity of vision which is often disturbingly amusing' – *Time Out*

Flamingo

Adam Zameenzad

My Friend Matt and Hena the Whore

A continent of permanent revolution, of marauding rebels and despotic governments, yet one of love and laughter, compassion and humanity: this is the Africa of today.

Nine-year-old Kimo, wide-eyed witness to its brutality, is starved out of his home village by drought. Desperate for help, he sets out for the big city of Bader in the company of his resourceful friends, the visionary Matt, pragmatic Hena and dreaming Golam. Their journey takes them through a country paralysed by the horrors of civil war, horrors which soon tighten their grip around the frail hopes of the starving foursome . . .

Buoyed up by laughter, weighed down by tragedy and violence, *My Friend Matt and Hena the Whore* is an impossibly touching, quite extraordinary accomplishment from an outstanding new writer.

'Truly astonishing' *i.D.*

'Outstanding . . . into this odyssey of nightmares and magic the author manages to weave a thread of humour which is the most remarkable achievement of his horrifying book' *Sunday Times*

'Beautifully written, imbued with enormous integrity and insight, his book is a plea for us to exercise humanity towards our fellow humans; it is in the characters' expressions of love and care that we are offered a glimmer of hope, both for the present and the future' *Time Out*

'It would be hard to overpraise the achievement . . . a truly remarkable novel' Adam Lively, *Punch*

Flamingo

Flamingo

Flamingo is a quality imprint publishing both fiction and non-fiction. Below are some recent titles.

Fiction
- [ ] Rich in Love *Josephine Humphreys* £3.99
- [ ] City of Blok *Simon Louvish* £3.99
- [ ] Deep Diving *Stephanie Conybeare* £3.99
- [ ] States of Emergency *André Brink* £3.95
- [ ] Rock Springs *Richard Ford* £3.95
- [ ] The Silence of the Sirens *Adelaida Morales* £3.95
- [ ] Playing Foxes *Helen Dixon* £3.95
- [ ] Blue Eyes, Black Hair *Marguerite Duras* £3.50

Non-fiction
- [ ] A Pike in the Basement *Simon Loftus* £3.95
- [ ] Solitude *Anthony Storr* £3.95
- [ ] A Leaf in the Wind *Peter Hudson* £3.99
- [ ] In the Land of Israel *Amos Oz* £3.99
- [ ] Taking it Like a Woman *Ann Oakley* £3.95
- [ ] Feeding the Rat *Al Alvarez* £3.95
- [ ] Uncommon Wisdom *Fritjof Capra* £4.95

You can buy Flamingo paperbacks at your local bookshop or newsagent. Or you can order them from Fontana Paperbacks, Cash Sales Department, Box 29, Douglas, Isle of Man. Please send a cheque, postal or money order (not currency) worth the purchase price plus 22p per book (or plus 22p per book if outside the UK).

NAME (Block letters) _____

ADDRESS_____

_____

_____